DEE SHULMAN has a degree in English from York University and went on to study Illustration at Harrow School of Art. She has written and/or illustrated about fifty books, but *Fever* is her first book for teenagers, which is surprising considering she lives on a campus in central London with about 760 of them.

feverbook.co.uk

FEVER

DEE SHULMAN

razOr
bill
PENGUIN

RAZORBILL

Published by the Penguin Group
Penguin Books Ltd, 80 Strand, London WC2R ORL, England
Penguin Group (USA) Inc., 375 Hudson Street, New York, New York 10014, USA
Penguin Group (Canada), 90 Eglinton Avenue East, Suite 700, Toronto, Ontario, Canada M4P 2Y3
(a division of Pearson Penguin Canada Inc.)
Penguin Ireland, 25 St Stephen's Green, Dublin 2, Ireland (a division of Penguin Books Ltd)
Penguin Group (Australia), 250 Camberwell Road, Camberwell, Victoria 3124, Australia
(a division of Pearson Australia Group Pty Ltd)
Penguin Books India Pvt Ltd, 11 Community Centre, Panchsheel Park, New Delhi – 110 017, India
Penguin Group (NZ), 67 Apollo Drive, Rosedale, Auckland 0632, New Zealand
(a division of Pearson New Zealand Ltd)
Penguin Books (South Africa) (Pty) Ltd, 24 Sturdee Avenue, Rosebank,
Johannesburg 2196, South Africa

Penguin Books Ltd, Registered Offices: 80 Strand, London WC2R ORL, England

penguin.com

First published 2012
001 – 10 9 8 7 6 5 4 3 2 1

Copyright © Dee Shulman, 2012
All rights reserved

The moral right of the author has been asserted

Set in Sabon MT 10.5/15.5 pt
Typeset by Palimpsest Book Production Limited, Falkirk, Stirlingshire
Made and printed in Great Britain by Clays Ltd, St Ives plc

British Library Cataloguing in Publication Data
A CIP catalogue record for this book is available from the British Library

ISBN: 978-0-141-34026-5

www.greenpenguin.co.uk

For Chris

Northamptonshire LRE	
Askews & Holts	

Prologue

Seth opened his eyes. The unbearable tremors had stopped. He sat up warily. No excruciating pain in his limbs. No dizziness. No crashing headache. The fever was completely gone.

He swung his legs carefully to the side of the thin mat he lay on, and looked around his shadowy cell. It was just as it should be – low wooden table littered with medicinal herbs and vials, fresh water in a cup. He squinted his eyes against the flickering light of a burning oil lamp. Its aura shimmered with a surprising prism of colours, unnerving him a little.

'Matt?' he called.

He expected his voice to come out husky and spent, but it sounded pure and full. He stood up – his legs felt strong. He walked over to the door. It was open.

Strange.

He moved out into the narrow passageway.

Empty.

The gladiatorial barracks should be throbbing with noise. Where was everyone?

He ran to Matthias's cell.

Also empty. A tunic lay across his mattress, and a pestle and mortar with some semi-crushed medication stood abandoned on the table by the small window.

Seth walked across to the window and looked out. Again, that strange spectrum of coloured light shimmering around the edges of the eerily empty practice arena. He glanced across it towards the gates. Where were the guards? They never left their post.

Without another thought, he fled from the building, across the deserted arena until he reached the huge wooden gates. Glancing behind him, he gave them an almighty shove. They clanked open. He slipped through quickly, before the sound could betray him, and continued to run, certain his captors wouldn't be far behind.

He knew where he was heading: their secret meeting place. He pictured her standing in the shadows of the trees. Waiting for him.

Livia. His Livia.

And then he froze, because he suddenly remembered. She wouldn't be there. Couldn't be there. She was gone forever.

He had watched her die.

PART I

Time is too slow for those who wait,
Too swift for those who fear,
Too long for those who grieve,
Too short for those who rejoice,
But for those who love, time is eternity.

– Henry van Dyke (1852–1933)

1

Delinquent

York, England

AD 2012

'*Eva, what is your problem?*'

I shrugged. Where to begin?

'So what were you doing when you were supposed to be at school?'

'Er – this and that.'

'What's that supposed to mean?'

Really? Do you really want to know, 'Dad'?

'Eva, what is going to happen to you?' Mum had finally joined the party.

How the hell did I know what was going to happen to me? But thanks, Mum, for reminding me that I had no future, and that you would always side with *him*.

I stared back at them. My mother and my stepfather, Colin. All I needed now was darling Ted to show up (his son, *not* my brother), to make it three against one.

'I'm so sick of this, Eva,' said Colin. 'Get out! I don't want to look at you –'

'The feeling's mutual,' I muttered as I shoved past him and stormed off to my room.

My first instinct was to pick up my guitar, turn up the amp and scream. But I didn't trust myself. I loved my guitar too much – it was my dad's – and all I wanted to do was smash something. I tried to get my breathing under control, but the rage was building. I needed to get out. I grabbed my jacket and slammed out of the house.

Then I ran . . . through the town, across the park, down the hill to the river. I ran along the path, ignoring the joggers, dog walkers, inevitable wolf whistles – I could shut out anything when I put my mind to it – until gradually the red suffocating heat started to subside, and I began to feel calmer.

I even managed a small humourless chuckle. Because for once Colin did have a genuine reason for being freaked.

I had been expelled *again*.

And I'd read enough to know that two expulsions meant you were pretty well washed up. And even though I hadn't turned up at school for weeks I couldn't help feeling this huge void opening up in front of me. My future.

My stomach churned. It was pretty scary being sixteen and washed up.

The last thing I wanted was to think about my life and how I'd got to this point. I just needed to keep running and block it all out, but my brain would not stop fizzing away uncontrollably.

My brain.

My brain was definitely at the core of the problem. The number of times I'd wished I was normal. But had I ever been normal? Happy? Like other kids?

I could only really remember when things started to unravel . . . when I realized that a gift could be a curse.

How old was I? About six, probably. My dad had been dead, I don't know – nearly a year, I guess . . . And although Mum's months of continuous crying were finally over her interest in me remained . . . intermittent. So I had plenty of time to amuse myself.

On this particular day, the TV was on as usual – Mum had shoved the remote in my hand and told me to stay put. But I'd had enough of TV. I'd read everything there was to read in the house (OK – she didn't have a lot of books) and I was bored.

I looked out of the window. Mum was in the garden, lying on a recliner, her eyes shut. I remember pressing my face to the window, willing her to look up and notice me. But of course she didn't. As I reluctantly turned away, I caught sight of her open laptop on the table. I wandered over to it and touched a key. It blinked into life. It was open on a web page: my mum had been ordering some wine. Wine wasn't very interesting to a six-year-old, but I had watched my mum typing so I had got the gist of the mechanics. I had also, it turned out, photo-graphically memorized quite a lot of what Mum had typed – like her bank details, her PIN and password. Within a couple of hours I had done a bit of shopping myself.

I was delighted when a few days later twenty-five packs of Dolly Mixtures, a hundred bottles of lemonade, a Labrador puppy and three Siamese kittens arrived. My mother was *not* delighted. Although I happily confessed to the shopping, she didn't believe me, assuming she'd been the victim of some iden-tity theft mess-up.

I wasn't allowed to keep any of my purchases, so I didn't do that again, but I'd discovered an awesome new world, a world where I had total control. To a small, lonely, powerless child this was mind-blowing.

By the time I was eight I could hack my way through most data security codes and firewalls, and although nobody had the least suspicion about what I was doing, I had the sense to cover my tracks pretty well. By then I knew that this activity wasn't strictly legal. But my motives were pure: I just enjoyed cracking codes – they fascinated me. I wasn't interested in people's secrets, their data, their financial status; I just got a buzz breaking open locked doors.

Needless to say, I wasn't that good around other eight-year-olds. Barbies just didn't do it for me. I liked the idea of having friends; I longed to have friends actually. I just couldn't fake normality well enough. I didn't understand that kids wouldn't want me to mathematically predict the outcome of any playground game before they started playing. Or that the whole point of The Memory Game was that you *didn't* remember what was on the reverse of every card. Pretty soon I stopped getting asked to play.

School was mostly excruciating. I sat for hour after endless hour listening to old facts and obsolete ideas. And things weren't much better at home . . . Colin just about endured me while Ted seemed to loathe me more each day.

I had dreamed of running away loads of times, but didn't really know how, so for several years I made do with virtual escape – I could customize any computer with undetectable pirated games, and found a lot of comfort in becoming someone else, someone with power, someone who could conquer legions of mythical enemies. The games became my *real* life.

They kept me sane . . . till I discovered an even more exciting world.

I was about eleven and had finally started bunking school. Not intentionally at first. One Monday morning I just couldn't bring myself to get off the bus at the school stop and by the Thursday I'd discovered the town library: banks of computers, shelves of books, nobody hassling you. How had this oasis managed to stay such a well-kept secret from me? It became my paradise. Day after day I sat in an inconspicuous corner, devouring information: the disintegration of Stalinism; social organization in Roman Britain; Russian; Latin; Greek; quantum theory; random genetics . . . just about anything and everything turned me on. When I got home, I'd continue my reading online until someone came in. Then I'd quickly erase my history, log out, shut down and put the TV on.

I genuinely believed I'd get away with it. I thought I'd covered all bases. I'd researched drawn-out illnesses with symptoms I could fairly easily fake, and forged a letter to the school from my mother claiming I had ME and needed to be excused indefinitely.

I used the same story when the librarian eventually challenged me. I thought she'd swallowed it. I'd even begun to trust her enough to have a couple of conversations about the Canadian legal system (she was Canadian), but she turned out to be a *total traitor*.

Three months after I entered paradise I was to be cast out again. One minute I was completely absorbed in a *Lancet* article about stem-cell research, the next minute I was being tapped on the shoulder by some appalling welfare officer.

For two hours I refused to speak. I knew that once I told them my name they'd call my parents and send me back to school. Unfortunately, when you're only eleven and you haven't received training in SAS counter-torture techniques, you don't stand up well to interrogation. I caved. I was taken home to Mum and Colin (massive row) and they sent me back to school. I received my first official warning.

This meant that if I did anything else *really bad* I would get kicked out of school.

My heart lifted! All I had to do now was come up with something big enough to get expelled. I began researching and plotting.

It turns out there's an actual list of expellable offences. Truancy (Number Six) I had successfully completed. I just had to choose my second crime. I drew the line at violence, bullying or supplying drugs. But Offence Number Seven was made for me – computer hacking! The main challenge was making it blindingly obvious that I was the only suspect.

It was quite a lot of fun. I got into the head teacher's email account and composed the perfect letter of resignation, which I mailed to everyone on the board of governors and to each member of staff. Then I sent out an email alert to all the pupils, advising them that school had been cancelled for the rest of the week. I left a neat, easy-to-follow trail back to my own login account, and four days later I was summoned. After submitting to an hour's worth of rant, I skipped out of the school and never looked back.

Actually, although I never looked back, looking forward didn't turn out to be that much better. Because the head teacher's fury was like a sneeze compared to my parents' anger. I was grounded for a week and then they packed me off to Downley Comprehensive . . .

Surprisingly, Downley Comp was OK at first. It was big, anonymous, and had enough disruptive pupils to keep the focus off me. I managed to be quietly invisible for nearly three years.

But sadly, when I hit fourteen, stray interest began to be a problem.

As if my life wasn't awkward enough, I had just started to develop *Disability Number Two*.

2

Escape

York, England

AD 2012

For some reason I suddenly lost my invisibility cloak. I had been working on being inconspicuous for so long that I almost believed I was invisible. I walked in the shadows, didn't make conversation, sat at the back, avoided all eye contact, but gradually I became aware of people looking at me. Boys started asking me stuff, inviting me to weekend events.

A small buried part of me really wanted the company, wanted to go with them, but an instinct told me it wasn't safe. They would find me out. So I tried ignoring them. They just persisted. I tried acerbic rudeness. They just laughed as though I was flirting. I cut my hair really short, and started wearing baggy clothes. Nothing worked. My distance seemed to just make them more avid. Then when Jason Drummond chucked Sophie Scott, saying he fancied me more, the girls stopped ignoring me too. Instead, they started to actively hate me. En masse. And girl bullying is no fun.

It was definitely time to leave.

I'd hoped I wouldn't need to resort to expulsion again. It was, after all, legal to leave school at sixteen. But I'd made the mistake of getting a bunch of A* GCSEs. I had radically improved Downley Comp's exam stats, and they were counting on my A-level results to do the same. So when I told the head I was leaving, he phoned my parents, and they started forcing me through the school gates every morning. I had to take evasive action. So I resorted to my little hacking gag again, and within two weeks I'd managed to get kicked out . . .

. . . *And* pick up a police record.

I stopped running and stood staring across the river.

I had just reviewed my life to date, and it was a pitiful catalogue of failure. I had managed to make a complete mess of everything. I was a criminal. I had failed at school – twice. I had failed to make a single friend. I had even failed to be loved by my own mother: quite an achievement.

Nobody really wanted me around.

I was shivering. It was getting cold. I knew I had to keep moving so I started to walk, mindlessly on and on, until I found my legs had carried me to my old sanctuary: the library.

I opened the door and wandered across to the seat in the corner. I sat down in front of the terminal. Someone had left a newspaper on the table next to the monitor. It was open at the job ads.

That's when it hit me. Like a bolt of lightning. I could get a job! I was sixteen now. And if I got a job, I could probably afford to move out – get away from my parents . . . and darling Ted!

I began to feel just a tiny flutter of optimism. What if I could get a job in a science lab? One with an electron microscope?

That would be OK. That would be more than OK. That would be cool.

With shaking fingers I started surfing. I keyed in: *research jobs – electron microscope*. Loads of technician jobs came up. My heart thumped as I trawled. Although most of them were in the States, there were a few in the UK . . .

For someone quite clever I guess I could be pretty stupid.

In what universe was I expecting anyone to invite a sixteen-year-old felon with no qualifications into their precious science lab?

Ad after ad was filled with lists of annoying requirements . . . stuff like 'three years' experience, blah blah . . . doctorate . . . relevant expertise . . .'

I didn't even have A levels. I'd be lucky if I could get a job making beds in a hotel. Angrily, I started deleting my search bar, and accidentally double-clicked on *electron microscope*. A new entry popped up.

St Magdalene's acquire an electron microscope . . . cached.

Without a lot of interest, I clicked on the page and started reading. The name St Magdalene's rang a little bell. It had come up before on one of my researches – ancient Roman burial sites or something . . .

I started reading.

St Magdalene's School in central London has just acquired a scanning electron microscope at a cost of £1.8 million. St Magdalene's is unique – the only school in the world where the pupils need an IQ score in excess of 170. This is off-the-scale genius level. They are also required to sit a four-day sequence of tests and interviews. It is consequently a small school, with very few places. Only the brilliant need apply.

Should such a school exist? Many educationalists question the elitism of such an establishment, insisting that it is in the interest of children and the system generally that schools cover a full spectrum of abilities. But the head teacher, Dr Terence Crispin, is adamant that St Magdalene's children need this rarefied environment to thrive . . .

It was the next line that made my stomach twist.

. . . Super-gifted children can have difficulties in mainstream education, and here they are understood and given scope . . .

I clicked on to the St Magdalene's School website.

It looked a bit like a medieval castle, built round a cobbled courtyard. Couldn't be more different from the purpose-built four-storey block that was Downley Comprehensive. I clicked on *Facilities* . . . and within a couple of seconds I was staring at their newly acquired microscope.

My heart missed a beat. I HAD to go there.

How did you apply? Feverishly, I searched through the contact info and application forms. Then suddenly I saw a line that made me want to be sick.

Fees: £10,000 per term.

Yeah, right.

I slammed my fist down on to the table. Someone coughed and I remembered where I was.

I hadn't cried for years. So I didn't recognize the tightness in my throat, until the tears started plopping down on to the keypad. I shut down and stormed out of the library.

It was late by the time I turned the key in the lock. I was hoping they'd all be in bed. Mum was waiting.

'Hi.' I tried to sound nonchalant.

Nonchalance was clearly not the right note.

'Eva – where *were* you? I've been going out of my mind. I was about to call the police . . .'

My heart sank. How had I managed to turn myself into a delinquent?

I sighed, slumped down on the sofa and put my head in my hands. I should have phoned. Should have taken my mobile. I looked at my mother. She was pale. Lined. Worried and angry.

She didn't have the faintest idea how to deal with me. I wanted to be angry with her, but instead I felt an unexpected wave of sympathy. She had been landed with a rubbish daughter who couldn't do the simplest thing right.

I had to get away. Give them all a break.

'Look – I'm sorry, Mum,' I whispered, and slowly climbed the stairs to my room.

I couldn't sleep, so I sat on my bed, and took out my laptop. I logged on and found myself Googling St Magdalene's again.

How was I going to find that kind of money? Rob a bank? I probably could. I could hack my way into most places – why not a bank? First I'd need to set up an account – then I'd have to transfer enough money into it to cover two years of fees – £60,000. Whoa!

My fingers started flying, rising to the challenge. And then abruptly I stopped.

What was I doing?

I may have had a criminal record but I wasn't actually a criminal, was I? I lay back against the pillows. No. I couldn't do it.

I clicked back to the St Magdalene site. Did another virtual tour of the science labs, the art history wing, the drama studios. I masochistically clicked back on the application page.

And then I saw it. A tiny little link labelled *Scholarships & Bursaries*. How had I missed this before?

A number of means-tested bursaries are available. They are awarded on the basis of academic ability and financial need. When a full bursary is offered, it will cover the cost of all tuition, equipment and boarding fees.

Boarding fees? A boarding school? A TOTAL escape . . .

I started filling out the application form then and there. It was pretty straightforward. I knew the difficult questions came later – if they invited you in.

At 3 a.m. I pressed the send button. At 4 a.m. I was lying in the dark trying not to hope too hard.

3

Control

Londinium

AD 152

Sethos Leontis's hopes were limited. Although some irrepressible part of him hoped to live to see another day, he knew he had little control over his destiny. A gladiator lived and died by the will of others.

Nevertheless Seth took what control he could: he had total possession of his body. It was honed. Ready. He had trained hard: harder than most of the others; harder than the lanista had pushed him, and Zeus knew the lanista's regime was savage.

He looked out across the practice arena. It was unusually peaceful. The rest of the gladiators were on the other side of the city now, feasting. They felt they justly deserved the banquet they were enjoying – one of the few pleasures of their dangerous lives. But for Seth, attending the banquet in some way indicated an acceptance of the world he'd been dragged into. He would never do that. He was not born to be a slave: fighting to survive; subject to the whim of the crowd; under the ruthless ownership of the maverick lanista, Tertius. He absently rubbed the tattoo on his arm, the tattoo that denoted his status. The muscles in his jaw flexed. He could not afford to lose his focus; anger was not helpful.

He had been blessed with strength, power, stamina and speed. But the gladiator he would be fighting tomorrow would probably possess most of these skills. And Sethos knew that if you intended to win, to live to see another day, you needed more than good skills. You needed an unshakeable determination, and absolute concentration. His concentration during a fight was so acute that it manifested as a kind of uncanny intuition. In practice, this meant that he could analyse his adversary so accurately, so quickly, that he was able to calculate the next move, and thus pre-empt it. This not only gave him a clinching advantage, it also made him mesmerizing to watch.

Sethos gazed out at the stone seats of the training arena. Later, when the feasting was over, the area would be swarming with citizens, all eager to meet tomorrow's winners and losers. He shook his head. He hated the ritual. Hated the status ambivalence. They weren't free men, yet they were fêted and adored.

The tiny squeak of a sandal behind him initiated his lightning reflexes and his dagger was out, his posture tense.

'Oh, it's you, Matt!' He sheathed his weapon and raised an arm in greeting. Matthias was his friend, a fellow Corinthian slave, captured on the same raid. Too slight to be a fighter, Matthias had made himself indispensable to the familia with his training in medicines. He carried clean towels, water and a flask of oil.

'Not at the banquet then?' Matthias clapped Sethos across the shoulders and gestured for him to sit.

'Are you surprised?'

'They are fools to gorge themselves so near a fight. They will slow their minds and bodies.'

As he spoke, Matthias steered his friend to a nearby bench, and began to rub oil into his shoulders. He knew every muscle in Seth's body, and slowly, methodically, made sure each one had been sufficiently warmed and loosened before moving on to the next. While his fingers worked, he saw again the drawings and charts his father had shown him: the bones; the muscle groups; the arteries and veins. But here he stopped his mind from wandering. He did not want to think about his father. He forced his mind back. Seth's skin was so much paler than it had been in Corinth – so much less sun here in Londinium. Though today, on this glorious June evening, you could almost imagine yourself back home: preparing for the honourable games, not this bestial gladiatorial circus. He had not known Sethos well at home, but since they had been thrown together, he now loved him like a brother.

Matthias had been up since dawn, preparing the fresh Sabine olive oil with juniper leaves. He would do the same tomorrow. It was his way of helping to keep his friend alive. He was rubbing down Seth's calves when the singing crowd started to make their way through the big stone gateway. They had clearly been drinking plenty of good wine: the party was loud and wild.

'Let's get out of here,' murmured Sethos, trying to stand, but Matthias hadn't finished and was too superstitious to stop now. He pushed his friend back down.

'Patience, Seth. Only a few moments more.'

They did not have a few moments.

'There he is! Sethos Leontis!' The crowd started to converge on them.

'Here, Sethos! Drink to your victory tomorrow!'

A cup of wine was pushed to his lips. He turned his mouth away, but hands were grabbing him, touching his oiled skin.

'Hey! Give him some air! Zeus! Do you want him to suffocate before he makes it to the fight!' shouted Matthias, trying to push them all back.

Just then Tertius and the rest of the familia came through into the arena.

The crowd became distracted. Some moved off to greet other heroes, but Sethos knew from experience that most of the women would stay here. As a *retiarius*, he wore virtually no armour, only a leather shoulder strap. So although he was strong, compared with the heavily armoured, sometimes massive opponents he faced, he needed to rely on his speed and agility. The women found this kind of fighting attractive, he supposed. He did not acknowledge that his physical beauty was another factor.

Reluctantly, Sethos flexed his shoulders, preparing to rise and face his admirers – there was no way the massage could be finished under these circumstances. But as he stood, he noticed a girl, head covered, standing just behind two older women. She was watching him, through heavy-lashed, dark almond eyes. Her eyes danced. She found his obvious discomfort amusing. The corners of her mouth twitched . . . her mouth – he had never seen a more lovely mouth: full lips, slightly parted over small white teeth. A tiny breeze lifted her head cover, and a strand of black hair escaped. As she pushed it back, the gold jewellery on her wrist caught the light.

Sethos found his legs moving towards her. She blushed but held his gaze. The two women she stood with gasped in pleasure, unaware that the object of his interest stood just behind them.

'Sethos Leontis! What an honour to meet you! We are such supporters! I cannot believe that one as young as you now holds eight wreaths! How is that possible?'

'The gods have been kind. So – you will be watching the fight tomorrow?' He spoke to them, but his eyes flicked over to the girl. She nodded imperceptibly.

'We will certainly be there!'

'May I know who my loyal supporters are?'

'Oh, of course! I am Rufina Agrippa, and this is Flavia Natalis . . .'

Sethos took each lady's hand in turn, and put it to his lips.

'And?' he prompted, shifting his gaze towards the almond eyes.

'Oh! The *child*! Adopted daughter of Flavia and Domitus Natalis – Livia . . .'

Livia's eyes shot fire. 'I am almost seventeen, Rufina! Hardly a child!'

This time it was Sethos's mouth that twitched. 'Livia Natalis – a pleasure!' he murmured, taking her hand and kissing it. Her skin smelled sweet, of rosewater and jasmine. He inhaled deeply, inconspicuously, but Rufina noted his interest and bristled.

'Livia, will your betrothed be accompanying you to the games tomorrow?'

Livia's cheeks burned. 'Cassius is *not* my betrothed. I have not yet accepted him!'

And then she bit her lip. She had said too much.

'Come, Livia, there are many others waiting to speak with Sethos Leontis. Perhaps, Sethos, in the event of your victory, we will meet again at tomorrow's banquet?'

Flavia Natalis extended her hand, which he dutifully put to his lips. 'It would be an honour.'

As they moved away, Sethos gazed after them, willing the girl to turn round. He had almost given up hope, when she suddenly turned and shot him a secret glance. He touched his forehead in a mock salute, and she smiled. He felt a wave of unfamiliar warmth.

As they disappeared through the archway into the crowd, Sethos marvelled at the liberty of Roman women. In Corinth, where he came from, a girl would never be allowed the freedom of the city, and as for such an open defiance of her family's marriage arrangements . . . He shuddered to think of the repercussions, and felt a flood of protective fear for this lovely girl.

'Seth – what *are* you thinking?' Matthias hissed in his ear.

Sethos started, suddenly remembering where he was.

'She's an unmarried Roman citizen!'

Matthias was so damned sharp. Seth's jaw clenched. He knew what Matthias was saying. *Remember who you are: a slave.* He had no rights in this city. The girl, Livia, was as out of his reach as the sun in the sky.

'Stick to married women!' Matthias murmured, as another wave of flushed female admirers pushed their way forward to greet him.

Sethos remained in the arena for another half-hour, answering questions, allowing the Roman women to flirt with him. The lanista was watching him. Sethos knew it was his duty to be charming: the more popular he was the bigger the audience. But later, when he spotted the lanista sitting back on one of the stone seats with a jug of wine, and a woman on his knee, he seized his opportunity to slip out.

Matthias wasn't far behind. He loved the women who clustered around Sethos, and his proximity to the star gave him many social advantages, but the night before a fight his loyalty to his friend had to come first. They headed to their barracks. Sethos poured two cups of water from a jug, handed one to Matthias and took the other with him as he stretched out on his narrow mat. Matthias squatted at one end of the bed, poured a little oil into his palms, and proceeded with the interrupted massage.

Sethos began to relax. The massage felt good. He allowed his mind to wander – to the girl with the almond eyes. He had encountered so many women since being torn from his home. Some beautiful, some exotic, some powerful – all of them married. They had chosen him, and had made discreet arrangements to meet with him. But he had never wanted to *know* any of them, or actively seek them out.

His interest in Livia therefore came as a shock – an alien emotion. And Matt was right – it certainly wasn't healthy. Distinctly unhealthy, in fact. To even entertain the idea of a relationship with this girl was suicide. Roman law would show him no mercy. But what difference did one more unhealthy addition make to his life? He was a gladiator, after all.

He opened his eyes. Yes. He was a gladiator, and he had a

big fight in a matter of hours. He couldn't afford to be distracted. He had to concentrate his mind. Matthias had begun pummelling the other leg. Sethos shut his eyes again, and reminded himself of the running order. Although the fight lists weren't yet published, he knew he would be facing Protix Canitis, a massive Gaul who hated Romans and Greeks alike. Protix was a savage fighter, and his passionate hatred would be an even match for Seth's speed and intuition. Seth fervently hoped that Protix had availed himself of plenty of wine today. He could use all the help he could get. Suddenly his desire to win tomorrow felt acute, overpowering his usual simple motive of self-preservation. He sat up, eyes wide.

'What is it?' asked Matthias.

'I have to win.'

'You will win. You always win.'

'I mean, I need to win –'

'That's good –'

'Because afterwards, I am going to see the girl: Livia.'

Matthias shook his head. 'The *one* woman in Londinium he can't have, he chooses . . . Seth – do you *want* to die? Or have you had so many blows to the head that your brain's stopped functioning? Leave her alone. No woman is worth a death sentence.'

'Apollo's flames, Matt! My life is a death sentence! Surely to die for a woman would be a more purposeful cause?'

Matthias whistled through his teeth in frustration. He hated it when his friend was reckless. He became unmanageable. And it wasn't easy keeping Seth alive at the best of times. He was too passionate, too angry, too charming. All these qualities made him vulnerable.

But Matthias also recognized that Seth was far too clever to be managed. He read people so accurately that he could almost hear their thoughts. It was safer to keep his counsel for now.

'Win your fight first – then decide what's worth dying for.'

Seth smiled, and slapped Matthias across the shoulders. 'That sounds like a plan.'

4

St Magdalene's

London

AD 2012

'So, Eva – your parents? They are not with you today. Are they enthusiastic about your application here?'

'Well – er –'

This interview was not going well. The pile of tests had gone fine – all pretty easy, but now I was sitting opposite the St Magdalene's headmaster, Dr Crispin, and I'd more or less given up.

I'd started messing up when he asked me what subjects I would be interested in studying. This shouldn't have been difficult. Not unless you happened to be some sort of weird misfit. Instead of just answering the question, I'd started to sweat: this was a topic I found it hard to be cool about. He'd just sat there waiting. Waiting for me to dig my own grave – which I obligingly did.

'I think it's crazy the way we're made to choose between arts or sciences or humanities – why should people only be allowed to be curious about one minute corner of the universe? There is so much to find out . . . If I had any control, I would be studying everything, anything . . .' I'd tailed off, coughed, and started again, hoping he would forget my little outburst.

'Sorry – I guess – well, the A levels I've been doing are maths, applied maths, biology, physics, chemistry . . .'

He'd stared at me for a moment, pursed his lips, and then written a load of notes on a pad. Not a good sign. Then – to finally seal my fate – he moved on to the personal stuff: my parents. And there was no way I was prepared to go there. I just couldn't help myself – I resorted to my fallback position: gazing out of the window. I knew it irritated the hell out of teachers. They called it *disengaged*. I called it *survival*.

He waited. I gazed. He finally cracked.

'I see. All right then, let me ask you something else. Perhaps you'd be good enough to tell me why you gave up on your previous secondary schools – er – North York High School and – er – Downley Comprehensive?'

How did he know *I'd* given up on *them*? Expulsion normally suggests it's the other way round. Was he giving me a chance to explain?

I tried to drag myself back to the room. Headmaster. St Magdalene's. A place I *really* wanted to be.

He was still talking. '. . . To lose one school could be regarded as a misfortune, but to lose two may begin to look like carelessness?'

I cleared my throat. 'Careless – but consistent,' I countered.

His sharp blue eyes were squinting at me through half-moon glasses. Suddenly his bony face broke into a smile. 'Yes, that is true . . . And here at St Magdalene's we have often found consistency to be an admirable virtue . . .

'We are also a little intrigued by your prodigious – how should I put this? – extracurricular abilities . . .'

I stared back at him, bewildered.

'With – ahem – computers . . .'

'Ah,' I said. Damn. I'd been hoping to keep the hacking quiet.

'I'd be interested to find out how long it takes you to get into my account, Ms Koretzky. Naturally, we have fashioned a considerable number of obstacles – it would be fascinating to learn how successfully . . .'

And this, it turned out, was his way of telling me I'd won a place at his school.

Two weeks later, I returned to St Magdalene's with a big suitcase, my acoustic guitar and a sick feeling in the pit of my stomach.

My mum and Colin had responded to the news with mixed feelings. Mostly they were relieved that someone was taking me off their hands. But being only too familiar with my record of past successes, they didn't think they'd have peace and quiet for very long. I couldn't blame them. I felt pretty much the same way.

Virtually everyone at St Mag's had been there since they were eleven, and most of them boarded as they came from all over the country. I'd read *Malory Towers* and *Harry Potter* so my expectation of boarding school was gilded in fantasy, but I didn't arrive filled with bubbling hope of friendship and adventure. I was way too realistic.

Which meant I was completely thrown by Ruby. Ruby was the girl chosen to show me around. She was also sixteen, tall, blonde, willowy, cool. Not like me at all – pale-skinned, dark-haired and weird. She smiled easily, laughed easily, talked easily.

'Right then, Eva, this is our boarding house.'

I looked up at the name carved in the stone above the front door.

'Isaac Newton,' I read.

'All the houses are named after influential thinkers connected with St Mag's.'

'What's Isaac Newton's connection?'

'They say he came and lectured here,' shrugged Ruby.

'But – but wasn't he around in the seventeenth century?'

'We've got earlier ones than him! I mean Omar, a boy in our year, is in Geoffrey Chaucer. Chaucer goes back *ages*! St Magdalene's has been around – God, I don't know – forever!'

As she talked, Ruby was leading me through the front door, along a narrow corridor and up a winding staircase. She was moving too fast for me to get a good look at the hundreds of pictures that lined the walls. Towards the end of the corridor, she suddenly stopped and flung open a door.

'This is your room.'

I stepped in cautiously. 'What? Don't we sleep in *dorms*?'

'Ha ha! You've been reading Enid Blyton, haven't you? I made that mistake! No – we get our own rooms, desks, PCs, showers . . . it's great.'

And she was right. It was great. Nothing fancy – no Hogwarts four-posters or anything. Although we'd just walked through a corridor that looked like it was centuries old, the bedrooms were surprisingly modern. All glass and light wood. We even had our own en-suite shower rooms! Ruby quickly showed me where to stow my things, how to double-lock my door so *nobody* could get in, and how to get out of the building after curfew. Essential stuff. Then she took me to her room.

'Wow!' I gasped. She'd transformed the place. The bed was covered in an intricately patterned Mexican blanket and loads of cushions. Not one scrap of the wall was visible through the mass of postcards, photos and posters. She had also added a couple of tall chrome lamps and a serious music system.

'Come and sit down,' she said, flopping on to her bed. I hesitantly sat down next her.

'OK, Eva! Tell me what brings you to St Mag's! I want to know *everything*!'

'Er,' I stalled. This was unexpected.

Ruby sat there waiting.

'Well – er –' I swallowed. It felt like I was back in the head-master's office. 'I f-found out about the school online and filled in an application form . . .' I shrugged, hoping that would be enough.

It wasn't. She just stared at me, waiting for the rest.

'What?' I asked, longing to get back to my own room.

'Oh, come on, Eva!'

I bit my lip nervously. 'What do you want to know?' I croaked.

'What school were you at before?'

'Downley Comprehensive.'

'And . . .?' she said, rolling her eyes.

'And what?'

'And – why did you leave?'

'I got myself expelled . . .'

'Expelled?'

Her shocked expression shut me up. Imagine her face if she found out I'd managed to get expelled twice.

She shook her head, leaned back against the pillows and waited for me to say something.

I didn't.

'Eva! How did you get expelled?'

I rolled my eyes. 'Long story . . .'

'I've got time.'

I just shook my head.

Ruby sighed, jumped off the bed and then began rifling around underneath it. A couple of seconds later she dragged out a tin, which she pulled up on to the bed and opened.

'My sister made these. I only offer them to totally monosyllabic new girls . . . Go on – help yourself!' she grinned.

Inside the tin was a pile of misshapen chocolate cookies. I took one.

'Thanks,' I mumbled.

'So – if you aren't going to spill about your evil past, at least tell me about your family. I've told you something about mine . . . I've got a sister. Actually, I've got two. Now – your turn . . . Your parents . . . Why didn't they bring you?'

I sat in silence for a couple of seconds. Officially chewing. Unofficially wondering how the hell I was going to get out of this room.

'*Eva!*' Ruby said in exasperation. 'I'm going to keep you here until you say something . . . so unless you want to live in silence on my sister's cookies for the rest of your life (and I can assure you they aren't *that* good), you might as well start talking.'

God, was she undercover Gestapo?

'So – what do you want to know?' I said warily.

'Your *parents?*'

'Well . . . I don't exactly have *parents* –' I muttered, making a move for the door.

She put an arm out to stop me. 'Hey! Don't go! I really didn't

32

mean to freak you out! I'm so sorry, I didn't realize you'd lost your parents – I'm such a tactless idiot.'

She looked so guilty I couldn't help relenting.

'No, Ruby – I didn't mean you to think – er – well – I do have parents – sort of . . .'

She just sat there, waiting for more. I sighed and sat back down.

'I have a mother. My dad died when I was small –'

'Oh, you poor thing! That's awful. Do you remember him?'

I stared at her, realizing that she was the first person who had ever asked me about him. I had spent years trying not to think about my dad. Mum had been so stricken when he died that I was never allowed to mention his name, so he had been my guilty secret. I had one beaten-up old photo of him, which I kept under the lining paper in my sock drawer. In desperate moments I'd pull out his picture and confide in him, and in truth when I was younger this had comforted me. But I eventually got too old to believe in the restorative power of an old photo. And the more dysfunctional my life became, the less able I felt to face him. I knew he'd be too disappointed in me. I hadn't looked at that photo in years.

I shook my head sadly.

Ruby was staring at me. 'You don't remember him at all?'

I sighed. 'Yes, I remember him . . . Moments . . . Riding high on his shoulders, his hands tight round my ankles . . . sitting in my car seat gazing at the back of his head . . .'

'How did he die?'

'Car crash.'

'So it's just you and your mum?'

'No.'

'Sorry – if you really don't want to talk about it . . .'

I took a deep breath.

'My mother remarried when I was seven.'

'I'm guessing he's not your favourite guy?'

I tried to picture Colin. Had I ever liked him?

'I think when he first turned up I wanted to like him . . . My dad had been dead a while – I didn't have replacement issues or anything . . . but he had a son of his own . . .'

'You've got a brother?'

'STEPbrother,' I corrected.

Why was I spilling like this?

'Oh my God, Eva! This is better than *Neighbours*. What's he like?'

I pressed my lips together. I'd said way too much. My palms were beginning to sweat.

'Aw, come *on*, Eva!' she pressed.

I sat in silence.

'OK, you've asked for it . . .' She grinned purposefully.

My heart started to thud. Oh God – was she turning on me already?

'Asked for what?' I croaked, my eyes darting wildly for the door.

'Since you are providing me with such an abysmally disappointing amount of information, you will now be subjected to . . .' She looked across at me and wiggled her eyebrows . . . 'a twenty-minute monologue – at least – about me and my family.'

I blinked.

'Ready to change your mind?'

I shook my head and grinned.

Ruby leaned back and crossed her legs.

'OK – just remember – you've only got yourself to blame . . .
Hmmm. Where to begin? OK. So – like I said I have two sisters,
two parents, a dog, three cats and a horse. We live in Suffolk
. . . well – our main family home is in Suffolk, though my father
has a flat he uses in London . . .'

I raised my eyebrows.

She grinned. 'He's a high court judge, so when they're in
session he stays in London. He sometimes takes me out to
dinner . . .'

'Is that allowed?'

'Yeah – they're pretty cool here about boarders. They need
some sort of email confirmation from the parent, and then you
just sign out. Maybe one evening you could come with me?'

I swallowed. A big lump had just formed in my throat. Ruby
and me. Like normal friends . . .

'It also means that when he's not in London, we've got somewhere empty to go after curfew!' she grinned wickedly.

'Wow!' I breathed. This was beginning to feel quite *St Trinian's*.

'What about your mum? Does she ever come with him?'

'Not really. She's not crazy about London. She says she can't
think properly here. She spends most of the time in her studio
at home – she's a conceptual artist. You may have heard of her
– Martha Gaine?'

Had I heard of her! I'd have had to be living on a different
planet not to have heard of her.

'Yeah, I've heard of her. I love that *Rain* installation she
did . . .'

Ruby looked at me, surprised. 'To be honest, Eva, I don't
really get her art! It all seems a bit random to me. Miranda
loves it, though.'

'Miranda?'

'My big sister. She's at university in the States, majoring in art history.'

'Did Miranda come here too?'

'No. She didn't pass the entrance exams. My father couldn't believe it. He came here when he was young, but he assured Miranda it wasn't nearly such a geeky school in his day.'

'Lucky for him you got in then!' I laughed.

She cocked her head to one side. 'It may not have been luck, Eva,' she whispered. 'I'm not sure I would have got in if he hadn't paid for the new philosophy wing.'

I sat in silence digesting this piece of information. She was watching me through narrowed eyes. I tried not to look shocked, but clearly failed.

'What disturbs you more, Eva? That he can afford to buy me a place, or that the school let him?'

I shrugged. 'Both. Neither. I think I'm trying to imagine a dad who cares that much! So are you glad you're here?'

'Yeah. It's OK. I just about keep up.'

A bell rang.

'Good, dinner time! Come on – I'll show you where we eat . . .'

5

Others

London

AD 2012

We crossed the quad to the dining room. It was wood-panelled, with big old portraits hanging on the walls, and chandeliers from the ceiling. Kids with trays were gradually filling the long tables and benches. We started queuing. The food didn't smell too bad. Way better than Downley Comp, but I knew I wouldn't be able to eat. I was too hyped. I took a glass of juice and a banana.

'Is that all you're having? God – you're not anorexic, are you?' asked Ruby, frowning.

'Anorexic? No – I just feel a bit –'

'Oh, yeah! Sorry – forgot – you've just arrived . . . That can make you feel sick. You'll be starving later, though. Here, take a couple of these – they've saved my life more than once . . .' She shoved two flapjacks on to my tray.

'Thanks,' I mumbled.

We carried our trays over to a half-full bench. The kids sitting there watched us as we unloaded our food.

'Hey, Rubes . . .' A tall boy with longish dark hair grinned up at us.

'Omar – this is Eva . . .'

She lightly ran her hand along the back of his shirt. He smiled at her, and then flicked a smile at me. While Ruby attacked her plate of food, Omar introduced me to the rest of the table. Everyone seemed so friendly I began to relax.

After supper, Ruby showed me the school library. It was unbelievable. The subject sections were in separate rooms, each with its own identity. We started with the biology area. It had a whole central aisle of life-sized skeletons . . . a human male, human female, human child, mouse, dog, elephant, iguana, macaw . . . there were at least thirty of them. The spaces of wall not covered in book shelving were filled with muscle charts, nerve charts, pressed flower and plant speci-mens, trays of butterflies . . . I just wanted to stand and stare, but Ruby was pulling me up a winding staircase into a circu-lar room.

'Physics,' she announced.

'Wow!' I breathed, as I gazed up at a domed ceiling twinkling with the stars and planets of our solar system.

'Cool, eh? And look at this . . . it's a space tracker – it charts the rapidly changing positions and distances between earth and all the other named planets . . . watch.' Ruby typed *Mercury* on to a keypad at the base of the instrument, and an arrow swivelled and pointed towards my feet.

'Hmmm,' I said. 'That's cool.'

'What are you thinking?' she asked.

'I'm thinking – that must be the trajectory of Mercury at the moment?'

'Oh God, Eva, you're the real thing, aren't you? When I first came up here and saw that the arrow pointed at a planet underneath me, I thought the machine was broken.'

'Why?'

'Because I assumed space was up there, in the sky . . . not all around us. When did you realize?'

I shrugged, but I was watching the screen racing through its calculation. For a few seconds it settled on 222,040,561 km. So that's how far away Mercury was. But then the arrow shifted a little and the numbers changed to 222,040,967 km. This was mind-blowing. Until then I hadn't really understood that the planets were all moving around so fast. Mercury had just moved 300 km in less than two seconds.

'Ruby, this is incredible!' I wanted to check out another planet, but she was hauling me off again, up a narrow staircase round and round at least a hundred steps, until we finally reached a small arched door.

We ducked our heads. I gasped. We were in an observatory. The ceiling and walls were made entirely of glass. In the centre of the room was a massive telescope, pointing up through the ceiling. And ranged around it, facing out towards the night sky, were another twelve smaller telescopes.

'I don't do astrophysics, Eva, so I can't remember what the different telescopes do. I think they all have different kinds of lenses or something. Oh – and Harry told me that we can also get data access to the really giant telescopes at NASA . . .'

In a daze, I walked across to the big telescope in the centre of the room, cautiously putting a hand out to touch it. But Ruby was looking at her watch.

'Eva, I have to show you the rest of the library and get you to the common room in ten minutes . . . I promise you – these will still be here tomorrow!'

I sighed, and let her drag me away. For the next ten minutes I was whisked through the art library – were those actual Titians on the wall? Through philosophy and ethics (it had a tented ceiling) . . . maths (the floor was also a chessboard) . . . chemistry (the walls were covered in formulae), English and drama (beanbags and sofas), languages (headphones and terminals), history (the books were all ranged round an enormous printing press), geography (globes like balloons hanging from the ceiling), Latin and Greek (incredible replica statues of gods dotted around the room), economics (a running screen along the wall charting real-time currency changes), and finally around the music section, which had cases filled with historic musical instruments, a couple going right back to the first century AD.

'If you get permission, you're allowed to have a go on them,' said Ruby, trying to hurry me through. 'Don't you think that kithara looks a bit like a guitar?'

'Ha – I don't s'pose they did many rock gigs in ancient Rome.'

'Is that what you're into? I saw you brought a guitar . . .'

I shrugged. 'Rock? Yeah, I guess so – I like lots of stuff . . .'

'Maybe you should hook up with Astrid – she'll probably be in the common room . . . She's cool – if she likes you!'

We had swung out of the library double doors and were heading across the quad.

'So – the common room . . .?'

'It's just a place the seniors hang out after 9 p.m. Until then

you're expected to be working or rehearsing or whatever . . .
OK, this is it . . .'

Ruby opened a door on to a room where about twenty
students were sprawled across sofas and chairs. Ruby strolled
towards the coffee machine. She found a couple of mugs and
started pouring coffee from the steaming jug.

'Eva – do you want milk, sugar?' she asked.

The room had gone kind of silent. I swallowed.

'Milk, thanks.' My voice came out in a sort of squeaky whisper. Why did she have to bring me here? I was so much happier
in the library.

I stood around for an eternity while she added milk and
stirred, and then found myself herded towards a big armchair.

'Sit,' she commanded and I sat. Ruby perched on the arm.

I leaned back and gratefully held on to the coffee cup she
handed me. At least it gave me something to do with my hands,
and more importantly something to focus on apart from the
twenty pairs of eyes all staring in my direction.

I was so busy looking down that I didn't notice Omar heading towards our chair until he'd perched himself on the other
arm.

'Hey, you two,' he smiled. 'How's the tour going?'

Ruby started filling him in, and I began to relax. Conversations around the room had started up again, and pretty soon I
considered it safe to look up over the rim of my mug and check
the place out.

It was a nice room – mood lighting, deep red walls. Even a
fireplace. One wall was covered by a big heavy curtain, which
made it feel cosier.

Ruby, who had been asking Omar about his football practice, suddenly nudged me and said, 'Do you want to see what's on the other side of that curtain?'

She was already walking over to it. I watched as she pulled it open.

'See?' she laughed. 'The room is actually way bigger! We just use this end most of the time, but for events – gigs, parties and stuff – we open up the whole space. Look – there's even a small stage at the far end. Next week we're planning a stand-up night. A couple of guys here,' and she raised an eyebrow at Omar, 'fancy themselves as comedians . . . Hey! Do you want me to put your name down for a slot?'

'You've gotta be joking,' I gasped, truly terrified.

She squawked with laughter. 'Yeah, Eva. I am . . . Sorry!'

As jokes go, that had *not* been funny. I tried to get my heart to slow down.

Omar gave me a nudge. 'Hey, Eva . . . it's OK. Relax!'

Relax! Huh. But I did my best.

And by the time I returned to my room that night I honestly felt like I had joined the human race at last. I had met about a thousand new people, and though I spent most of the time listening to their conversations, not actually talking myself, I had still felt – well – comfortable. I didn't need to pretend, I didn't have to hide. For the first time ever I didn't feel like some sort of impostor. It was like I had finally arrived home.

I unpacked my case, and caught myself looking forward to the next day – another first. I felt this weird need to laugh out loud. Luckily, I just about managed to stop myself. I put on my pyjamas, brushed my teeth, turned out the light, got under the duvet and shut my eyes. Then I opened them again. I put the light on, found my phone and texted my mother.

Hi Mum. All good. Love Eva.

I plugged in the phone charger, turned out the light and fell asleep.

6

Gladiator

Londinium

AD 152

The amphitheatre was heaving with people. Armour was polished, weapons oiled and sharpened. The gladiators were ready. They began processing on to the fresh new sand towards the governor Cnaeus Papirius Aelianus.

'Hail Aelianus! Those who are about to die salute you.'

The crowd was cheering and shouting. Sethos bowed but avoided looking directly into the crowd. He didn't want to see individuals. He preferred them as a braying faceless mass. As he processed with the other gladiators round the arena, he flexed his fingers. In his left hand he carried the net, and in his right the trident. His sharpened dagger was slung through his belt. Though it was evening, the sun was still so hot his fingers were finding it hard to keep purchase on their weapons. He would need to sand them again.

When the gladiators had finished their slow procession, they gathered behind the big wooden gates, while the musicians played. Sethos knew that in a few moments he would be fighting for his life. He closed his eyes and concentrated on his body, stilling it, preparing himself. Others resharpened swords, or spat on armour, or roared. He stood apart, silent, contained. Nobody touched him. He created an invisible barrier around himself, which inexplicably all the other gladiators respected. The horns sounded and Sethos knew it was time.

He opened his eyes. Matthias was now standing beside him. They slapped each other's right hand, just as the gate opened. Tertius, his owner, yelled at the gladiators to get the hell out there, so moments later Seth was running across the arena with the rest of the combatants.

Protix Canitis, his massive, heavily armoured opponent, lumbered towards him, shaking his sword at the crowd. People cheered with delight. Sethos knew it was his turn to greet the audience. Raising his chin, he did his wry mock salute and grinned. The crowd went wild.

'*SETHOS LEONTIS! SETHOS LEONTIS! SETHOS LEONTIS!*' they chanted.

But he wasn't listening. He had gone to the place in his head where he could function most effectively. He began dancing round his opponent. The Gaul swivelled clumsily, but Sethos knew that this man was not clumsy. He was feigning. Protix played an early show of ungainliness to make himself look more dexterous later when he jabbed accurately. And Protix was lethally accurate. He lulled his opponents into a false sense of complacency until they were taking stupid risks to go in for the kill. Sethos knew better. He had watched Protix fight. He understood the technique – admired it. So he danced and watched. He knew Protix wanted to wait for him to tire, but Seth was very fit. Protix was going to have a long wait. And Sethos was a very patient man.

At last Protix saw that he'd have to be a little more proactive. The crowd was getting restless. But he knew that the moment he lunged he became vulnerable to the net. Once he was netted he was helpless, so he had to avoid that.

His game plan was to disarm Sethos first, and then go in for the kill. Sethos understood this, so he kept a tight hold of his trident, and swirled the net, so there was no way the Gaul could catch it. Protix was much slower in his armour than Sethos, so speed was something he could not compete with.

Sethos darted around his opponent, biding his time. He was waiting for his opportunity. Protix had two vulnerable spots: his neck – the gap between his helmet and breastplate – and under the arm. An injury in either of these places would finish the fight. Unlike Protix, Sethos didn't have a game plan. He was infinitely flexible when it came to fighting. But he did have one objective. And that was to win: to get his opponent down, and the dagger to his throat. He would try to do this with as little injury to either of them as possible. It was never his intention to kill, or to inflict fatal wounds. The lanistas preferred their fighters alive. But nobody had any real control over the crowd, and they were the ones who decided the final outcome.

Both Seth and Protix were aware that they needed to start fighting in earnest or the crowd would grow savage. Protix was still waiting for Sethos to tire, so Sethos realized it was his job to provide the entertainment. He started jabbing at the giant with his trident. Protix roared and thrashed out with his sword. But his moves were predictable, and Sethos appeared to anticipate each thrust even before Protix himself had decided where to aim. Seth's ability to predict moves had the crowd entranced. They clapped appreciatively. Frustrated and hot, Protix paused in his thrashing. The crowd jeered. This riled him, and he began aiming wildly; the more he thrashed, the more Sethos danced and ducked.

'*SETHOS! SETHOS!*' the crowd cheered, which fuelled Protix's anger. He was becoming uncontrolled and indiscriminate, blundering around the arena like a drunk. The crowd booed ruthlessly, which enraged him further. Suddenly he turned and roared furiously at the auditorium, at which point Sethos threw his trident. It hit Protix in the neck, not too deep but agonizing. Protix bellowed, grabbed the trident, and holding it between both hands, prepared to snap it in half. The crowd whooped.

Sethos had been counting on this move, so just as Protix flexed to snap the trident, he shot his net out. Protix flailed frantically, caught in the net.

'Got you!' breathed Sethos. But as he moved in to use his dagger, a flash of gold in the crowd momentarily distracted him. Glancing towards it, he found himself staring straight into a pair of almond eyes.

The eyes widened in horror, because in that one moment of distraction Protix had swung his sword free and was suddenly slicing hard through leather into Seth's shoulder. White pain seared through him as blood gushed from the wound, the impact of the blow propelling Sethos backwards. But his reflexes were acute, and he recovered his balance just in time to stop himself falling. Before Protix had a chance to register that his opponent had not been immobilized, Sethos had twisted the net around Protix's sword, incapacitating it. At the same time Seth's right hand had unsheathed the dagger at his belt. Instantly it was touching Protix's throat – and the fight was won.

Sethos stood victorious, his left arm hanging limply, dripping blood, his right hand at Protix's throat, waiting for the verdict. He turned his eyes towards the governor. The crowd was wildly yelling, 'DIE! DIE! DIE!'

Cnaeus Papirius Aelianus was not a sentimental man, and he understood his citizens. He swiftly glanced around at them and nodded, then slowly turned his thumb. Protix was to receive no mercy.

At that moment Sethos hated them all. He hated their insatiable desire for blood. It made him sick. He dropped his gaze to the man at his feet, and looked through the helmet into the eyes of the Gaul.

'May your journey be swift,' he whispered, and with one quick, precise movement plunged a fatal blow deep into Protix's neck. The Gaul slumped forward against Seth's legs. As he did so, the jarring caused Seth's shoulder to flame with pain. He slowly bent to wipe his dagger in the sand, sheathed it, and started back towards the wooden gate. But a few steps in, his eyes began to swim, his legs gave way and he staggered. The lanista and Matthias ran into the arena to help him, but they couldn't reach him in time. The last thing Sethos saw that day was the sand rising up to meet him.

7

Friends

St Magdalene's

AD 2012

I was woken by a light knock on the door.

'Hey, Eva! You coming to breakfast?'

I lay blinking awake, trying to make sense of where I was and what I was hearing. St Magdalene's. My first morning. A few seconds later I was stumbling over to the door.

Ruby stood there, grinning.

I opened the door wider and she ducked in. A part of me just couldn't believe Ruby still wanted to hang out with me.

'Honestly, Eva, if it wasn't for me, you'd probably starve to death!' she said, collapsing on to my bed. 'Now put some clothes on – we haven't got all day!'

I splashed my face with cold water, shoved on a pair of jeans and a T-shirt, grabbed a sweatshirt and followed her out.

The atmosphere at breakfast was much more desultory than it had been last night. People wandered in bleary-eyed. Nobody talked much. Nobody except Ruby, who was as animated this morning as she had been last night.

I sat with my hands round a mug of coffee, willing myself awake.

Ruby plonked a plate of eggs in front of me. I groaned.

'Eva – you've gotta eat! What is the matter with you?'

'Ruby! It's the crack of dawn. My mouth hasn't woken up yet. It can't be expected to chew food . . . Give me a break here!' I mumbled.

She sighed deeply.

I looked at her and weakened. 'OK, OK!' I piled up a forkful of scrambled egg and shoved it in my mouth. 'Happy?'

She rolled her eyes and looked pointedly at the rest of the plate.

'Ruby! I've had some egg. I'll be fine!'

'It's a long morning, Eva. You need sustenance.'

I frowned. Nobody had ever cared about me eating before. As I ate, Omar wandered in. Ruby waved him over.

She grabbed his hand as he sat down. They smiled at each other.

'Hey, Rubes! Hey, Eva!'

I was trying to swallow, so I nodded hi.

'So d'ya have your timetable yet?' he asked me.

I swallowed the mouthful down. 'Gotta pick it up at eight thirty from the office.'

'Do you know where the office is?' Omar asked.

'Er – is it the room by the arch?'

'There are about a hundred arches, Eva.' He grinned. 'Do you want me to take you?'

'Ahem! Who has been given the job of settling Eva in?' interrupted Ruby. 'Don't worry, Eva – I'm on it!' She playfully dug Omar in the ribs, and that was when I knew for sure they were a couple.

I finished my food, we stacked our plates, and Ruby carted me off to the office.

When I got my timetable, I couldn't believe it. I was down to do maths, further maths, applied maths, physics, chemistry and biology. This was already more than I'd hoped for. But I was also timetabled for history of art, Latin, Greek, philosophy, ethics and politics.

I couldn't wipe the grin off my face.

'What's with you, Eva?' Ruby asked, peering down at my timetable.

'Oh my God! That's the fullest timetable I've *ever* seen . . . you're on nearly every period six days a week! Must be some sort of error. Come on – let's go and sort it out . . .'

'No, Ruby. I don't think it's a mistake . . . I sort of asked for it – I wanted it . . . I can't believe he listened . . .' I was awestruck.

'Aw, Eva! Are you going to turn out to be a total nerd?' groaned Ruby. I looked up at her in alarm, my stomach clenched.

But she was smiling. 'Come on then. We're in the same biology class – and Dr Franklin does *not* like to be kept waiting!'

Biology was one of the only classes I had with Ruby, but she made sure I knew where to go for everything else. And within a few days I had got the hang of my timetable: which teachers were scary, which were chilled. There were never more than twelve students in a group, and it didn't take me long to find out that you couldn't spend a lesson gazing out of the window.

'So, Eva, what do you make of *Le Déjeuner sur l'herbe*? Was

Manet genuinely surprised by the hostile response this painting received?'

'Does anyone *anticipate* hostility?' I muttered, a question close to my heart. Then I did my best to consider the question.

'Sure – it looks provocative to paint a nude woman sitting between three fully clothed men, but Manet based his composition on a Titian painting, didn't he? Maybe the picture is a simple homage to an old master? Maybe he didn't realize that by substituting nineteenth-century Paris fashion for shepherd robes he was transforming a rural idyll into a hugely controversial vision?'

'Oh, come on, Eva,' Omar interjected. 'Surely the Father of Impressionism couldn't have painted all those pictures because he was too naive to know any better?'

'OK, Omar, Eva. Good questions. We have to wrap up this session now, but I'd like you all to continue the argument in an essay: "The Progenitor – Visionary or Accidental Innovator?"'

Omar gave me a no-hard-feelings shoulder squeeze as we wandered out of the classroom. Ruby was waiting for us.

'Hey, Rubes,' I grinned, taking her arm. Omar took her other arm, and we headed over to the dining hall. Ruby and Omar were an easy couple to hang out with. They were good together, laughed a lot and seemed totally OK with having an extra guest at their party.

We queued up at the lunch counter.

'So how was German, Ruby?' I asked.

'Oh . . . I've got a *massive* pile of Goethe to translate tonight. I don't think I'll ever get to bed.'

'Have you talked to the Crisp about switching?' asked Omar.

'Come and do art history – it's cool!' I added.

'Eva! How can you say that? Did you hear the essay title we've just been given?' snorted Omar.

I looked at him. I'd thought he was as into art history as I was, and I'd been quite looking forward to writing that essay.

'Yeah . . . guess you're right,' I mumbled, biting my lip. I'd nearly let my guard down again. St Mag's was getting me way too relaxed.

Later that evening, I was sitting at my desk, just about to start researching bromine and chlorine oxides for my chemistry essay on stratospheric ozone loss, when Ruby burst into my room.

'Eva, you're not ready!'

I turned round, confused. 'Ready for what?'

'The stand-up gig. Duh! They're starting in fifteen minutes.'

'But – aren't you on German translation all night?'

'You can't be serious? This event is a once-in-a-lifetime. German can wait! I'll crib Mia's tomorrow.'

She picked up my trainers and threw them at me. 'Now please get a move on . . . I really don't want to miss the beginning.'

I obediently put on my shoes and ran across the quad after her.

The common room was heaving when we arrived, but Omar had saved us a couple of places near the front.

'Nervous?' I asked him.

'Course not,' he grinned.

'Yeah, right!' laughed Ruby.

At 9.15 the audience quietened down expectantly, and we all looked towards the stage. A few people shuffled on to it, forming a huddle and casting regular furtive, slightly embarrassed glances in our direction.

'What's going on, Omar?' I hissed.

He shrugged.

'What time are you on?' whispered Ruby.

He shrugged again.

'Whose idea *was* this?' I asked, thinking longingly of my desk and stratospheric ozone loss.

'I dunno! I just put my name on a list!'

We all sat around waiting for something to happen.

Fortunately, at last something did. A tall girl with spiky hair and a collection of piercings strode towards the stage.

'Astrid, Astrid, Astrid!' people started to chant.

She looked across at the crowd and frowned. Then she approached the huddle on the stage.

'OK, guys – what's going down?'

They all shook their heads.

'Well – who's in charge?'

They turned to each other and shrugged dejectedly.

She rolled her eyes, then headed towards the back corner of the stage and pulled out a microphone and stand. She plugged the mic into an amp and hauled them to the front of the stage.

'Anyone got a piece of paper?' she bellowed into the crowd.

A crumpled sheet made its way forward.

Astrid collected it, then pulled a pencil out of her pocket and started taking down the names of all the guys who'd signed up for a spot.

'Now – let's get this show on the road!'

The room went silent.

'Ahem . . . Ladies and gentlemen. Put your hands together for the hottest comedy on the circuit. There are ten names on my list – let's say five minutes each? First up: *Karl*! Take it away!'

The room erupted in applause, Karl began a rambling joke about hedgehogs, tarmac and spiky pancakes – and the event was saved.

As we headed back to our rooms later that night, my cheeks ached from laughing so much. I think everyone left feeling the same way. It had been an awesome night. Not because anyone had done any brilliant stand-up – in fact the comedy had been terrible – it was just that we were all there to have a good time.

'What would have happened if Astrid hadn't shown up?' laughed Ruby. 'It would have been awful. She totally nailed the evening, didn't she?'

I nodded.

'She's pretty cool, isn't she?'

'Yeah.' Cool but kind of scary.

'Omar somehow pulled it off, didn't he?'

I laughed. He'd been dire, of course, but by then we would have screamed with laughter at anything.

I went to bed really impressed that ten boys had been prepared to make total fools of themselves for our entertainment. The evening had definitely been worth leaving my desk for.

8

Patterns

St Magdalene's

AD 2012

As the days turned into weeks, it began to feel as if I was start-ing to belong somewhere at last – waking up each day feeling optimistic. For some reason Ruby still seemed to want to be my friend. Every morning she'd swing by my room and we'd head off to breakfast together. And although I didn't chat with anyone easily like she did, her buoyant sociability was relaxing. All I had to do was smile and nod from time to time, and it almost felt like I was part of the gang.

Of course there were times I wished Ruby didn't have to be involved in *every* event on campus, and sometimes longed for my desk and laptop. But I liked the novelty of feeling part of a group, and I found it pretty easy to work when I got back – I just had to listen out for the prowling footsteps of the house matrons, and be ready to switch out my light.

Now half-term was looming and I was counting off the days with dread. A whole week at home was going to be grim.

'So – do you have any special plans for half-term?' asked

Ruby as we wandered across the quad from biology.

'No – not really,' I mumbled. I did *not* want to think about it.

'I'm planning to teach Omar to ride a horse,' she giggled.

'Is Omar going back with you?'

'Yeah! He lives too far away to go home. I just hope my mother's gentle with him . . .'

'Gentle?'

'She can be a bit of a nightmare if you don't quite measure up to her exacting standards.'

'He's a good art historian – she should like that.'

'That will probably be his downfall – she loathes art academics. She thinks they're all so bogged down in analysis that they don't know how to respond to anything when they see it. She can be pretty savage when she gets going.'

'But isn't your sister doing art history at uni?'

'Yep. Poor Miranda thought Mum would be delighted. She's spent her life trying to impress her. I gave up years ago!'

'Does Omar know what he's letting himself in for?'

Ruby rolled her eyes. 'I suppose I should probably warn him . . .'

'No time like the present . . . Hi, Omar!'

Omar had just joined us in the lunch queue.

'Warn me of what?' he asked, spooning Bolognese on to his pasta.

'Hey! Don't look at me!' I laughed.

We sat down and started eating. Omar's eyes were on Ruby. 'Is there something you wanted to share?'

Ruby smiled. 'Eva thinks you should be given some strategy advice on dealing with my mother . . .'

Omar looked alarmed. 'What do I need to know?' he asked slowly.

Ruby considered for a second.

'Hmm . . . well, she's – er – quite a . . . large personality . . . You'll be fine if you say as little as possible,' she said finally. 'Then she'll have nothing to pounce on.'

'Sounds ominous,' breathed Omar.

'Anyway – I'm going to teach you to ride. That should keep us out of her way.'

Omar nodded. 'So, Eva, what are you doing for half-term?'

'Going home,' I muttered.

'Where's that?'

'York.' I could hardly bear to say it.

Ruby squeezed my hand. 'Poor Eva . . . our half-term will probably be heaven compared with yours.'

'So why don't you invite Eva to come back with us then?'

'What?' I spluttered.

'Omar! That's such a cool idea! Why didn't I think of it? We've loads of room, and Eva would totally dilute the mother effect. Anyway Mum's bound to like Eva – she's always preferred the super-clever . . .'

'Thanks very much,' sniffed Omar. 'That's really gonna help my confidence!'

'So how about it, Eva?' Ruby was smiling at me. So was Omar.

OK – this was obviously the answer to a prayer, but something about it made me uneasy. I stalled.

'Th-thanks, Ruby – sounds great – but I'd better –'

'You'd better what? Check how many thumbscrews your brother's got lined up before you can decide? Come on, Eva! You know you'll have a much better time with us.'

'Ruby – I –'

'Shhh, Eva, I'm busy . . .'

Busy texting.

'Good – that's that. Right, Eva. No negotiation. It's arranged.'

Just like that. My half-term was taken care of. I rang my mother later that evening, and couldn't help noticing the slight note of relief in her voice. Which was nothing compared to the relief in mine.

As it turned out, my misgivings were unfounded. We had a great time.

I really liked Martha Gaine. She was acerbic but funny – well, she made me laugh, anyway. I didn't meet Ruby's dad because he'd had to travel abroad on a case, but I met her younger sister, Jess, who was really sweet.

I even got to ride on the horse. Ruby took us each out a couple of times. I loved it – the height, the speed.

'Bloody hell, Eva – is there anything you can't do?'

'What do you mean?'

'Well – you've just picked this up so quickly. Galloping isn't meant to be something you master on your first lesson.'

I shrugged. It didn't feel like a skill I'd picked up. It just felt natural.

Later the three of us took Jessie for a long leaf-scrunching walk through the woods on the edge of their estate . . . Yeah – ESTATE: Ruby's house was seriously enormous. And beautiful . . . gabled, covered in ivy, surrounded by gardens.

On our last day there, Martha invited us to look around her studio – an amazing glass-roofed building on the far side of the stables.

I don't know what I was expecting – but this definitely wasn't it. Martha Gaine's installations were big abstract events using projection, water, flames, even ice. So I suppose I was expecting her studio to be full of that stuff, but the walls were covered in delicate drawings of leaves, feathers, bones, rocks. She had shelves of tiny things in jars – insects, sweets, dolls' house furniture . . . seemingly random items, neatly arranged.

When she noticed me peering at them, she just waved a hand and said, 'My inspirations come from surprising places sometimes.'

I nodded, glancing across at Omar. He was staring at a jar of tiny berries. Unfortunately, he had taken Ruby's advice so literally that he had hardly said a word to Martha the whole week. She must have thought he was practically mute. And weirdly, although that was the role I normally played around people – and although Ruby had briefed me as well as Omar to keep a low profile around her mother – I found I couldn't seem to stay silent. Martha had a kind of aggressive energy that was really infectious.

Later that evening, when we were heading back to St Mag's on the train, I couldn't help asking Ruby if the whole *mad mother* thing had just been a joke to terrify us.

'Honestly, Eva – I've never seen her so mellow.'

'I wouldn't exactly call her mellow!' snorted Omar.

'Trust me, Omar. That was mellow.'

I gazed out at the dark shapes of trees blurring past our window. I wondered if Martha Gaine had ever done a piece on *Speed*. Or *Time*. Or *Motion*.

My mind started filling up with Martha-style imagery, so it came as a bit of a shock when Omar touched me on the shoulder and started hauling our luggage off the rack.

It was pretty late and we were quite tired by the time we got ourselves back to school.

As Ruby and I parted at my door, I found myself reaching out and giving her a hug.

'Thanks, Rubes, I had a really great week.'

She wasn't to know, of course, that a hug from me was a momentous leap into the realms of human contact. I couldn't remember the last time I had spontaneously touched anyone. I vaguely wondered if this was the first time ever.

'Hey, Eva – thanks for coming, babe! It would have been torture without you. You saw how relaxed Omar was!'

I grinned. 'Poor Omar!'

She shook her head and laughed.

''Night, Eva.'

I went to sleep feeling happier than I had in years. I was at a perfect school, I had a perfect best friend and I had just successfully avoided a horrific week with my darling step-brother, Ted. Could life get any better?

The next morning I floated through physics, chemistry, ethics and philosophy, and didn't catch up with Ruby and Omar till lunchtime.

'Hey, Eva! Look at these!'

Ruby was running through the photos she'd taken over the week. They were laughing at a shot of Omar trying to mount Ruby's horse.

I plonked down my tray of chicken curry, and leaned over them. Omar was scrolling through the set.

'Oh, that's a lovely one of you, Eva,' he said, enlarging one of me laughing with Jessie.

'Aaah – doesn't Jessie look sweet in those pyjamas!' I murmured, tucking into my food.

'And this is a good one too.' Omar shoved the camera over. It had stopped on a photo Ruby had taken of Omar and me leaning against the stable wall.

'Can you email me that picture, Rubes?' he added.

'Sure,' she said. 'I can send you the whole set.'

Then she suddenly scraped back her chair. 'Hey – look at the time! I'm supposed to be at the pool. What have you got now?'

'Athletics,' Omar and I said in unison.

I looked at him. 'I thought you did football?'

'Just switched,' he shrugged.

A tiny alarm went off in my head then, but I ignored it.

'OK – well, I'll see you there. I've left my kit in my room.' I picked up my tray and stood. 'Catch you two later!' I grinned and left.

We weren't officially allowed in our rooms during the day, so I sprinted back, picked up my kitbag, and was just turning to leave when Omar was suddenly blocking the doorway.

'Omar?' I gasped. 'You gave me a fri–' But I never got to finish that sentence because his arms were suddenly banded round me.

'Oh, Eva,' he breathed, forcing me back into the room. Then he was kissing me.

'OMAR – What are you doing?' I tried to push him away. He seemed genuinely surprised.

'Come on, Eva – you must feel the same way –'

'NO! What are you talking about?'

'Eva! I'm crazy about you.'

'What?'

'I can't deal with it any more.'

'But you and Ruby –'

'Yeah, Ruby's great – of course I really like her – but you're the –'

'I am the *what*?' I was truly horrified. He took my face in his hands and started trying to kiss me again.

'*Omar* – stop!' I spluttered, 'I *never* gave you any reason –'

'Eva –' His voice suddenly broke as he looked at me, kind of pleading. 'Eva – please! I've been going crazy ever since – ever since you walked into the dining room that first evening . . . I knew then –'

'Omar – please! Ruby –'

'Look, Eva, I don't give a damn about Ruby –'

And guess who should walk in at that moment? Yep – Ruby walked in at that moment, and then ran straight out again. I chased after her, of course, trying to explain. But she refused to stop. Refused to talk to me. She just turned round and looked at me like I was the worst kind of traitor. Which is exactly how I felt.

I spent the whole afternoon feeling sick. I avoided all eye contact with Omar during athletics, and then wandered miserably through the rest of my lessons. At the end of the day I went and knocked on Ruby's door. I could hear her crying inside, but she refused to let me in. I went back to my room and just sat there, gazing at the wall.

How could I have let this happen? Why didn't I see it coming? I was supposed to be clever and here I was in the same old mess.

Only this time it was much, much worse. I really cared about

Ruby. And Omar. I had actually started believing in them as friends.

When would I get it into my stupid head that I couldn't have friends?

That evening Ruby split up with Omar ... publicly ... in the dining room, in front of everyone. By the time dinner was over, I don't suppose there was anybody in the whole school who didn't know what had happened, or who the poisonous witch was who had caused the catastrophe.

I know I shouldn't have been surprised. It was, after all, a pattern I was familiar with, a recurring pattern that made chaos theory seem benign. And it was one I had no control over whatsoever.

9

Fall

Londinium

AD 152

The massive arena crowd gasped when the gladiator fell. They had just watched his skilful victory: there lay the massive Gaul, dead and bleeding. Surely Sethos Leontis could not fall? He was invincible, the god of gladiators, the holder of wreaths. The pattern could not have been broken . . . So why was he lying so still on the sand?

Sethos did not lie there for long. Matthias and Tertius were rushing towards him, closely followed by four other gladiators from their familia. Together they carried him away. Seth's injury would be a wound to the whole familia. They needed him. His popularity brought in huge crowds and the consequent wealth. His victories were their victories. He had just won them the further glory of a ninth wreath, though he would not be there to collect it.

He must not die.

Matthias had never before seen Seth lose concentration, but he had caught the moment, had followed the source of his friend's distraction, and he cursed the gods for sending the dark-haired girl into Seth's life, into the arena that day. If Seth died . . .

They laid the limp body of his friend on to his bed-mat.

Matthias cut off the leather shoulder strap. He prayed that the meagre protection this afforded had prevented too much damage, that the profusion of blood belied a shallow wound. He washed his hands and pressed down hard on the gash, causing a scream of pain from his now momentarily conscious friend. Seth's eyes darted wildly around and then glazed over. He fell back. Matthias shouted for his assistants to collect his salves and powders, boiled water and clean towels. While he waited, pressing with all his strength across his friend's shoulder, he watched in despair as Seth's blood pumped on to the sheets beneath him. Matthias tried calming himself by muttering incantations. He had little belief in the spells that so many of his fellow physicians relied on, but he was prepared to try anything.

As he crouched beside Sethos, he tried to imagine life without him. He could not. He would not. The towels and water arrived and he started methodically cleaning around the gash. Ye gods, the Gaul had driven his sword in deep. Matthias pushed the friend in himself down and summoned the physician. He began his inventory: the heart sounded weak, but if he could staunch the bleeding it might be strong enough to hold out. The damage to the tissue, muscle and bone around the shoulder was extensive. Muscles were ripped, and the bone had been shattered. He would need to salve the wound, laboriously excavate it for loose bone fragments and then splint the area to promote bone fusion. But first he had to stop the bleeding. If Seth lost any more blood, he would not survive.

Matthias got a table set up next to him and he selected the phials of cobwebs. He stuffed three circular wads deep into the wound, then spread them along the channel of the gash, keeping his pressure to the edges. He held his breath . . . and gradually the flow of blood ceased. Matthias could breathe again. Although this was just the first hurdle, he felt a small spark of hope. Maybe Sethos could be saved.

Suddenly Seth began to shake. His body was going into shock. Matthias felt his friend's hands – they were ice cold.

'*Blankets!*' he shouted. The assistants ran off to find covers, and returned seconds later. They piled them on to the prone figure.

'*Careful, you idiots! Not on the shoulder!*' screamed Matthias.

Matthias listened again to Seth's heart. The beats were erratic and weak. This was critical. He couldn't begin his surgery unless Seth's heart was stable. He would go into total shock and then die. Matthias began to panic. He knew that the longer Sethos lay there with an open wound the risks of contamination were multiplying. And when the wound became poisoned, fever would follow. Sethos could not survive a fever in this weakened state. But if Matthias went ahead with the surgery and Sethos went into shock, he'd die within minutes.

'Father,' he whispered, 'what would you do?'

Never did Matthias feel the need for his father's guidance more than now. Although he had treated several seriously wounded gladiators over the last two years, not one had meant this much to him, and it had been easier to be objective. So if a gladiator died, Matthias had not blamed himself. But he knew that if Sethos did not survive, he would never forgive himself. He and Sethos had been captured in the same raid. Together they had stood in chains and been forced to witness the slaughter of their families. They were irrevocably bound.

'Father, please?'

But his father did not answer. He was far from this world, wandering the Elysian Fields, free at last. Matthias envied him.

He crouched down next to the mattress and touched Seth's cheek. It was less clammy. He listened to Seth's chest. The heartbeat was more stable.

'Right!' he said purposefully. 'Aurelius, I'll need more light – fetch me as many lamps as you can carry. Telemachus, I'll need you to help Aurelius hold the light steady.'

When the oil lamps were lit, Matthias lined four along the table edge as near to the damaged shoulder as he could get them, and then he positioned his two assistants above the shoulder area to cast a more accurate glow.

He held his surgical instruments into a flame to purify them, and then began the painstaking job of clearing the fragments from the wound.

Seth's breathing became laboured. Sweat began to pour from him, so Matthias threw the blankets to the floor, and continued working.

Gladiators wandered in and out during the surgery, looked across at him, and mostly shook their heads.

'He was a brave fighter.'

'One of the best.'

'He's not dead yet!' spat Matthias. 'Now get out of my light.'

Matthias had picked out the last tiny fragment of bone, and was cleaning the wound with water when the lanista strode over, carrying the wreath Sethos had won. He propped it up against the table.

'Will he make it?' he asked.

Matthias shrugged and carried on swabbing Seth's shoulder. 'It is in the hands of the gods.'

'If Sethos dies, I will hold you personally responsible, Matthias. I can't afford to lose him.'

Matthias swallowed the bitter response that sprang to his lips, and did his best to keep his fingers still.

The lanista strode out again, and Matthias reapplied cobwebs into the cleaned wound, and then mixed a poultice of honey, burnt dill seeds and rosemary, which he spread over the area. Then he bandaged the shoulder with clean cotton gauze.

'Right, Telemachus, we need to splint the shoulder now. Can you hold these battens still while I secure them?'

Finally the shoulder was clamped, but Matthias felt no relief. Seth's breathing was shallow and uneven, his forehead was burning and he shivered continuously.

'Sethos is cold, Matthias, we should cover him!' whispered Telemachus.

'The fever has set in,' Matthias sighed. 'Fetch bowls of water and clean cloths.'

If Sethos had been conscious, Matthias would have given him a draught with purslane and chamomile, but there was no way to make him swallow, so Matthias turned instead to a treatment his father swore by, and trickled tepid water all over the body.

Sethos began to shiver profusely and Telemachus tried to cover him.

Matthias pushed him away angrily. 'Feel his cheeks – is he cold?'

Telemachus put his hand to Seth's face and felt the burning skin.

'It is the fever that causes him to shake. His body is over-heated.'

Sethos began to moan, and then to shout. 'Help me – Matthias! Help me –'

'I am here, brother –'

Sethos was writhing and twisting as the pain seared through him. 'Matt!' he panted. 'I am hurt –'

'I know, Seth.' Matthias and his two assistants had to hold him down with all their strength. 'Please try to lie back. Your shoulder is too unstable –'

But Sethos was not receptive to reason. 'Matt – are you there? I – need –'

'Sshh, Seth. Drink, brother.' Matthias held a cup of opium to his friend's lips. Seth tried to drink, but his body was convulsing, and he was gagging for breath.

'Matthias!' he gasped. 'I – I –' And then his eyes rolled upwards and he fell back, unconscious.

Matthias sat vigil all night, trying to hold his friend still when he tossed, anxious that the wound would open.

At the fourth hour after midnight, the bleeding began again, and Matthias had to swab it and apply more cobwebs. He rebound the wound and watched.

Sethos did not look good. His pallor was sickly white, sweat beaded his brow and he moaned incoherently. Matthias feared he would not make it through till dawn.

As he watched, he wondered about his treatments. Were there better herbs to apply? Should he have stitched the wound? It was such a gaping gash he feared closing it too soon. He had seen poison sewn into bad wounds . . . a sure way to kill a friend.

By morning he was feeling desperate, unequal to the task of saving Sethos. He was just nineteen. He did not know enough.

So when the lanista strode into the cell with a stranger Matthias prayed it was a physician.

'Matthias, this is Domitus Natalis.'

The deliberate pause and imperceptible nod Tertius gave Matthias indicated that he was in the presence of someone important.

Matthias bowed.

'Domitus Natalis was at the arena yesterday when Sethos Leontis fell. He has, this morning, generously offered him a room in his villa, with his own physician in attendance.'

Matthias was speechless.

'Actually,' admitted Domitus, 'it was my wife who persuaded me – she is the one with the kind heart. Such a sentimental woman!'

Although Matthias had no status and therefore no choice in this decision, he felt deeply torn.

'B-but I don't know if it's safe to move him. His heart is so weak, he has lost so much blood and the fever rages. Every movement reopens the shoulder wound . . .'

Domitus gave Sethos a cursory glance, and said, 'He'll die if he stays in this putrid cell. I'll send a litter within the hour.'

The lanista slapped Matthias across the back. 'Lets you off the hook, eh? Besides, we're heading for Aquitania the day after tomorrow, and can you see Sethos making it through that journey?'

Matthias swallowed. There was no way Seth would be in any condition to travel. He had to see this as the miraculous intervention of the gods.

'Would you wish me to stay with him?' he asked without hope.

'Don't be a fool, man. Your job is with the familia. Sethos will be looked after. I hear Domitus's physician treats the procurator himself!'

Matthias sighed, and prepared to bid farewell to his dearest friend.

10

Distraction

St Magdelene's

AD 2012

Ruby had a new best friend: Mia. I couldn't pretend it didn't hurt. Neither could I pretend that there hadn't been a part of me waiting for this to happen.

And in a way that thought was weirdly consoling. I had survived as a loner for sixteen years, so I knew I could do it again. I didn't actually *need* Ruby. Nobody was better at living without friends than me – I was the expert. And I guess although it was hard to see Ruby hanging out with Mia at least it helped with the guilt. Ruby was clearly OK. I had been easily replaced.

I still felt sick about Omar, though, and there was nothing I could do about that. Except ignore him – which wasn't easy, given the number of times he tried to talk to me. But he hadn't reckoned on my skill in this area. Shutting people out was, after all, my specialist subject. I could keep my head down better than anyone. Plus I had immense stamina. It only took a few weeks for Omar to finally give up.

Unfortunately, Omar wasn't the last. After him there was Dominic. Then Karl . . .

My new solitary state seemed to have triggered an immediate chain reaction. I started having to avoid all social situations – the common room, film nights, room parties. But it was trickier avoiding academic ones. And the worst academic situation turned out to be the paired tutorial – a St Mag's special.

Normal lessons were fine, safe: between eight and twelve in a group, and usually a fair mix of boys and girls. Paired tutorials, on the other hand, were a lottery. We had a paired tutorial every week with a teacher in each subject – very dangerous if the other student turned out to be a boy because at some point the two of you could end up being left alone in a room, or worse, walking back through the school grounds without the safety of the group.

After a couple of months I decided that lottery odds weren't good enough: too unpredictable and way too stressful. If I was to avoid any more excruciating amorous declarations, I needed something a bit more reliable. It didn't take me long to work out what I had to do (hack into the senior master's timetable grid and make the necessary alterations) but it took me a bit longer to actually do it.

Hacking into the account was insultingly easy – his password and PIN were obvious (middle name and date of birth), but the head of IT had added some irritating firewalls to protect the grid. They took me a couple of evenings to decipher, which impressed me enough to be more on my guard once I'd skipped through them. Cunning adversaries could be sneaky. And I was right to be careful. He had laid a couple of ingenious little spyware and key-logging traps. I liked this guy. Anyway, it meant

I had to be quick, circuitous and undetectable. Plus I had to remember to log in very late every Thursday night, so that I could make the amendments undetected each week, just before the new timetable was posted.

Once I'd sorted out the tutorial problem, my life got more on track – I could breathe again in lessons and tutorials. Which was a good thing.

Another good thing was St Mag's' awesome new toy: a quantum particle microscope. It was totally mind-blowing. The electron microscope had been able to detect an incredible variety of micro-organisms, but this could monitor neutrons! It could record variations in gravity. It could even track bacterial and viral movement. Quarks now had substance. Indecipherable specks on the electron microscope could now be observed as pulsating elaborate forms.

All the science teachers were fighting over it, but Dr Franklin turned out to be the winner because hers was the only lab big enough to house it. And somehow I managed to persuade her to let me stay and watch while they set it up. Which meant they got used to me hanging around while they experimented with its functionality. So the new microscope kept me happy and preoccupied for some time.

But sadly not all the time. It seemed that however long I stayed in the lab, however hard I worked in lessons, however long I sat at my desk, I was still left with an annoying amount of brooding time. Ruby's disappearance from my life had seen to that.

Until I found a couple of unexpected distractions.

The first, I kind of fell into by mistake. I was trying to dodge Karl after Latin one day, so I scooted out of the lesson under the cover of a gang of girls. It turned out they were heading off to the drama studio for an audition. I just went along with the group, and somehow ended up being persuaded to audition too.

So I was now in the school play . . . *Hamlet*! I suddenly had lines to learn and rehearsals to go to, usually accompanied by a gang of other cast members, so not much opportunity for solitary chats. And pretty soon the rehearsals stopped being just a distraction. I started to really enjoy them. You came in, took off your shoes, put on your training clothes and left all the baggage outside. There were no judgements. No annoying innuendos – well, I guess mostly because Dr Kidd, the drama teacher, would have done his nut. But most of all I loved being someone else for a change.

Then one lunchtime, as we were all leaving a rehearsal, Astrid came up to me casually and said, 'You sing pretty well – do you play anything?'

'You mean – like an instrument?'

'Yeah.'

'Just a bit of guitar . . .'

She grinned. 'Great! Let's have a jam later.'

'Yeah, OK.'

Later was one of my favourite words. It showed intention without commitment. It could mean *in an hour* or it could mean *in twelve years*. Nice and open. I used it regularly myself to get out of stuff. So when Astrid said, 'Let's have a jam later,' I didn't worry about it . . . until I was being slapped on the shoulder at supper that night.

'You coming or what?'

Astrid was standing there, a gig bag strapped to her back,

with Sadie, a small blonde girl from my philosophy class. Bang went the twelve-year theory.

'Er – I've only got my acoustic guitar here,' I stammered lamely.

'That's cool – there's a Strat in the studio.'

'I-I'm not very good . . .'

'Well, you're not going to improve sitting there. Just get off your chair, would you? We don't have all night.'

So I got off my chair, cleared my plate and reluctantly followed them through the quad into one of the music studios.

'Wow!'

The room was big, soundproofed and had a complete studio set up: drum kit, amps, mics . . .

Sadie went straight over to the drums and started bashing around while Astrid pulled a red Stratocaster off a guitar stand and handed it to me. Then she unzipped the gig bag she had slung across her back and took out a black Gibson bass.

Astrid – it turned out – was a scarily good bass player. She effortlessly slid up and down the fret-board, while I shrank into a corner, vaguely attempting to get the Strat strings in tune. This was going to be hell.

'Er – Astrid . . . I don't think . . .' I croaked.

'Here, Eva,' she said, throwing me a scrawled page of lyrics.

I bit my lip and looked at the song. The chords were pencilled above the words. Hmmm, nothing too tricky . . . possibly I could just about get my fingers round them . . .

She briefly showed me how the tune went, and Sadie knocked out the beat. Pretty soon we were actually jamming together. By the end of the evening we'd played through two songs and I was even adding the vocals.

'I like the way you sing, Eva,' Astrid said as we headed back to our rooms.

'Better than I play,' I mumbled.

'You could improve . . .'

'Yeah – practice makes perfect, right?'

'No – I mean – you have *no* technique. You need a couple of lessons.'

She was right. I had basically taught myself out of a chord book and, given the lack of enthusiasm at home for anything noisy, I hadn't really pursued it very hard.

'So where am I supposed to get lessons?'

'Duh! Me, of course!'

'You?'

'Why not? And in return – you can help me with sodding Latin translation!'

'Deal!' I grinned.

11

Destiny

Londinium

AD 152

Seth's eyes did not open as he was carried on a litter through the streets of Londinium. Neither did he wake when he was taken into the cool marble chamber at the back of the Natalis villa.

He was oblivious to the gentle hands that bathed him and laid him to rest on a couch with smooth cotton sheets. Later that morning, Domitus summoned his physician, Tychon, the Greek.

Tychon arrived with a small entourage. He bowed deeply to Domitus Natalis, who met him at the bedside.

Before touching Sethos, Tychon asked for water to wash his hands. This was surprising enough, but then after rinsing them he proceeded to douse them in vinegar. Domitus suppressed a patronizing chuckle. He assumed that the Greek was observing some strange ritual homage to a foreign set of gods. He had no idea that he was actually in the presence of one of the most innovative healers of the time. Tychon had discovered, through a series of monitored trials, that vinegar – acetum – proved a very effective cleansing agent, and he now insisted that no surgery was performed without its use. Once he had thoroughly cleaned his own hands, he passed the jar to his assistants who washed their own. Tychon then lifted the gauze and web padding covering Seth's shoulder. He shook his head pessimistically when he observed the raging heat and swelling surrounding the gash.

The entire Natalis household gathered to hear his summary.

'At this point I can tell you that the wound is very deep, and there is likely to be extensive muscle and nerve damage. I cannot say for sure until I look inside, but I suspect the bone has been partially shattered. The site is tumescent and hot, which means I will have to eviscerate the wound again, to try and clear out the poison, but I imagine he has already lost a lot of blood, which means his state will be weak. His heart rhythm is not powerful or regular, and he is submerged in fever. I will do my best to try and restore him, but I have to say his chances of survival are slim.'

As the physician spoke, Domitus Natalis nodded gravely. He had a lot of money invested in Sethos Leontis, though he hadn't mentioned this to his wife, Flavia, particularly as most of the money was originally hers. Flavia was the daughter of a rich man, and Domitus had done well in the marriage. If she were to find out about his precarious investments, her father could demand a divorce, which would leave Domitus practically destitute. But the gods had been smiling on him because it was she who had suggested nursing the gladiator here at the villa.

'What can we do to help push the odds in Leontis's favour?' he asked his physician.

'Well, after I have cleaned, stitched and dressed the wound, his future will be in the hands of the gods, of course, but a day and night watch would be helpful. His fever rages, and he will need careful nursing. Do you have slaves with any medical expertise?'

'I could supervise the watch,' said Flavia quickly.

'And I could assist if you would like, Mother,' added Livia.

Domitus smiled gratefully at his women. They really were very useful at times.

'That is good,' nodded Tychon. 'Well, I had better get to work. The longer I stand here, the more the poisons spread. I will need plenty of boiled water, as many clean cloths as you can muster and all the lamps you have. That marble table in the corner would be the perfect surface for my instruments . . .'

His assistants were already carrying the table over to the bed. Flavia went off to organize the delivery of cloths and the boiling of water. Domitus retired to his study.

Sethos lay oblivious as Tychon laid out his instruments and medications. He was also unaware that the girl who had distracted him in the arena now hovered in the doorway. She watched attentively as the physician placed all his instruments in the boiling water, and then as he fished them out with long metal tongs.

He carefully peeled away the padding on Sethos's shoulder, and with smaller tongs lifted out all the sodden pieces of web wadding Matthias had stuffed into the gash. Tychon then nodded to his assistants and they suddenly clamped hard on to Sethos's wrists and legs, while their mentor uncorked the bottle he had washed his hands from earlier. The sharp smell of vinegar pervaded the room, and he poured the liquid liberally into the wound. Sethos screamed, and began thrashing wildly, but the assistants had him securely pinned down. Livia covered her ears, then slipped from the doorway.

When she returned later, Sethos lay still and pale, fresh gauze now covering his shoulder. The doctor was placing his instruments back in their cases. His assistants were wiping blood from the floor.

'Does he live?' she whispered.

'Just about,' said the physician. 'He's heavily sedated. He won't wake up for a while. I'll be back again this evening to check on him. In the meantime, keep him cool, with fans and water. He will be thirsty, so try to drip the water between his lips – like this. Tonight I will leave you some herbs to give him if he wakes.'

As Tychon and his entourage left the room, Livia pulled up a stool and sat next to the couch. Very lightly, she touched Seth's forehead. It was burning. Carefully picking up the cloth from the bowl of water next to the bed, she squeezed out the excess and dripped the rest on to his forehead. The liquid ran down his face into his hair, across his cheeks, over his lips. He flinched, but his eyes did not open.

'Ah, Livia.' Flavia strode in. 'I'll take the first watch. You run along now and practise your kithara. We are expecting you to play well tonight at the banquet.'

Without a word, Livia stood and walked over to the door. But she didn't leave immediately, hovering instead for a moment, concealed by the curtain that hung behind the door frame.

Flavia sat down, and began gently – sensuously – to bathe Seth's face and chest with water. Livia heard Flavia sigh quietly, then saw her lift Seth's nearest hand and take it in both of hers.

With wide eyes, Livia watched as Flavia slowly brought Seth's hand up to her lips and, one by one, kissed his fingers.

For the second time that day Livia took herself from Seth's doorway. This time she ran past a series of mystified slaves through the villa towards the furthest part of the garden. Once shrouded by the hanging foliage of the cherry trees, she threw herself on the ground and sobbed. And there she would have stayed if the handmaid, Ochira, hadn't come out on a mission to pick bay leaves for the cook. Livia shrank in the shadows till she passed and then dodged quickly, circuitously, back through the house and into the sanctuary of her bedchamber.

Her kithara leaned against the wall. She picked it up and settled down on the couch with it nestled comfortably on her lap. She ran her fingers along the strings distractedly, and tried not to think. Her fingers began plucking soothing melodies, tunes that brought her comfort and fresh resolve. The tight band of anguish in her throat gradually relaxed, and unconsciously her voice picked up the melodies while her hands weaved intricate harmonies around them.

Domitus, who was in his study checking through the latest shipment inventory, heard the sweet notes as they floated through the marble atrium, and was proud of Livia's accomplishments. She had a strangely compelling voice and was a gifted player: a credit to him. Though he had no ear for music himself, he could see how her playing captivated an audience. Cassius Malchus, the procurator himself, had been bewitched. So bewitched, in fact, that the very first time he heard her play at their Matralia banquet, he had proposed marriage.

Domitus chuckled. He could not have planned it better. And now Cassius was to be the honoured guest tonight. It was imperative that Livia charmed him once more because that evening they would be sealing the betrothal and discussing the settlement. Domitus felt sure that the more enchanting her playing, the better the marriage terms would be for him. The hefty dowry Cassius would expect was a small price to pay for the future power their union promised. Cassius had people in all the right places, and ways of helping awkward situations disappear. The wedding would be worth every dupondius.

The fact that Livia knew nothing of this other motive did not trouble Domitus at all.

12

Vanquished

OK – I was really enjoying the whole band thing. We were practising twice a week, and we had ten songs working really well. My guitar playing had definitely improved – well, Astrid was a ruthless teacher so I had no choice. Her Latin translation, on the other hand, hadn't. Sure, she was getting great marks now, but that was because I was doing it for her. She just couldn't be bothered with it.

'It's totally pointless.'

'Why is it any more pointless than, say, music?'

'God, Eva! Perhaps you haven't spotted it yet, but – er – Latin's a dead language.'

'Yeah, but –'

'You can't argue, Eva! That stuff's two thousand years out of date! Life's way too short!'

She was probably right, and life was definitely way too short to waste time arguing about it with her; so I just carried on translating Virgil and left her to get on with the important things – like downloading Livid Turkey song lyrics.

'OK, done!' I yawned, throwing my pen down.

She glanced across at the page. 'Good – that gives us an hour to practise. Big gig tomorrow.'

I froze. 'What did you say?'

'Gig. Tomorrow. Common room. Come on.'

She was shoving me out of her room. I refused to be shoved.

'Er, sorry, Astrid . . . Rewind please.'

'How many times would you like me to tell you?'

I did not sign up for this. It was one thing doing the songs and enjoying the playing; it was quite another actually performing . . . to an audience. An audience of people I had been doing everything to avoid for months.

'No way, Astrid.' I stood against her wall with my arms folded.

Astrid wasn't paying any attention. She was on her mobile.

'Sadie – my room, now!'

Within two minutes I had both of them dragging me off to the music studio. Resistance was futile. I consoled myself with the thought that I had a whole night to plot my escape.

But the next morning I still hadn't worked out my exit strategy. The day did not start well. I had barely walked into breakfast when they started on me.

'The whole point of playing music is to perform!'

'What is your problem, Eva? The music's good!'

'It's gonna be fun!'

'Oh, come *onnnnnnn*! It's a great opportunity!'

By suppertime Astrid, who had somehow picked up that I wasn't exactly gagging for this opportunity, had managed to galvanize most of our year into guarding all school exits. She was also sticking to me like glue.

By 9 p.m. she was pushing me through the quad into the common room. My heart sank. The place was crammed. Sadie was already on the stage, tightening her cymbals. The mics and the guitars were all in place.

'When did you set the stuff up?' I hissed.

'Sadie and I sound-checked at lunchtime. Would have been much easier with you, of course – but you seemed intent on your macaroni cheese . . .'

By the time she pulled me on to the stage, rage had completely taken the place of anxiety. I was incandescent. Which unfortunately played right into her hands because the first song was her angry one about a psycho stalker.

By the end of it, I'd worked out my rage. It helped that nobody was throwing bruised bananas at us. In fact they were clapping surprisingly enthusiastically.

I was just about to start singing the second song when I spotted Ruby. She was pulling Mia by the arm and heading for the door. Pointedly. Message received.

I bit my lip, took a deep breath and tried to put her out of my mind. I discovered if I shut my eyes I could pretend that there was no audience at all and just concentrate on the music. It worked so well that I was completely taken by surprise when they started cheering. By the fifth song I'd just about worked up to singing with my eyes open, and by the end of the set, though I hate to admit it, I was actually quite enjoying myself.

Of course Astrid was sickeningly smug, but I just about forgave her when she dealt with all the social stuff afterwards. I just coiled cables, packed up the guitars and stole away.

I thought that would be the end of it. Ha.

I was crunching my way through some honey-wheat loops the next morning, avoiding all eye contact, when a familiar face loomed in front of me.

'Astrid.' I sighed.

She plonked her plate of eggs and bacon on the table, and sat down opposite me.

'Great news!' she slurred as she negotiated a forkful. 'We've got a regular spot! Every Thursday evening. They loved us!'

13

Vigil

Londinium

AD 152

The arena crowd was cheering, screaming his name. Seth was covered in blood, staring down at the eight defeated gladiators groaning at his feet. He was tired . . . so tired . . . but he raised his arm in salute and then turned to leave. Why was the sand so hot? Too hot . . . It was burning his feet. He looked down and saw that the sand had melted away . . . he was standing in a pit of fire. The flames were rising higher. The heat was unbearable, coursing through his body . . . pulling him down . . . As he fell, the flames licked at his skin, eating into his flesh . . .

'Please,' he shouted into the crowd. 'Please . . . help me . . .'

But he found he had no voice. They couldn't hear him . . . they weren't listening. They were shouting his name . . . 'Sethos Leontis . . . Sethos Leontis . . .'

Through the red flames he searched their faces, looking for someone . . . a face he needed to see. But as he cast wildly around he saw that the faces had changed, distorted into vacant eyeless skulls. Wide black mouths now screamed for his blood . . .

'Die, Sethos Leontis!' a voice bellowed behind him. He turned and there was Protix towering over him, ten feet tall, wielding a sword of flame. It was a relief to see him. The great Gaul was here to kill him, to take him away from this flaming hell. He watched impatiently as Protix brandished his sword, and thrust it into his shoulder. Again and again . . . But he was not dying. Why did it not end?

'Stop . . .' he cried weakly.

He felt cool hands on his forehead, dousing the fire, but the flames still raged in his shoulder and the heat made him so thirsty.

'Water,' he croaked.

And as if by some miracle his lips were no longer parched; he could feel water on his tongue. He opened his eyes. His vision was blurred. Where was the fire? Where was the cadaverous head of Protix the Gaul? He blinked. The light was not red. It was cool and blue and shadowy. He tried to make sense of his vision. He could swear that he was looking into the almond eyes of his dreams.

He tried to speak her name.

'Livia?'

Gentle hands lifted his head and helped him sip from a cup. When a trickle escaped, he felt the lightest touch gather the drop of water and touch it to his chapped lips. He shut his eyes and rested his head against her cool arm, suddenly catching a whisper of a familiar scent, rosewater and jasmine. But he was so confused by fever, pain and opium that he could not make sense of this dream, and fell back again, exhausted.

His dreams continued to swirl between the terrifying heat of the fiery arena and the deep chill of night, where the cold would grip him, racking his body with convulsive shaking, his teeth grinding as he searched in vain for shelter. The demons would lurk in the shadows, waiting for him, fire flicking from their eyes. But just as he feared he would be lost forever, sweet music would float through the darkness, charming his demons away, lifting the night and bathing the world in light.

Light. He needed to see the light.

He opened his eyes. Clear eyes gazed back at him.

This time they did not swim and sway away. He reached a shaking hand up and touched her face.

'Are you real?' he whispered.

She smiled.

He gazed at her face, transfixed: so beautiful.

'Have you returned to us, Sethos Leontis?' she whispered.

'Where have I been?' he croaked.

She smiled again. 'A place I couldn't follow.'

He shook his head. 'Livia,' he breathed. 'You were there . . . in my dreams. You saved me.'

'No, Sethos, I nearly killed you.'

She lifted his head and helped him drink from the cup. He sipped cool water, and felt it soothe his scorched throat.

'Where am I?'

His eyes took in the unfamiliar room. He could see dawn breaking through a small high window. His eyes continued round. He started as he caught sight of an old woman slumped on a stool by the door.

'That is just Vibia, the cook . . . my chaperone.'

Vibia stirred. Seth watched as Livia walked over to her and whispered something. The old woman stretched, stood up painfully, and hobbled out of the room.

'What did you say to her?' he asked.

'I suggested she find you something to eat . . .'

Seth lay gazing at the apparition next to him, wondering if he was trapped inside some beautiful fevered dream. How was it possible that he was here, with the girl who had swum in and out of his consciousness since he first met her?

'This is your house?'

'This is the villa of Domitus and Flavia Natalis. My adopted family.'

She spoke Latin, but her accent was unusual. 'You are not Roman born?'

'No,' she said simply. 'And neither are you?'

'Of course not,' he answered with unconcealed bitterness. 'I was dragged from Corinth in chains.'

'Well, I am glad you found your way here.' She smiled.

He looked at her in wonder. Suddenly his years of hatred and anger seemed to dissolve. There had been a reason for it all: a reason he had been torn from his home; a reason he had fought and won all those battles in the arena; a reason he was here in this cold and barbaric land . . .

Livia.

He opened his mouth to speak again, but Livia gently laid a finger on his lips. The cook had returned with some vegetable broth.

'Thank you, Vibia. Now you may get on with your other duties. I can help our guest with the soup.'

Vibia wavered uncertainly at the door, but left.

Sethos smiled. Somehow Livia, with one look, had persuaded the old cook to relinquish her chaperone duties. Impressive.

She held the broth in her hands. He tried to sit up.

'No, don't move!' cried Livia. Too late. He had forgotten his shoulder. Searing pain threw him panting back on to the couch. He clenched his eyes shut, trying to recover.

She rested her cool hand on his damp forehead and stroked the hair off his face. It felt good – more than good. He didn't want it to stop.

Suddenly her hand jerked away.

'Livia!' An imperious voice filled the room. 'Where is Vibia?'

'I released her,' the girl answered calmly.

Seth expected some kind of dangerous response. Unmarried Roman girls should never be unaccompanied, but for some reason Livia's quiet answer seemed to be adequate.

'His fever seems to have lessened,' Livia added, as the woman Sethos recognized as her mother strode towards them.

'I'll take over now, Livia,' she said sharply. 'You go and rest. And don't forget our meeting with Cassius at noon. We have much to discuss and very little time to plan the wedding banquet. Wear all your jewellery, and tell Ochira to dress your hair. She has nimble fingers.'

Seth's eyes flew open at the word 'wedding'. He just caught the expression that flitted across Livia's face, and didn't know how to interpret it. All he knew was that he felt a sharp stab of pain that had nothing to do with the jangling wound at his shoulder. How could he have forgotten? She was betrothed to another man.

Livia carefully placed the bowl of broth on the table, stood up and turned away from the bed. As she walked to the door, Seth followed her with his eyes, but she did not turn round.

'Sethos Leontis, it is good to finally see you awake.' Flavia was gazing down at him, running her finger across his jaw.

93

Sethos closed his eyes, remembering the cool touch of Livia's hand on his hair. He heard a quiet sigh and then felt warm lips touching his.

Flavia Natalis was kissing him . . .

The shock of the realization stunned him. He was unable to move. He barely had the strength to turn his head away. He could not even sit up, let alone walk out. He was powerless: a captive in her house.

Sethos was not used to feeling weak. True, this wasn't the first powerful woman who had wanted him. There had been many others, but he had never been kissed without his consent because, despite his lack of citizenship, he had always held his status. Here, now, his powerlessness dishonoured him.

And suddenly he understood the fleeting expression on Livia's face. It had carried a warning.

As Flavia's lips touched Seth's, her pulse raced. She had risked much to suggest to her husband that the gladiator be brought here. Her attraction to him was a kind of sickness, she knew. But many Roman wives succumbed to longings outside the marriage, and they managed to find justification for their affairs. She was sure she could. After all, her husband saw other women, though she knew that there was one rule for men and quite another for their wives.

In the eighteen years she had been married to Domitus she had never been sufficiently tempted to stray. Not because she loved him. She didn't. He was thirty years older than she was and chosen for her by her father, but she'd always considered she had too much to lose: a beautiful villa with plenty of slaves and the freedom to come and go as she pleased. Her husband didn't beat her, and he hadn't abandoned her when she had failed to produce children, so she had much to be grateful for. In addition he was out a great deal . . .

And now Sethos Leontis was lying here in her house . . . so breathtakingly beautiful . . . conscious at last . . .

'Madam, the physician is outside.' Vibia was standing at the door. Flavia shot her a thunderous look, and quickly stood up. How long had she been there? How much had she seen? How easily could she be silenced?

As these thoughts raged through her head, the physician entered the room. 'Ah, Tychon – welcome!' She smiled graciously. 'Our patient is much improved this morning.'

Tychon nodded respectfully and led his assistants purposefully towards the bedside. Flavia could do little more than make a dignified exit.

Seth breathed a sigh of relief, but it wasn't long before he realized he had just exchanged one form of torture for another.

Tychon started removing the dressings. Seth's shoulder was still inflamed and jarring from his earlier attempt to sit up, so when the physician began pulling at the blood-encrusted bandages he could barely suppress the gasps of pain. And when at last he felt cool air against his shoulder, he panted with relief. It was over.

Not quite. He opened his eyes with surprise at the sudden clamping iron grips of the physician's assistants on his arms and legs. What was going on?

This time, as the fire-water made contact with the aching gash on his shoulder, he could not hold back the scream. His body writhed under the fast grip of two strong men, trapping him, stilling him, while the physician worked on, unconcerned.

'Sethos Leontis, the gods have been merciful!' he murmured

soothingly. Then he turned to his assistants. 'The fever is much reduced, as is the heat in his shoulder. See how the dark red area of swelling around the wound is somewhat diminished? The poisons are seeping to the surface . . .' As he explained, Tychon pushed his fingers firmly and deliberately on the inflamed skin around the stitching, forcing pus and blood from the wound. Sethos screamed again.

'He has naturally lost a lot of blood, but we need to prevent the blood around the site from stagnating, so it is necessary to perform some judicious blood-letting, which will ease its course.'

Seth had frequently witnessed blood-letting in the barracks. Matthias swore by it. But he did not relish the prospect, and gritted his teeth in anticipation.

Tychon picked out a small fine knife from his box of instruments. He examined it against the light, and then held the blade into the flame of a burning lamp.

Seth swallowed. The assistants continued to hold him fast, so he knew there was no escape.

The physician then took a delicate horn cup, and placed it near the wound. Seth shut his eyes, and tried to force his mind away from the room. He gasped as the knife slashed through his skin, and then felt the pressure as Tychon forced the blood from this new wound into the cup. He had to endure the procedure seven more times. Three further cuts around the wound area, two on his left arm, through the vein at the crook of his elbow and wrist, and two into his torso. When Tychon had finished, he doused the cuts in his fire-water, redressed the shoulder wound, made Sethos drink some gritty bitter medicine, and left, promising to return the next day.

'Ah, good,' groaned Seth. 'Something more to look forward to,'

As he lay trying to focus away from the raging pain, Seth realized that in truth he was deeply grateful to this man, along with Matthias, for saving his life. Because now he genuinely had something – or rather someone – to live for.

Or had he dreamed her? His mind felt hazy as he tried to clarify his thoughts, and he began to feel his body floating. He could not stop it, and tried gripping on to the sides of the couch, but his hands slipped and he drifted away.

14

The Betrothed

Londinium

AD 152

Cassius Malchus, Livia's betrothed, sat in his office with Blandus, his chief accountant. Blandus was unrolling scrolls and Cassius was checking the columns of figures. Each scroll contained an audit of the taxes that had been collected from the Britannia provinces over the last three months – a heavily edited audit.

As procurator, Cassius was responsible for the money's collection, distribution and reallocation. It was an eminent and honourable position, suiting a man of high integrity. Unfortunately, as an unscrupulous, acquisitive tyrant, Cassius did not quite conform to this ideal, and so the role of procurator afforded him an immense and devastating power.

With control of such wealth, he could buy anyone he wanted. And he knew that anyone was corruptible if the stakes were high enough.

Blandus, his clever accountant, had been in Cassius's debt for the thirteen years since Cassius had stumbled on his fraudulent merchant tax-skimming activities. By the time he came to Cassius's attention, Blandus had accrued a small fortune. The Roman sentence for such a crime was banishment and the seizing of all property. Instead, Cassius offered Blandus the mighty and lucrative position of chief accountant. In order to fulfil his new post, Blandus simply had to continue with his creative paperwork, but on a much, much larger scale.

And Cassius knew he could utterly depend on Blandus's loyalty. Not simply because Blandus had so much at stake financially, but because Blandus wanted to live, and nobody understood the depth and breadth of Cassius's ruthlessness better than he did. If he were to try and extricate himself from the threads that bound him, neither he and his wife, nor his two little daughters, would survive the night.

When Cassius had finished signing the province's tax audits, Blandus cleared his throat.

'We have encountered a small problem with the olive merchant, Janus.'

Cassius inclined his head towards Blandus and waited.

'He has expressed a certain – er – unease regarding his – er – *insurance* tax.'

Cassius shrugged. 'Then he can expect his first visit from the special guard tomorrow.'

Cassius's special guard needed specific skills. His three most talented – Otho, Pontius and Rufus – were standing wordlessly just outside his door. Nobody would get past them uninvited. These three had served him since their legion days. Cassius, then their captain, had caught them viciously beating a couple of other soldiers over a gambling debt. He had immediately recognized in them the sadistic bloodlust that made them perfect for his service. Again, instead of meting out punishment, he enlisted them into his employment. He further cemented their commitment and obedience by procuring them wives with good dowries.

They were savage, callous fighters, which made them not only efficient, powerful guards, but also perfect tax collectors. Although Cassius did not require his special guard for the official tax collection, they were responsible for the enforcement of his additional 'insurance' tax: the tax that shop owners and merchants paid to protect their property from fire and vandalism . . . events which would inexplicably visit their properties if they didn't pay up. Usually a warehouse of ruined stock would be enough to loosen a merchant's purse strings, but if he continued to refuse protection payment, it would not be long before a family member was found floating face down in the Tamesis, Londinium's deep and vast river. A third visit from the special guard was rarely necessary.

Although Cassius had a huge and complicated network of agents serving him, these were the three who had performed for him the longest and most diligently. They loved their work, and he valued them.

Cassius was just sealing the final scroll when Otho knocked deferentially on the door and entered.

'What is it, man?' asked Cassius, frowning.

'Sir – Domitus Natalis and the ladies Flavia and Livia await your pleasure.'

'Ah, thank you, Otho. Show them into the atrium, and offer them spiced wine. I'll be there directly.'

Cassius carried the scrolls over to his strongbox and turned the heavy iron key. 'Blandus, would you authorize some additional funds? My wedding banquet is to be a state occasion worthy of an emperor.'

15

Cell Mutation

St Magdalene's

AD 2012

Seven a.m. Friday morning.

'Nooo!' I groaned as the alarm ripped through my oblivion. I was not ready to face the day. This Thursday-night-gig thing, followed by my 4 a.m. appointment with the school computer network, was beginning to get wearing.

I decided that an extra half-hour in bed was worth the trade for breakfast. So I reset my alarm.

When I woke the second time, I remembered that I had something really cool to get up for. A visiting professor of pathogenic virology was coming in to talk to us. It was an area of microbiology that I'd just got hooked on. I jumped out of bed and headed for the shower.

It was a bright November morning. I managed to be first into the biology lab, so I got myself my favourite seat at the front and started reading through my virology notes. By the time I lifted my head again the whole class had arrived and Dr Franklin was bringing our visitor through.

'Good morning, guys! This is Professor Ambrose. He has been working with pathogenic viruses at the New York University Microbiology Research Department. We are very lucky to welcome such an eminent scientist, and today he intends to talk to you about the cytopathic effect on cell metabolism . . .'

Bliss! I glanced round the class to share my delight, and noticed that not everyone was as excited by the prospect as me. In fact I caught quite a few eye-rolls. It was becoming alarmingly clear that I was one of the geekiest biology students here.

For me, the next forty minutes just flew past. We were using our new quantum particle microscope to check out the subtle and extreme varieties of virion shape and their replication patterns, as well as their cytopathic effect. It was hard to believe how deadly some of them could be because the way a virus transformed a cell could be so beautiful.

When the bell went, everyone stood up to file out. I hung around. I wanted to clarify syncytium formation, which we'd touched on briefly.

'Professor Ambrose?'

'Ah – it's Eva, isn't it?'

I nodded. 'Er – I was just wondering if you had a moment?'

'Certainly.' He turned to Dr Franklin. 'If that fits in with your schedule?'

'It's lunch break – so if your stomach can stand the delay?'

'Of course – don't worry about me. But I wouldn't want to keep you.'

'Oh, no problem, I have some slides to prepare for this afternoon – I'll be just over there in my office.'

'Thank you so much, Professor!' I gushed.

Professor Ambrose had a way of explaining things that was

so clear and open that each explanation led to another question, until suddenly he was rummaging in his bag and taking out a small case. He opened it carefully, and inside were some sealed glass vials, droppers and slides. He hesitated slightly, and looked at me as if to check that I was genuinely interested before continuing.

'I didn't have time to show these to the class, but given your enthusiasm and aptitude, perhaps you'd care to take a look . . .'

I was in heaven.

When the first slide was in place, he motioned me to look at the screened computer image. 'What do you see?'

I peered closely.

'Nothing unusual . . . just normal T-cells?'

'Good. Now keep watching . . .'

He then took one of the tiny vials and syringed an invisible amount on to the slide.

I watched as the T-cells were joined by tiny, spiked thread-like structures. Not a shape we'd looked at earlier.

'What are they?' I asked.

'Just watch carefully . . .'

I blinked and the screen went blank. 'Hmmm – something's gone wrong with the transmission –'

'No – the transmission is fine.'

'But –'

'Watch again – this time at a discernible speed.'

He had recorded the event on to the hard drive, which he now replayed – 300 per cent slower.

Again I watched the screen. I saw the bouncing T-cells being joined by the spiky threads. Within a moment the threads had attached themselves to the T-cells, and were worming their way through the narrow cell receptors into the central cell cavity. The threads now wriggled inside the cell. Suddenly they were splitting. Two threads became four and so on, until each T-cell was a pulsating mass of threads. The T-cells started to grow as the reproducing threads continued to multiply. The cells grew and grew and then quite suddenly seemed to simultaneously explode. I stared at the screen. It was completely empty.

'What just happened?' I whispered. I had never seen anything like it.

'What do you think happened?' he asked.

'Well – it's impossible – but it looked as though the cells just ... disappeared.'

'What you have just seen –'

'Professor Ambrose.' Dr Franklin was striding towards us. 'I really think Eva has tested your patience long enough! Come now, before the dining staff give up on us entirely – as it is we have probably missed any chance at the chocolate brownies!'

A flicker of impatience crossed Professor Ambrose's face, but he smiled genially.

'Ah, thank you for your solicitous hospitality.' He turned back to me. 'Eva, maybe we could continue our conversation after lunch?'

I nodded, trying to work out whether I could get out of maths.

Dr Franklin frowned. 'Do you have a free period at 2 p.m., Eva?'

'Well – er – not exactly, but –'

'Maybe I can prevail upon Professor Ambrose to come back and visit us another time then?' said Dr Franklin.

'It would be my pleasure,' smiled the professor, as Dr Franklin steered him firmly towards the door.

But just as they were about to step outside, he turned round suddenly. 'I can leave my things here till after lunch?' he asked, gesturing to the slides and vials.

'Absolutely, Professor! Eva, you can release the lock when you leave, can't you?'

'Of course, Dr Franklin.'

'But you'd really better hurry now. You've got less than twenty minutes to eat before your next lesson starts.'

Dr Franklin opened the lab door and led the professor off to the dining room, leaving me alone in the lab.

I looked at my pile of books. And then at the microscope.

Of course, at that point, I should have packed up my stuff and gone to lunch . . . but I didn't.

16

Hallucination

Londinium

AD 152

That scent. He knew it. He breathed deeply, turning his face towards it and opening his eyes.

She was there. Sitting on the stool next to him. But her face was turned away, her eyes gazing out of the window at the moon, her expression troubled.

'Livia?' he whispered.

Her eyes darted back to him and her face broke into an exquisite smile.

'Hello, Sethos,' she breathed. She looked anxiously towards the door, then bent her head so that her lips almost touched his ear. 'Vibia has given us a few minutes . . .'

'You have persuasive powers . . .' he smiled, reaching for her hand.

'Actually, I think her actions are more in defiance of Flavia than concern for me. She doesn't approve of Flavia's . . . er . . . interest.'

He shut his eyes and tried to swallow the bile that rose in his throat at the memory of Flavia's approach that morning.

'Are you thirsty?' asked Livia, misinterpreting his movement. She picked up the cup from the table, and gently lifted his head, helping him to drink. He did not take his eyes from her face.

'Flavia is dangerous, Seth. If she wants something, she *will* get it.'

'Livia,' he choked, 'you're the only one I want, the only one I'll ever want . . .'

'Seth,' she breathed as she held the cup to his lips. 'You are weak with pain and fever. You don't know whether you wake or dream. And you do not know me . . .'

With wild eyes, he swallowed down the water. 'Livia . . . tell me you don't feel the same way . . .'

He held her eyes with his and found his answer there. But he also saw that she was struggling against it.

'Livia,' he urged, 'we cannot let fear defeat us.'

Gently, Livia lowered his head, and turned to replace the cup on the table. As she took her hands away, he felt an instant pang of loss. Instinctively, he reached out for her, and as if by some miracle, he now felt his hand encased in both of hers. He sighed contentedly, bringing her hands up to his cheek. Her scent made him dizzy. He brushed her fingers with his lips, then lifted his eyes to her face and saw that she was weeping.

'Seth,' she choked, 'this is impossible –'

'Shhh – no! Don't say that . . .' He kissed her fingers. 'We're meant to be together.' Seth frowned as he spoke these words. Where had this conviction come from? He despised sentimentality, but recognized that this wasn't sentiment. This girl had simply and completely realigned his universe. For years his life had centred entirely, relentlessly, on physical survival. He had done everything to cauterize all unhelpful thoughts and emotions. Hope, trust, love – banished. He knew that his survival had depended on this rigorous denial. Yet now, suddenly he was relinquishing himself, aligning himself with another. And instead of fearing for his survival, he felt as though his survival now depended on it. He couldn't live without her.

But she was gazing past him, shaking her head. 'This shouldn't be happening,' she breathed.

'I knew as soon as I saw you,' he whispered, seeing again her face in the arena.

'But, Sethos, everything is against it – us . . . more than you could know.'

'There will be a way. We just need time.'

'We have no time. I have to leave. If I stay here, I will be married . . .'

He flinched. 'When?'

Her voice was dead. 'The date is set. The wedding is in less than two weeks.'

'Two weeks?' he repeated stupidly.

'Cassius Malchus does not wish to wait.'

Cassius Malchus. That name was familiar.

'Nobody defies him. He is a powerful man.'

'How powerful?'

'He is procurator.'

'I don't fear the procurator,' rasped Sethos. 'I only fear – losing you . . .'

'I am already lost, Sethos,' she whispered.

His chest heaved as she spoke, causing the pain to rage in his shoulder. His mouth was dry. He felt the fever as it threatened to carry his consciousness away again, and he fought against it.

Her mouth twisted when she saw how he struggled. She soaked a cloth in water and gently wiped the sweat from his face.

'Shhh . . . it's all right,' she soothed. 'I am here now . . .'

Seth pushed against the fever, but it swallowed him again. He didn't know how many times he tried to resurface, but every time he opened his eyes, it seemed he would be drinking bitter potions, and then he would be swallowed away again, thrust back once more into dark dreams. Somewhere far away, in the light, he could feel her waiting for him, but he couldn't reach her, his limbs were weighed down . . .

From time to time, other voices drifted in and out of his consciousness, and sometimes he thought he heard his own voice, muttering, screaming, shouting . . .

Then, occasionally, the colour of his dreams changed . . . the reds and blacks of his nightmares became imbued with soft blues and yellows. Words transformed into songs, and music chased away the shadows. He would drift contentedly across peaceful waters on to warm sands.

Now he lay by the lapping sparkling waves of Corinth. The sun was high in the clear blue sky. He shielded his eyes against the dazzling light.

'Sorry, I didn't mean to startle you!'

He opened his eyes. 'Livia?'

He wasn't in Corinth. He was here in this room. Livia stood in front of him, holding an oil lamp. A halo of light enveloped her. He reached out. She moved closer and took his hand.

'Thank you,' he whispered.

'For what?' she asked.

'For being here . . . for being . . .'

She touched his face, but she wasn't smiling. 'Seth, I have to go.'

'Livia – please –'

'I cannot stay. I have to get far, far away. And you have to let me go . . . or he will kill you.'

Sethos laughed savagely. 'Do you think I am afraid of him? I have faced death every day for years. It holds no terror. We will go away together –'

'Then he will kill us both . . . or have us killed. He has many friends and they will do anything he asks,' she said bitterly. 'We can't win.'

'Livia, I have won eight wreaths . . .'

'Nine,' she corrected.

He shook his head. 'I will not be beaten,' he spat as he took a deep jagged breath. Bracing himself, and cursing the drugs that made his head so heavy, he began heaving himself off the mattress. He didn't expect the sickening dizziness as the pain in his shoulder flared; nor did he expect her reaction.

'Seth – what are you doing?' she gasped, forcing him back down with both her hands. 'You will open your shoulder, and never recover . . .'

'Livia,' he groaned as he lay back against the couch, weak and spent. 'I need to regain my strength . . . I need to train.'

She shook her head sadly. 'Not now. Now you need to rest. You will regain your strength, Seth,' she said, gently stroking his face. She let her fingers wander across his chest. The taut muscles were testament to her statement. He caught her hand as it traced the contours of his skin, and pulled her towards him. He kissed her hair, and she lifted her chin to look at him. As their eyes met, he felt his gut tighten with emotion. Instinctively, his hand reached out and pulled her face towards his. He closed his eyes and his lips sought hers. As their mouths touched, he sighed, and instantly they were inhaling each other's breath, hearts beating out a heavy urgent rhythm. At last, dizzy and gasping, Livia pulled away. They both felt the loss instantly and she returned, this time kissing him softly, tenderly.

Her lips brushed over his eyes, his cheeks, his chin, his neck, while he breathed in her heady scent. Once again their mouths met; this time the intensity of their passion made their breathing hoarse and heavy. Seth groaned and she started away.

'Did I hurt you?'

'Oh, Livia!' he breathed, pulling her roughly back. 'You have done what no gladiator could do – you have torn out my heart . . .'

'I am so sorry,' she wept, tears spilling from her eyes as they kissed once more.

Their senses sharpened, they both heard the movement outside at the same time. The kitchen slaves were preparing for the day. She touched his lips with her fingers and was gone.

Her absence felt like a hole opening up inside him. He willed her back, but she did not return. So he closed his eyes and began to plan.

If what she said about Cassius was true, they would need to leave Britannia, and cross the seas. He allowed himself to dream briefly of taking her to Corinth. But he did not want to bring the wrath of Rome down on to his homeland. They would probably be safer travelling into the barbarian lands still untouched by the Romans, though he knew there were good reasons for Roman absence from such places . . . either the land was merciless and inhospitable or – more likely – the inhabitants were. He didn't particularly want to impose the risk of either on Livia. But he didn't see any other choice.

He would not allow himself to consider the difficulty of a wounded, branded gladiator and a young, beautiful Roman girl travelling through hostile territory. The odds were stacked against them, but he was no stranger to terrible odds.

He had saved some money and a number of valuable jewels – generous gifts from admirers – which were buried safely at the barracks. He would need to return there to retrieve them. So he had to get himself off this bed.

Clenching his teeth against the pain, he tried once more to pull himself up. He ignored the tearing heat in his shoulder, and the hot blood as it seeped through the dressing across his chest. But he could not ignore the black mist that now spread across his eyes.

Later, when Flavia arrived at his side, he was hot, delirious and covered in blood. Concerned, she called for Tychon, the physician, who couldn't understand how the stitches had torn. He sewed the wound again, and this time braced the shoulder to the bed. Then he administered a fresh draught of opium, which Seth, through the fever, struggled against swallowing. He had to keep his mind clear. But despite his gladiatorial prowess, he was easily overpowered by an elderly Greek physician, and could not stop himself slipping away.

At dusk, Seth woke with a start. He was confused. He had been dreaming of journeys . . . collecting his belongings . . . the barracks.

'Matthias?' he croaked.

'Who is Matthias?' a man's voice asked, without much interest.

Sethos turned towards the voice. His head throbbed and he could barely open his eyes, but he could just make out two men standing at his bedside. Men he did not recognize.

'I believe Matthias was the name of the incompetent slave at the barracks doing his best to kill the gladiator,' chuckled the other man.

Seth's eyes narrowed at this insult. He felt his hand clench into a fist.

'Ah, Sethos Leontis . . .' A voice he did recognize. His eyes moved towards the imperious figure of Flavia Natalis. She stood beneath the window, her eyes shooting a warning. But her presence simply amplified for Seth the yawning absence of the one person he needed to see. His eyes darted around the room distractedly, searching for her. But Livia was not there.

'Now that you are conscious,' continued Flavia, 'I think it would be appropriate for you to meet and thank the man who has saved your life: Domitus Natalis, your host; my husband.'

She smiled and walked over to the tall, thin man who had just insulted Seth's best friend.

Domitus patted her hand and waited. Flavia's eyes widened pointedly at Sethos.

He swallowed down the bile and mumbled his thanks.

'You are doubly honoured this evening, as we also welcome our exalted guest Cassius Malchus . . . soon to be so much more than a guest! Our future son.'

Seth's eyes darted up at the name. Future son? He looked ten years older than Flavia. He stared into the hooded eyes of his hated rival: a broad-shouldered man, clearly an ex-soldier by his stance, with a full, slightly twisted mouth, a large wide nose and a heavy head of greying hair. Seth almost retched at the idea of this man touching Livia.

Cassius was growing restless. 'Where is my bride, anyway? I haven't come here to stare at a sick slave . . . I assume Livia will be singing tonight?' He was propelling Domitus from the room.

Seth's knuckles whitened, and he tried to get control of his breathing as he watched the two men make their way towards the doorway.

Flavia stood at the window, watching him. She sighed deeply. She had seen enough. For days now, Seth's feverish mumblings had alerted her to his preoccupations, but she had hoped his words were just the result of delirious ravings. Only now she had observed the conscious effort he made to control his animosity towards Cassius. And it wasn't difficult to guess the reason. She was not a stupid woman. She knew that Livia was exceptionally beautiful, and that the girl had a quality that drew people towards her. Had not she and Domitus themselves been captivated by her?

There was no doubt about it. Sethos Leontis was in love with her daughter.

Flavia bit her lip, trying to suppress the sharp intake of breath that threatened to betray her. In her heart, she had known yesterday when she had kissed him that he did not want her. But she had been sure that in time she could win him. Now she knew she could not. Jealousy was a cold companion. It clawed into her soul and filled her with bitterness. As she followed the men out, she decided she would need to act quickly.

Through desperate dreams Seth could distantly hear a strange sensuous song weaving its cadences around intricate plucked notes. Some part of his consciousness knew it was Livia. Her voice called him, reminded him that there was something he needed to do.

He woke with a start. It was dark. Her scent filled the room.

'Livia?' he whispered.

He felt her lips against his ear. 'Seth, I have no time. They know about us . . . I'm to be married in the morning. Guards are on their way . . . I have to run.'

'Livia,' he gasped, 'I'm coming with you –'

'No, Sethos. You can't. I'll come back for you . . . I love you . . .'

And she was gone.

He tried to get up and follow her, but he was now braced to the bed. He lay helpless and bereft, a boiling rage growing in his chest.

17

Trap

Londinium

AD 152

'Sethos.'

Seth didn't want to open his eyes.

He had been flailing in a swirling, sickening chaos of despair and fury. And right in the epicentre of his nightmare storm had stood Livia: small . . . disappearing. As he tossed and turned, the darkness suddenly blazed with white flashes of fear. Livia was screaming. She was screaming his name . . . His heart thudded as he fought against the brace that bound him to the bed. He felt more a prisoner than he ever had as a gladiator. His helplessness was drowning him, taking away his very identity. He had nothing . . . he was nothing.

'Sethos, wake up!'

This was not the voice he longed to hear. He turned his face away.

'Quickly, Sethos, I have a message – from Livia.'

His eyes shot open. Vibia, the old cook, crouched anxiously by his side.

'She was caught, escaping . . . and married –'

'When?' he gasped.

'Yesterday. You have been well sedated –'

'Where is she?'

'She has been taken to Cassius's villa.'

'Oh ye gods . . .' he groaned. It was unendurable.

Seth thrust an arm across his eyes. He couldn't bear to face Vibia. He couldn't bear to face himself. He had failed Livia when she needed him most. And now he saw nothing but darkness, all hope extinguished.

'Sethos Leontis – all is not lost,' hissed Vibia, her eyes darting towards the door.

Seth stirred.

'I have a niece – house-slave in Cassius's house. She can be trusted . . .'

'But, Vibia –'

Vibia suddenly pulled herself upright, and spoke more loudly. 'I will fetch you some bread directly. It is good to see you awake.'

She flashed him a warning with her eyes and stood to leave.

'Ah, Vibia – the food will need to wait,' said Flavia as she strode towards the bed. 'The surgeon is here.'

'Of course, Madam,' said Vibia as she left the room.

Seth closed his eyes in anticipation of his latest visitors. He tried to ignore the cool, proprietorial touch of Flavia's fingers on his arm, but when he sensed the Greek standing over him, examining the dressing, his whole body tensed.

Tychon cleared his throat deferentially.

'Madam, I will need some time to make an examination of the gladiator. I'll call the house-slave to let you know when I have finished.'

'Very well,' Flavia snorted and left the room, shutting the door firmly behind her.

When it was clear that she was no longer within earshot, Tychon spoke to Sethos in Greek.

'What ails you, man? You are consistently fighting against my medicine. You have the strength of ten stallions and yet you are still swamped in fever. You fight against the draughts to help you sleep, you have forced your wound open twice now . . . the skin around it is thin and cannot be stitched indefinitely. You have to allow it to heal. Do you want to live? Or have your years as a gladiator made you weary of life?'

Seth shook his head. 'I want to live, Tychon. I need my strength back. I have to get out of here . . . I can't be strapped down like an animal –'

'If I take away the brace, the wound will not heal.'

'Do I need to be braced to the bed? Could you not brace around the shoulder so that I can sit up and move about? My legs still work . . . my hands . . .'

Tychon scratched his head and thought.

'Well – let me see how the stitching is holding and how the swelling is doing . . .'

Seth prepared himself for the dressing change, but today the searing pain of the fire-water, and the torturous meticulous swabbing and probing helped to sharpen his mind. He was determined to get himself strong enough to rescue Livia from her prison.

Tychon had not brought any assistants today, so he decided against blood-letting. Seth breathed his thanks to Zeus for this small mercy. When the wound had been redressed, instead of strapping him once more to the bed, Tychon called Vibia.

'Could you find me clean linen and tear it in strips, so wide and so long,' he said, gesturing with his hands.

Vibia nodded and left. When she returned with a neat pile of cream-coloured linen, Tychon laid the strips out carefully on the marble table next to the bed.

'Thank you, Vibia. Now could you stay and help me for a moment?'

With her help, Tychon gently raised Sethos into a sitting position. Seth gasped as the pain in his shoulder flared.

'Remember this was your idea,' warned Tychon.

'I'm fine,' panted Sethos.

Now Tychon gently folded Seth's left arm into his body, and began strapping linen around his shoulder and arm until they were tightly bound. When he had tied off the last strip of linen, he stood in front of Seth with his arms folded.

'You must not attempt to use this hand. Move with caution. Do everything in your power to prevent the shoulder jarring. I do not want to be restitching the wound again. If you feel an intense heat in the shoulder, you must send word immediately. You will swallow the sedatives I am supplying at night without demur, and you will take the blood-cleansing herbs I am preparing, three times a day. Do not let me down, Sethos.'

'Thank you,' whispered Seth.

'I'll see you out,' said Vibia.

Seth sat on the side of the bed, breathing raggedly. The pain was settling into the familiar bearable throb, and his mind was clearer than it had been for days . . . or was it weeks? He could not remember how long he had been here.

Vibia returned with bread, dried fruit and some warm honeyed wine. Seth ate and drank gratefully. It was strange finally seeing this room from a different angle. It was, he realized, a beautiful room: airy, with painted pale-blue walls. Small simple scroll patterns were picked out in white. The floor was tiled, in a simple grey-and-white geometric pattern, and the grey marble of the table was delicately threaded with blue. The couch-like bed he had been lying on had a scrolled end, and it too was painted grey.

After he had finished his breakfast, he put the plate and cup on the table by the bed, and leaning on it for support, pushed himself up to stand. It wasn't a painfree operation, and he felt dizzy, but once he was upright he was pleased with himself. He took a few steps. A wave of nausea sent him stumbling back to the bed, but he did not stay there long. He took a few more deep breaths and pushed himself upright once more.

He needed to drive himself hard if he was ever to regain his strength, so he forced himself to walk round the room. Every time his legs felt weak, he leaned against the cool blue wall; every time his head began to swim, he crouched on the floor until it passed. He had done three circuits, and was just resting against the wall, when Flavia suddenly walked in.

She gasped when she saw him upright, and then smiled.

'Sethos! How splendid to see you standing!'

'If the gods are willing, you will soon be free of me!' He could feel her eyes on him, and tried to smile lightly, but his lips would not cooperate.

'Sethos,' Flavia whispered, drawing very close, and touching him lightly on the chin. 'It is good to see the gladiator fire burning in your breast again.'

Her hand moved down to his chest, and Sethos tried to

submit without flinching. Then she strode over to the bell and called Vibia.

'Fetch a bowl with some warm scented water, some drying cloths and some juniper oil.'

The thought of bathing filled Seth with joy, but he feared Flavia didn't intend to leave him alone to wash. Her fingers rested on his arm.

He considered his options. Was he fit enough to leave right now? The physician would obviously say no, but Seth knew himself to be pretty resilient. Then he remembered that Tychon had mentioned that the gladiatorial familia was away from the barracks for at least two more weeks. He knew he would be unable to totally fend for himself yet. He also knew that if he refused Flavia, his life here would be untenable. Spurned Roman wives would be revenged . . .

He had to face it – he was trapped.

Vibia knocked and entered, carrying a large bowl that sent a glorious aroma through the whole room. But she did not set the bowl on the table and leave. She gestured with her head towards the door.

'I have brought Ochira to help me bathe the gladiator, Madam,' said Vibia with a meaningful smile. Ochira, a large full-faced girl, tiptoed in behind her, carrying towels and oils and a fresh tunic.

Flavia was furious. She had been trumped by the old slave-woman, and it would be unseemly for her to do anything other than leave.

'Thank you, Vibia,' she hissed as she stormed out.

Seth raised a silent prayer of gratitude, and smiled at his deliverer. He was suddenly filled with an unexpected rush of optimism. With Vibia's help, why shouldn't he and Livia make it out of Londinium? He flexed his good shoulder and shut his eyes. If he trained hard, he could regain his strength, and then he would be fit enough to take on Cassius.

The warm scented water soothed his skin and as the day's miseries washed away, he breathed deeply, daring to dream of the day he and Livia could finally be together.

18

Heat

St Magdalene's

AD 2012

I shut the biology lab door and went back to the screen. I was intrigued. Invaded cells did not just disappear. I'd seen cells explode, but there would always be the visible remains, plus the multiplied virus or bacteria swimming off to invade further cells. Never this total evaporation.

I needed to watch it one more time. Quickly I set it to replay, this time 500 per cent slower – as slow as it was programmed to go.

But the speed reduction didn't provide any more information. The total disappearance happened just as before, only a bit more slowly.

I turned away from the screen in frustration and nearly fell over Professor Ambrose's open case on the floor. As I glanced at it, I realized he hadn't put the vial and dropper away. They were still on the table by the microscope. My heart started to thud as I looked at them, the decision already made.

If I was going to replicate the experiment, I would need some normal T-cells . . .

Easy, I had a body full of them. I quickly took a compass out of my bag, jabbed it into my finger and smeared the blood on to a new slide. Then I picked up the tiny vial, added a drop to the surface, placed it under the microscope and refocused the lens.

'I don't believe it!' I breathed as I watched the replay. Even in slow motion it all happened so fast: invasion, replication, multiplication, explosion . . . evaporation . . . then a completely still and empty screen.

I stared at it for a few minutes. This was pure science so there had to be a logical explanation. I must have missed something. I stood up to repeat the experiment again.

I found a fresh slide, grabbed my compass, stabbed my finger, picked up the vial –

'Eva Koretsky! What are you still doing here?' Dr Franklin and Professor Ambrose were back. I'd been so lost in my own thoughts that I jumped in surprise. The contents of the precious vial spilled down my fingers and on to the floor.

'Oh God! I am sorry!' I gasped.

Professor Ambrose was staring at the half-empty bottle, his face frozen.

'Eva, you know these labs are out of bounds when there is no member of staff present. I hope that sample wasn't anything too valuable, Professor Ambrose?'

I held my breath.

Professor Ambrose stared for a few moments at the tiny pool of liquid on the floor. Then without looking up, he said quietly, 'No, no – I have infinite supplies.'

'Well, that's a relief. OK, Eva – you'd better get off quickly to lunch.'

'I am so sorry. I'll go as soon as I've cleared this up.'

'You'd better go now, Eva,' said Professor Ambrose, gently propelling me towards the door. 'I can do this. Dr Franklin, do you have a paper towel?'

She went off to fetch one.

'Well, um – thank you, Professor Ambrose. Sorry,' I mumbled as I pulled open the door. 'Er – goodbye then.'

'Goodbye, Eva. I'm sure it won't be long before we meet again.'

I had six minutes. I sprinted across to the empty dining hall, but I had missed lunch. So I made straight for maths, my head filled with questions.

By the end of the lesson I was feeling a bit light-headed. Must get something to eat before my rehearsal, I decided, as I collected up my stuff and stood up. Too fast. Head rush. I wobbled unglamorously, and Rob Wilmer steadied me.

'You OK?' he asked.

'Missed lunch . . . And breakfast, now I think of it. I'll be fine.'

'Here –'

He handed me half a Mars bar.

I picked the fluff off. 'Thanks,' I said gratefully.

About half an hour into art history I started to feel hot. Really hot. I pulled off my hoody, but I was still sweating. I wiped my forehead. I was burning up.

I totally didn't have time for flu. Before I could finish the thought my stomach started churning. God, I was going to puke. Bloody Mars bar! How long had it been in Rob's pocket?

I stood up quickly. Mistake. The whole room began to spin violently. I tried to get it to stop long enough for me to locate the door. But as I searched for it, my vision began to cloud and everything started to darken. By the time I heard the crash I knew it was me, hitting the floor.

19
Rage

Londinium

AD 152

Seth put the same drive, energy and intensity into his recovery as he had into his arena battles. He pushed through pain, fatigue, shaking limbs and daily blood-lettings; denying his body any mercy. He was driven not only by the need to regain his strength and fitness, but also by shame. His failure to prevent Livia's abduction consumed him. He had regularly witnessed gladiatorial shame at a badly lost fight, but this was the first time he truly understood the sickening sense of dishonour. Though for him this dishonour was worse. In the arena the gladiator let only himself down, whereas Seth had failed some-body else – the girl he professed to love.

His ruthless training was punctuated by regular visits from Flavia. Sometimes she simply stood against a wall, watching, her eyes greedily enjoying him. Sometimes she would stand just behind him, inhaling him. When she was sure they would not be disturbed, she would lean her head on to his shoulder and kiss along his neck, or run her hands across his back, through his dark hair, along his jaw, across his lips. Seth would shut his eyes and stand absolutely still, like a wild animal trapped by a predator. He did not flinch; he simply submitted until she sighed with frustration and strode out. As the door closed behind her, he would allow himself a momentary shudder and resume his exercise.

On the morning of the sixth day, shortly after Tychon had finished his torturous dressing change and blood-letting, Vibia slipped into his room. She waited until she was sure the physician and his assistant were definitely out of the building, made sure that the door was firmly closed, then crept over to the bed and whispered, 'I have word.'

Seth leaned into her and she breathed her message. He sighed deeply and nodded, watching in glazed abstraction as she picked up the empty water cup and his finished breakfast dish and left the room. When he heard the door close, Seth blinked, raised himself painfully from the bed, and began his leg squats.

For the next two hours he sweated through his training: one-armed floor presses, sprinting on the spot, rope-skipping, lifting makeshift weights (marble candlesticks and stools), lunges and parries. He wouldn't have been able to say whether his thumping heart rate was the result of exercise or anticipation.

At midday Vibia arrived with a bowl of warm water and oils, and began helping him to wash and shave. Seth had always been completely relaxed about his nakedness until Flavia had begun her daily assaults. Now his eyes and ears were alert for any sign of intrusion. Vibia had timed her visit well. She had just helped him into his tunic, when Flavia swept in.

'Vibia!' she hissed. 'What are you doing here?'

'Excuse me, Madam, do you have need of me?'

Gathering up the bowl, towel and old tunic, Vibia backed out of the room without daring to look at her mistress. Flavia's stony expression was ominous.

'Lady, I am so sorry,' said Seth. 'The fault was mine. My movements are still restricted and I asked Vibia for assistance.'

Flavia snorted. 'The cook should be in the kitchen, unless otherwise instructed. However, I shall not be lunching at home on this occasion, so I will overlook her transgression . . . for your sake.'

Flavia's eyes met Seth's and he understood their meaning. Vibia's fate was now dangerously bound up with his own. He swallowed bitterly, every cell in his body resisting the powerlessness of his situation, and despising the threatening authority the woman wielded.

'Thank you, Madam,' he breathed between clenched teeth.

Flavia smiled, leaned into him and kissed him hard on the mouth. He shut his eyes tight, did his best to conjure Livia, and . . . kissed her back. Gasping with pleasure, Flavia ran her hands through his hair, around his neck, pulling him closer.

When she stopped for breath, she touched his lips, laughing softly.

'Sethos, my sweet, I cannot stay! I shall be late for Tavinia! But fear not, we will continue later . . .'

She kissed him once more and glided out of the room.

'Ochira!' she called. 'My cloak!'

Within five minutes, Flavia and Ochira had left the villa, and Seth stood, his fists clenched, trying to control the seething anger curling round his chest.

The door creaked open and he started, but it was Vibia, carrying a toga and cloak.

Sethos gaped at the garments.

'A toga?' he breathed, uncertain.

'You cannot walk out of this house in your slave's tunic, and these will conceal your tattoos and injured shoulder.'

The Roman toga was a symbol of citizenship and honour, and the wearing of one without authority was almost blasphemous. In addition, Seth had no idea how to put one on. But Vibia, despite her stiffening fingers, had had years of practice, and within moments she was smoothing its folds around him. He inhaled sharply as she swung the heavy dark cloak over his braced shoulder.

'Sorry,' she muttered, fastening the clasp. 'But you will find the hood a useful addition.'

When she was finished, she stood back.

'Good,' she nodded approvingly. 'You look like a true Roman citizen.'

He smiled wryly at her. They both knew what an ambivalent compliment this was to him; he loathed most Roman citizens.

Then Vibia touched his arm. 'Sethos, whatever you see, do not reveal yourself. All our lives depend on that.'

Seth's eyes narrowed speculatively. He knew a warning when he heard one, and he began to feel dread creeping through him.

Vibia stepped briefly out of the room, checked that there was nobody around, then beckoned for him to follow. She led him out through the garden and side opening, gesturing for him to wait while she moved cautiously on to the street beyond. When she was sure the way was clear, she turned to him, nodding silently, and he was suddenly out on the street, alone.

This was Seth's first taste of freedom since his capture in Corinth. A gladiator slave never walked through the streets of

Londinium unless he was chained and guarded. But he didn't waste time savouring his liberty, because he was aware that however blissful it was to feel his body unencumbered by shackles, the sweetness was threaded with the bitter certainty that if he were caught impersonating a Roman citizen he would be shown absolutely no mercy. And he was walking right into the lion's den: the forum.

It was a reckless plan: the forum was the centre of Londinium's commercial and political life. It would be seething with people. Everybody who was anybody met there. And here he was, Sethos Leontis, the famous gladiator, heading straight for it.

But Seth understood the Roman psyche. Slaves were invisible; subhuman. So even though he had been a fêted slave, a beacon in the arena, he doubted if many people had taken the trouble to look at his face. In any case most of the vast arena crowd sat too far away to see any gladiator clearly, so he felt fairly confident in his disguise. The only people he had to fear were those who actually knew him. Fortunately, his gladiatorial familia was not yet back from Aquitania, but he had to admit there were several Roman ladies who knew him fairly intimately. He pushed this thought away.

The Natalis villa was a short walk from the forum, and as he did his best to move swiftly but without hurry (as Vibia had instructed) he considered the message he'd received from Vibia's niece, Sabina.

Sabina was to accompany Livia from Cassius's house at noon to visit the forum shops. This would be Livia's first outing since the marriage. Cassius, it seemed, had decided that she could be trusted with this small freedom, though of course Sabina and a guard would be there to watch her. Seth tried not to imagine how Livia had convinced Cassius that she was trustworthy. The same way he had convinced Flavia?

He knew that the best he could hope for was little more than a glimpse of her, but the thought of that glimpse had sustained him through his morning. It never occurred to him to question the sanity of the plan. He needed to see her like a plant needed water.

The walk to the forum passed without incident and, as he drew close, he pulled the cloak's hood over his head. It was a cool but dry August day, so the weather didn't warrant it, which made him slightly uneasy, but the hood shadowed his face nicely, and on reflection, this was probably the safer option. The combined weight of the cloak and the toga chafed his shoulder painfully, and each step further jarred the wound, but Seth's attention was elsewhere. His eyes were skimming the throngs of people, scanning for danger, scanning for Livia.

And then he saw her. Standing at the baker's stall, nibbling on an almond cake. Her face was turned away, but he knew her at once. Her hair was covered in a beautiful lilac silk, embroidered in gold; her tunic was heavy and white with an elegant purple trim. Three jewelled bracelets sparkled on her wrist, and – with a stab of pain – Sethos saw the large glittering betrothal ring on her finger. The whole ensemble proclaimed Livia as the wife of a very rich man. But she was exuding an air of such misery that his heart ached. She ate without tasting. She was not interested in the food: her eyes were glancing nervously around.

Seth didn't need to try and attract her attention because almost as soon as he'd spotted her, as if by some magnetic compulsion, her eyes found his. She froze. And so did he – the smile of pleasure at seeing her suddenly eclipsed by a new emotion: fury. Her face was a catalogue of injuries – a healing but swollen cut along her cheek, bruising along her jaw, lips cracked and swollen. Seth's breathing became jagged, and his eyes darted quickly over the rest of her to check for further injuries, but her robes were designed to reveal nothing.

Wildly, Seth started towards her, but her eyes widened in fear and silently indicated to her left. She was identifying her guard, a heavy, belligerent-looking man with coarse red hair and a soldier's stance. He did nothing to conceal the dagger at his waist and the sword slung across his back.

Seth had no weapon, an injured shoulder and a duty to all involved to remain concealed. He fought with himself, wrestling down the overwhelming impulse to kill the guard and rescue the girl. But he had learned years ago that a fighter has to control his anger. He had to remain measured. Too many lives were at stake.

As Seth edged towards her, Livia suddenly reached a hand out to the guard.

'Otho, my husband Cassius expressly asked me to buy him a new set of dice. I am a little dizzy . . . would you be good enough to purchase them for me? I saw a beautiful games store over by those steps. I will stay here with Sabina.'

Livia pulled a purse from her waist, and handed the guard three coins.

The guard did not look like a man who cared whether his prisoner was dizzy or not, yet Seth watched in amazement as Otho turned and strode off towards the stall. Immediately Seth ran forwards and pulled Livia towards him. He felt the shuddering sob as she leaned against his chest.

He looked down at her face. 'Who did this to you?' he hissed.

'Cassius is my husband now,' she whispered simply.

'I'll kill him!' Seth rasped.

Livia shook her head. 'Seth, you have no idea what kind of man he is.'

Seth looked at her damaged face and thought he probably did.

'I have to take you away, my love,' he groaned.

'Not now. Not yet!' she warned, brushing a tear angrily from her cheek.

'Madam!' Sabina's eyes were wild with anxiety. 'We are so exposed, and Otho will be returning any moment.'

Seth's fists clenched as he tried to control his breathing. His adrenalin was pumping; he was in fight mode, and was not dealing well with this forced inaction.

Livia put a hand on his arm, warning restraint.

'Livia, when can I see you again?'

'Mistress! Otho is coming! Now!'

'Go, Sethos. I will send word.'

He could not bring himself to leave her.

'Please, my own sweet Seth . . .' she choked, and turned away.

He moved into the shadows and helplessly watched his lovely Livia drift out of reach. It was unbearable. He needed to run, to expend the destructive energy that was building in his chest. But Roman citizens draped in togas and cloaks did not run. They walked briskly and purposefully.

Every cell in his body railed against the discipline of walking away, but he had immense self-control. He had to survive. He had a job to do, and thinking about how he would carry it out occupied his mind so completely that he arrived back at the

Natalis villa without noticing the journey. But as soon as he found himself in the garden, Vibia was upon him, hauling the cloak and toga away and hissing for him to get back inside. Flavia had returned home.

She was waiting for him when he reached his room, anger emanating from every pore. '*Sethos Leontis, where have you been?*'

Seth's eyes narrowed momentarily as he suppressed the revulsion he felt for this woman and the power she wielded over them all, but then he regained control and remembered his script.

'I was in the garden, lady, picking you this.'

As he handed Flavia the polished red apple Vibia had slipped into his hand a moment previously, Seth watched the most dramatic mood change he had ever witnessed.

Delight transformed Flavia from imperious tyrant to flirtatious coquette. 'Oh, Seth,' she breathed. 'How thoughtful.'

Then she swept over to the bedroom door, locked it and took him in her arms. As she kissed him, Seth closed his eyes and thought only of Livia.

20

Secrets

Londinium

AD 152

Eight difficult days had passed since Seth had seen Livia. In that time he had endured five conjugal visits from Flavia, thirty-two hours of gruelling training and seven blood-lettings. He was now sitting on the side of his couch submitting to yet another dressing change, doing his best to suppress overwhelming agitation.

As Tychon was about to begin the slow business of rebracing his shoulder, Seth suddenly turned to the physician and begged him to reconsider.

'Tychon, it's impossible to train properly with one arm. And I am beholden to the women of the house for even the smallest tasks. I need to be released!'

He did not mention that a braced shoulder heavily encumbered his disguise as a Roman citizen, a disguise he was planning to use again in about half an hour. Neither did he add that his ability to flee Londinium and his role as Livia's protector would be dangerously compromised by such a handicap.

Tychon shook his head gravely. 'Patience, Sethos! The skin and muscle tears are healing, but the bone takes longer. If I do not brace your shoulder, you will never have the use of this arm again. Are you aware of what that will mean? Your usefulness in any capacity will be over.'

Tychon had never put his case more starkly.

Sethos swallowed and said no more. Instead he allowed his mind to dwell on happier thoughts: Livia's letters. He had received two. Both had been written in Greek. Seth smiled. Roman ladies did not make a habit of learning Greek, but then, he reminded himself, Livia wasn't born Roman. He had been deeply grateful, of course, because he could not read or write in Latin.

He had burned both letters immediately, which had been hard: to burn his only physical connection with her seemed sacrilegious, but keeping the letters was too dangerous. For everyone involved. Anyway, he'd memorized every word. The letter he'd received yesterday was the one he now reread in his mind.

> My dear love.
> The meadow behind the temple of Jupiter.
> Dusk tomorrow.
> I long to see you.
> Yours ever,
> L

She would be chaperoned, of course, by Vibia's niece, Sabina, and two guards, who would be stationed outside the temple while Livia 'prayed'. With Sabina's help, Livia was planning to slip out unnoticed and meet him. His stomach twisted. He didn't trust the plan, fearing it would put her in too much danger, but she was sure she could do it. She knew the layout of the temple well.

He was so engrossed in his thoughts he hardly noticed the doctor leave and Vibia arrive with water and a fresh tunic of fine grey wool.

Quickly, she helped him shave and change, and was just lifting the bowl of water to return it to the kitchen when Flavia swept into the room.

'Madam –' began Vibia.

'Thank you, Vibia, run along now.'

Seth's heart sank. Flavia was supposed to be visiting her sister. Why hadn't she left?

'Seth, my own sweet Seth,' she whispered, kissing his mouth.

He tried not to choke. Flavia had just stolen the very words Livia had used in the forum. Hadn't she taken enough? He had washed and changed, done all in his power to cleanse himself of Flavia before meeting the girl he loved, and now everything was tainted.

He felt sick with shame and disgust. He pushed Flavia away and leaned against the wall, panting.

'What is it, Sethos?' she asked. 'Are you ill?'

He nodded mutely, an arm across his eyes. Then he slid down the wall to the floor and put his head his hands.

'Vibia,' called Flavia, 'send for the doctor.'

Vibia came in and peered at Sethos on the floor. 'Of course, Madam,' she began. 'Ahem . . . the master has just returned home, and asks if you're ready?'

'Ready?'

'For the visit to your sister's house?'

Flavia gasped. Her obsession with her new lover had made her forgetful. She hurried out of the room.

Vibia stood over Sethos. 'Do you still need the doctor?'

He shook his head slowly.

As soon as Flavia and Domitus had left, Vibia helped Seth on with a cloak.

'No need for the toga today. It's nearly dark. Now go!'

Seth crept through the garden and out of the villa. He knew the way to the Apollo temple. He kept his head down, and avoided eye contact. As soon as he was able, he took the smaller, less populated streets.

Within fifteen minutes he was skirting the temple and slipping through the trees towards the edge of the clearing. Vibia had honed the plan and suggested they meet on the wooded side of a huge oak tree. It would provide them with good cover. Seth now leaned against it, praying to the gods he no longer believed in that Livia would make it.

And then she was there, running through the trees towards him. He raced to greet her, and they tumbled breathlessly into each other's arms.

'Livia,' he groaned as he buried his head in her fragrant hair. 'My Livia.'

She threaded her arms under his cloak and wound them round his waist, closing her eyes and breathing in his scent.

'Oh, Sethos, how I've missed you . . . and we only have a few minutes before –'

He stopped her speech with his lips. The days of longing and loss, of fear and frustration, all transformed into a single moment of bliss. As he kissed her, his fingers ran down her beautiful long neck, along her spine. He wanted to know every detail of her: kiss every part of her. His lips skimmed the length of her neck, pausing when they reached the embroidered edge of her silk tunic. He hated that tunic, for coming between them. He pulled her gently to the ground, unfastening his cloak and spreading it beneath them. Then he folded her into his arms and kissed her, gazing into her lovely eyes, holding them, memorizing them in order to nourish him until their next stolen moment.

'Sethos,' she murmured, when they paused briefly for breath. 'I have news. Cassius is planning a business trip to Camulodunum in two days. He will be taking most of his guards with him.'

'So that is when we shall leave. I will find a way of returning to the barracks to collect money. I also have several jewels for bribes . . .'

'Sethos, I don't think I can ask you to do this for me. It will be too dangerous for you. It is safer for me to leave alone. I have options you don't have. If we are caught, you will be whipped and executed. I cannot let you risk your life for me.'

'Livia . . . You are my life. Without you, my life is nothing. I do not want it.'

'But, Sethos, think. Within a year or two you might be freed. You have money saved. You could return to Corinth, buy some land, have a good life. How can I take your future away from you?'

'You are my present and my future, Livia. Now please – let's not waste our precious time arguing. As soon as you know exactly when Cassius is leaving, send word with Sabina. We should meet when it's dark, near the harbour. Our best chance is to get passage on a merchant ship heading north. I'll try and find out what I can.'

'Sabina has a good network of friends around the harbour too . . . Sethos –'

'What is it? What do you see?'

'Sabina's signal . . . I have to run.' Livia held his face in her hands and kissed him one last time. 'I love you. Keep well. And safe. Goodbye.'

Sethos watched as she slipped back into the temple, and waited until he'd seen the whole party leave. Then he set off himself.

Despite the fact that he would no doubt have to face Flavia again that night, he now felt so elated that nothing could mar his excitement. He had heard the familia would be returning within the next day or two, so he had to try and retrieve his box of treasures from their buried site. The barracks would be deserted now, and he could swing by on his way back. It would take no time.

Then everything would be in place for their flight. In just two days he and Livia would be together again.

21

Drifting

St Magdalene's

AD 2012

I was vaguely aware of being carried out of the art history room, but I couldn't open my eyes. Not sweating any more, I was freezing. Shivering. My teeth chattered uncontrollably. I could hear people calling me, from a great distance, but my mouth felt too far away to answer, my tongue too heavy to pick up. I drifted.

Sirens woke me up briefly. I was on a narrow bed. Something was covering my nose and mouth. I felt so sick. Was that motion I felt, or dizziness?

I was being wheeled through dazzling corridors. Pounding steps. Reverberating clanging. The light was too bright. The smell of pain all around. Head hammering. Someone close by was groaning. Was it me?

22

Collapse

Londinium

AD 152

Matthias was tired and depressed after his long sea journey, but glad to be back in Londinium. At least here he could get clean, and the food was decent. And he wasn't in constant fear for his life.

He'd had a miserable time. They had endured three barbarian raids during their tour, and although a party of gladiators proved a lethal mistake to target (no barbarian survived the attacks), Matthias had nonetheless been terrified. He had no combat skills whatsoever.

And his skills as a physician had been sorely tested. There had been so many injuries to treat. In addition to the wounds following the barbarian attacks, there were more than usual in the arena. The gladiators had left Londinium with heavy hearts, superstitious to be travelling without their star fighter. Seth had made them all feel lucky, and without him they believed the trip ill-omened. Tertius's savage exhortations to fight like men were ineffectual against such fear. And fear made them inattentive.

Within a week, two fighters were mortally wounded and Matthias had been unable to save them.

Tertius had been furious: gladiators were expensive to buy, train and accommodate, so the loss was costly. Mercifully, he blamed their deaths on their own incompetence and weakness, not on Matthias.

But their loss had made Matthias long for news of Seth. While everyone missed Sethos the gladiator, and prayed for his return to health, Matthias missed Sethos the friend. He felt anchorless without him.

For the past eight weeks he'd had no news of Seth. Now that they were back, the first thing he asked the lanista was whether he had received word of his favourite fighter.

'Patience, Matthias. A messenger has been dispatched to the Natalis house. We will hear soon enough!'

Matthias spent the afternoon grinding dill and poppy seeds, pounding acorum root, and checking and sorting his depleted stores. It was nearly dark by the time he was ready to write the list of items he needed to restock. He lit his lamp and began the painstaking inventory. Two hours later the lamp began to sputter and fade. He cursed. He would have to wheedle more oil from Brude, the surly Pict slave guarding the tallow and oil store. Sighing, he picked up his sputtering lamp and set forth to do battle.

'Anyone would think it was his own personal stock,' Matthias grumbled as he finally hurried back across the arena towards his room. His lamp was now casting a warm bright glow, making the dark edges of the arena more shadowy and sinister. He had almost reached the doorway when he heard a strange rasping sound. He stood motionless, peering into the darkness.

He could just make out the outline of a shape crawling slowly towards him. He gasped in fright. He had a healthy fear of the spirit world and his instinct was to run and hide. But he held his ground a moment longer. The shape had stopped moving. It had collapsed in a heap, and was still.

At last curiosity got the better of him, and he moved cautiously towards the dark shape, holding the lamp high. As he crept closer, he knew he was looking at a man. A bleeding, broken man. A man clearly dying.

He turned the body over, and choked.

'S-Sethos! Oh, Seth, brother . . . What happened to you?'

Seth's face was covered in blood and bruises. His eyelids flickered. He was trying to speak.

Matt leaned in to hear.

'C-Cassius –' Seth rasped.

'Cassius? Who's Cassius, Seth?'

Seth's eyes had shut. He was struggling for breath.

'Did Cassius do this to you?'

Seth tried to swallow. 'She's . . . dead. Matthias . . . L-Livia's dead.'

And then his body began to convulse, and he said no more.

23

Fever

St Magdalene's

AD 2012

Why was I lying on snow? So cold. Huge polar bears padding towards me. I shivered, but couldn't move. A howling wind screamed around my ears. I wanted it to stop. It was making my head throb. I had to get away, but I couldn't see where I was going . . . My eyes were shut against the screaming wind. I tried to open them. I had to. With a supreme effort I pushed the muscles in my eyelids upwards. I couldn't make sense of what I saw. I gazed around wildly. I was in a hospital bed, attached by wires to tubes and monitors that seemed to fill the room. The polar bears were bearing down on me. 'No!' I screamed, and as I stared the massive bears shrank and reshaped into . . . doctors. And then they shape-shifted again . . . white wolves . . . and then disappeared. Darkness . . . Now I was running. Running from the snow . . . running into the mouth of a black tunnel . . . The brightness snuffed out. Running away from the light into the darkness . . . All around me darkness. No air . . . Only darkness and heat . . . I turned back, but there was no way out . . .

'Somebody help me!' I shouted, but I couldn't hear my voice. All I could hear was the rhythmic beeping . . . a monitor . . . now the beep was stuttering . . . people running, calling, shouting, 'She's crashing –'

I was being hit, my chest hurt, I couldn't breathe –

'*Clear!* Give me 200 –'

'No pulse –'

'*Clear* – give me 250 –'

'V-fib–'

'More charge – 300 –'

'Flatline . . .'

PART II

Parallon

There could be an infinite number of universes each with a different law of physics. Big Bangs probably take place all the time. Our Universe co-exists with other membranes, other universes which are also in the process of expansion. Our Universe could be just one bubble floating in an ocean of other bubbles.

Michio Kaku, City University of New York

24

Otherness

Seth was running from the barracks. Why were the gates unguarded? Why were the streets deserted? Surely it was only a matter of time before someone noticed he was missing and came after him?

His muscles felt strong; his head clear. He flexed his injured shoulder. No pain. No stiffness. He looked down at it . . . Barely a scar.

How was that possible?

He surveyed the emptiness around him and an uneasiness crept over his skin. The only sounds were the whisper of his sandalled feet as he sprang along the paving, and the rhythmic beating of his heart.

Everything felt wrong. Very wrong.

Had some catastrophe hit Londinium?

His pulse, normally so slow, so measured, began to quicken.

Survival had been his focus for so long that it was more than an instinct. It defined him. And survival meant escape. He needed to keep running, and so he moved ever forward, legs pushing mechanically, eyes darting left and right.

He knew where he was headed. Although it hardly represented a place of safety, it was the only place he wanted to be.

He could just see the temple of Apollo ahead, which meant he was nearly there. He gazed up briefly and its marble pillars, sparkling in the light, dazzled him. The walls surrounding the temple grounds seemed to shimmer slightly as he moved his head. Did he still have a fever, after all? He put his hand up to his forehead. Warm but not hot. His body didn't ache or shiver.

He ran on, concentrating on the temple ahead. A strange prismatic lustre hovered above the road in the distance. Must be some sort of mirage. He slowed and the effect reduced. He picked up his pace again, until he was passing the temple, and could just glimpse the dappled green meadow sloping away from the building. His stomach twisted. He sprinted forward. There it was, soft grass, dusted with wild summer flowers, tall shady trees . . . long dark shadows, flecked with dusky sunlight.

He ran towards the place. Their oak tree.

But she wasn't there. The meadow was empty. No sound. Not even a birdsong. Just shimmering shady greens. He crouched under the tree, touching the bark, the grass, the ground, anything that could connect him back to her. But nothing of her remained.

He wandered restlessly, trying to re-create moments from their snatched time together. But all that came back to him was the final image of her. The one he didn't want to accept. At last he sat on the ground under the tree and wept, feeling his solitude like a blanket of ice encasing him.

He must have slept, because when he opened his eyes again, it was dusk. He was stiff. The ground was hard. He stood up and glanced about. It was as though the meadow was rematerializing around him. He stopped moving and just stared ahead. Everything stabilized. He did a sudden turn again, wanting to catch the effect, and sure enough – as his eyes scanned round the meadow, the trees seemed to shimmer into definition. He walked slowly back to the temple, pausing next to a sparkling marble column. He reached out with his fingertips. It was solid and smooth. He stared past it, into the shady portico: deserted.

He moved away, towards the road. By the time he got back to the huge barracks gate, it was completely dark. He had no idea why he had returned to his own prison. It seemed suicidal . . . But maybe that was the point? He had, after all, lost his purpose to live.

He pushed open the wooden gates and walked straight across the practice arena, no longer creeping in the shadows. He didn't care if he was found now. But nobody came after him. He looked in on his cell . . . it was just as he'd left it. He was painfully aware of the sound of his own breathing, his own heartbeat. Sounds normally masked by men arguing, chains clanking, guards beating.

He wandered through the gladiatorial cells: all empty. He moved on to the lanista's quarters: also abandoned. Usually there were slaves in constant activity: cooking, cleaning, hammering, running to and fro . . . But for the first time ever, Seth was free to explore the building.

It was vastly superior to the cells occupied by the gladiators: large rooms, paved floors, a kitchen filled with fruit, bread, hanging game. There was even a stew cooking on the stove. Seth realized he was starving, so he took a bowl from the shelf, and spooned some into it. It smelled mouth-watering. Looking around for something to drink, he spotted a jug filled with honeyed wine on the table. He picked it up, poured some into the cup next to it, and took a long draught. Then he carried the bowl, cup and jug off to his cell. When he had finished his meal, he stretched out on to his mattress and tried to sleep. But it was too quiet. He didn't want to listen to the only sound – his thudding heart, a painful reminder that he was alive when she was dead.

Was this empty solitude his punishment for loving her? Or for letting her die?

Well, so be it. He deserved his fate.

25

Reflection

'S-Seth?'

Seth opened his eyes. Morning light was struggling through his tiny window. He sat up and blinked. Matthias was standing at the door of his cell, his face frozen, his eyes wide.

'MATTHIAS!' Seth gasped, jumping off the mattress and bounding towards him. 'By Zeus, it's good to see you!'

He tried to hug his friend, but Matt jumped back, as though struck by lightning.

'What is it? What's wrong?'

'Seth?' breathed Matthias. 'H-how can this be possible?'

Seth swallowed. Matthias was still staring at him with wild, terrified eyes.

'Matt?'

'W-what are you?' Matt whispered hoarsely.

Seth frowned. 'What do you mean?'

'Seth – look at yourself.'

Seth looked down. Everything appeared exactly as he expected. Tunic in place, arms, legs, feet . . . He looked back at Matt questioningly.

'Y-your shoulder . . .'

Seth flexed his shoulder. Perfect . . . but the uneasiness that he'd suppressed yesterday began to claw its way back into his consciousness.

'Y-your leg?'

His leg? Ah, yes. The new knife wound . . . He rubbed a thumb along his calf – it was completely healed.

Matt tentatively reached across and laid his hand across Seth's chest. Feeling the steady beat of his heart.

'This isn't possible, Seth. You shouldn't be here. Don't you remember anything? Crawling back to the barracks? I couldn't do anything to help you. Y-you stopped breathing . . . your heart stopped beating . . . Y-you . . . died!'

Seth slowly shook his head.

He did remember.

He had known since he had woken yesterday that the world had made some sort of unsettling shift. It was the same – and not the same. The deserted barracks . . . the familiar roads . . . the light . . . the shimmering . . .

Now he forced himself to face the question he had been pushing away.

He did not feel dead, but he had no idea how being dead was meant to feel.

And . . . if he *was* dead – what was he doing in Londinium? Shouldn't he be in Hades by now? And – more significantly still – *what was Matthias doing here?*

Matthias was pacing round the small room, frowning.

Seth watched him.

Neither of them could find the words to frame the chaos of their thoughts.

At last Matt picked up the flask of honeyed wine that Seth

had brought back from the lanista's house and put it to his lips, swallowing all that was left.

He wiped his mouth on the back of his hand, cleared his throat and said, 'Seth – I think I am dead too.'

26

Dark Dreams

London

AD 2012

Running again . . . fear driving me on . . . Something terrible behind me, chasing me through the darkness . . . And yet there in the distance – surrounded by light . . . bright . . . dazzling . . . drawing me . . . forward . . . The darkness breathing . . . swirling . . . gaining on me – swallowing the air . . . shadowy fingers extending – reaching . . . Arms grabbing me, binding me . . . no escape . . . No!

I tried to scream.

No sound. My throat hurt. Something was in my mouth. I reached up to touch it. My hand heavy, the skin pulling. Restraining arms. I opened my eyes . . .

I was in a hospital bed. Monitors beeping, and tubes everywhere, in my hand, in my mouth, in my nose . . . and doctors and nurses . . . But . . . but someone was missing. I looked around the room wildly, trying to remember a face . . . I flailed around in my throbbing head, but all I could remember was . . . terror. My heart pounded in my raw chest, each breath hurting.

'Whoa – that was a close one!' said one of the doctors, frowning.

He was looking at me strangely. Then he was taking my blood pressure, and temperature, writing stuff down, murmuring to the other white-coated figures bustling around my bed.

I closed my eyes. I couldn't make sense of this . . . Too much effort. I allowed myself to drift away. Oblivion. Bliss.

When I next opened my eyes, most of the tubes were gone. There was just a gentle rhythmic beep coming from the monitor beside me. Peaceful. Someone was standing over me.

'Good morning, Eva!'

I blinked.

'I'm Dr Falana. Do you know where you are?'

I looked around: beds; monitors; green curtains; nurses. Not exactly rocket science. 'Hospital?'

Was that me speaking? More of a rasp than a voice.

'That's right! Good. You are at Guy's Hospital. So, how are you feeling this morning?'

I lay there for a second, trying to interpret the question. How was I feeling?

The pounding headache was gone. So was the sickness. Carefully, I moved my legs. The awful aching in my limbs had subsided. My throat felt like someone had been shredding it with a cheese grater, and my chest felt like a bus had backed into it, but otherwise –

'Great!' I beamed, sitting up. OK – dizzy, but nothing I couldn't handle.

He shook his head. 'I've been a haematologist for fifteen years, and I have never seen a deterioration or indeed a recovery like yours.'

Recovery. That was a word I liked.

'So, am I OK now?'

'Well . . . you're certainly a lot better . . .'

'So – what was it? Some sort of weird flu thing?'

'Hmmm . . . something like that . . .' His eyes darted towards the door, uncomfortably. He looked like he was planning a quick getaway.

'So – flu then?'

He was avoiding eye contact. My gut tightened. 'Is there something you're not telling me?'

He cleared his throat. I braced myself. 'Well – to be perfectly honest, Eva, we – er – have no idea . . .'

'Oh, come on!'

His jaw jutted out defensively. 'Your symptoms were indicative of a really virulent bacterial or viral infection, but the blood results were so . . . anomalous . . . that we have been unable to use the data.'

'Anomalous results? Is that the medical term for lab cockup?' I smirked.

His eyes moved shiftily. God, I was right!

'A thorough lab investigation is already under way. In their defence I don't think they've ever produced such a sequence of discrepant data before. And in your case we could have really done with some coherent, consistent analysis.'

'So what are you telling me? That your lab messed up, and you don't know what I've got?'

'Well – on the plus side I can tell you that your most recent blood test indicates a complete absence of infection.'

'So that's good, right?'

'Yes! It's excellent . . . though last night . . .'

'Last night?'

He chewed his lip, and stared at the floor.

'Last night?' I prompted.

'Well – last night . . . you were in total organ failure . . . In fact – we –'

God – why couldn't he finish a sentence?

'In fact you –'

'WHAT?'

'Well, we . . . for a moment there . . . we thought we'd lost you . . .'

I swallowed.

He took a step nearer and gently lifted up my eyelids, peering into my eyes with a torch. 'Your parents –'

'My parents?'

'They're waiting outside . . .'

Oh NO.

'Your mother assures us that you've had all your vaccinations, you've not been exposed to any weird tropical diseases . . .'

I could feel my eyes widen as he spoke . . . Weird tropical diseases?

Actually, I had been exposed to something very weird . . . in the school biology lab. It all came back to me in sharp focus: the strange multiplying threads; the spilled vial . . . A professor of virology . . .

'So – could this have been caused by a virus?' I croaked.

'Whatever you have – had – I don't see how it could have been a virus. Your blood is showing no raised antibodies. A virus as powerful as that would leave a massive aftermath. And although you are severely weakened by the episode, all your organs seem to be functioning normally. It just doesn't make sense.'

While Dr Falana stared at my notes, my mind raced. It didn't make sense, but surely it was too much of a coincidence to ignore?

So what had I been exposed to then? And if it wasn't a virus, what the hell was it? Did Professor Ambrose know how dangerous it was? And if he did, why didn't he warn me? My tumbling thoughts were interrupted by a familiar voice.

'Eva! How are you?'

'Mum?' She was suddenly by my bed, looking fifty years older.

'We were so worried!' Her eyes flicked over to the door. Colin was hovering there, looking distinctly uncomfortable.

Wow! Things must have been serious to have brought Colin down.

'Is Ted here too?' I asked warily.

'No – no . . . Er, he stayed at home to – man the fort.'

'How long have you been here?' I realized suddenly that I had no idea how long I'd been here.

'Well, the school phoned yesterday afternoon to tell us you were in hospital, and by the time we got here I thought we were . . . too late. It was all so sudden. And they don't seem to know what it was. But thank goodness you're better,' she said, patting me awkwardly.

I nodded thoughtfully. 'So – I only got sick yesterday?'

'A twelve-hour bug, I suppose.' She was looking at me with unexpected warmth. 'We're taking you home with us to recuperate.'

Home? Back with Colin and Ted? No way. I was definitely not up to that.

'Honestly, Mum, I'm fine. And I've got loads of work – we've got mocks coming up . . .'

She was shaking her head, smiling. 'I just don't understand you, Eva. Most kids your age would give anything for a few days off school.'

'You know me, Mum – always been the odd one,' I mumbled.

A nurse arrived to check my blood pressure, and I was saved from any further awkward discussions about my immediate future.

27

Revelation

Matt and Seth slowly walked across the practice arena. They moved in silence, because they could not bring themselves to risk putting into words thoughts that had barely begun to have shape.

At last Seth spoke. 'I can see that I should not be here, Matt . . . that I should be – dead. I remember the wounds, the fever . . . everything. But the point is, I *can't* be dead . . .'

'Why's that, Seth?' said Matt flatly.

'Because, brother, *you* are here!' Seth clapped him on the shoulder.

Matt stopped walking and turned to face him.

'I found you collapsed in the arena. You'd been trying to crawl back to the barracks. You remember that?'

Of course he remembered. Though there was so much about that night he couldn't bring himself to think about.

'We carried you into your cell. You were already delirious . . . raving with fever – more dead than alive, even then. Covered in blood and bruises, broken ribs, knife slashes across your chest, broken jaw, broken nose. Your shoulder was dislocated and the wound had opened up again, and you had that deep gash along your leg.

'I was so angry with you – getting injured again. Of course I started cleaning off the blood . . . Your injuries were tumescent with poisons . . . I . . . poulticed . . . mixed fever-reducing drafts, but none of my remedies made any difference. Within a couple of hours you had sunk so far into fever that you didn't even have the strength to turn your head. As a last resort, I tried one final attempt to release some blood around the wound sites . . .'

'At least I can be grateful to the fever for something – I didn't have to consciously endure your blood-letting,' smiled Seth.

'Even unconscious you did everything to avoid it,' growled Matt. 'You still managed to flail around so much that my knife slipped and I ended up doing a bit of blood-letting on myself!'

He held up his hand. No sign of a cut now.

'A taste of your own medicine!' chuckled Seth.

'Maybe it was the shock of it . . . I don't know. But almost immediately you stopped writhing . . . Suddenly perfectly still. And then I realized why . . . you had stopped breathing.

'I just sat there, trying to accept that you had gone. I remember thinking that I should go and tell someone you were dead . . . but then I felt a surprising heat down my back, and the light grew suddenly brighter. I thought that maybe someone had brought in a flaming torch. I looked round, but the room was empty . . .

'So I wondered if perhaps it was your spirit leaving your body. But the heat was in my own body. I stood up and a terrible dizziness took hold of me. I stumbled to my own cell and lay down, exhausted. I remember little else . . . just pain, sickness and heat . . . And then I woke up – here.'

Seth nodded slowly. He thought Matt was probably right. They were both dead.

28

Elysium

Matt and Seth were sitting in the lanista's kitchen, drinking wine and eating bread and olives.

'Do you think this could be Elysium?' pondered Matt.

Seth shook his head.

'But what if we were so confused by fever that we passed over the river of Lethe without noticing?'

'Does this look like Elysium? Where are the fields, the nymphs and the perpetual music? No, Matt – this is Londinium. Well, somewhere very like it . . .'

'But what if we just haven't found the fields and nymphs yet? We haven't explored very far –'

Suddenly Seth gasped, leaped off his chair and practically crashed into the doorway in his hurry to get out of the room.

'Where are you going?' Matt shouted.

'To find Livia,' he called back. 'I don't know what this place is, but if we are dead it means she must be here somewhere too.'

He sprinted through the barracks gate and on to the wide road that led to the centre of the city. Dawn was breaking, gently lighting large silent villas, and small closed-up shops. He passed two inns, and the bathhouse . . . then stopped in his tracks. The bathhouse looked wrong. Everything about it was wrong. Wrong height. Wrong colour. Where were the columns that supported the entrance? What were those strange reflective panels punctuating the facade? And why was the building so tall? Seth's heart began to hammer in his chest.

He walked up to the building and brushed it with his fingertips. It shimmered slightly, as did everything, but it felt solid enough. He moved cautiously on, past three more buildings he didn't recognize, towards the forum. He gasped. Instead of the forum, with its open square and basilica, materializing before him was a huge marrow-shaped structure. Not only did it shimmer eerily, but it reflected the sky.

He gazed in disbelief. It obeyed none of the structural rules of any building he had ever seen. It looked neither stable nor balanced. How did it stay upright? How many slaves would it have taken to build?

And what was it doing here?

His stomach clenched. If he couldn't find the forum, would he be able to find Livia?

He veered away from the giant marrow and ran towards the Natalis house.

Seth skidded to a stop. He'd found it, and it was just as he remembered it, glowing in the rising sun.

Only no slaves swept the portico. No one came out to question the unannounced stranger. He walked straight through the main door, and into the room where Livia had sat by his bedside. He shut his eyes, remembering her there, willing her back. But she did not join him.

He ran through the house, slamming doors, pulling back

curtains, desperate . . . convinced that if he looked hard enough she would materialize.

But she didn't appear.

He refused to give up. The conviction that she must be here somewhere in this strange afterlife drove him on and on. When he had been through the house three times, and was hoarse with calling her name, he explored the large courtyard garden. It was just as he remembered it. Fruit hung heavy and ripe from small pruned trees. Vegetables and herbs grew in neat rows on one side; scented flowers on the other. But Livia wasn't there.

Wildly, he began running through the streets he no longer knew. Though some remained determinedly Roman, others were flanked by giant glittering structures that darkened the morning sky. How would he ever find her here?

Despite the whisper of despair that was beginning to spread through his veins, his strong legs carried him quickly and efficiently towards the most prestigious road Londinium offered.

Villas big enough for Caesars, Seth thought savagely.

He knew which one he sought. The ostentatious one with the golden eagle statues outside: the palace of the procurator Cassius Malchus. This was where Cassius had brought Livia. Seth's breathing quickened and rage rumbled in his chest.

Everything about the place made his flesh crawl. But at least there was some comfort in knowing that it was still here, and no strange building had taken its place. Was it possible Livia might be inside?

Despite the fact that he hadn't seen anyone at all, he moved into the shadows, creeping up the large steps and into the huge pillared entrance portico. He cautiously reached out and pushed one of the doors open. It creaked slightly.

Slipping inside, he whistled softly through his teeth as he gazed around. Although Livia had described it to him, it was still impressive. The villa was built around a massive open central atrium, which bathed everything in light. The effect was heightened because the walls and columns were of sparkling white polished marble, and the turquoise mosaicked floor was inset with golden birds glinting in the sunlight.

Within the atrium was a large carved fountain, with stone lion-footed benches surrounding it. Carefully shaped Mediterranean fruit trees grew in the corners, and in this bright light, the whole effect reminded him of home. And this made him curse Cassius more. As if he weren't guilty of enough crimes!

Footsteps suddenly sounded outside the building. Adrenalin pumped through his veins.

Cassius?

It never occurred to Seth to run or hide. Apart from Livia, there was nobody he wanted to meet more than Cassius. He pulled the dagger from his waist, his chest heaving with anticipation. He had spent years in the arena, but he had never felt this burning desire to fight. Rage seared through him as he stood facing the door, rigid, ready to spring.

As soon as the door opened, he lunged.

'*Seth!* What are you doing?' gasped Matthias.

Seth's reflexes were, fortunately, sharp. He landed like a cat, a hair's breadth away from his friend; the dagger, which had been set to rip through his enemy, now frozen at Matthias's throat.

'Forgive me!' panted Seth, relaxing his stance and withdrawing the knife.

He'd left a small nick on Matt's skin, and a thin line of blood trickled down his neck.

'Zeus! Dying once was enough,' Matthias grumbled, straightening up.

But Seth was staring at his friend's throat. The cut he'd just made was . . . closing as he watched. Soon all sign of it had disappeared.

What *was* this place?

Seth instantly flipped his dagger and experimentally slashed himself along the length of his forearm.

'Have you gone completely mad?' shouted Matthias, reaching out to stop him.

'Just watch, Matt.'

Seth had been hoping that the cut would be painless; it wasn't. And as the blood seeped across his arm and started dripping on to the mosaic floor, he began to doubt his new theory. But then, as they continued to watch, the skin around the gash started to knit itself together, and within a few seconds it was completely healed: no sign that it had ever been broken.

'By Hercules!' breathed Matt, frozen, staring. And then he started to laugh . . . and jump and cheer around the room.

'Seth, do you see what this means? We are immortal! We are gods!'

29

Epiphany

St Magdalene's

November AD 2012

I was sitting on the edge of my hospital bed, waiting. The consultant had officially discharged me ten minutes ago, and I was desperate to get out of the place. After a trillion blood tests, numerous ECGs, MRIs and CT scans, I had definitely had enough. But they wouldn't let me leave. Not until someone arrived to pick me up.

And that someone was Rose Marley, the school matron. She had been to visit me a couple of times, and she turned out to be OK. Really OK, in fact.

A week ago, when I mentioned to her that I'd prefer to get back to school than go home, she gave me this sort of quizzical look, but didn't ask a single awkward question. I suspect the pleading in my eyes may have given her a hint of my desperation, though she didn't refer to it.

She had even dealt with the unappealing job of breaking the news to my mother.

'Ah, good morning! You must be Mrs Koretsky. How lovely to meet you.'

'Actually, no. My name is Brewer . . . Jane Brewer. I – er – remarried.'

Rose Marley shot me an unobtrusive glance, as she apologized to my mother for the slip.

'Oh, I am so sorry, Mrs Brewer, I must have missed that on Eva's notes.'

Because it wasn't there. I had told the school as little as possible about my family.

'I can't begin to imagine how relieved you must be to see Eva so much better,' she went on seamlessly.

'Well, yes. It is a relief,' smiled my mother.

'It is great news to everyone at St Magdalene's too. We were terribly concerned. And of course she's such an extraordinarily gifted girl . . .'

My mother looked uncomfortable. She certainly didn't see my brand of extraordinary as a gift.

'Well – er – yes . . .'

'In fact the headmaster is so concerned for her health that he has suggested she spend the first couple of weeks after her discharge from hospital in the school medical wing with me. Then, should there be any sign of relapse, we can act immediately – we are, after all, only ten minutes away from the hospital . . . which, as you've probably gathered, has the country's leading haematology unit. Aren't we fortunate to be so well placed?'

I shot a surprised glance at Rose Marley. This was slightly beyond the call of duty. The medical wing? Why did I need to stay there? Or was this just her ruse to get my mother off my back? Must be. Excellent strategy. There was no way my mum could insist I travel all the way up to York with her, after that little speech. How could she put my life in such jeopardy?

I suppose if I had believed for a minute that my mother *genuinely* wanted to take me back to York to look after me, I might have felt a bit guilty, but as I watched her face, I could see nothing but relief. She was one hundred per cent grateful to Rose Marley for taking responsibility for me. So was I . . . No Colin. No Ted. I was going back to school. After that neat little victory, my respect for Rose Marley was immense.

And now, as I sat on my hospital bed contemplating the great escape, I heard the sound I'd been waiting for . . . Rose Marley at the end of the corridor chatting to the nurses at the desk. I picked up the small bag of possessions I had accumulated since being here, and headed down to meet her.

I'd only managed a few metres when I had to steady myself against the wall. How could twelve steps have made me so dizzy? I slid down to the floor and put my head between my knees. This was not good. I hoped that the nurses were so engrossed in their conversation that they hadn't spotted me.

No such luck. Before I had got myself upright again, I felt strong arms bundling me into a wheelchair. Annoyingly, I was too nauseous to resist.

I then got wheeled into an ambulance, and horror of horrors, publicly wheeled out again across St Magdalene's quad to the medical wing. Completely humiliating. And to make it worse I just didn't have the energy to object.

Had Rose Marley known all along that I wasn't quite as much better as I thought I was? Because she was acting like it was completely normal to be a total weakling. And for two weeks

I was hopeless. She helped me in and out of the shower, even helped me eat when I was just too tired to hold the fork.

Being with Rose in the medical block turned out to be surprisingly soothing. Maybe it was her easy presence . . . Maybe it was the place itself . . . the particular blue of the walls – a lovely pale cerulean – which felt somehow familiar and comforting. Or maybe it was just relief that my room didn't feel too much like a hospital. OK, there was the emergency bell on the wall, and the table of medical stuff – blood-pressure cuff, sick bowl, oxygen canister, drip stand. But there were also a couple of beautiful Dufy prints above the bed. And a big window looking out over the quad. As well as a good-sized desk, a lamp, a laptop and wireless Internet. What more did a girl need?

And I did get stronger. By the second week I was managing to do morning lessons, and by the third I took on a couple of afternoons as well. Frustratingly, exhaustion made concentration harder, so my assignments were definitely suffering, but Rose said that I needed to add patience to my list of qualifications.

'Huh!' I said back.

But I was glad to be hanging around someone who treated me like everything was completely normal, because when I went into classes everyone else acted like I was an unstable chemical – on the brink of spontaneous combustion. Teachers kept saying, 'Are you all right?', 'You can sit this one out, Eva', 'Don't crowd her, guys!', 'Well DONE! That was terrific!' And students kept offering to get my lunch and carry my bag. Although it was kind of touching, I loathed all the attention. So it was a massive relief when I finally managed the whole day of school, and people started to forget my little near-death experience.

At the end of that third week I moved out of the medical centre and returned to my own room. I was more or less ready to resume the pattern of my school life: lessons, tutorials, band practices, even *Hamlet* rehearsals. Dr Kidd had rehearsed an understudy, but he seemed happy enough to take me back – I couldn't believe it.

So it was as though everything was back to normal.

But it wasn't.

Those days in hospital had shaken me much more than I admitted to anyone. Something inside me had changed . . .

And now, even five weeks later, I was still feeling pretty weak and tired. I was sure that Rose was right; I just needed to be patient. But I promised myself that as soon as my energy returned I would start researching that damned virus.

30

Home

'Seth, we have to name this place . . .'

Seth and Matt were lying on the ground in the practice arena, gazing up at the stars. They had been living here for so long, and still had no name for it.

'Londinium?' suggested Seth sarcastically.

'We both know that we're not in Londinium,' answered Matt, unruffled. 'I still think this is Elysium.'

'Come on, Matt!' Seth spat. 'Elysium is the destination of the good and heroic –'

'Well, you're heroic! I never saw a braver gladiator –'

'Matt! A *hero* wins wars and fights *noble* battles. He isn't a tattooed slave, forced to fight like an animal in a ring.'

'A man can fight nobly in the arena –'

'No, Matt, he can't. There was only one noble fight I craved . . . but I have been denied it.'

Matt stared back at him, questioningly.

'The fight to rid the world of Cassius Malchus.'

Matthias sighed. Why couldn't Seth simply embrace his new world? He himself had welcomed it with open arms – each day punctuated by new wonders:

'Seth, Seth – watch this!' And Seth would have to patiently

witness Matt standing in front of a table, as he willed the evening banquet to appear. Anything Matt thought of would materialize. Cooked chickens, loaves of bread, rice cakes, soups, stews . . . jugs of wine, sparkling goblets . . .

First it was food, then clothes, wall hangings, scrolls, medicines . . . And while Matt enjoyed the days creating, Seth spent his time searching for Livia, or running and training. He didn't need partners to train against; he challenged himself. He erected a post in the arena, and practised his strikes and parries against it. He set himself daily running challenges, testing his speed and stamina. If he didn't keep moving, desolation would overwhelm him. Wherever he ran, his eyes never gave up searching.

He had started to define certain parts as theirs: their temple, their barracks, their arena. He didn't feel nearly so comfortable running in the alien areas. The structures there felt ominous and uncanny. Their surfaces didn't make sense. Neither did their height or their function. So he gave them a wide berth . . . Until the day he decided to confront the river.

Since his arrival, Seth had been avoiding the River Tamesis – it was the last place he had seen Livia alive, and he hadn't had the strength to face it. But as time went on, and he had clearly run out of places to look, he knew he couldn't avoid it any longer.

He rounded the last corner, and there it was, sparkling in the sunlight. He frowned. The river looked different – smaller somehow. Perhaps because it was now flanked by taller, more alien structures? Some instinct made him move into the shadow of the shimmering building he had stopped by. Had he heard something?

He must have, because a few moments later three men emerged from a building next to the water.

People.

There were others.

His heart raced. Maybe they had seen Livia?

But could he speak to them? Would they recognize him as a slave? Seth cursed – his tattoos would give him away immediately. If only he'd worn a cloak. Almost before the thought was complete, he felt his shoulders shrouded in fine wool – he looked down to find he was draped in an exact replica of the cloak Vibia had lent him. Seth smiled. He'd forgotten he could do that.

But he remained hidden. If there was one thing the years of slavery had taught him, it was caution. From this position he could watch and listen, unobserved.

The trio wandered over to the riverside and looked down at the water. One laughed and pointed. They were wearing strange, unfamiliar garments – legs and arms completely encased in fabric, despite the heat of the day. One was bearded.

Maybe he's Greek? thought Seth hopefully. Most of the Romans he'd met were clean-shaven.

He crept closer to see if he could catch a shred of conversation. They were speaking a tongue he had never encountered. Not Greek then. Where could they be from?

As he watched them from his shadowy corner, the taller of the three men suddenly lifted his eyes and appeared to stare directly at him. Instinctively, Seth spun away and ran.

By the time he got back to his cell, he was bathed in sweat and gasping with thirst. He had just poured some water into a cup, and was swallowing it gratefully, when Matthias came bounding in.

'Seth – it's time to move.'

'Was I followed?' breathed Seth, darting to the window.

'Followed? Who could possibly be following you?'

Seth scanned the arena, looking for movement.

'The three men . . .'

'What three men?'

'Down by the river. I saw people . . .'

'There are others?' Matt was elated.

'I don't think they were friendly.'

Matthias came and joined him at the window. 'Even more reason then . . .'

'Reason for what?'

'To move! I've found us somewhere else. We're living here like slaves, but now we are free. We need to move on.'

'Here's good enough for me,' said Seth, striding to the table and pouring the remains of the water over his head.

'Seth, brother, you might feel you belong here, but I do not. I wasn't born to live like an animal – and neither were you.'

'I have lived like an animal for too long to know the difference.'

'Seth – all that's over now.'

'Nothing is over, Matt. It just continues. Each day, each night – nothing changes. The pain just goes on and on. Look around – there is emptiness everywhere . . . You must see it?'

'I don't see it, Seth, I really don't. When I look around, I see a place full of opportunity. Especially if there are others as you say . . . How long must you stay in the dark? How long must you grieve for this girl?'

'My grief will go on as long as I go on.'

'Apollo's blood, Seth! She's *gone*! But *you* are here.'

'*Who* is here? Who *am* I, Matthias? I am no longer Sethos, the Corinthian, Neither am I Sethos Leontis, winner of nine wreaths. He died in a gladiatorial barracks. I don't know who or what I am now, but I am no longer that person . . .'

Matthias shook his head and pulled his friend to his feet. 'Come.'

He dragged Seth through the great wooden doors of the barracks towards the western end of the city. The Roman buildings they knew gradually faded out. Seth stared around him. No strange structures dominated this part of the landscape . . . In fact nothing did. It was empty: featureless sky and ground. Matthias smiled.

'Nearly there,' he grinned.

'Nearly where?' muttered Seth, glancing around him irritably.

They walked on a little further, and gradually a small olive grove appeared on the horizon, the leaves fluttering softly in the breeze. And sparkling just beyond the trees was a huge white building.

'All right, my friend – this is it!'

'This is what, exactly?'

'Our new home!'

They were standing in front of – well – a palace . . . a sumptuously decorated palace.

'What do you mean, Matthias?'

Matthias didn't answer, but pulled his friend through the columned entrance into a marbled atrium. There was a bubbling fountain at the centre, with a pair of glistening marble statues facing each other across it.

Seth walked round them silently and then started chuckling. Something he hadn't done for – he didn't know how long.

'How tall have you made yourself?'

'Oh, I just added an inch or two! What do you think? Good likenesses?'

'In that we both look like gods, you mean?'

'Why not?' grinned Matthias. 'Here, we are gods. Now come and see your practice arena! I haven't forgotten anything!'

He dragged Seth out to a large space at the side of the palace. He'd exactly replicated the arena at the barracks. Only the ground was smoother, the post newer; the training weapons clean and sparkling on their frame.

Seth smiled.

Sensing a lightening of spirit, Matthias grabbed him by the arm and started moving back towards the villa. 'Just wait till you see your chamber!'

They padded along beautiful mosaic floors, past a lush internal garden containing every tree and shrub they had ever talked about from home, a bathhouse with hot and cold spa, a comfortable living and dining area, and finally arrived at two carved wooden doors.

'The one on the left is yours.'

It was a huge room with a large bed at one end. Heavy curtains hung at the windows and across the door – reminding Seth of the room he had stayed in at the Natalis villa. Beautiful . . . painful . . . empty.

He shook his head, slapped Matthias on the shoulder and backed away. Then he turned and ran.

'Seth, what's wrong? We can change anything you don't like – hey, wait!'

But nobody could chase Seth when he began to run.

31
Match

London

AD 2012

'Earth to Starship Koretsky. Any life on board?'

I jumped about a foot in the air. Astrid was standing at my door with her arms folded.

'God, Astrid! What are you doing here?'

'Er – excuse me? What are *you* doing here?'

I looked at my watch. Oh no! Our band practice started half an hour ago.

'Aw, Astrid, I am *sooooo* sorry! Why didn't you phone?'

'I did. About twenty times.'

My phone was stuffed in my bag. On silent. Oops. Twenty-one missed calls.

'I can't decide whether to be annoyed that you forgot about band practice because you were *working*, or relieved that you aren't lying in a dead heap on the floor . . . I think annoyed is winning.'

'Thought it might be,' I said, shutting my laptop and following her out of the building. 'You should have thrown me out of the band weeks ago, Astrid. I am not worthy.'

'True. Don't think we haven't been looking for a suitable replacement.'

I darted her a quick look. She was grinning.

But the truth was, I had been pretty useless. We'd had hardly any band practices since I'd got back from hospital, and even those had been half the usual length.

As it turned out, though, tonight we actually managed to keep going for two full hours. While I'd been languishing in hospital, Astrid had been writing some great new songs, and the melodies were in the perfect key for my voice, so not too tricky to sing. We ended up working through loads of material and I left the music block shattered but ecstatic. It could only mean one thing. I was getting stronger.

Which was just as well, because I still had a lot to do tonight.

Astrid had been wrong about one thing. I hadn't been working when she'd arrived. Well – not in the conventional sense. I was actually researching . . .

Viruses.

I was determined to find out what I'd been looking at with Professor Ambrose. Because I was pretty certain that whatever it was had nearly killed me.

Given that he was a virologist, it seemed reasonable to assume that we had been looking at a virus, although I couldn't exactly remember whether he'd categorically told me it was.

Anyway, for days now I had been trawling for unusual viruses.

There were thousands to wade through – many of them deeply unpleasant, and it was hard to know where to begin identifying mine. So I started with symptoms: fever, headache, collapse, nausea, vomiting. This eliminated quite a few.

The second factor that seemed to be significant was shape.

I knew virus shapes were variable. Most seemed to be spherical, some were spherical and spiky, but virtually none looked like threads – let alone spiky threads.

Which was why when I found the Ebola virus I knew I was in the company of a really hot contender. It produced almost identical symptoms to mine, and though I couldn't see any actual spikes it was definitely thread-like. I had been in the middle of trying some Ebola image enhancements when Astrid had arrived at my door. Surely anyone would have lost track of time under the circumstances?

Which meant that although it had been really good to practise, I was pretty desperate to get back to my screen.

I waited until after official lights-out, hauled my laptop into bed with me and started it up again.

Scrolling down the page for Ebola information, I suddenly felt a shiver run right down my spine . . . fatality rate between 50 per cent and 89 per cent.

This was a pretty bad virus.

Which certainly added to its list of credentials. OK – the shape was a bit different, but maybe that could be due to lower magnification?

But why would Professor Ambrose be messing around with the Ebola virus? And why did he want me to see it? And why didn't he tell me what it was?

I was idly scrolling down the page when I suddenly jerked to a stop. My heart raced as I read:

> . . . this devastating and virulent virus can have an extremely rapid
> incubation period . . .

I quickly scrolled down a bit further:

> . . . Symptom onset can start within forty-eight hours of infection,
> though incubation can take up to twenty-one days.

Forty-eight hours to twenty-one days? Way too slow. I had been
infected and got sick within two hours.

So Ebola was out of the running. As was everything else I
looked at. The viral proliferation I had seen on that slide, even
slowed down 500 times, was way quicker than anything I had
managed to turn up.

I carried on trawling through another thirty viruses, but none
of them came anywhere near fitting the profile.

It wasn't until I realized that the amorphous shapes floating
in front of my face were no longer viruses on a screen, but blobs
on the inside of my eyelids, that I decided to turn out the light
and go to sleep.

32

End

Seth ran blindly on, away from Matthias and his glittering fake palace, until his legs had carried him to the temple of Jupiter and *their* meadow. His and Livia's.

It was a mistake. He felt more alone than ever. He leaned against a temple column, gazing across at the grass, and was filled with such a sense of desolation and loss that he began smashing his head against the marble in despair. The pain felt good, the blood that trickled down his cheek felt real . . . but he was still here. He stopped and stared at the blood-spattered marble. He stared until the blood began to disappear. Then his eyes followed the length of the column up towards its ionic capitol. Above the pillar was a frieze, and above the frieze was the cornice.

He started to climb. The marble was smooth, but the patterned ridges gave him finger and foot holds. Before long he stood swaying at the apex of the building, surveying the city below him. In the distance he could see the barracks and the arena, nestling between the tall, strange alien constructions. Out beyond the barracks he could just make out the fort, but beyond that there was nothing at all, just sky and ground. He moved his eyes back over the city. Could he see Matt's new house and tree-filled garden standing alone in its solitary splendour? Suddenly a flash of gold glinted in sunlight. His heart leaped for a moment, remembering the glint of Livia's bracelet, but then he recognized the source . . . it was one of the golden eagles decorating Cassius's villa.

Seeing it made him snarl with hatred. Desolation overwhelmed him once more, and he jumped.

The sensation of falling was exhilarating. Hitting the ground wasn't. It was excruciating. He did lose consciousness briefly, so when he woke spread-eagled at the foot of the temple he was confused. He wondered if he had finally arrived at Elysium.

But a soft, mocking laugh suggested otherwise. Seth sat up and found himself staring straight into the hard, crystal-grey eyes of the tall stranger he had run from earlier.

Within a moment Seth was on his feet, assuming the taut defensive position that defined his gladiatorial style.

The stranger flinched, and moved back a step.

'Who are you?' rasped Seth, without relaxing his stance.

The stranger frowned. 'Who am *I*?'

Seth noted that the man spoke Latin with a strong, vaguely familiar accent.

There was a brief pause, while each considered the other. Then the stranger leaned against one of the pillars and said, 'I am Zackary. But more to the point – who are you?'

'I am Sethos Leontis of Corinth.'

'You came here from *Corinth*?' spluttered Zackary.

'No, Londinium.'

Zackary nodded slowly. 'And how did you get here?'

Seth shrugged. 'I have no idea.'

Zackary stared at him, stroking his chin.

'What is this place?' asked Seth quietly.

Zackary continued to regard him with narrowed eyes. 'Parallon,' he said finally.

'Parallon?'

Before Seth could ask more, Zackary continued. 'And you shouldn't be here.'

'I did not choose it,' spat Seth bitterly. 'I'd do anything to be free of it.'

'You'd really choose death over all this?' asked Zackary in surprise.

'Yes.'

'Well, you'll never achieve it jumping off buildings! You clearly know nothing.'

Seth had known, in his heart. He had just allowed hope to override knowledge. And he had no desire to stand around being scorned by this man, so he turned and started to stride away. But Zackary caught him by the shoulder.

'I can help you,' he said.

'No, you can't,' hissed Seth, shaking him off.

'You really want to end this?'

Seth turned to him, exasperated.

'Well – come on then. No time like the present.'

Seth reluctantly followed Zackary back along the dusty Roman road, through unexplored streets filled with unfamiliar buildings, until they were by the river. This time the place was deserted. He followed Zackary down a short flight of steps until they were standing right on the riverbank. Zackary moved forward a few paces, and then beckoned Seth into position.

'All you need to do now is jump,' he said nonchalantly, challenging Seth with his eyes.

Seth gazed back at him sceptically.

'I promise!' said Zackary. 'And if you are as in love with your mortality as you seem to be, you won't be disappointed.'

Seth gazed across the water. A light mist shrouded its surface, making the bank on the opposite shore indistinct. He wasn't aware of the slight breeze as he made his decision. All he felt was a small sigh of hope as he took off his sandals and jumped.

He didn't try to swim. His body was so primed to survive that it took all his strength to stop himself, but within moments of entering the water he felt an enormous pull, sucking him down. A part of his brain was surprised. He hadn't expected this; he had thought it might be harder to stop himself floating, but now he found he had no strength against this force. It was a much more powerful pull than the weight of his clothes or any underwater current, and while he swirled and twisted, he realized that he was caught in a strange vortex, dragging him downwards.

As he descended, he was gradually overwhelmed by a sense of physical recognition. Death: he was reliving his own death, shaking and sweating, jagged pain hammering against every bone, every muscle, every nerve. He couldn't scream, he couldn't breathe, he couldn't escape; he could only endure as it raged through his body . . . twisting him, turning him, spiralling him, annihilating him . . . And then . . . the pain stopped, and he was drifting . . .

Had he actually died at last? Had he finally found his way to the underworld?

No. He had found his way back to the water surface and was bumping against the bank of the river.

He cursed the stranger, Zackary, as he pulled himself out of the water and shivered. Then he stared up at the sky, puzzled. It should have been afternoon, but it felt later. The shadows were long. Evening. He gazed around. Everything was familiar but wrong: the bridge, the boats – all smaller than the ones he had just left. And he was surrounded by clamour . . . and the stench of burning meat and dead fish. People bustled and bartered and shouted around him. Dogs barked. Builders hammered. Where was the quiet, shimmering emptiness of – what was it Zackary had called it – Parallon? Here everything was abrasive and loud . . .

Londinium. He had found his way back to Londinium. Strangely bewildering and – presumably – hostile. He had almost forgotten the cringing fear of an escaped gladiator, but now here he was, suddenly surrounded by soldiers and citizens; all ready to seize a missing slave. He would need to be careful.

33

Return

Seth slithered into the shadows, waiting and watching. Once Londinium's dusk had turned into night, he was ready to move. But he wasn't sure what to do, or where to go. He felt strangely indecisive. Weak almost. He looked down at his wet tunic, his bare feet, and wondered why he didn't feel cold – just curiously numb. He was tempted to simply stay where he was, but in the end he did what he always did: headed back to the barracks.

Guards paced in front of the great gates as they had always done, confirming that he had indeed found his way back to Londinium. And assuming all was as it had always been, there would be another guard stationed on the other side of the gates. He hovered in the shadows opposite, trying to work out what to do. His brain was fuzzy. All he really felt like doing was lying down and sleeping. He slid noiselessly to the ground, but felt no sensation of the cold hard stone beneath him. He felt drugged, but knew he needed to keep his mind alert.

His plan was to get back into his own cell. He wasn't sure why he had to do this, especially when every atom of his body was urging him back towards the river. But he had fought his body's inclinations long enough to resist this temptation. He laughed silently and mirthlessly: never had he imagined that he would one day be trying to break back into his own prison. Now he knew for sure that he was mad.

At last he saw his moment. It was the hour for the watch to change. He heard the three new guards making their way through the practice arena towards the gates. This meant they were to open any second. It was dark; he was lithe. He would do his best to slip between them, as quick as a cat, and hope that they didn't notice.

The gate opened and Seth darted between the men. He'd judged it well. Not one of them sensed his presence. Cautiously, he crept on through the practice arena towards his cell. There was a huge amount of activity in the barracks – people running back and forth, voices raised in argument, someone whistling, a couple of men fighting . . . Seth recognized Telemachus, carrying towels and bowls, and followed him at a discreet distance.

Telemachus headed straight for Seth's cell and disappeared inside. Catching up with him, Seth peered round the door frame – and nearly gasped out loud.

He was looking through the gloom at himself, lying on the mattress, moaning, and shaking with fever. Aurelius was kneeling over him, waving a large stretched linen fan, while Telemachus crouched down next to the mattress, wiping away the lines of sweat as they formed, the body beneath him unconscious of any of these services.

'He's not going to make it this time, is he?' whispered Aurelius to Telemachus.

But before Telemachus had a chance to answer, Matthias had appeared, looking pale and gaunt.

'Any change?'

'He worsens every minute. Though the vomiting has

stopped, his breathing is laboured, his pulse acutely high . . . I don't think –'

'You don't think what, Aurelius? That you're up to the job of keeping him alive? Well, get out then! Hand me that fan and leave . . .'

'Matthias,' soothed Telemachus, 'you're tired – you need to rest –'

'I don't need to rest. I'm going to let some more blood . . . maybe this time it will draw the poison out. Telemachus, can you hold the light . . .'

Seth didn't really want to watch this – he was already feeling weak and queasy and he knew only too well what his other self was about to be subjected to, so he slid down against the door frame until he was sitting on the floor. The effort had exhausted him. His strength was waning. Every physical instinct was pulling him back to the river, but his will was strong, and he needed to stay. He glanced towards the bed. From this position he had a perfect view of Matt's face as he bent over and worked. He felt a sudden rush of love and guilt as he watched the concentration and intensity on his friend's face, struggling to save his life. He wasn't expecting the sudden violent response from his other self when Matthias inserted the knife near the old shoulder wound. He watched his over-strong, unconscious body flailing wildly, sending the bowl of collected blood crashing across the floor, and the knife spiking into Matthias's left hand.

'Zeus!' hissed Matthias, sucking his injured palm. He tore off a strip of linen from the pile of cloths on the table and wrapped it round the cut, and was about to resume the blood-letting when the now prone body gasped, shuddered and went perfectly still.

'Seth?' whispered Matthias urgently. The laboured breathing had stopped.

'SETH!' he shouted, pulling the body up into the light and putting his ear against the silent heart.

'SETH! Stay with me!' he rasped, as he gently laid the body back down.

Telemachus moved towards Matthias, and laid a hand on his shoulder. 'He's gone to a better place, Matthias.'

But Matthias didn't respond. He just crouched over the body of his friend and stared down.

After a while, Telemachus left the cell. Matthias didn't notice. Seth watched his friend's misery until he could stand it no longer. He hauled himself up to his feet, and made his way slowly over to Matt. The distance seemed suddenly enormous, the effort of walking immense.

'Matt,' he said. But his voice was apparently inaudible.

Seth put his hand out to touch Matthias, but he couldn't feel Matt's tunic under his fingers. He looked down at his hand and stared. All he could make out was the whisper of an outline, the translucent memory of a shape – as though he'd been rubbed out. But something in the contact touched Matthias, because he flinched, and suddenly turned his face towards Seth, his eyes wide, as if trying to see something in the dark.

'Seth?' he breathed, and put a hand out as if to touch him.

Seth watched in horror as Matt's hand passed straight through his own body. Then Matthias stumbled towards the door. It looked as though his legs wouldn't carry him.

'Matt, let me help you,' cried Seth, but again the words hung in the air and held no sound.

He followed Matt into his cell, and watched him lie down on his own mattress. The fever had already taken hold. Seth slid to a crouch and stared in horror as Matt, gripped by pain, started tossing and shaking.

'HELP! Telemachus . . . Aurelius!' Seth shouted, but of course nobody came running. Nobody heard.

He sat by Matthias's bed, watching his friend dying. The numbness and sorrow had driven away any instinct to return to the river, to Parallon. Then, in his delirium, Matthias moaned his name.

'I am here!' said Seth pointlessly. Matthias couldn't hear him, would never hear him again . . . except in Parallon.

Parallon. The thought registered vaguely in Seth's numbed brain. He tried to focus. He really should try to get back. Matt would be waiting for him. And suddenly, for the first time, he realized Matt needed him. He'd been so consumed by grief that he had abandoned his friend. If he didn't return, Matthias would be completely alone.

But he was so tired. So weak.

'Call yourself a fighter?' some deep part of his consciousness challenged. 'Get up and move.'

He summoned all his strength and pulled himself up. The effort made him dizzy and nauseous, but he pushed on and out of the barracks. He could feel that his time was running out. He was halfway across the arena when he heard footsteps running up behind him. He turned just in time to see Aurelius on exactly the same trajectory as his own. Before Seth had time to take evasive action, Aurelius was on top of him. He stood gasping for a second, stunned. Aurelius had just sliced through him, encountering no resistance at all. He was as insubstantial now as air. He stumbled on, and arrived at the gates just in time to hear Aurelius and the guards in conversation.

'Sethos is dead!'

'He was a brave fighter. The familia will miss him.'

'So will the women.'

Aurelius nodded sadly, then hurried on to the lanista's quarters with his news, so he missed the rest of the guards' murmured conversation.

'Are you thinking what I'm thinking?'

'I'm thinking it's interesting that Cassius Malchus withdrew his financial stake in Sethos Leontis this morning.'

Seth snarled. Cassius Malchus. The man he hated above all others. He hadn't known Cassius had money invested in his arena successes. The thought that his own gladiatorial victories had only helped to make Cassius more rich and powerful filled him with such rage that the heat of it fuelled him forward. He was not going to let himself disappear here now, weak and unavenged.

His resolve gave him the strength to hurl himself at the guards. He cut right between them and then through the gates without even stirring the air. Then he forced his legs onwards, calling on every last shred of energy to push himself. He was barely conscious when he finally made it to the river. Praying he wasn't too late, he threw himself in.

34

Light

Seth opened his eyes to feel his body bobbing against a hard rough surface. He looked around in confusion, and inadvertently gulped a mouthful of river water. Coughing and shivering, he dragged himself out of the water on to the bank. He was freezing, soaking wet and exhausted. Where had he landed this time? He felt too cold to function, so he just sat there for a few moments, trying to clear his head.

At last a coherent thought occurred to him: *I need to get dry*. This thought was instantly followed by the comfort of a fresh dry tunic, and the weight of a huge warm woollen cloak over his shoulders. He was no longer in any doubt that he had returned to Parallon.

The sandals he had slipped off earlier were no longer there, so he created a new pair and put them on. As he worked the buckles, he noted with relief how solid his hands looked again. He had not enjoyed feeling like a shadow, and was suddenly extremely grateful to be back.

He was ready now to go and face Matthias. But as he stood to move away he heard sounds.

Voices. Laughter. He crept silently along the bank and up the steps. Crouching in the shadow of a huge building, he saw them. Seth counted eleven people sitting at round white tables on a wooden deck. Each table had a flickering light in its centre. They were drinking from transparent vessels, chatting in the strange language he'd heard last time. Smiling.

And Zackary was weaving between them all, agreeing, laughing, listening. Seth crept nearer. He felt like a beggar looking through a window at a family celebration. And he knew suddenly, that in some significant way, all these people belonged here . . . and he didn't. Hadn't Zackary implied something like that to him earlier? Who was Zackary? And how did he know so much about this world? Seth vowed to find out.

At last Zackary yawned, waved at the group he'd been chatting to, and moved away from them towards a tall glistening tower of a building. Without a second thought, Seth crept after him.

He watched from the shadows as Zackary climbed the three steps up to the large entrance porch, and faced an imposing black door. But instead of pushing it open, he seemed to draw a pattern with his fingers on a smooth buttoned panel beside it. The door slid open and Zackary disappeared inside. Could Seth follow? Should he?

What did he have to lose?

Zackary represented no physical threat whatsoever. He was slight and clearly lacked muscle. But physical prowess was virtually irrelevant in Parallon. In truth, what Seth was trying not to dwell on was the growing conviction that Zackary wielded some sort of power here, a power far more compelling than mere gladiatorial strength.

He hovered for a moment, uncertain. Could he slip past the tables of people without being noticed? He felt the odds were good, so choosing a moment of raucous mirth, he soundlessly darted across the deck and up the steps to the door. He tried pushing it open. It was locked.

He found the panel Zackary had touched, and tapped it with his fingers. Nothing happened. He saw that the buttons had symbols stamped on them. Some sort of coded entrance? He began pressing the buttons randomly, but the door remained locked. He shut his eyes, trying to picture exactly what he had seen Zackary do . . . There had been a pattern he had traced. Seth did his best to imitate it. On the third attempt, the door suddenly emitted a long low sound and slid open. Seth stumbled forward and the door hummed shut behind him.

He was standing in a white entrance hall. Coloured rectangular hangings decorated the walls. There was a panelled door to his left, and a staircase ahead.

He stood absolutely still, listening. Where was Zackary now? He heard the faintest footfall above him. Good. That placed him out of immediate danger of discovery. He had no idea whether he and Zackary were alone, but he had to explore inside.

Very quietly, he pushed the panelled door open and gasped. Nothing he had ever seen prepared him for the cacophony of colour and invention before him. A huge rectangular screen, alive with moving pictures and patterns, dominated the room. On either side of it were additional smaller screens, but they were black and still. Along the opposite wall were long white tables, on which several large cylindrical instruments were arranged around two further screens. The third wall was covered in coloured buttons twinkling across boxes of silver.

Seth stood by the door and stared.

And then his legs began moving on an inexorable trajectory, drawn by the compelling magnetism of the colour and movement on the large screen in front of him. His heart hammering against his chest, he watched in dispassionate wonder as his hand reached out to touch the screen's surface. As his fingers made contact, a sudden warmth spread instantly through his hand, along his arm and across his body. No – not a warmth . . . a heat. A burning heat . . . An impossible heat. The room started to sway and spin around him. He shut his eyes, tried to tear himself away, but his fingers were now clamped in position. Millions of images and sounds flashed across his brain, faster and faster until he couldn't follow, couldn't breathe, couldn't take any more . . . Someone was howling, filling the space with terror, and then a blinding white pain exploded in his head . . . And he lost consciousness.

35

Blind Alleys

London

AD 2012

It was when Dr Franklin was talking about unusual monocyte responses in biology that I suddenly wondered if I had been missing something vital. To tell the truth I was frustrated. I had been drawing one blank after another on my virus hunt, and I wasn't used to this kind of failure. My research strategies had been meticulously thorough. And I had now literally trawled through every independent research institute in the world. I had to be missing something. However close I got to symptom and virion shape, two hours' incubation was proving too hard an act to follow.

Even the Hong Kong Institute of Biochemical Medicine, where they were doing some incredible research on some pretty sensational (scary) viruses, offered me nothing. Which was deeply annoying considering how long it took me to hack into their system.

So where was *my* virus?

I gazed back at the board. Dr Franklin was drawing a

diagram of a typical immune response. The immune system had actually been one of the things that turned me on to micro-biology when I was eleven. I'd loved the idea of this microscopic army doing its best to defend its world (me) against alien inva-sion. And then when I discovered how many different microscopic jobs there were for the cells to do, I was even more blown away.

And I hadn't stopped finding it distractingly cool. So as I watched Dr Franklin drawing her T-cells and monocytes attack-ing the invading infection, I suddenly wondered why I hadn't seen any sign of defensive action when I'd witnessed the cell invasion with Professor Ambrose. No T-cell activation, no B-cell activation, no macrophagic action and definitely no monocyte response.

I put up my hand.

'Dr Franklin, could speed of infection suppress an immune response?'

'I think all infections would induce some sort of immune response, Eva. As you know, lymphocytes sense an invasion and head off to meet it. If the infection proliferates too fast, obvi-ously the attackers can get overwhelmed, but there will always be evidence of raised numbers of white cells during and after an infection.'

But the attack I'd witnessed hadn't obeyed any of the usual rules. It had been so focused . . . so deliberate . . . so specifically targeted . . .

'Dr Franklin,' I gasped, 'what if the infection directly bombards the T-cell itself – would that deactivate its defence response?'

'Stealth attack? Nice. A pre-emptive strike directly on the

defence cells . . . Hmmm. There is only one virus I know that goes straight for the T-cell . . .'

I held my breath.

'The HIV virus.'

I sighed. I knew for sure that my virus wasn't anything like HIV.

So clearly HIV wasn't the only cunning virus.

The bell rang. End of lesson. End of day. I packed up my books, wondering if there was another tack I should be taking in this dead-end research of mine. I stood up and bumped straight into Harry, who was standing just behind me.

'Oops, sorry, Harry,' I said, trying to stay upright. He had reached out his hands to steady me.

'Hey, Eva, you were miles away. Are you OK?'

'Yeah, fine,' I said, stepping carefully out from his arms.

'Well, we'd better get going or we'll be late.'

I frowned at him. 'Late? Haven't we finished for the day?'

'Er . . . *Hamlet* rehearsal, Eva.'

He was smiling and shaking his head at me, like I was an idiot child. Which wasn't so far off the truth. What was wrong with me?

As we walked across the quad to the drama studio, we caught up with Astrid, George and Louis on their way from English.

I caught a look between Astrid and Harry, and I suddenly realized Astrid had given him the job of herding me there.

Sudden sick realization flooded through me. Harry wasn't the only one Astrid had primed. The day before yesterday it had been Omar. As if it wasn't awkward enough that Omar was now turning up every day to *Hamlet* rehearsals because Felix had been sacked for bad attendance. Now it seemed Astrid had got him to represent the art history contingent in her new Get Eva To Rehearsals campaign.

But I was pretty sure that Omar's agreeing to act as my alarm clock was more due to his general awe of Astrid than any attempt to get close to me again. He'd started hanging out with Verity Sutton and seemed genuinely happy with her. And to be honest it was nice to be able to talk to him again. I'd kind of missed him. Ruby too, of course, but she still refused to even look at me. Thank God she wasn't in *Hamlet*.

After rehearsal I had a philosophy essay and a physics experiment to write up, so I had to give my virus research a miss that night. Which was a bit of a relief really. I was hitting too many brick walls. I knew I was missing something – but what?

I was so preoccupied by my frustration that the following morning I found myself wandering out of the Greek class at the end of the lesson without my textbook.

I'd reached the door by the time Dr Mylne's voice cut through my cluttered thoughts.

'Planning to write your Plato essay without the source text, Eva?' he queried, glancing at the book lying on my desk.

I stood at the door, frowning.

'Eva, are you OK?'

I tried to shake myself back into the here and now. 'Yes, fine. Sorry, Dr Mylne,' I mumbled, grabbing the book and stuffing it into my bag.

But I left the room feeling suddenly much more purposeful. Dr Mylne had made me realize that I had been on the wrong track. In my obsessive search for equivalent viruses I'd failed to think about the source: the vial.

I needed to find Professor Ambrose.

36

Overload

Seth heard himself breathing. So . . . he was alive then. His pounding head was testament to that. He twitched a hand and tried to work out where he was. Images were echoing through his mind, images of things he recognized but didn't know.

Where was he? The arena? He tentatively reached a hand out. No. This wasn't the arena. No sand. He was horizontal. Flat on his back. Eyes shut. Hard surface beneath him. Completely drained.

He drifted off for a while, and woke with a start. He was moving. Someone had grabbed his legs and was dragging him along the ground.

He groaned. Tried to focus. His mind was so confused he couldn't think where he was. Had he just been injured in the arena? Was Protix dead? No, that happened long ago . . .

Gradually, his head began to clear. He now knew for certain that he wasn't in the arena because he was being hauled down a flight of steps.

'Aggh!' he gasped, raising his arms to protect his head.

He opened his eyes and looked up. 'Zackary?' he croaked.

Zackary turned to face him, and in that instant Seth knew that Zackary was going to kill him.

He tried to reason with himself. You couldn't die on Parallon, could you?

Even in his weakened state, Seth's survival instinct flared. He suddenly knew where they were heading. The river.

Zackary was grunting with the effort, and gasping for breath, but they were practically there now. Seth's eyes darted wildly for something to grab on to. He needed a wall, a post, anything to help halt Zackary's progress.

And because this was Parallon, and Seth had willed it, a wooden post appeared next to him, which he grabbed with both arms.

Zackary stumbled and almost lost his hold on Seth's feet, which gave Seth the moment he needed to kick against his captor and unbalance him. As Zackary fell backwards, Seth jumped to his feet, and willed a dagger into his hand.

Zackary stood up slowly and faced Seth coldly. 'Surely you know that a dagger won't help you now?'

Seth's eyes widened. Zackary wasn't speaking in Latin. He was using the alien language Seth had heard him use with those other people earlier. Yet inexplicably some part of his brain now understood the words.

'I no longer need it,' breathed Seth in Zackary's tongue, as he threw the dagger to the ground.

Zackary's eyes narrowed. He took in the taut physique of the man standing before him, and knew Seth was right. His eyes flickered around. Searching for an ally.

Seth regarded him uneasily. 'Why do you hate me?' he asked quietly.

Zackary stared back at him. 'Wrong question, Sethos.'

Seth's jaw flexed with anger, but he stood and waited. At last Zackary spoke again.

'I don't hate you,' he snorted. 'How could I? You are now the nearest thing to me that has ever existed . . .'

Seth was baffled. What was Zackary saying? It didn't make any sense.

'So why do you want me dead?'

'Better question. Simple answer: there's no room in Parallon for us both.'

'Is that why you sent me back to Londinium?'

'I didn't *send* you back to Londinium, but I assumed that's where you would go.' Zackary shook his head. 'Which is why I don't understand how you survived. You were there too long . . .'

'Just one night –'

'An entire night in your own time? Shouldn't be possible. I have measured two hours as the longest survivable stay. Did you not feel yourself disappear? Your life ebb away?'

Seth shrugged, trying not to remember the appalling struggle to force himself back to the river.

Zackary was staring at him. 'You either have incredible strength or you were uncannily lucky. It is the primary instinct to return to your own death, which is why you arrived there. But your stay was so long, you should have become trapped in your own time.'

'Trapped?'

'Once you are trapped, you never get out. You remain a ghost forever.'

Seth nodded. 'And you assumed that's what would happen to me.'

'Of course.' Zackary continued to stare. 'So why did you come back? I thought you'd had enough of Parallon.'

Seth was on the point of telling him about Matthias when it occurred to him to keep quiet. Zackary didn't know anything about his friend, and Seth was fairly certain that it was in Matt's best interest to keep it that way.

'So,' said Zackary quietly, 'not only do you survive the visit, you survive the vortex. You come back, you break into my office, hook into my terminal and . . .'

'. . . Somehow acquire a little knowledge a gladiator slave does not normally have much need for,' finished Seth.

Zackary shook his head. 'Slight understatement.'

'Zackary –'

'Sethos,' said Zackary, holding up his hands. 'I need to think. Leave me now. We'll speak again in the morning. Meet me here at eleven.'

'Eleven? How will I judge the hour?'

'Oh, for God's sake, Sethos, this is Parallon. Get yourself a watch.'

37

Restored

When Seth returned to their palace, he found Matthias in his chamber, fast asleep. But his friend had laid out a huge feast on the table in the dining room. Seth's chest tightened as he pictured Matt sitting alone, waiting for him to return. He sighed, took a plate and selected a radish salad, and a slice of duck in oyster sauce.

He ate thoughtfully, trying to make sense of what had happened to him. Could he really speak an entirely new language without having been taught? And what else did he now know? Picking up a stray olive, he suddenly caught sight of the new accessory glinting on his wrist. It had appeared there when he had thought of a watch at Zackary's command. Now it silently displayed the time and he could read it easily – as though he'd never been without it.

He shook his head. He was just too tired to think any more, so he swallowed down a large cup of water, and padded off to his chamber. Within moments he was asleep under a thickly embroidered cover, on his soft new bed.

By the time Matthias emerged the next morning, Sethos was already training in the practice arena. Seth paused in his attack on the post to grin across at his friend.

'Thank you for this,' he said, gesturing around the arena, 'and for the banquet last night. I'm sorry I was back too late to share it with you.'

Matthias's eyebrows shot up in surprise. He had become so accustomed to Seth's monosyllabic despair that he hardly recognized the warm, gracious boy now smiling before him.

'Seth, what happened yesterday? You were gone the whole night. Where were you?' he asked tentatively.

Seth gazed back at his friend, wondering what on earth he could tell him. The shattering insights he had suddenly acquired, insights he still hadn't assimilated himself, now formed such a huge gulf between the two of them that he didn't know how to begin to bridge it. So he stood indecisively for a moment, wondering if there was some small part he could share.

'I found out what this place is called.'

'Thank the gods,' laughed Matthias. 'Now come and have some breakfast.'

Seth was not late for his appointment. He arrived to find Zackary sitting on the steps to his house, broodily gazing out at the river. Seth sat down next to him, and Zackary passed him a one-handled cup filled with a steaming hot liquid.

'Mmm . . . coffee! Thanks,' said Seth automatically. Then he stared down at his mug. How did he know what it was? He had never seen a mug, never tasted coffee, and yet when he sipped it, it was exactly as he expected. Delicious.

He glanced across at Zackary's resigned expression, and began to grasp that he had somehow acquired a lot more knowledge than simply the ability to speak a new language.

And he had no idea what the parameters of this new knowledge were. He had not known he could speak English until Zackary had used it to speak to him. He did not know he knew what coffee was, until just now.

Seth looked around him, testing his knowledge: Zackary was wearing *jeans* and a *T-shirt*, garments that had been peculiar, unfamiliar and nameless to him yesterday. Now they appeared normal . . . right. He looked down at his tunic. It didn't feel wrong exactly, just suddenly less appropriate. He frowned.

Zackary sniggered gently at his confusion and shoved a neat pile of clothing on to his lap. 'Might as well get it over with. You can't wear a dress for the rest of your life.'

Seth didn't laugh. He glanced coolly at Zackary, and wondered irritably where he was from.

The answer was in his head before he'd finished framing the question: London. And without pushing that thought, he found he knew that London was what Londinium would become. Had become. Seth's breathing quickened, as he realized that his whole sense of stable, measurable, sequential time was suddenly spiralling out of control.

Zackary sensed his discomfort and turned to him. 'What's nettled the gladiator then? Not the coffee or the clothes, I'm guessing.'

'What year is it now?' Seth asked huskily.

Zackary blinked back at him. 'Oh, come on, gladiator! You can do better than that.'

Seth frowned. He had landed on Parallon and found himself with another damned lanista. Zackary wasn't hot-blooded and vicious like Tertius, but Seth recognized that same strand of ruthless indifference. And like Tertius, Zackary enjoyed goading him.

But Seth refused to get riled. Instead he considered Zackary's comment – and instantly realized his question had been a stupid one.

'We are living outside time here, aren't we?' he breathed. How had he known that?

Zackary nodded.

'Have you been back to visit your time?'

'Of course.'

'And others?'

'Many others.' Zackary turned his face sharply to look at Seth. 'And so will you.'

'Oh no,' murmured Seth, shaking his head. 'Not me.'

Zackary raised an eyebrow, and stood up. 'OK, time to go inside,' he said briskly. 'There are some things I want you to see.'

Seth stood up, but didn't move. What was Zackary up to? Last night this man had tried to kill him, and Seth knew with blinding certainty that he now had no intention of dying.

Zackary stood by his open doorway, waiting. 'Gladiator too scared to come in?' he mocked.

'What am I doing here, Zackary?' hissed Sethos.

'You'll see soon enough,' said Zackary smoothly. 'Now come, I don't have much time.'

Seth roared with laughter. 'Of course not. Time's such a precious commodity here!'

Zackary stared coldly at him. 'You have no idea.'

Seth gazed back at him furiously, and then turned to leave.

'Fine! Run away . . . Oh mighty and courageous gladiator!' jeered Zackary. 'And when you are brave enough to return and ask the right questions, I'll be waiting.'

Seth snorted with rage and strode from the house. He hadn't gone far when he felt a hand grip his shoulder. He swung round, his eyes narrowing dangerously.

'Before you leave, you must swear not to tell anybody about the vortex.'

Seth gritted his teeth. 'Who would I tell?'

'Sethos, tell *no one*,' Zackary repeated. 'Life in Parallon absolutely depends on your silence.'

Seth frowned. He had stronger loyalties than the one he was now being expected to honour. And yet – something about the intensity of Zackary's words rang true. He hesitated one moment more and then nodded.

'All right,' he murmured. 'I swear.'

38

Contact

London

AD 2012

The *Hamlet* rehearsal finished a bit early, so instead of going straight to supper, I sped back to my room to embark on my latest line of enquiry: Professor Ambrose – virologist.

I remembered that when Dr Franklin had first introduced him to us in biology she'd said he worked at the New York University Microbiology Research Department, so I started by Googling it.

Looked impressive.

I clicked on *Research Teams*, kicking myself for not starting with Professor Ambrose earlier, and for not including university research units in my big virus search. I suddenly had the feeling that universities would be much more likely places to experiment with viruses than privately funded laboratories.

But the really great thing about universities was that they tended to list the names of *everyone* on their research and teaching teams, which meant I could look for Ambrose completely legally.

Absolutely no hacking required.

Easy . . . In theory. If Professor Ambrose had appeared on any of the lists.

I started, obviously enough, with the virology department. No sign of him. So I broadened my horizons and trawled through the entire microbiology unit. When he didn't appear on any of their many research teams, I opened out even further. I visited cell biology, biochemistry, even medical parasitology.

He wasn't there at all.

Not one to be easily daunted, I decided to do a simple Google name search: *Professor Ambrose virology*.

I got one vaguely relevant hit. A Dr Ambrose who had contributed to a paper on *Host Factors in Malaria*.

Could this be my Professor Ambrose? There was no photo. It wasn't the area of research he had talked to us about. It wasn't much to go on, but I was at least on a trail . . . Until I discovered that he was a she: Dr Caroline Ambrose.

I spent a while longer exploring various unrelated Ambroses: Belinda Ambrose, a historian who had written a paper on the American Civil War, a couple of lawyers, a poet and a housing officer.

Then I finally had to admit to myself that I had drawn another blank.

'Eva! What are you doing here?'

I jumped. 'Astrid?' Oh God! What had I missed now?

She was standing at the door, shaking her head.

'S-sorry, Astrid,' I said, hurrying to stand up. 'Where am I meant to be?'

'Eva, you're gonna get sick again if you keep forgetting to eat . . . What is wrong with you?'

She was hauling me towards the dining room. We reached it just as they were clearing away the food, but I managed to grab a bowl of cold pasta and an apple.

'Aren't *you* getting anything?' I asked as Astrid guided me across the room to a table. Rob, Harry and George were sitting there with empty plates, and Sadie was guarding a full tray of food. This turned out to be Astrid's. Which meant she had stopped eating to come and get me. I was embarrassed. And touched.

They were chatting about the *Hamlet* rehearsal, but I was too preoccupied to join in.

'Well, Eva?'

I jerked back into the present. I was walking back to my room, with Astrid propelling me by the elbow.

'Sorry, Astrid, what did you say?'

'Eva!' she spluttered. '*Where are you?*'

I blinked at her. I had to. Her face was about a centimetre in front of mine.

I sighed. 'Thing is, Astrid, there is something I just can't work out . . . and it's really bugging me . . .'

'Eva – have you considered the hypothesis that if *you* can't work it out, maybe there *is* no answer?' she smirked.

I rolled my eyes.

'What subject?'

I glanced up at her. Should I confide? Could I? It was so dangerous to trust anyone. Look where it had got me. But Astrid had been so . . . cool.

'Oh, for God's sake, Eva? What's the big secret?'

And I thought . . . there was no big secret. What was my problem?

So I told her, about my virus, and Professor Ambrose's vial, and my fruitless researches.

She stood there, looking extremely sceptical. 'Eva – you have to admit it – disappearing viruses followed by disappearing professors sounds just a teeny bit . . . *crazy*?'

I was so regretting this.

'So what's old Frankie's take on all this?'

'Whose?'

Astrid rolled her eyes. 'Dr Franklin's . . . I mean – how did *she* find the Prof?'

Silence.

'You *have* asked her, Eva?'

'Of course not! Why would I do that?'

'Duh! How much time could you have saved yourself?'

I looked at her blankly. I suppose she was right. I could have asked Dr Franklin.

But I never asked anyone for help. The last adult I'd trusted was the librarian who'd reported me to social services. The thought of confiding in Dr Franklin actually made me want to throw up.

Astrid was frowning at me. Then she said quietly, 'Eva – not everyone's out to get you, you know.'

I narrowed my eyes.

''Cept Will and Harry and George!' she laughed. 'They seem pretty determined. Anywhere. Any time. Any place, if I'm any judge. But I reckon you can probably fend them off.'

We had arrived back at my building.

'Now get to bed, Eva, and in the morning – do me a favour and talk to your biology teacher.'

Which is exactly what I did.

I caught up with Dr Franklin at the end of the lesson. It was lunchtime and most people were heading for the dining room. I walked out of the lab just behind her. I had decided to leave it to fate. If she detoured to the staffroom, then I would just forget about it. If she headed the same way as me, I'd ask her. She didn't detour, so I was committed.

'Er – Dr Franklin?'

'Hi, Eva! Everything OK?'

'Yeah, sure . . . . er, I was just wondering . . . about Professor Ambrose.'

She frowned for a moment. I guess we get quite a lot of guest speakers at St Mag's.

'The virologist,' I prompted.

'Ah, yes, of course! You got on well with him, didn't you?'

I decided not to answer that one.

'The thing is – there's a virology question I wanted to run by him, and – er – I was wondering if you had his contact details?'

'Hmmm. Let me think. I'll see if I have an email address for him. I'm trying to remember how he got in touch . . .'

'Oh. He contacted you then?'

'Yep. He said he was in the country for a lecture tour, and would we like St Mag's to be included. He sent me a couple of papers to look through, so I'm bound to have an email address. I'll have a look tonight.'

'Thanks so much, Dr Franklin.'

Annoyingly, Astrid caught the tail end of that little exchange, which meant she spent the whole lunch hour with a smug grin on her face. I had to just sit there and suck it up.

Thankfully she'd got over it by the time we did our band practice that evening. In fact I was the one with the smug grin because I managed to get to the music block before either Sadie or Astrid. I wasn't quite so smug when I discovered they were only late because they'd swung by my room to pick me up.

Anyway, we played well together – best practice we'd had since my time out. So I was pretty buoyant when I headed back to my room.

Buoyant but tired. Definitely due an early night. The only urgent stuff left to do was some physics homework and a Latin vocab list I'd promised to email Astrid for a test the next day.

The physics took no time, so I opened my laptop to get online.

My inbox was blinking.

A message from Dr Franklin. Yay.

Hi Eva,

Unfortunately I don't have an email address for Professor Ambrose. I remember now that he made his initial approach by phone. He couriered a couple of research papers over the week before his visit, but they contain no contact details.

I've photocopied the articles for you, in case they answer any of your questions. You can collect them from me in class tomorrow.

A. F.

Damn.

39

Company

After his face-off with Zackary, Sethos did his best to continue with his routine – training, running, and searching for Livia – while completely avoiding the river and its surrounding area.

As he ran, his mind seethed with new questions and answers. Questions about Parallon; about London; about the end of Londinium; the demise of Latin; and the origin of English. He wondered how he could be dead and alive at the same time. He wondered if his Londinium existed at the same time as Zackary's London. If he and Zackary were both to travel across to their deaths simultaneously, then surely both times would exist concurrently? Or did time only exist if you were there to witness it? Did the real world, his old world, actually exist at all? Did Parallon? And where, between these worlds and time, was Livia?

Of course he had to keep most of his thoughts from Matthias. Matt knew nothing of Zackary, the vortex or Seth's newfound knowledge, and Seth had to keep it that way. Knowledge would make Matthias too vulnerable.

But if Matthias suspected Seth was keeping something from him, he did not dare bring it up. He was so delighted to have his animated friend back, he was not going to question why.

Then one evening Seth returned sweaty and tired from a

particularly long run, to find Matthias waiting in front of the house, bursting with excitement.

'Seth, I have just seen people! Lots of them!'

'You were by the river?' asked Seth cautiously.

'No! I'll show you . . . only . . .'

'What?' asked Seth.

'They were wearing such strange garments . . . and they spoke . . .'

Seth sighed.

'Let me bathe, and then I'll take a look,' Seth called as he strode to the bathhouse. Stripping off his damp tunic, he wondered idly what Matthias would say if he installed a shower.

When he emerged again, Matthias gasped. 'Seth! You're dressed like them . . .'

'I think it would be best if you were too,' suggested Seth gently.

Matthias frowned but complied. Seth showed him how to use a zip and thread a belt through his jeans. Matthias just stared, baffled.

'When . . . How did you learn all this?' he breathed.

Sethos realized he would have to come up with some sort of explanation, but he needed time to prepare himself.

'I'll tell you later,' he promised.

Matthias shook his head in exasperation, but didn't argue. He was too excited. 'Come on then,' he said, dragging Seth outside.

Their villa was west of central Parallon, out beyond the temple and meadow. Sethos preferred to run in that area. But Matthias was leading him east, in the direction of Cassius's house – Seth's least favourite district.

Just before they reached Cassius's road, Matthias veered right, crossed two more streets, then stopped. They were facing a grassy square. Seth could tell the tall shimmering buildings surrounding the square were Edwardian. Whenever a new piece of knowledge suddenly presented itself in his mind, Seth shuddered slightly. It was difficult to get used to. Matthias was pointing to the far corner.

'Over there,' he whispered.

'A café,' breathed Seth, knowing and saying the word for the first time. Tables spilled out on to the grass . . . And people sat at the tables. He didn't recognize any of them as the ones he'd seen by the river.

There were as many women as men, and most looked about their age, some maybe a couple of years older. And Matt had been right. None of them were dressed like Romans. Seth was relieved they'd changed their own clothes. He felt surprisingly comfortable in his jeans and trainers.

Matthias was grinning, and it was all Seth could do to stop him running straight across the square and pulling up a chair.

'Stay in the shadows, Matt. We have no idea who they are.'

But Matt had completely lost his fear of capture, and his sense of immortality had invested him with a reckless confidence. He refused to step back. Seth now regretted that he hadn't warned Matt about Zackary.

'Matt –' he began, but it was too late. One of the girls had spotted him, and was waving.

Matthias returned the wave, and started to head over. When Seth didn't join him, he turned back and pulled his friend into the light.

*

Later that night Matt and Seth walked back to the villa in silence.

As soon as they were through the front door, Matthias stormed off to his room, and with a deep sigh, Seth slipped into his own.

Unwilling to dwell on Matt's terrible mood, Seth lay back on his bed, gazing up at the ceiling, and began wondering about the Parallon population. Most of the people they'd met that night had arrived quite recently. Some had known each other before, like he and Matt, whereas others were strangers.

So what brought them here?

What was the link they all shar–

He never got to finish that thought because Matthias suddenly burst in on him, shouting.

'So – what was that all about? How could you do that to me?'

Seth dragged himself away from his own questions to face this new onslaught. But he was genuinely bewildered.

'What did I do to you, brother?'

Matt stared at him in disbelief.

'How can you pretend not to know? All those people! All those girls! Smiling, waving. It was as if we'd arrived in Elysium. And then we sat at the table and . . . I didn't understand a single word they were saying.'

'Matt – I tried to –'

'But *you* did!' Matt ploughed on. '*You* – who claimed not to want to go there at all – have obviously been sneaking off without telling me, and *secretly* getting them to teach you their language!'

'No, Matt . . . it's not like that –'

'You sat there pretending to look as though you'd rather be anywhere else in the world, with all the women in the place clamouring around you . . .'

'Matt – they were just –'

'And I couldn't even say a simple "I like your hair" without having to ask you to translate for me.'

'Matt, I –'

'You made me look like a dumb fool.'

Matt threw himself down on the edge of the bed and glowered at the floor.

Seth sat up and took a deep breath. It was time to talk. 'You remember the night I didn't come home?' he began.

Matt frowned at the sudden shift in topic, but nodded reluctantly.

'Well . . .' Seth hesitated. How could he explain this? He didn't have the Greek vocabulary. He knew, because his recently enlightened intellect knew, that his brain had somehow downloaded a vast amount of information directly from a computer terminal. He also knew that Zackary had been both surprised and horrified by the occurrence. Although he had no idea exactly how much he knew, he was quite sure it was substantial. So substantial that Zackary wanted him dead. Which was one of the main reasons he had said nothing to Matt. The other reason was that he didn't know how it had happened. From what he now knew of computers, this physical transference of information shouldn't have been possible.

Matthias was getting impatient.

'That night, I – accidentally – opened a – a – box . . . lost consciousness . . . and when I woke up, I could speak English

224

. . .' It sounded preposterous, but it was as near the truth as he could manage.

Fortunately, Matthias had spent long enough in Parallon to be able to accept the preposterous.

'Like . . . Pandora's box?' he breathed.

'I suppose so . . .' hedged Seth.

'So why didn't you take *me* there? If I had found the box, I would have shared it with you!'

Seth sat gazing at his friend. 'Because the man guarding the box tried to kill me,' he said at last.

'But you can't be killed in Par . . .' Matt's words died on his lips when he saw Seth's expression.

'Well, who was this man?'

Seth pressed his lips together, and shook his head. 'I don't know.' At least that was true. Zackary's role in Parallon was still a mystery to him. Matthias said nothing for a minute or two. He knew from experience that if Seth didn't want to tell him something, he would never be able to force it out of him.

At last Matthias sighed deeply, and stood up.

'All right then,' he growled. 'But you're going to teach me English! Starting tomorrow morning.'

40

Reflections

Seth was cooking soup. The conventional way: assembling ingredients, crushing spices, chopping onions, heating and stirring. As a small child, he had enjoyed helping Acantha, the kitchen slave, as she prepared the family's meals. Matthias couldn't understand why Seth would bother spending so much time crushing and blending, when they could click their fingers and create a ready-made meal. But Seth enjoyed the process. He found it soothing. He had so many thoughts whirring through his mind all the time that he needed calming activities. He now ran for the first two hours of each day before returning to the villa to bathe, wake Matt and eat breakfast with him. Then he would spend a couple of hours teaching Matt English – as he'd been doing every day since that night at the café.

The lessons were going quite well. Seth was a patient teacher, and Matthias had a pressing incentive so he worked hard. In fact Matt's English was now good enough for him to enjoy visiting the café every day.

He usually set off shortly after Seth began training, which suited them both well. Seth hated an audience, and Matthias could hardly bear to watch him practise any more. He simply couldn't understand why he was still doing it. Seth had hated being a gladiator; he had never enjoyed the combat. So what drove him to continue? Combat skills were irrelevant in Parallon, surely?

Of course, there was another reason Matt couldn't bear to witness Seth's relentless training. Deep down he feared that Seth still harboured the need to be avenged for Livia's death. And until that day, his friend would never find peace. And as Matt was fairly certain Seth would not be seeing Cassius again, he was grimly aware that Sethos would be fighting against himself forever.

They never talked of Livia now. She was a forbidden subject. As was Cassius and The Night Seth Disappeared. But their relationship could shoulder these taboo areas. It had evolved. They respected each other, and they allowed each other plenty of privacy.

Seth's soup was simmering nicely, sending aromatic reminders of another kitchen and another life. But he would not allow his mind to retreat again. As he sprinkled fennel leaves on to the beans, he wondered idly whether Matt would be coming home to eat this meal. And as if on cue, he heard the front door slam.

'Hi, Seth,' called Matthias breezily. 'Something smells good!'

'I'm in the kitch–' Seth's eyes widened.

'Meet Georgia and Clare. I've brought them back to eat with us tonight.'

This was the first time anyone had ever come into their villa. It had been their cocoon, their private sanctuary, and suddenly Matthias had opened the door and brought Parallon in.

Seth weighed up the acute sense of shock at this invasion against his innate sense of courtesy. Matthias affected nonchalance while the girls watched Seth warily, sensing his discomfort.

But Seth had quick reactions and he had been brought up to honour the laws of hospitality.

'Welcome, Clare . . . Georgia. I hope you're hungry.'

They both nodded, mesmerized by his smile. Matthias watched ruefully as he witnessed the familiar devastating effect Seth had on the girls. He was beginning to regret bringing them back already. Georgia had definitely been interested in him until she'd walked into the kitchen and seen his friend.

Seth turned to the food. He needed to boost the quantities. He obviously couldn't start adding and cooking from scratch, but the beauty of Parallon meant that quantities could be increased at will. He decided to add a simple fish course – coriander and spearmint mullet with lemon juice. The only desserts he had encountered were at the Natalis house. So, despite the jolt of pain the memories still caused, he concentrated his mind and within a few moments remembered the delicious plate Livia had once brought him, laid out with stuffed dates and almond cake. He conjured it now, and the aroma was so evocative that it almost took his breath away.

Clare happened to put her head round the kitchen door just in time to catch Seth's tortured expression as he wrestled with the memory.

'Er – I j-just wondered if there was anything I could do to h-help?'

He shook his head, unable to trust his voice. She retreated quickly.

Seth took a couple of deep breaths and once more relegated his memories to that safe dark corner of his consciousness. He ladled soup into bowls and brought them through to the dining room, where the others were already seated. The atmosphere was tense. Seth remained silent, but Matthias talked enough for them both.

As soon as they had finished the soup, Seth returned to the kitchen for the fish. But when he placed the terracotta plates in front of the girls they stared down at the tableware, confused.

'Oops! I don't seem to have a fork,' said Georgia with a nervous laugh.

Matthias looked dismayed. What on earth was a fork? But Seth, frowning in surprise, knew instantly what they required and conjured four of them. Matthias threw him a questioning look. Seth shrugged and started using his. Fortunately, Matthias's years as a physician meant that he was pretty adept with his hands, so once he had watched the others wielding theirs, he picked it up pretty fast.

When Seth brought out the final course, Georgia's eyes widened with delight. The cake looked delicious. He cut everyone a slice and then sat down to taste it himself. He was instantly transported back to that room in the Natalis house, gazing across at Livia as she held the aromatic plate for him. He had playfully fed some cake to her. She loved almonds and he loved to watch her eat. When they had finished the cake, she had licked the crumbs from his fingers . . .

Matthias cleared his throat. 'Seth, why don't you show Clare around the rest of the villa?'

Seth dragged himself back to the present.

'Oh, I'd love to see it!' said Clare, jumping up.

'Of course,' said Seth, glancing sharply at Matthias. He stood and led Clare outside to show her his herb garden. At his invitation, she crushed different leaves between her fingers and sniffed the scents appreciatively.

'How lovely! I've lived in a city all my life and have never grown anything.'

'London?'

'Yes.'

'What year was it when you . . . left?'

'1969.'

'Zeus!' he breathed unconsciously.

'Zeus? Seth – when do you come from?'

'I come from a time quite a lot earlier than yours. But here time is different. People don't seem to arrive in any consecutive time order . . . It is very perplexing.'

'Seth . . . I need to know – and Georgia keeps changing the subject . . . Tell me . . . please . . . do you know why we are here?' She fixed him with a steady gaze.

He bit his lip. It wasn't a question he could answer.

'Seth – I need you to tell me the truth . . . Are we dead?'

He looked down at his hands, and then braced himself. 'I know little more of this world than you. But yes, Clare . . . In your time I believe you are dead.'

She slumped down on a low wall and stared at a rosemary bush. Tears were rolling down her cheeks. She shook her head. 'Why, though? I'm too young . . . I'm still at school. I haven't done anything yet . . .'

Seth sat down on the wall next to her and put an arm round her. She was sobbing now.

'Clare,' he said quietly. 'You are dead in your time, but here you are alive.'

'But I still had so much to do –' she choked.

Seth wished Matthias was sitting here instead of him. Matthias was so bewitched by his new life that he would have been much more comforting. He tried to remember some of his friend's arguments.

'Clare, you can do anything you want in Parallon. And you have all the time you need. You won't age, you'll remain strong and healthy . . .'

She sniffed, and nodded, trying to wipe her tears away with her hand.

'And Matt would say we are more alive here than we ever were there.'

She nodded again, and tried a watery smile. 'It's true . . . I do feel well. Better. The fever made me so weak.'

Seth snapped round at the word *fever*. 'You were sick?' he asked.

Clare blinked at the sudden change of tone. She nodded.

'Could you describe it? The fever, I mean.'

'Well – it was awful! I couldn't move. Then there was the agonizing headache, vomiting, awful dreams and – I don't remember much else . . . just waking up here.'

Seth nodded, and started pacing around the herb garden.

'Seth?'

He turned.

'I've got another question . . .'

Seth paused in his pacing and waited.

'Well – if we are dead – where's everyone else?' she whispered.

'There are many people here now,' he answered, avoiding the point.

'Yes, I know – but where are all the others? My grandparents? Shakespeare? I don't know – Queen Victoria?'

Clare had just asked the question that had plagued Seth since he'd arrived here. He had, after all, been searching for Livia since that day. Where was she? And where *were* all the others – Sophocles? His own parents? His slaughtered brother and sister?

'I don't know,' he rasped. 'But – I am beginning to think there might be a pattern. Come.'

Clare followed him back through the atrium into the living room, and he threw open the door. Matthias and Georgia jerked apart.

'Seth! Could we have some privacy please?'

'Sorry, Matthias – I just need to ask Georgia something.'

Georgia smoothed out her hair and raised her eyebrows. 'What do you want to know?'

Seth realized it was not an easy question. He stood for a moment, deliberating. How best to put it?

'Seth?'

'Georgia . . . how did you die?'

41

Mosaic

London

AD 2012

'Are you *ever* coming, Astrid?'

'Hey, chill, Eva! You can't rush a treacle tart. Anyone would think you actually wanted to go on this trip.' She gave me one of her looks.

'Stop smirking,' I said grumpily. 'I'm not the only one who's excited.'

'Aw, sorry, Eva, I forgot about – er – Dr Mylne, Dr Crispin and a couple of nerds from Year Nine . . .'

I huffed, folded my arms and glanced longingly out of the dining-room window across the quad to the assembly point.

'OK – we are now officially late. Mylne, Andropolus, Edwards and the Crisp have all arrived.'

Astrid groaned, shovelled the last spoonful of tart into her mouth, and took her plate to the counter.

We weren't quite the last. Ruby and her new boyfriend, Dominic Patel, wandered over just after us. All four teachers frowned at them in unison.

The classics and history departments – four teachers and twenty-four students – had teamed up for this particular school trip, and the anticipation among the staff was palpable. Most of the students looked about as enthusiastic as Astrid.

'OK,' announced Dr Mylne as he finished checking the register, 'we're going to walk to the site. It'll take us about fifteen minutes. When we get there, you will all be issued with safety instructions and hard hats.

'I don't need to tell you what an incredible opportunity we've been given. It is very rare these days for a building to be demolished over the old Londinium site, and the archaeologists have uncovered not only the foundations of what appears to be a Roman palace, but many rich Roman artefacts, which I'm hoping we'll have an opportunity to see as well.

'As I'm sure you know, school trips are never normally allowed on to an active site like this, but I happen to be a personal friend of Allan Hardcastle, one of the site directors, and I promised him that you would be exceptionally well behaved.'

He gazed round at us pointedly. One or two of us looked back enthusiastically. Some just yawned. Well – we did get The Behaviour Speech before every school trip. And St Mag's did *a lot* of trips – theatres, concerts, art galleries, museums – so most kids were pretty blasé. Not me, though . . . I was still in awe of it all. Which meant I was right behind Dr Mylne as he set off purposefully through the school archway. Astrid rolled her eyes and wandered in beside me.

Dr Mylne paced quickly along City Road, then across London Wall, and on to Moorgate. We followed. Others straggled.

When he paused by Bank Station to count everyone again,

Astrid folded her arms. 'Fifteen minutes was somewhat optimistic,' she hissed.

'It's only taking so long because we have to keep waiting for everyone to catch up.'

I had to admit I was grateful for the stops. Partly because I still found walking exhausting and needed to rest. But also because I loved this part of London; it was a bit like an architect's catalogue displaying hundreds of different building shapes and styles, all side by side, in no coherent order.

When everyone was present and correct, we headed off again.

'At last,' breathed Astrid. We had arrived in front of – well – a dusty building site really, with lots of tarpaulins covering different sections.

Dr Mylne scooted off to announce our presence, and returned a few minutes later with his friend Allan Hardcastle. They were both carrying big boxes of helmets. Astrid was happier once she had a hard hat on – she liked dressing up, particularly in fluoro orange, which these were.

Then we were herded very carefully along some small rectangular ridges.

'We think these would have been the palace storerooms,' said Allan Hardcastle.

'How can you tell?' asked one of the Year Nine boys.

'God, I hate coming on these trips with the kids,' muttered Astrid in my ear. 'They always slow the thing down so much.'

'Well – firstly, the dimensions,' our guide continued. 'And secondly, we've found lots of pottery remains – probably water and wine vessels. They are currently being pieced together by the Finds Coordinator.'

We peered into the two smallish areas, but it was quite hard to imagine them stacked with food and wine. Actually, it was almost impossible to imagine them as rooms at all.

'If you step carefully up to this ridge here,' Allan Hardcastle was saying, 'you will be standing along the remains of one of the palace's external walls.'

We followed him up on to a higher ridge, and I looked down towards what would have been the palace interior. I could make out dusty paved floors about two metres below our ridge. I glanced across the site. It was a network grid of similar ridges – most rising to the same height as the one we stood on – the remains of the internal walls. I tried really hard to picture the sort of building it would have been.

'Good Lord!' I heard Dr Mylne exclaim ahead. 'The structure of the fountain is almost completely intact!'

Allan Hardcastle was nodding proudly. 'You can even make out the bird carvings around it. Whoever owned this palace clearly liked his birds – we've uncovered the remains of two huge eagle statues. We think they probably flanked the original front doors.'

'Can we see them?' asked Rob Wilmer. Rob was obviously on the side of the enthusiasts. He went up a notch in my estimation.

'Hopefully. If they haven't already been bagged and sent off to the British Museum. I'll need to check with the Finds Coordinator.

'Now, if you step down in single file, you can take a closer look at these carvings. They are exquisite . . .'

I followed behind Dr Mylne. Although there were loads of pieces missing, I could suddenly envisage exactly what the fountain would have looked like. In fact I got such a powerful sense of it that I could almost see it as it would have been . . . glistening, polished marble . . . the light catching the surface.

'Have we seen slides of this fountain before?' I asked Dr Mylne.

'No, of course not, Eva. It's only just been unearthed.'

'Something similar? It's incredibly familiar,' I persisted.

He shook his head. 'Well, certainly not in my class. I've never seen a fountain so elaborately decorated with birds. It's extraordinary.'

I was beginning to feel distinctly uneasy. I was sure I'd seen this fountain before, and if not in Dr Mylne's classroom, then where? School library? Online? But as Dr Mylne said – it had been hidden under successive buildings for the past two thousand years. So there was no way I could have seen pictures of this one. There had to be another one just like it. I trawled my brain for visual references. I was usually so good at remembering source information.

'Come on, Eva,' hissed Astrid. I blinked and realized I was the only one still standing by the fountain. Everyone else had moved on. Astrid pulled me up on to the wall next to her and we picked our way across to join the group.

Allan Hardcastle was leading. 'Over here is the area that I'm most excited about,' he beamed as he walked carefully round what was left of the central atrium and along another stretch of wall. We all filed after him.

'Bunch up together along here,' he said, indicating a section of wall, while he dropped cautiously down on to the floor below. It was completely covered by a big white tarpaulin.

We watched from our higher vantage point as he carefully

rolled back the material. He was gradually revealing a beautiful turquoise mosaic floor.

'Now you know why I said the owner of this palace was seriously fond of his birds! Look at these . . .'

I stared down at the pattern of glinting golden birds on intricate foliage, set against the rich turquoise stone, and suddenly my heart started to pound, my stomach churned and I knew I was about to throw up. Oh God – this was so not the time to be sick. I had to get to a bathroom, but my legs were now too heavy to lift. Like dead weights. When I tried to turn, instead of a coherent movement, I could feel myself swaying. I had to stay focused – my brain tried to cling on to the words Allan Hardcastle was saying, but his voice had become all distant and echoey. I tried to concentrate on his face . . . but he was disappearing . . . darkening . . . and before I could take any further action I was falling into blackness.

42

Statistics

'Seth! It's nearly morning. Aren't you ever going to bed?'

'Yes, Matt, in a minute. I just need to work this out.'

Seth was sitting at the kitchen table with a pile of papers and charts scattered all around him.

Matthias stood at the kitchen door, shaking his head. Georgia appeared behind him.

'Seth, you'll regret it tomorrow. How will you have the energy to go running?' she said.

Georgia and Clare had moved into the palace a few weeks after that first dinner. Matthias had added a new wing, and had given them each a large room. To his slight annoyance, they had both instantly redecorated. Georgia had recoloured her walls black and silver, and Clare had covered hers with pictures of the Beatles and Rolling Stones. She had also acquired a lime-green record player and played them all the singles and LPs that she had loved. Georgia, who had left London in 1982, quickly added a pile of *her* favourites: The Stranglers, Adam Ant and Squeeze – which Matt found marginally harder to appreciate.

A couple of months later Matt had expanded the palace further for three more of his friends from the café: Blake, Emerson and Tamara.

Matthias was in his element. He now hosted fabulous parties and such lively dinners that their home had become a social hub. Although Seth didn't share Matt's enthusiasm for entertainment, he would sometimes put in an appearance. He now spent most of his days working on his new research project.

Tonight he had come home planning to collate his findings, but the rooms were all filled with people and the music was too loud for him to concentrate. So he'd had to wait until the party wound down and peace reigned once more.

Seth had been systematically gathering information. Since that first evening with Clare and Georgia, his preoccupations had changed. Until then his entire focus had been on searching for Livia or contriving ways to cauterize the pain of her absence. But now his quest had taken a new turn.

He had started casually questioning the people who drifted in and out of the house. Once he had exhausted this supply of subjects he had moved on to the café, and then to the shops. After that he had accosted general passers-by. His natural reluctance to initiate conversation was conquered by his curiosity to find out more about this mysterious fever. He had now charted the comments of hundreds of people.

As soon as he heard Georgia and Matt finally shut their bedroom doors, he set to work collating all the information he'd been gathering.

PARALLON STUDY OF 543 PEOPLE

AGE	MALE	FEMALE	SYMPTOMS	LENGTH OF FEVER	TRANSMISSION (Number of linked cases)	CUT OR WOUND
16	31	27	Fever, sickness, headache, weakness	Unsure: <12 hrs?	12	2
17	39	35	Fever, sickness, headache, weakness	Unsure: <12 hrs?	36	6
18	47	41	Fever, sickness, headache, weakness	Unsure: <12 hrs?	46	12
19	43	44	Fever, sickness, headache, weakness	Unsure: <12 hrs?	38	14
20	39	33	Fever, sickness, headache, weakness	Unsure: <12 hrs?	24	6
21	31	29	Fever, sickness, headache, weakness	Unsure: <12 hrs?	28	4
22	29	27	Fever, sickness, headache, weakness	Unsure: <12 hrs?	24	2
23	24	21	Fever, sickness, headache, weakness	Unsure: <12 hrs?	16	0
24-44	2	1	Light fever, some sickness, headache, weakness	Between 4 & 13 months	2	0
TOTAL	285	258			226	46

He sat staring at the chart, checking the information against his notes. He thought he could hear Clare laughing. Then he heard Emerson's voice.

'Is Clare with Emerson?' he wondered.

Seth hardly knew Emerson. Or Blake and Tamara for that matter. They tended to be more solitary and quiet. He thought it probably wouldn't be long before they moved out. The palace could be exhausting.

But not as exhausting as the insoluble puzzle he grappled with.

He now understood some of what the figures in front of him represented – it was pretty obvious, for example, that the fever was the key. But the key to what door? And why did the door lead here?

Earlier that day, when he'd found Matthias unexpectedly alone, Seth had shown him the data.

'Matt – as a physician . . . what would you consider a reasonable cause of fever?'

Matt sat and considered. 'Well – I was taught to assume that most fevers are due to a disorder in the blood: either the blood is too heavy, or too stagnant, or it holds too much heat. But I'm guessing your question is to do with the particular fever that preceded our arrival here?'

Seth smiled. Matthias could hardly have been unaware of his little project.

'Of course I've thought about it, Sethos. My feeling is that since we both suffered such profusions of heat, the whole illness was clearly the result of overheated blood.'

'But from what I understand,' argued Seth, 'the fever is not a disorder in itself, but a symptom. And I was wondering if it could be the symptom of a very profound infection?'

'Infection?' Matthias looked bewildered.

Seth winced, realizing too late that the whole concept of infection was an alien one to Matt.

'Er – I mean – poison . . . some sort of profound poisoning?'

'But the poison would need some kind of access to get into the body.'

'Like a wound?'

'A wound? I was thinking about bad meat or a poisoned draught – but yes, I suppose a wound . . .'

'Which both you and I had . . .'

'You were the one with the wounds, Seth, not me –'

'But did you not tell me yourself that your blood-letting knife slipped and cut you?'

Seth could not mention that he had himself witnessed the event, as his own ghost.

Matt was silent for a moment. 'You're right, Seth.'

'Well, no. I'm not. I thought I was on to something, but only a few of the people I've talked to have any recollection of a cut or wound. So that can't be the answer.' Seth's brow furrowed with frustration.

Matthias sighed. 'Seth, brother, why does it matter? We're here now: safe and well in this wonderful new world, surrounded by interesting and entertaining people. We can do what we want, when we want. We are not slaves. We suffer no pain. We are young forever. What difference does it make how we came here?'

Seth gazed at Matthias and tried to think of an answer.

He couldn't tell Matt that Livia was at the centre of his quest. He had lost her, and he would go on searching until he understood why.

43

Fall

London

AD 2012

I groaned, and turned my head.

'Great stunt, Eva. Wish I'd thought of it.'

I rolled my eyes. Astrid was grinning down at me. I tried to smile back – my mouth refused to cooperate.

'What happened?' I croaked, closing my eyes again. My head hurt.

'Well. It was a genius ploy. One minute you were standing next to me on a crumbly bit of old wall, looking down at some mouldy bits of mosaic; the next minute you were diving off it – well, swaying off it, to be totally accurate.

'But if I'd known how much you wanted to get out of the trip I could have come up with a marginally better plan. For example, I would have tried to avoid the bit that involved diving head first off a two-metre wall.'

'Oh no! I didn't fall on to the mosaic, did I?' God, I hoped I hadn't damaged anything.

'Well, on to a big pile of tarpaulin. Caused a bit of a diversion – all the hard hats came running! Anyway – some first-aider turned up, checked you hadn't broken your neck, and carried you in here. An ambulance is on its way.'

'No way!' I wailed. 'I'm fine. I want to go back and look at the site.'

I tried to sit up. Astrid pushed me down. 'Eva, no one in their right mind is going to let you wander on to their precious site again! Imagine the damage you could cause!' She actually sniggered when she said that. 'So just get over it. Anyway, the trip is due to end in – approximately thirty seconds. If you're lucky, we'll get a visit from –'

'Dr Crispin,' I gulped as the tall figure of our headmaster strode towards us.

'Hello, Eva. Good to see you awake. You gave us all a bit of a turn, I must say . . . especially poor old Allan Hardcastle.'

As I lay there trying to focus on his face, something was trickling into my eye. I tried to blink it away. I wanted to look attentive, but it was getting distracting. I put my hand up quickly to wipe my face. It came back wet and sticky. With blood.

Astrid raised an eyebrow at me, and gave me her *try-and-get-out-of-this-one* look.

She was right. I couldn't get out of it. I ended up in A & E, getting seven stitches on my head, and five for a gash I hadn't even noticed on my arm.

When I finally put the light out and climbed into bed that night, I tried to remember what I had been looking at when I blacked out. For some reason my heart started to race, and my stomach twisted in fear. I fumbled for the light and stared in relief around the familiar room. I'd never been bothered by the dark before, but tonight there was no way I was going to switch that light out again.

44

Vortex

Seth ran over to Zackary's house and knocked on the door. He had done exactly the same thing yesterday. And the day before. It had been his daily pattern for the past five months.

As usual, he got no answer. And as usual he cursed. He cursed Zackary for being absent, and he cursed himself for walking away all those months ago. Because he finally had to admit that he needed Zackary. He could go no further in his search without him.

But Zackary had disappeared.

Seth sighed deeply and turned to walk away yet again, trying to suppress his growing desperation.

Suddenly he heard the front door slide open behind him. He swung round, then gasped.

Zackary was standing at the door, wrapped in a towel, his hair dripping water on to the floor.

But Seth was staring at his face. 'Zackary! What happened to you?'

Apart from looking cold and tired, the man looked . . . older. At least ten years older. His face was drawn, his forehead furrowed. His eyes more hollow.

'I've been away for a while,' Zackary replied.

'Surely not long enough to . . .'

'. . . to have aged this much?'

Seth stared at him in discomfort.

'Time folds, Sethos.'

'Time folds?' This concept did ring a faint bell.

'How long was I away from Parallon?'

'Well, I've been knocking on your door for five months.'

Zackary nodded. 'That was careless. I'd meant to be away only a few hours. I imagine you've been getting – a little impatient.'

Seth rolled his eyes.

'Good to see you've got rid of the skirt,' Zackary smirked, glancing at Seth's jeans. 'I suppose you'd better come in.'

Zackary left the door open and headed upstairs. Seth hesitated a moment, then shut the door behind him and followed.

'Coffee?'

'Sure,' said Seth.

Zackary started moving methodically around the kitchen. It was an airy room, filled with polished steel appliances. Seth sat down at the large table, and watched as Zackary picked up a box of filter papers, peeled one from the packet and placed it carefully into a coffee machine. Then he spooned three scoops from a jar of coffee, into the filter. He took the glass jug and meticulously measured water into it, then slowly poured it into the barrel of the machine. Finally he switched it on to brew.

Seth started to understand how frustrated Matthias got with him when he insisted on cooking meals, instead of instantly creating them. He was desperate to speak to Zackary and felt the man was deliberately stalling.

While the coffee was making its interminable progress, drip by drip through the filter paper, Zackary took a shallow pan, which he lightly oiled and then placed on the steel cooker. When the pan was hot, he pulled out a box of eggs and started breaking them into the pan.

'Breakfast?'

'No, thank you,' said Seth through gritted teeth. He was doing his best to stay calm. He had waited this long to talk – he knew he could wait a little longer.

When Zackary finally sat down in front of his plate of eggs and two slices of buttered toast, Seth opened his mouth to speak.

'Zackary –'

'Sethos, pour the coffee, would you? There's milk in the fridge.'

Seth bit his lip, stood up, poured coffee into mugs, brought the carton of milk on to the table and sat down again.

'Zackary . . .'

Zackary was chewing ruminatively and gazing out of the window. He didn't appear to be listening.

'I have a couple of questions.'

'Are they the right questions, though, Sethos?'

Seth snapped, 'How do I know what the right questions are? How can there be right questions? What is a wrong question? You challenge me to come up with the right questions, then you disappear for months. When you finally come back, you're more patronizing than ever. Zeus – are you even going to bother listening to me ask the wrong question or am I wasting my time?'

Zackary put his fork down on the plate, turned his face to Seth and raised his eyebrows.

In a voice as hard and cold as ice, he said, 'Some patience and a little respect would not go amiss. I returned this morning, after twelve years away, hungry, weary and a little cold. I certainly wasn't planning on subjecting myself to a visit from a wild, over-excited gladiator as my homecoming treat. Now settle down, give me a few minutes to reassemble my thoughts and then I will listen to your questions.'

Sethos was like a coiled spring. He had already run his usual two hours this morning, yet now he felt he needed to run two more. His body buzzed with excess adrenalin. Could he wait five more minutes? He wasn't sure he could. So he paced.

Zackary slowly sipped his coffee and continued to gaze out of the window. At last he turned his head to Seth, and indicated himself ready.

Seth took a deep breath. 'Zackary, why are we here?'

He gazed back at Seth meditatively. 'I know why I am here, but I can't say I know why you are.'

'Where should I be?'

Zackary shrugged carelessly. 'Londinium, of course.'

Seth was fighting the urge to walk out of the kitchen and slam out of the house. But contrary to Zackary's accusation, he *did* possess considerable self-control. He breathed slowly, counted to ten, and then continued.

'From the research I have done, everyone here appears to have died from the same cause. A virulent fever. It is the unique factor we all have in common.'

Zackary stared at Seth. 'You have been busy.'

'I need to understand this fever . . . this infection . . .'

'Why?'

'Well, clearly not every kind of death ends in Parallon. There has to be something about this particular infection.'

'So how do you propose to find out?'

'Well, I was hoping you –'

'You were hoping what? That I would have all the answers? I'm sorry, Sethos.'

Seth glared at Zackary. 'You do know why we're here.'

Zackary stared abstractedly out of the window. 'Yes and no. Like you, there are many questions I can't answer.'

'Are your questions so different from mine?'

'Our journeys are very different . . . but who knows? Perhaps our paths intersect.'

Seth tried to suppress his irritation with Zackary's indirect and evasive responses.

'What journey am I on then?' he snapped.

'How can I answer that?' smiled Zackary. 'What journey do you think you are on?'

'I want to know why we are here. How could a fever bring us to another world? What is this infection? How is it transmitted? And . . . where is everyone else?'

'Everyone else?'

'The people who didn't die of fever.'

'All excellent questions. Many of the answers you will find if you continue researching with the rigour with which you have begun. But I suspect you are searching for a *resolution* you will never find. Perhaps we are not on such different paths, you and I.'

'It isn't resolution I seek, Zackary. It's answers.'

Zackary stared at Seth thoughtfully. 'OK . . . So what do you want to find out?'

'How do I identify the infection?'

'You already know this. To identify an infection, first you have to understand it. What kind of pathogen is it? Macro-parasitic? Bacterial? Viral? Fungal? Prional? What does it look like? How is it spread? What is its incubation? Once you have identified it and named it, you may begin the task of locating the cause. And eventually you should be able to discover the source.

'But before you begin on this laborious and time-consuming course of action, you need to ask yourself why you are doing it.'

'Because I want to understand.'

'And how do you think this enlightenment will serve you? You cannot save yourself.'

'I know that. I am not after salvation.'

Zackary sighed deeply. 'So be it. I suppose I will have to teach you how to travel.'

'Travel?'

'Sethos! What possible use are you if you have to repeat everything I say? When will you start activating your brain to actually process the copious information you have been inadvertently granted?'

Seth stood in front of Zackary, burning with fury. Yes, Zackary was right – he *was* stupid . . . stupid to come back here and hope for any help. What was he thinking? He hated the man. And to make matters worse, Zackary was completely impervious to his anger.

'Sethos – surely you understood that to do this research you would need to travel across to the source?'

'You mean back through the vortex?' breathed Seth.

'Why else have you come to see me?'

'I *stupidly* thought you might be able to help me!'

Zackary laughed. 'Come back when you're ready to take what I do have to offer,' he said, picking up the empty coffee mugs and taking them over to the sink.

Seth very nearly did leave. He got as far as the door. And then he stopped, took a few more deep breaths, and turned round. When he spoke, his voice was very controlled.

'I need access to blood: infected blood and non-infected blood. And access to equipment and instruments that will help me identify the pathogen.'

Zackary was standing by the sink with his back to Seth. 'Good,' he said.

Then he rinsed out the mugs and placed them carefully on the draining board. When he had finished, he dried his hands on a cloth, folded it neatly and turned slowly round to face Seth.

'Let me ask you what you know about the vortex.'

Seth stood for a moment, considering. 'Well – I suppose it's a kind of wormhole? A short-cut through space-time?'

Zackary nodded imperceptibly. 'But once you travel through it to the corporeal world, you return to your human state: your cells become vulnerable. They age and die as rapidly as they would have when you lived in Londinium. If you are injured and you cannot make it back to the vortex, you will be unable to return here.

'However, and this is interesting, the further you travel from your original time, the greater your strength will be in that world. This could be a particular advantage to you. But be careful, because weaknesses are amplified as well as attributes.

'And I must remind you particularly . . . the flip side of courage is recklessness. You have an impulsive nature, which needs to be tempered.'

Seth clenched and unclenched his fists. He would not let Zackary rile him.

'Sethos, you are very young, so I don't know if I can convey to you the immense and terrible power the vortex represents. Your very knowledge of it has doubled the risks to both worlds.'

'Is that why you wanted me dead?'

'One of several reasons – yes. Knowledge can be a dangerous gift. And knowledge of this magnitude . . .' Zackary shook his head and frowned. 'The vortex is an absolutely unique doorway – if it were to be wrongly accessed, the results would be . . . catastrophic.'

'I swore an oath. I have told no one.'

Zackary nodded slowly and sighed. 'Well then – have you decided where you wish to travel to?'

With all the control and humility he could draw on, Seth braced himself. 'Where do you suggest I go?'

'Finally! The right question,' said Zackary, with a twitch of a smile. 'Hmmm . . . you will need to be somewhere with access to a random study group.'

'Not too random. My target group is aged sixteen to twenty-three.'

'Interesting. And you will require an environment where your youthful appearance doesn't draw too much attention. All right then, we'd better begin. But before I let you loose on an unsuspecting public, you need a little induction into time travel.'

PART III

He passed the flaming bounds of space and time:
The living throne, the sapphire-blaze,
Where angels tremble while they gaze,
He saw; but blasted with excess of light,
Closed his eyes in endless night.

Thomas Gray

45

Displacement

The Christmas holidays were finally over and I was on a train headed back south to St Mag's. I gazed out at the fading light, trying to look forward rather than back.

I'd spent the last two weeks holed up in my room, under a duvet, with a pile of books and my laptop. Of course, the books were all subject-specific (virology) plus I'd managed to hook into the WiFi of the house next door, so I'd sorted myself with unlimited research opportunities.

I'd gone home, expecting my main Christmas preoccupations to be avoiding Ted, and getting on with my research, but I soon found I had a more pressing objective: trying to keep warm. Either my months at St Mag's had turned me soft, or the illness had done something weird to my personal thermostat.

York was definitely a few degrees colder than London and there was a bit of snow around, but the house had central heating, and though it was kind of draughty, the cold had never bothered me before. But I found the only place I could stay without shivering was my bed.

Of course, I would have tried to spend as much time in my room as possible even if there'd been a freak December heatwave – my room was the most fortified, Ted-proof part of the house. But I honestly couldn't sit downstairs for more than ten minutes before my teeth started chattering.

The first couple of days Mum let me bring my duvet downstairs, but Colin couldn't stand the untidiness of the living room with me and a duvet cluttering it up, so I gratefully retired to my room and stayed there. The happy little threesome had grown so used to my absence while I was at school that they found it pretty easy to forget all about me for hours at a time. Which obviously suited me. As long as my door was jammed shut, I found I could actually start to relax. And when they were watching movies, the TV was loud enough for me to take my guitar out and practise.

I had this tune kicking around my head . . . it had been niggling away at me for weeks, but I'd had so much on my mind that I hadn't let it surface. Now with so few other distractions, I'd started paying it a bit more attention. I knew it had to be a melody I'd heard somewhere, though one I couldn't place. But it was a nice tune; sort of haunting, so I decided to jot it down, try to write some lyrics and ask Astrid if she recognized it when I got back to St Mag's. A few days after Christmas, I'd just about nailed it, and was strumming quietly through the final chorus, when I heard Mum outside my room.

'Eva? Can I come in?'

I propped the guitar against the wall, and cautiously unjammed the door.

'Hey,' I said, 'everything OK?'

She hovered for a moment or two, then walked in and perched on the end of my bed. I hugged my knees opposite her, waiting.

She stared out of the window – big flakes of snow were swirling silently across the inky sky. She was frowning, pressing her lips together. I was curious. Mum did not make a habit of popping up to my room. Nor did she do girly chats. She definitely had something on her mind. I waited.

'Eva . . .'

She was going all red. Oh God, what had I done now?

'Mum?'

'Er – Colin and I – are – er . . . well – ahem . . .'

'Colin and you . . . ?'

'Eva . . . Oh . . . I just don't know how to put this . . .'

'Just spit it out, Mum.'

'OK then.' She took a deep breath. 'Eva, I'm pregnant.'

Whoa. I wasn't expecting that one.

'C-congratulations,' I spluttered. What else could I say? 'Er – have you told Ted?'

Her eyes darted nervously towards the door. Clearly not. I wasn't surprised. You didn't need a degree in psychology to guess he would not take it well. I just hoped they would save that little bombshell till I was two hundred miles away.

I was vaguely wondering why she'd decided to mention it to me . . . when all became clear.

'So . . . Colin figured that as you – er – only come back for the holidays now, you wouldn't mind swapping rooms. You're hardly here, and babies take up so much space,' she ended, smiling lamely.

I couldn't think of one word to say. And even if I could have, my mouth wouldn't have cooperated. So I just blinked at my mother, wondering if she had ever, once, put me first.

But I knew the answer. It wasn't that she couldn't put other people first. She'd put my dad first, then Colin and Ted, and now – an embryo . . .

So why – after all these years – did I expect anything else? My room wasn't big, but it was the only place I had. And the junk room (the one I'd be swapping it for) was more of a cell than a room: it barely fitted a bed. Definitely no place to put a guitar. I bit my lip and traced patterns on the duvet with my finger.

'Sure,' I mumbled, picking up the nearest virology book and staring at it until she left.

My hands were shaking, and the more I tried to read the words in front of me, the more my vision blurred. I squeezed my eyes shut, but tears trickled through and plopped messily on to the smooth pages on my lap. I wiped them away furiously, hating myself for being so needy. I was nearly seventeen for God's sake. When was I going to grow up? What lame part of me still held on to the need for my mother to care about me? It was pathetic. I got up, strode to the bathroom, washed my face, and vowed that this would be the last holiday I spent here. It was insane coming back to cringe in a corner. Surely I could get a holiday job and find a place to stay in London?

That thought cheered me up a lot. It actually sustained me through the last few strained days.

And here I was now, watching the miles whizz past the window. The train had just stopped at Stevenage, which meant I'd be clearing the remaining part of the journey in under half an hour.

'Eva?' I jumped as a hand brushed my shoulder.

'Rob!' I smiled.

Rob Wilmer. One of the good guys from St Mag's. Tall, blond, freckly. Had never made a move on me. Nice.

'Is this seat taken?' he asked, squinting at the reserved ticket on the back of the seat opposite me.

'The woman sitting there just got off, so I think you're safe,' I grinned.

He stowed his case and came and sat down.

'You live in Stevenage?' I asked.

'It's my nearest station,' he said.

'So – pretty close to St Mag's?'

'My parents travel a lot. That's why I board.'

I nodded. Small talk was not one of my great talents and I had now officially run out of questions. I picked up my book again to prevent an embarrassing silence. But Rob, it turned out, was a bit more skilful in the conversation department.

'So – how was your Christmas?'

'Could have been worse.'

Marginally.

'I see!' he laughed. 'St Mag's is a welcome escape?'

'You have no idea,' I breathed.

'Are you – er – back to normal now?'

What?

'I mean – you know – recovered. From your illness?'

I nodded. I really didn't want to talk about my health.

'So – looking forward to an action-packed term?'

I smiled. 'Yep. You?'

'Of course! Well . . . how are you finding St Mag's? Living up to expectations?'

'I guess . . .' I said warily.

'Like it?'

'Yeah. A lot better than where I was before.'

Uh-oh. Too much information.

'Where were you before?'

'Nowhere . . . just my local comp . . .'

He raised his eyebrows. 'Care to elaborate?'

'Not much to tell.' I bit my lip.

His eyes narrowed. 'Sure,' he grinned. 'Anyway – I've got far more important questions to ask . . . like, is there a buffet car on this train? *I am starving!*'

I pointed him in the right direction, and pulled out my book again. I was pretty sure we'd be hitting London before he got back.

I was wrong.

'Hope you like muffins. That's about all they had left.'

He was looming over me with two polystyrene cups and a squashy bag. The train jerked and he expertly avoided being thrown on to my lap, but he didn't manage to prevent scalding tea spilling all over his hands.

'Geez, that's hot!' he breathed.

I fumbled in my pockets and managed to find a reasonably clean, slightly shredded tissue, which mopped up most of it.

He sat down and handed me a cup, a pile of sugar sachets and a cake.

'Thanks! How much do I owe you?' I asked.

'Hey – it's the beginning of term. I'm loaded!' he shrugged. 'You can get them next time.'

I glanced at his face, checking for subtext. I made it absolute policy not to accept gifts from boys. But this felt OK. He was nonchalantly breaking off bits of muffin and chewing them, gazing out of the window, totally chilled. I relaxed. Maybe this time it would be all right.

46

New Year

St Magdalene's

January AD 2013

Talk about hitting the ground running. I had just about managed to get my suitcase heaved on to my bed when Astrid swung into my room.

'Happy New Year, babes!' she grinned, handing me a sheet of paper. 'I printed this off for you.'

'The *Hamlet* rehearsal schedule?' I skimmed over it. Pretty full on. But not surprising really, considering how soon we were putting on the show.

'Thanks,' I said, slightly surprised by her efficiency. Then I remembered she was on a mission to try and get *me* more efficient.

'So . . .' she said, pointing to all the evening slots, 'this means rescheduling our band practices. You know we've got a gig Thursday week . . .'

'Uh-huh,' I said, wondering where this was leading.

'Well – luckily, I've managed to book the practice studio for 6.45 every day till then.'

'But, Astrid, you've just shown me the *Hamlet* schedule. We're rehearsing nearly every evening –'

'Exactly!'

Silence. 'Astrid – you *can't* mean . . . Not . . . 6.45 *a.m.*?'

She ducked her head down then and made a dash for the door.

'Astrid . . .' I whined, but she was gone.

It was 8.50 a.m. and we'd been on Astrid's punishing early morning band practice regime for eight days. Eight very long days. I could not get through another morning without coffee, so I was sprinting from the music block across the quad to the dining room, willing it to still be open.

As I skidded past the headmaster's office, I slid to a stop. Running in corridors is strictly forbidden at St Mag's, but it wasn't the school rule that made me stop so suddenly. I could hear Dr Crispin talking to someone. Nothing unusual about that, he had a lot of visitors, but for some inexplicable reason I was suddenly desperate to find out who was in there.

I hovered, weighing up my need for a coffee against this bizarre curiosity. Then I thought I heard the visitor's voice, but my head went all echoey and dizzy, and I realized my need for coffee was extremely urgent. I was just setting off again when Ruby suddenly pushed past me, gave me a hard stare and knocked on the head's door. I stood gaping as she disappeared inside.

47

Collision Path

London

January AD *2013*

Sethos Leontis sat in a red leather chair facing Terence Crispin, the headmaster of St Magdalene's. Although he had been able to answer all the questions Dr Crispin threw at him, Seth knew he didn't actually need any display of intellect. In this twenty-first-century world the power of his natural magnetism had grown exponentially. He didn't often consciously employ it, but it did come in useful from time to time. Like earlier this morning, when he had climbed out of the river, soaking wet and freezing.

He knew that he would die of hypothermia if he didn't get warm quickly, so he simply walked into the nearest café and asked the girl behind the counter for some clothes.

Elena (she wore a name badge) blinked back at him, smiled, and immediately disappeared out through the kitchen, appearing moments later with some jeans, a sweater, a pair of shoes and a parka.

'My ex left in a hurry,' she grinned.

As Seth reached across the counter to take them, she suddenly registered that he was dripping wet. She quickly opened the hatch and led him up a narrow back staircase to her flat, insisting he took a hot shower. He thanked her, promising to return the clothes as soon as he could.

True to his word, he had brought them back a couple of hours later, having retrieved the trunk full of clothes from left luggage that he and Zackary had prepared on their last visit. But she wouldn't have minded if he hadn't. She would have done almost anything for him. The combination of his beauty and the time-amplification of his magnetism made him virtually impossible to resist. This, added to his now extrasensory intuition, meant that he could read people's intentions, and even divert them where necessary.

So now as he sat in the headmaster's office he didn't really have the patience for all the form-filling. He needed to get into the school and at the quantum microscope.

This place was perfect. Seth couldn't quite believe it when Zackary had found it: a school with all the resources of a serious research laboratory, an entire population of his target age group, and up to two years of research time.

He had already met and won over the science staff, but he knew his meeting with the headmaster was the crucial one.

Terence Crispin regarded the strangely compelling boy sitting opposite him, and was on the point of asking him where exactly he came from, when he suddenly found his pen writing answers he had not heard, his head nodding earnestly and his mouth smiling delightedly. What an asset a boy of this quality would be to the school. Within a few minutes, the paperwork was all done. Dr Crispin picked up his phone and called his secretary.

'Marcia, could you rustle up a nice sixth-former to come and look after our new student? Preferably someone who's done this sort of thing before.'

'Of course, headmaster.'

Five minutes later Ruby Garcia, who had way better things to do than show yet another new student around St Mag's, entered Dr Crispin's office.

'Ah, Ruby, how nice to see you! Allow me to introduce Seth Leontis.'

The boy who had been sitting in the red leather chair stood up and turned to face her. He lifted his startling blue eyes and gave her a smile that seemed to erase all previous thought. She found her legs walking quickly, unconsciously, towards him. Her impulse to touch him was so strong that for the first time in her life she initiated a handshake. And as her fingers grasped his, she felt a shiver of such profound delight that she knew with complete certainty that she and Seth Leontis were meant for each other. Her whole existence had been leading to this moment, this boy, and their shared future together. She smiled happily. She was so over Dominic Patel.

48

Electricity

Dr Isaacs let us out a bit late from philosophy, so I had to run across the quad to get to biology in time. God, it was freezing today – my hands were practically blue by the time I got there. I quickly pushed through the heavy glass door into the lab, and looked anxiously towards the front desk. Good. Dr Franklin hadn't arrived yet.

Rob Wilmer was sitting near the front. He turned and waved, gesturing to the empty seat next to him. I smiled. He smiled back, just a bit too enthusiastically. Damn. I liked Rob. Since our little train journey we'd sat on the same table for a couple of lessons and a few meals. He was funny and he made me laugh. Was he about to go and spoil it? I sighed and sat down. I had been really looking forward to this session, and now my stomach twisted anxiously.

The door swung open again. I turned, expecting Dr Franklin.

I was wrong. Someone was hovering by the entrance, uncertain.

'Oh, yeah – the new student – what's his name?' murmured Rob.

'New student – in January?'

I couldn't see him clearly because he was silhouetted against the light, but he somehow looked too tall, too broad-shouldered, to be a St Mag's boy.

It wasn't so long since I'd been that person: new and uncomfortable. I winced. A part of me wanted to jump up and help him cross the excruciating boundary into the class. But there was no way I could risk the attention an action like that would bring me. I had to keep my head down.

I needn't have worried, though. Ruby was right behind him.

'OK, everyone. This is Seth Leontis! Seth – this is biology!' She did a big gesture around the lab. 'Come and sit down!' she said, dragging him proprietorially over to a bench and patting the seat next to her. But before he sat down, Dr Franklin arrived.

'Sorry I'm a bit late, guys. Ah, good – I see you're taking care of our new student, Ruby. Seth's just joined us at St Magdalene's, so please make him welcome.'

Seth smiled back at Dr Franklin, then glanced quickly around at the rest of us.

His eyes stopped and widened when he saw me. My mouth went dry.

I dropped my gaze quickly. For some reason my heart was thumping. Why?

I avoided all eye contact for the rest of the lesson. But I found it abnormally difficult to concentrate on the pathogenic microbes we were looking at.

He reminded me of someone, but I had no idea who. Surely if I'd met him I would have remembered . . . he was definitely memorable: kind of extraordinary eyes . . . deep blue – luminous. And his movements were weirdly graceful given his height. He had none of the awkward stoopiness that most of us had. His face told you he was our age – but he just didn't look like a kid.

I really wanted to look at him again – just to confirm my accuracy (in the interest of science, of course) – but I didn't dare. Instead I tried really hard to think *pathogenic microbes*.

At last the lunch bell went. I was getting all my stuff together and did a quick glance towards the back of the class just in time to see Ruby pushing the new boy out of the door. I felt a little pang of . . . what? No. Absolutely not. No way!

'Come on, Eva – we'll get stuck at the back of the lunch queue.' Rob was standing there, patiently waiting for me. I stuffed my lab coat into my bag, and stood up. We headed off to lunch.

I was just shoving the last forkful of lasagne into my mouth when Louis and George came bounding over.

'Eva – it's nearly 1.30!'

'Well done, boys, you can tell the time.'

'Ha ha! Does the word *rehearsal* ring any bells?'

God – *Hamlet* rehearsal. I swigged my water, stacked my tray, and followed them through to the theatre.

Dr Kidd was up a ladder fixing a light when we got on stage. 'Start warming up, I'll be right down,' he called.

No one was embarrassed about running on the spot, or waving their arms around – stuff that outside drama would be excruciating.

'I don't believe it!' said Dr Kidd. 'Everyone is here. Must be a record! Don't suppose it has anything to do with the fact that we will be performing this show to the whole school next week?'

My stomach flipped over. Aggh! Could I do this?

I had a chance to settle my nerves because the first two scenes he wanted to run were ones I wasn't in, so I sat in the auditorium watching – while my mind wandered.

Who was the mysterious Seth? What was he doing turning up halfway through the syllabus? And more importantly – what was he doing to my inner chi?

'Eva, in your own time . . .'

I surfaced. Back in the theatre . . . Dr Kidd . . . his patience straining.

'Oops, sorry, Dr Kidd –'

'Good of you to join us . . . The *Madness* scene?'

I had been cast as Hamlet's (kind of) girlfriend, Ophelia: just one of the people who goes stark raving mad in the play. I wasn't sure quite how to take that particular casting decision – but I was doing my best to rise to the challenge. Going mad publicly is not easy. Especially with the abandon that Dr Kidd was after. But there was something about Ophelia's madness that I could tune into: maybe it was her powerlessness? She was stuck in a world that she had no control over – I could really identify with that.

I tried not to think about all the other kids watching. It was going to be mortifying. But then it suddenly struck me. Maybe mortifying could be a good thing? Maybe this was just what I needed to help sort out my relationship issues? Because there was *nothing* cool or attractive about going mad on stage. If I did it convincingly enough, boys would definitely start leaving me alone . . . and girls might even start talking to me again.

I resolved to make my madness spectacular.

And, gratifyingly, Dr Kidd was quite pleased with my efforts. 'Good, Eva – you're really beginning to inhabit the role. OK, everyone – the call for tonight's technical rehearsal is 4.30 p.m. DON'T be late.'

We trooped out of the theatre – blinking in the sunlight.

Will (Hamlet) caught up with me as I strode off towards my art history class.

'Er, Eva, d'ya want to just go through our scene at some point before we run it tomorrow?'

My heart sank.

'Which scene?' I asked, knowing full well which one he meant.

'Er – Act three, Scene one,' he said quickly, chewing a nail. What a surprise . . . the *Get thee to a nunnery* scene. The one where he manages to grip me a bit tighter and longer every time we run it. So – my efforts at deranged madness this lunchtime hadn't worked on him yet. I'd either have to try harder . . . or . . . give up drama. I sighed.

He was waiting for an answer.

'Sorry, Will, I don't think I'm going to have time. I've got band practice . . . and I have to get on with – er – Dr Franklin's essay. Hey, we'll be fine. Don't worry.'

I steered quickly away towards art history.

I was a bit late. The room was dark, and Dr Lofts had started on her Cézanne presentation. I quickly felt my way to an empty seat. I hoped I hadn't missed too much. I found his paintings strangely soothing. However transient his subjects – women, fruit, trees – Cézanne managed to give them a kind of timeless permanence. They remained fixed forever, anchored, unchanging.

If only life was like that. If only *my* life was like that. I couldn't rely on anything or anyone being there for any length of time. I took a deep breath, willing Cézanne's world order to permeate my own.

'Lights please, Amit.' Dr Lofts's voice broke through my meditation. I blinked in confusion, suddenly remembering where I was. And as I turned to look around me, I noticed who was sitting beside me. He turned at exactly the same moment and our eyes met again.

He swallowed, and his face twisted into an expression of – what? Pain? Shock? I looked quickly away, stunned. Had my reputation here got so bad that he'd already heard?

And then I remembered Ruby. Of course. He was hanging out with her. What had she said? I really thought she was over the Omar fiasco by now.

I leaned forward on to my elbows, and let my hair fall across my face so for the rest of the lesson I couldn't catch even the smallest glimpse of him next to me. But his presence burned. What was the matter with me? This was not rational. Maybe Ophelia was getting to me . . . maybe I should stop trying to inhabit the role? Maybe I was *actually* going insane? Never did a forty-minute lesson feel so long. When the bell finally went, I didn't look left or right, I just made straight for the door. Once out in the quad I leaned against a wall to regain my equilibrium, and by the time Rob strolled out, I was back to normal.

Maths was fine. Seth wasn't there. I could enjoy my differential equations. Then during the short break before rehearsal, I dashed back to my room to change. As I emerged, Ruby was shutting her door.

'Hey, Eva!' she said.

'Er – hi!'

'Off to a rehearsal?'

'Yep.'

'See you later then.'

Ruby was talking to me? Wow. She hadn't spoken a word to me in months. I was grateful, though. Being avoided all the time is bad for your karma.

I headed off to the theatre. Technical rehearsals were all about entries, exits, lighting, sound and costume cues. Which meant while Dr Kidd was focusing lights I had plenty of time to think about stuff that was bothering me. And I used my time constructively. First I checked I knew all my lines. This was definitely priority number one. Next I read through the biology essay for tomorrow (the one I'd told Will I hadn't written). It was OK. Ready to hand in. I glanced at the stage. They were still trying to sort out the *Ghost* scene. I wouldn't be needed for a while. I rifled through my bag. I could get on with some stochastic differential equations, but they weren't due in till next week. Which left me plenty of time to concentrate on more pressing worries. Like why had I started thinking about the weird new guy *again*? I *really* didn't like distractions. I had to get him out of my head. Which wasn't going to be easy. He shared at least two subjects with me. What if he was doing physics and chemistry as well?

49

Macroshock

St Magdalene's

AD 2013

Six thirty a.m. The alarm hauled me into the new day. I wasn't ready. I'd had a horrible night – filled with nightmares, from which I jolted awake, heart pounding, drenched in sweat. When I tried to remember the details, I couldn't. All I could remember was my own fear.

Now my head was throbbing, my mouth was dry, and the light bulb seemed too bright to be allowed. I dressed, filled my toothmug with water, swilled it down, and then made my weary way to band practice. We ran through the set a couple of times and then stopped in time for assembly. Which I just couldn't face, so I took the inconspicuous route to physics.

I wanted to go over my notes on quantum algorithms. We had a visiting lecturer coming today to talk to us about his theory of quantum logic gates, which was going to be mind-blowing. I needed to get focused.

As it turned out, I was so completely zoned into my notes that I didn't notice people start to arrive. It wasn't until I got whammed by an electric current that I was jolted into the present. And I mean literally jolted. I found myself gasping as I turned to see – guess who – getting into the seat next to mine. His elbow had touched my shoulder as he moved across. I rubbed at my tingling skin in confusion. Ruby was pulling up the chair on his other side. She shot me a look that bore no relation to her friendliness last night.

I turned away from her and tried to make some space between me and electricity boy. I couldn't face another session like art history, so I scanned the room for empty seats. There was one in the front row. I collected my stuff and had just stood up to move, when our teacher Dr Chad strode in with the guest speaker. I sat down again. I took a few deep breaths, and shifted my seat as far from Seth as I could get without actually sitting on Kumal's lap. I put my hands on either side of my head (horse-style blinkers), avoided any possible physical contact, and blocked him out. Somehow I managed to concentrate on physics.

The guest was from a research lab in Queensland. He was exploring and experimenting with the energy spectrum of molecules. Awesome stuff. And when the bell went he proposed a forum for questions afterwards, for anyone who didn't have to rush off for another lesson. Luckily, my Latin tutorial had been cancelled so I had a free. Unluckily, so did Seth. But he kept his distance, and I made sure I avoided all possible eye contact.

It seemed like five minutes later the bell rang again, and this time I did have to go – it was chemistry with Dr Burleigh, and nobody was late for Dr Burleigh.

I packed my books up and hurried quickly across the quad.

I could hear footsteps behind me. I didn't need to turn round to know who it was. I could feel his presence gaining on me.

'Livia, wait!' He reached out his arm and touched my shoulder. Again the electric jolt. I shivered, and turned.

'My name's Ev—' I began, and then I was staring into his incredibly blue eyes and my voice stuck in my throat. I just stood there, frozen.

'Who are you?' I whispered.

'Seth, Seth — wait!' shouted Ruby, running up behind us, stuffing a ring binder into her bag. 'Aren't you coming to history?' Seth's hand dropped from my shoulder. Ruby eyed me dangerously. I looked down at the ground.

'No, I've got chemistry,' he said.

'But I'm sure —' she started, then shook her head. 'No, I must have got that wrong . . . you'd better hurry then — Burleigh is savage about time.'

She headed off, and Seth picked up his pace so we were walking together. I kept my eyes to the ground and hugged my bag of books to my chest. Something about the way he'd looked at me had triggered something . . . a memory? A dream? But I couldn't place it.

I can honestly say I cannot remember what happened in chemistry. Something had short-circuited in my brain and I couldn't focus. Seth was sitting behind me and — again — it was like he was radiating something, some sort of powerful magnetic energy. Which took all my concentration to resist.

You can't spend a whole lesson resisting magnetic energy and making sense of the adiabatic process. Just not possible. And then, although I had a Seth-free afternoon, my mind kept drifting back to him, so by the end of the day I decided I had to visit the senior tutor and sort out a timetable change. I could not be in classes with this boy. He was messing with my mind.

I had nearly reached the staffroom when I heard a shout behind me. 'Eva! Wrong direction!'

I turned. Astrid was striding across the quad towards the music block. I looked at my watch. Nearly 4.30. We had a final band practice for the gig tonight. Our first gig in ages. In fact the first since my hospital debacle. I did an about-turn, and caught up. I'd have to do my best to sort out something before school tomorrow.

We were trying out my new song tonight. I had finally plucked up the courage to play it to Astrid on Tuesday.

'God, Eva!' Astrid had shaken her head.

I knew it. She was going to savage it. I was stupid to play it to her – I couldn't write songs.

'Rubbish, isn't it?' I sighed, putting the guitar down.

'No, Eva. It isn't. I didn't know you even had . . . those kinds of feelings. Anyone I know?'

I laughed. 'No one I know. Sadly.'

All I did know was that for some reason I had agreed to sing it tonight.

50

Lost

St Magdalene's

AD 2013

Sitting through a chemistry lesson, with *her* just a touch away, had been almost more than Seth could bear. It felt like some sort of malevolent god's idea of a joke. To have stumbled on her here, the girl he had loved so completely and lost so agonizingly, after all that time searching, only to find that she had somehow become inaccessible . . . no longer his. She had a different name. She didn't know him. He was a total stranger to her. It was unendurable.

When the bell for the end of the lesson sounded, and she'd run from the room without a glance, all he could do was watch her disappear, the sick feeling of loss swamping his growing sense of frustration.

By the end of the day, his mood had deepened from bleak to black. He slowly gathered together his books, wondering whether there was any point trying to find her. And then that loud, tall blonde girl was suddenly by his side.

'Seth!' she gushed. 'How was your afternoon?'

'Fine,' he muttered, striding towards the door. He had decided that – yes – he would try and find her.

'Seth, wait! You must come and have tea.'

The blonde had somehow got hold of him again.

'Tea?' he repeated.

'Come on!' she said, hauling him across the quad towards the dining room. He scanned the quad for Livia, but there was no sign of her. Maybe she was in the dining room? He allowed himself to be dragged towards it. There were loads of people in there, all queuing for drinks. His eyes searched the room.

Ruby was pulling him towards the counter. He suddenly realized how irritated she was making him.

'Look, I'm not thirsty,' he said and strode out.

Ruby gazed impotently after him. Should she follow? She felt an overwhelming compulsion to: she wanted him so much – even when he was striding in the opposite direction. Her feet started spontaneously following when she heard a shout behind her.

'Hey, Rubes.' Harry was waving her over to his table. 'Bring your tea and come and sit with us!'

She wavered for a moment, and then decided it had to be the cooler option. She got herself a cup of tea and a bun, and sat down.

But they were all talking about the damned play. *Hamlet.* Which for some idiot reason she hadn't got a part in. Not that she really wanted one, though she would have made a perfect Ophelia. Mia thought so too. So did her father. And he was a high court judge, for God's sake. Dr Kidd clearly didn't know that Ophelia was meant to be blonde and willowy. Hadn't he seen the picture on the cover of the book? It could have been a portrait of her. And who had got the stupid role? Er – Eva, of course. It was always sodding Eva.

'Are you?'

Harry was staring at her. He was obviously waiting for an answer.

'Am I what, Harry?'

'Are you coming to the gig tonight? In the common room?'

'Oh – I dunno . . .'

'But you've gotta come. We're all going to be there, after the *Hamlet* rehearsal. I'm taking Seth along – you know, the new guy. He's in the room next to mine. He's so cool. And man – he's so fit! I walked in there, this morning, to check he knew where to get breakfast, and he had just got out the shower. The room was pretty dark, but even so you could see he had these – like – immense muscles! Totally awesome! Anyway, I promised the Crisp that I'd – you know – look after him.'

'But Crispin asked *me* to look after him!' gasped Ruby.

'Sounds like he can look after himself!' snorted Jack.

'I wouldn't want to mess with him, that's for sure! So – you coming later, Rubes?'

'Right. Well, yeah. I might come along. At nine, is it?'

Ruby finished her tea and headed for her room. She would go to the gig, and she was going to spend the next four hours making sure that Seth Leontis wasn't interested in looking at anything or anyone else.

While Ruby face-masked, deep-conditioned and waxed, Seth was running: his default activity. Harry had shown him the school playing fields at break, and he had known they would be his lifeline in this strange world.

As he ran, he tried to clear his mind. He had come here to

do his research. He must not be derailed by a girl who wasn't, definitely wasn't, the love of his life. Livia was dead.

So how could this girl, this Eva, look so completely like her? And why was it that every girl in the school seemed interested in him except her? Even as a gladiator slave, Seth had never actually experienced an unresponsive woman. He didn't recognize the feeling of rejection that he was wrestling with.

Maybe he should just go back to Parallon. This was proving to be a very bad idea. How could he do his research if he was this distracted?

Yes. He should leave before he got any more obsessed. Find another lab. Another time.

But. But. He didn't want to. He wanted to be near her. He needed to be.

He felt so alone, so bleak, that he suddenly missed Matthias; though he wouldn't be able to discuss this with him – Matt had no idea he was here. Zackary had made him swear. However long his research was going to take, he planned to be no more than a few minutes away from Parallon. Matt would never know – if Seth didn't cave now. And anyway he and Matt had made a pact. Seth had agreed never to mention Livia's name again.

Seth thought briefly about confiding in Zackary. Very briefly. He knew Zackary would be anything but sympathetic. He would be furious. First, because Seth hadn't managed to stay more than two days in London without revealing himself to be emotionally unstable: wasn't he always lecturing him about detachment? And second, because he would have wasted Zackary's valuable time and effort in a totally failed research project.

Seth ran on and on until the pure physical rhythm of his heart, breath and pounding feet soothed the tangled chaos of his thoughts. Four hours later he returned to his room soaked in sweat, but calmer.

51

Shadow

Seth might not have been quite so calm if he had known that Matthias was not actually in Parallon. In fact Matt was in London as well – no more than two miles away, curled up on a soft but slightly lumpy sofa with Elena, the girl from the café who had lent Seth the clothes.

Matthias wasn't stupid. And lately he had been getting just a little bit suspicious of Seth's activities. Or lack of them. Seth was not a man to hang around the villa looking exhausted. He had a daily rigorous routine – running at dawn, followed by an afternoon of training – whatever other enticements or distractions Matthias tempted him with. In fact Seth had been so reliable in his activities for so long that this new pattern was definitely noteworthy. So Matthias had been concerned. He hadn't wanted Seth sinking back into that gloom it had taken him so long to get rid of.

Despite the number of other people and distractions in Matthias's life, Seth still came first. Matt liked Georgia, and he was also quite interested in Clare since it looked as though Seth clearly wasn't. In fact as far as girls were concerned, Matthias was generally interested. Ardent, even. If a girl showed a glimmer of interest in him, he was quick to respond. He didn't really understand why Georgia got angry when he spent the evening with Clare, or Hannah, or Becca. He didn't see it as disloyalty at all. They had all the time in the world with no constraints. Why not enjoy it?

Matthias had always liked girls – in the purely physical sense. But he'd never want to fall in love with any of them. And he certainly didn't think much of marriage. Even in Londinium, his dreams for freedom weren't about ownership of land, or liberty to take a wife. They were about freedom to do what he wanted. And now, in Parallon, he could do absolutely what he wanted. And he was determined to enjoy it. Why hadn't Seth been able to see it that way? Why was he always on some sort of mission?

But Seth was the only person who really mattered to Matthias. The only one he actually loved.

So what had been going on with him? Matt knew that there was something Seth wasn't telling him. And he became determined to find out what it was.

So at dawn one morning, he had followed Seth out of the villa. Seth was wearing his running vest and shorts. There was no way he would have been able to follow on foot; Seth ran like the wind. For a second Matthias had felt defeated, until he remembered Georgia's Ford Anglia, parked in the driveway. Fortunately, she had taught him to drive it, though until that moment he hadn't really seen the point. Matthias picked up the keys from the table by the front door, and jumped in. Seth had been still just about visible so, keeping a safe distance, Matthias had started up the engine and shadowed him. Seth ran straight to the river.

Matthias saw a tall lean man waiting for him. They talked

for a couple of moments and then walked out on to the river-bank. Matthias parked the car on the other side of the bridge, and got out as quietly as possible. Then he crept along the bank towards them. He saw them standing at the edge of the river one minute, and the next, they had disappeared. He darted along to the place they had been standing and looked down into the river. No sign of them. He felt an anxious twist in his gut. Was Seth suicidal again? He was on the verge of jumping in himself when suddenly he saw the two men bobbing on the surface. He had ducked behind a pile of barrels, and watched as they hauled themselves on to the riverbank, shaking water everywhere.

Then Matthias had frowned. They were wearing completely different clothes.

The two of them disappeared into a tall building, and about ten minutes later Seth had emerged again, wearing a dry set of running clothes – shorts and a vest top. Matthias didn't bother shadowing him this time. He was pretty sure where Seth would be heading. Home.

He had got there a few minutes before Seth.

'Coffee?' he'd asked nonchalantly as Seth wandered into the kitchen.

Seth had done his best to conceal his surprise at seeing Matthias up so early.

'Yes, thanks,' he said, throwing himself down on a chair.

'Where did you go?' asked Matt as casually as he could.

'Usual,' said Seth noncommittally.

Matthias nodded. Clearly, Seth wasn't going to tell.

The next morning, he was already in the Ford Anglia by the time Seth had emerged in his running gear. Matt repeated the same sequence of actions – only this time, when Seth and the stranger jumped in the river, he jumped in a moment later. He'd wished he hadn't as soon as he felt the ghastly power of the vortex, pulling him violently downwards.

Just one terrified thought had sustained him throughout the ordeal: he mustn't lose Sethos.

52

Warning

St Magdalene's

AD 2013

Our final band practice went well. I just had time to dash back to my room for a quick shower and change of clothes, before heading off to the common room for sound-check. I debated passing by the dining room and grabbing something to eat, but decided a shower was the priority. I was on the point of stepping under the jet when there was a knock on the door. Damn. I thought about ignoring it, but it was probably Rose Marley. She did these random checks on me. I couldn't *not* answer, or she'd go and get one of the security guys to use his master key. So I turned off the shower, wrapped myself in a towel and opened the door.

Mistake.

It wasn't Rose; it was Ruby. Yes – the Ruby who hadn't visited my room since the day she caught Omar trying to kiss me.

'Eva, I need to talk to you.'

'Sure, Ruby,' I answered, frowning.

She threw herself down on my bed. I stood where I was, right by the open door, in nothing but a towel. Something about her expression made me feel I might be looking for a quick escape.

'Seth Leontis,' she said finally.

God, she was doing a good line in cryptic conversation.

'Yeah?'

'So what's going on, Eva?'

'What?'

'Don't give me that innocent look! What's going on between you and Seth?'

'N-n-nothing, Ruby –'

'Yeah – like I'm going to believe that! I've seen the way he looks at you.'

'Ruby – he's been at the school for five minutes. He's not looking at me any differently from anyone else. We've probably exchanged three words . . . And that was only because he thought I was someone else.'

She looked suddenly relieved. But she didn't smile. 'OK . . . Well, just keep it that way.'

'So – are you two going out together then?'

'We will be . . . If you don't get in the way.'

'I'm not putting myself in anyone's way, Ruby,' I protested. '. . . I never have,' I added quietly.

I probably shouldn't have.

'Yeah! Right!' she spat, jumping off the bed, pushing past me, and slamming the door behind her.

53

Scars

'Man! How many showers do you take in a day?'

Harry was banging on the glass of the cubicle. Seth took a moment to surface. He had gone into one of his pre-arena meditative states, and he felt disorientated when he opened his eyes. Where was he?

'Seth? Are you coming? The gig will be starting in ten minutes.'

Gig? Oh, yes. He'd agreed to attend it tonight. The boy, Harry, had been so insistent.

Seth stepped out of the shower and grabbed a towel. He heard Harry gasp.

'What's wrong?'

'H-how did you get all those scars, man?'

Seth froze for a moment. His scars had been part of him for so long that he was unaware of them. Especially since they now gave him no trouble. He glanced down and shrugged.

'Fighting,' he said simply.

Harry's eyes widened and he whistled softly through his teeth. He sat on Seth's bed, trying not to watch as Seth unself-consciously dried himself and put on some clothes. A few minutes later they were crossing the quad along with most of the rest of the upper school, and by the time they had squeezed their way into the common room the band was tuning up.

Almost as soon as Seth had made it through the door, he felt himself being grabbed from behind. Anyone who knew Seth in Londinium would have known better. His reflexes were danger-ously sharp and his survival instinct was so acute that it was always his first impulse. His hand shot out and threw his assail-ant across the room.

Fortunately, it was so crowded that the assailant (Ruby) didn't actually hit the ground. She just crashed into a load of Year Tens.

'Hey, Ruby! What happened to you?' said Harry as he helped her to a less horizontal position. 'Did you trip?'

Ruby was rubbing her arm. What did just happen? Surely Seth hadn't just swatted her away? She gazed at him in shock. He was looking at her in bewilderment, and encouraged by his obvious lack of hostility, she began making her way back to him. But then the band started their first song and Seth's eyes darted instantly towards the stage.

He had spent the last four hours realigning his emotional climate, and within a split second he was back in the claws of torment. There she was, his own personal demon-angel, singing . . . singing a tune he knew. One that had soothed his nightmares during the shadowy delirious weeks he had spent on that couch in the Natalis villa. He found himself moving through the crowd so that he was nearer the small stage, his eyes continuously fixed on her face. She sang with her eyes closed. She didn't need to look at her hands as they played the chords: the guitar was like an extension of her. Then suddenly the driving rhythms fell away. All the instruments dropped out of the song, and it was just her voice, whispering the notes with a heartbreakingly pure sweetness. She held the microphone as though it were her lifeline: her only friend. The crowd was completely transfixed. Then as the melody ended and the guitars and the drums steamed back in, she opened her eyes, and they met his.

54

Fracture

St Magdalene's

AD 2013

Why did I agree to start the set with my new song? What was I thinking?

Astrid said it would make me less nervous if I got it over and done with. And because she was usually right about stuff like that, I didn't argue. And it was going OK . . . In fact I was really there, inside the music; inside the place where the song had sprung from, when suddenly I opened my eyes and he was right in front of me. And in that instant I knew that the song was about him. For him.

But I'd written it before I'd even set eyes on Seth. Damn. Damn. Damn. What was going on in my head? I was genuinely going crazy. And here I was, on stage, in the middle of a song, completely distracted by this boy who was standing there looking straight at me. A boy I am pretty sure I had been dreaming about.

God. Oh God. Now I couldn't remember the words I was supposed to be singing. Luckily, my hands just kept playing the chorus chords, while I tried to get myself together. Poor Astrid was repeating the bass riff in the hope that I would at some point find my way back to the song and move on to the final verse, while Sadie valiantly kept the rhythm going. How could I let them down like this? I forced myself to take a deep breath, and turned my back on the mesmerizing boy. Astrid rolled her eyes and flicked me one of her long-suffering grins, and casually broke the spell. I started singing again. I got through the final verse by keeping my eyes off the audience. Then for some incomprehensible reason, when I finished the song, the applause was immense. Surely they noticed what a complete mess I'd made of it?

But somehow the applause gave me the strength to get through the rest of the set. That – and keeping my eyes shut or focused firmly on my guitar pedals. I could not afford to catch sight of that boy again.

When it was all over, I managed to continue keeping my head down, by dealing with all the gear. I was just coiling the last cable when I felt a jolt go through my whole body. I gasped and thought I was going to pass out. I leaned against the wall, panting, wondering what possible scientific explanation there could be for power to generate from a coil of disconnected cable, when I realized that he was standing next to me, looking horrified.

'Seth?' I croaked.

I was feeling so dizzy, I slid down to the floor and leaned my head on my knees.

He sat down next to me. 'Livia, what just happened?' he whispered. 'Are you all right?'

His voice. What was it about his voice?

I stared at him for a second, probably looking like a complete idiot, then tried to remember what he'd just said. I shook my head.

'Don't know . . . Shock of some sort. I'll be OK in a minute.'

'Look, Livia –'

'Seth . . .' Every time I said his name it felt like he belonged to me a little bit more. Which I liked. Quite a lot. Trouble was, Ruby had already claimed him, and he was only interested in me because he thought I was someone else. I suppose I had to put him out of his misery.

'Seth, my name – it's Eva.'

He nodded. But he looked like he didn't believe me. He just kept staring at me.

'It is you . . . I know it's you,' he whispered. 'That song – why did you choose that song . . .'

I looked at him, stared into his eyes, and felt this weird connection.

'I – er – didn't choose it. I . . . wrote it.'

Or did I? The tune had been drifting around my subconscious for weeks. Had I invented it, or had I heard it somewhere?

'That was the song that carried me back . . . when I was lost . . .' His voice cracked as he spoke. I glanced up at his face and the bewildered expression I read there made me want to reach out and comfort him. Before my brain had caught up with that instinct, my fingers were touching his face. The heat, the sheer physical power of the contact took my breath away for a moment, but it wasn't until his hand folded over mine that the dizzying faintness overwhelmed me once more. I leaned against the wall, panting. I had to shut my eyes until the room settled back down. This was so embarrassing. When

I opened my eyes again, he was looking at me so anxiously that it made me smile.

'Sorry, Seth, I've been ill. It's cool, I'll be fine in a –'

He was close. So close. I could practically taste his breath. I inhaled deeply . . . as though I could drink him into my lungs. I wanted . . . I wanted to . . . I wanted to melt into him . . . lose myself there.

'Seth?' I breathed, touching his face again. And again . . . the heat . . . the dizziness. I dropped my hand and leaned my head back, shutting my eyes. What was the matter with me? Now was so not the time to have a damned relapse. I forced my eyes open and he was staring at me with such intensity . . . such frustration.

'I'm sorry, Seth,' I whispered, 'I'm not usually –'

'Livia – please . . . please remember,' he urged, his voice choking with emotion.

I closed my eyes again, something brushing against my consciousness. His voice . . . reminding me of something . . . somewhere . . .

'Seth! Where have you been? I've been looking everywhere.' Ruby was suddenly charging over. When she got close enough to spot me on the floor on his other side, she couldn't have looked more livid.

'Eva,' she spat, 'haven't you got to be somewhere? Sign some autographs? Pick up your Brit Award?'

Whoa! Caustic. I blinked up at her, wondering in what universe I had ever thought she was my best friend. I was used to dealing with a certain level of hostility, but it still really hurt coming from her. She was looking down at me with undisguised loathing. Her face was positively distorted by it.

I had to get the hell out of here. I took a deep breath to steady myself. Although I still felt pretty dizzy and could have done with a couple more minutes sitting propped up against the wall, I pushed away from the floor with my hands and tried to get myself vertical.

'Come on, Seth,' said Ruby. 'Mia's having a little gathering in her room – Jack's smuggled in some wine . . . we've only got twenty minutes before curfew.'

She was dragging him away. I sighed. At least that meant I could sink back down to the floor, which is really where I needed to be right now. I put my head back down on my knees and shut my eyes. But a moment later they snapped open.

'You go to the party, Ruby, I'm staying here for a while.' Seth was still here.

'With her?' choked Ruby.

'Yes.'

'Can't you tell she's just faking? She was fine on stage, everyone looking at her. Did you spot that? Now suddenly you arrive, and she's too weak to get off the floor. Perleeeease!'

'Ruby –' I began, but she was just getting into her stride.

'Is it some kind of game with you, Eva? Taking other girls' boyfriends? Some sort of power trip? You don't really want these boys. You just want to take them away from everyone else. As if you don't already have everything! Brains. Beauty. Talent. Why can't you just leave something for someone else? How can you get a kick out of messing with other people's happiness?'

As if this scene wasn't horrible enough, Ruby's voice was so loud it had attracted the handful of people still milling around the common room. Including Astrid, who made her way over.

'Hey, Eva? What's going on?'

'Nothing, Astrid,' I sighed.

'Nothing, Astrid!' mimicked Ruby. 'Little invalid girl here has just pulled one of her *damsel-in-distress* routines for Seth.'

'What damsel-in-distress routines?' hissed Astrid dangerously.

'"Oooh, I'm too sick for school, but OK to be in *Hamlet*, or in a band . . ."'

'Ruby – you've got it so wrong! I don't know what –'

'Oh, save it for someone who believes you!'

By this time Rob had joined the fray. 'So, Ruby, you're saying that Eva was just faking it when she ended up in hospital? Because I was there, in art history, the day she collapsed. The paramedics took an hour trying to get her stable enough to make the ten-minute ambulance ride to hospital. Were they faking it too?'

'God, she's got to you too, hasn't she, Rob? She's like a bloody siren. She reels you in. Then she'll spit you out.'

'I seem to remember it was you who spat Eva out, wasn't it, Ruby?' said Astrid quietly.

'After she *stole my boyfriend*! It's her speciality. Haven't you noticed?' shouted Ruby, storming out of the common room.

There was a long silence while everyone tried to pretend they weren't all standing around the evil-siren-intent-on-stealing-and-spitting-people-out.

I put my head back down on my knees and prayed for them to just go away and leave me alone.

'Hey, Eva. Are you OK?' Rob squeezed himself in front of Seth and squatted down on the floor next to me.

'Yeah,' I sighed.

'You were great tonight. Really great,' he said.

'Thanks,' I smiled.

'Come on, Eva,' said Astrid. 'Time for the invalid siren witch to get to bed! Rob, can you help me get her back to her room? She's having one of her fragile turns.'

As they hauled me to my feet, I kept my face down and avoided all eye contact. I couldn't bear to look at anyone, especially Seth.

'Thanks so much, guys,' I breathed as they supported me back to my room. I curled up on my bed.

'Night, Eva,' laughed Astrid, clicking off the light.

55

Truth

St Magdalene's

AD 2013

Huh! All right for Astrid to find the whole thing funny. I was dying here. I shut my eyes, longing for oblivion. I did *not* want to think about the catastrophe of an evening I had just been the centre of. But of course, when you *don't* want to think about something, it's the only thing that keeps bobbing around your head, taunting you, daring you to touch it. And because I had the sort of brain that could recall exact information, I remembered every single detail. Every savage word. Did Ruby really think I was such a totally manipulative witch? Did she really think I had everything?

I hauled myself out of bed, switched on the light, and looked in the mirror, trying to find any resemblance to the girl Ruby described. I just saw the usual black eyes staring back at me.

No. I really didn't get it. I slumped back down on the bed, remembering the rest of her attack. She had been so venomous. And so public. I tried not to think about all those people who'd witnessed the awful scene. People I had cautiously started to care about.

Of course, there was one particular witness I really could have done without . . . Seth Leontis. I had to admit it . . . I *really* didn't want *him* to think I was an evil siren. So I suppose Ruby was right. This time I actually was interested in her boyfriend. More than interested. Obsessed. And of course I couldn't take him from Ruby. She had got there first, and had unequivocally claimed him. She had also made it pretty clear that she wouldn't be letting go. I had no rights in this situation.

Who was I kidding? There was no *situation* now. Ruby had totally made sure of that. Even if Seth had been remotely interested before – and that was only because he thought I was somebody else – he definitely wouldn't be now.

I tried to shake off my despair. In a way I should be grateful that Ruby had got her strike in so early, before I had the chance to fall any deeper into this hopeless, stupid infatuation. After all, hadn't I known all along that it was only a matter of time before Ruby filled him in on all my failings?

I groaned. I would have to face all these people tomorrow.

56

Dress

St Magdalene's

AD 2013

I must have finally got to sleep because my alarm woke me up the next morning. And I was starving. Damn. Probably because I'd missed supper last night. But did I have the strength to deal with the dining room? I was feeling pretty shaky after last night's little relapse, but from experience I knew skipping breakfast wasn't going to help.

I was still debating the pros and cons when my door burst open. There was only one person who didn't believe in the simple formality of knocking.

'Astrid.'

'How's the patient this morning?' she bellowed.

'The patient's hearing is still intact,' I said, wincing.

'That's good. I wouldn't want you missing your cues tonight.'

'Oh my God! *Hamlet* dress rehearsal!'

'So let's get the evil siren nourished, shall we? Long day ahead.'

'Aw, Astrid – could you grab me something? I just can't face it.'

'Eva! I didn't have you down as a wuss! Now please don't be pathetic – and if the whereabouts of a certain crazy-ass blonde has any bearing on your decision, she's already scoffed down her breakfast and left the dining room, so you're certainly safe for the time being!'

That cheered me up a bit. I sighed, finished dressing and followed Astrid out into the quad. It was another really cold day, so although I was in no hurry to reach the dining room, we had to run or freeze. For Astrid there was no contest.

The dining room was surprisingly full. I think it was because it was so cold outside nobody wanted to leave. As we walked in, the desultory morning babble suddenly faded. The room went quiet. Oh God, why had I come? Ruby had probably made a whole school announcement: 'Beware! Evil Boyfriend Snatcher on the prowl.'

I froze, and clutched the door frame. Could I slip out again before Astrid noticed?

I had just started reversing, when someone shouted, 'Great gig last night!'

Then a boy started singing one of our tunes, with spoon-on-table accompaniment. He was soon joined by a load of other spoons, and some rather hideous backing vocals. Astrid and I just stood there, grinning. When the song was over, the entire dining hall was cheering.

All through breakfast I kept my eyes firmly on my plate unless someone asked me a direct question. Then I focused on not allowing anything to catch my peripheral vision. I managed to get through the whole experience without seeing Seth – so I don't know whether it was simply successful avoidance, or that he wasn't there.

By the end of the morning I had begun to relax. I had double maths, applied maths and philosophy: all subjects that Seth mercifully didn't take.

Dr Isaacs had set up a debate between Will and Sadie, representing Marx and Nietzsche's views on religion. They were arguing so well that the class ran over, so I was late for biology.

I crept quietly into a seat at the back and tried to clear my mind for science. Should have been easy; would have been easy if I hadn't caught sight of Seth sitting in the second row, with Ruby very close beside him. From this position I could watch him without drawing any attention to myself.

He had a stillness that was almost uncanny. My eyes flicked over the backs of everyone else. The room was alive with little fidgety movements: Ruby twined her hair round her fingers, Amit leaned on one hand and then the other, Rob shifted his weight and doodled . . . Seth sat perfectly still and straight. Almost as though he were a sprinter waiting for the sound of the starting pistol. Still but taut. I scanned across the row. His shoulders were almost twice the width of Rob's. His black hair curled down on to his neck in a way that made me want to reach out and smooth it.

I tried to drag my head away from Seth and back towards biology. Dr Franklin had started talking about double-stranded RNA viruses, which clicked my mind back into focus. She was comparing their replication rates with those of a DNA virus. And this instantly triggered one of my insoluble Professor Ambrose questions. I didn't give myself time to hesitate; I just put up my hand.

'Dr Franklin, have you ever encountered a virus that can replicate really quickly – say three hundred times observable motion?'

Dr Franklin frowned. But I was on a roll and ploughed on regardless. 'One that can cause an entire T-cell to – er – evaporate . . . within less than a millisecond?'

Dr Franklin stared at me as though I had finally lost the plot. Then she laughed. 'Eva, it's not like you to confuse science fiction with credible hypothesis. Discounting the speed of replication, no pathogen can cause a cell to disappear. Cells can explode, become consumed, but as you know, matter itself cannot cease to be.'

I narrowed my eyes. She was right. It didn't make sense. I bit my pencil and shook my head. What *had* I seen that day?

I pulled myself back to the present. Dr Franklin was writing a theorem on the whiteboard for us to copy down. I glanced at it, and froze. Seth was not copying from the board – he was staring at me.

But I had to tear my attention away from him because Dr Franklin was talking again.

'If anyone is particularly interested in viral invasion,' she glanced pointedly in my direction, 'this lunchtime I will be preparing some Adenovirus slides for a lecture on *Host Entry and Replication*. Fortunately, the replication rate of this particular virus is clearly discernible!'

Hey, I was used to sarcasm. I could take it. So instead of worrying about feeling humiliated, I was busy making timetable calculations. The *Hamlet* rehearsal was at 1.30, which meant that I had at least forty minutes.

When the bell went, I sprinted to the dining room, grabbed a slice of pizza and headed straight back to the biology lab, hoping Dr Franklin would be working on her slides before she took her lunch break.

But she wasn't there. I sat by the quantum microscope and gazed at it. Of course I was tempted to check out what she had going on under there, but I wasn't going to touch the damn thing until she got back. I had learned my lesson. Instead I nibbled on my slice of pizza, and waited.

Suddenly I sensed someone else in the room behind me. I knew who it was instantly. I could feel the heat of his presence all the way down my spine.

So I knew better than to turn round. But when I felt him lightly touch my shoulder, the heat travelled through me like electricity. Not strong enough to send me spinning, but strong enough to raise my heart rate.

I turned.

'Liv— Eva —'

He was fixing me with his incredible eyes, and for a moment I was transported out of the biology lab – into sunshine . . . and trees . . . I could actually smell grass . . .

I shut my eyes. Something very weird was happening to my head, and it was beginning to really freak me out.

'Eva, Seth!' Dr Franklin came striding through the door, thankfully breaking the spell.

'Well – you two got here quickly! Oh – I see you brought your lunch with you, Eva. Not strictly legal, as you know, but . . .' She shrugged, and started fixing the magnification on the microscope. I moved to the other side of her so that I could do my best to concentrate.

As we watched the progress of the virus, I couldn't help noticing that Seth's biological preoccupations were similar to mine. He was as fascinated by the path and behaviour of the virus as I was. But my heart sank when he asked Dr Franklin if she had any comparative viral slides to demonstrate contrasting replication speeds. I knew he'd just overstepped the mark. Dr Franklin was not a woman who took kindly to being diverted from her agenda. And comparative replication speeds definitely wasn't on it.

To my utter disbelief, though, she nodded and produced *seven* comparative samples. I was still reeling with shock when Seth started quizzing her about the Hep B slide she'd just focused.

'Could the pregenome RNA serve as a template for the viral reverse transcriptase and for production of the DNA genome?'

I blinked, suddenly realizing that Seth Leontis was *very* serious about biology. Even Dr Franklin looked impressed, and scurried away to find a book he should read. As she handed it to him, her wristwatch caught my eye. Oh God – it was 1.45 and I was *really* late for my rehearsal. I apologized and ran.

Dr Kidd was furious, naturally, and kept me back for ten minutes at the end to make sure I understood just how furious, which meant I was then late for art history.

Fortunately, Dr Lofts was still messing around with her PowerPoint cables so I quickly grabbed the empty seat next to Rob and managed to keep my eyes facing the front for the whole triple period. Not once did I look for – or at – Seth Leontis.

Impressive self-control I'd call that.

When Dr Lofts finally wrapped up the lesson, I managed to stop myself glancing around the room by putting an inordinate amount of attention into packing up my bag. But the job didn't quite distract me from the growing awareness that Rob was sitting motionless beside me, his head in his hands.

'Hey, what's up?' I asked.

He sighed dejectedly. 'There's no way I can do the essay. I just don't get the difference between Naturalism and Realism.'

He was looking at me plaintively. If he genuinely didn't have a clue, then he was right – he'd have a nightmare doing the assignment, so I sat down again and unpacked my books.

'Aw, thanks, Eva,' he grinned.

But as I was doing my best to explain the two movements my eyes flicked involuntarily across to the door. I had felt his presence – and sure enough – there stood Seth, waiting for me. I was so torn. There was nothing I wanted more than to skip over and join him, but I knew I couldn't. For so many reasons.

I turned back to Rob, to Naturalism and Realism, and by the time I felt confident that he knew what he was doing, Seth was gone. Of course that had been my intention, but his absence left me feeling strangely hollow.

Rob was happily oblivious. 'Thanks so much, Eva,' he gushed, putting his notebook away. 'You coming for some tea?'

I looked down at my watch. Aghh! I was now officially late for the *Hamlet* dress rehearsal! I ran across the quad to the theatre and arrived panting and sweaty. Astrid, already in costume and make-up, raised her eyebrows and tossed me my dress. I flung it on, dashing into the auditorium just as Dr Kidd was beginning the vocal warm-up. I slipped behind Astrid, hoping that her height would shield my entrance. Thankfully, Dr Kidd was a bit more preoccupied with the intermittent output of the smoke machine than my lateness, so I was spared his sarcastic irritation.

By the time we had done a physical warm-up, the smoke machine was working, and we were good to go. In fact I should have said, 'the smoke machine was good to go', because – as it turned out – the rest of us weren't.

The dress rehearsal could only be described as – awful. We all stumbled on our lines; Laertes completely forgot to come on in the funeral scene; Hamlet lost his dagger and then managed to skip thirty pages; Polonius accidentally pulled the curtain down while he was hiding behind it; and Claudius stepped on Gertrude's train, sending her flying across the stage. Dr Kidd was doing everything in his power to stay civilized, but by the end he looked almost suicidal.

We were treated to a very long speech about responsibility: the show was in our hands. We would be letting each other down if we didn't work as a team, and we were to spend the rest of the night, if necessary, making sure we knew our lines and our cues. I didn't really need to be told. There was no way I could face the humiliation of standing on a stage the next day unless those words were tattooed on my brain. I thought I knew my lines – I think we all did. But nerves seemed to make them disappear. So by the time I put the light out that night I reckon I knew just about everyone's lines.

I prepared for *Hamlet*-style dreams.

I was not disappointed. The night was filled with them.

But the dreams weren't about standing on stage and not knowing my lines. I'd been expecting that. I could have handled that. No . . . I managed to conjure up a whole different order of pre-show nightmares . . . It was like my subconscious was totally *obsessed* with the death scenes.

Hamlet is a play crammed with deaths, so I guess I shouldn't have been totally surprised. But weirdly, you'd think my brain might have been mildly preoccupied with Ophelia's death scene, given that I had to rely on Will and Harry to carry me on stage in the dark without tripping over and dropping me on the floor.

But for some reason, my dreams didn't have much to do with our version of *Hamlet* at all. Instead my warped subconscious had cooked up a total bloodbath, full of daggers and swords and paralysing fear. I was trapped, cornered and bleeding. And then Hamlet was there, leaning over me, calling my name. Only he wasn't calling me Ophelia, he was calling me Livia. And he wasn't played by Will any more. He was played by . . . Seth.

57

Impact

London

AD 2013

The first time Matthias followed Seth out of Parallon into twenty-first-century London, he barely survived the experience. When he surfaced and landed on the concrete riverbank, he was so consumed with the need to follow Seth that he blindly hurled himself through a chaotic stream of traffic, desperate to keep him in sight.

As he ran, he saw, out of the corner of his eye, as though in slow motion, a motorbike roaring to the point on the road his body now occupied. He could hear the brakes screeching, but he was unused to seeing things moving so fast, and couldn't jump out of the way in time. Horrified, he watched the driver fly over the handlebars as the motorbike skidded on to its side, clipping into Matthias as it continued its trajectory. The impact threw him across the tarmac, but as he fell his eyes followed the riderless bike as it continued its inexorable skid until it was ploughing straight into its driver, who was now clumsily staggering in an effort to get clear.

Dazed, Matthias sat up. He was bleeding quite heavily. His collision with the ground had grazed the side of his face, arm, hand and leg. He stared at the gash on his arm, waiting for it to close up and disappear. When it simply continued to bleed, the shocking realization finally dawned. He was a long way from home. And immortality.

What had he done?

He stared at his arm, allowing a part of his brain to observe that the bleeding was slowing. At last the latent physician in him took stock. He examined his hand and leg. Surface cuts and grazes. Nothing serious. He could feel blood on his face, but felt sure the injury was minor. Gingerly, he stood up and stumbled towards the tangled mess of motorbike and man.

He heaved the bike off the driver's body and surveyed the aftermath with dismay. He leaned over the man's torn bloodstained shirt and felt for a heartbeat. There was a faint pulse, but the ugly twist of his body suggested serious spinal damage. Blood was oozing from a head injury into the dome of his helmet, and more urgently a fountain of blood was literally pumping from an artery in his leg. Matthias had seen similar injuries on gladiators, and knew that the man would soon bleed to death unless he could stop it. Oblivious to the people beginning to gather, he ripped apart the denim of the trouser leg and held his own injured hand hard against the pulsing source of blood flow. Using his teeth and his good hand he tore a strip off his own sopping T-shirt and tried to make a tourniquet. He tied the strip tightly round the leg above the wound, and breathed a sigh of relief as the bleeding began to subside. But this small success was fairly irrelevant. He was pretty sure the man was dying: the colour of his skin, the position of the body, the weakness of his pulse . . . And it was Matthias's fault. He had never been directly responsible for another person's death before, and it made him feel sick.

'Has anyone called an ambulance?' he heard someone ask.

He didn't understand the question, so he continued to kneel next to the dying man, protecting him from prying eyes.

Suddenly the man started to shake and pant. His body writhed and sweat poured off him. Matthias watched with a vague sense of déjà vu.

'What's happening to him?' someone gasped.

Matthias knew. He had seen this before: in the Londinium gladiatorial barracks. He was suddenly reliving the impotent torture of watching Seth die of fever.

By the time the biker stopped breathing and was still, Matthias's sense of his own helpless culpability was almost intolerable. He stared down at the man, willing him back to life, willing time to reverse, willing himself back to Parallon where he was safe and could do no more harm. His wretched vigil was interrupted by a high-pitched wailing sound, and he turned his head to see where it was coming from. A large white vehicle with a blue flashing light was trying to get through the slow traffic towards them. The bystanders muttered impatiently.

'About time!'

'It's a disgrace how long it's taken!'

Matthias turned back to the body. He stared. It had changed. Somehow less substantial. He blinked. He wasn't imagining it. The biker was . . . disappearing. And Matthias suddenly understood. Without looking back he started to run.

By the time the ambulance arrived there was no sign of the dead man. Or Matthias. All the paramedics found were a pile of leather, a gaggle of bewildered bystanders and a bike-wreck.

58

Arrival

Matthias ran as fast as he could back towards the river. He didn't look right or left. He was definitely not looking for Seth; he just wanted to return to Parallon as fast as possible.

When he reached the spot he'd emerged from earlier that day, he jumped straight into the water and almost laughed with relief when he felt the powerful pull of the vortex dragging him back.

He embraced the crushing, breath-puncturing strength of the spiralling water, because its agonizing power meant he could surrender himself, his guilt and the awful responsibility that was sitting on his chest. In this all-consuming maelstrom, no feeling had any power except the physical certainty that there was a force much bigger, much stronger and much more powerful than anything he could contain. And this surrender of self freed him. By the time he felt the cocoon of water burst open and his body being released on to the water's surface, his guilt had been washed away. He was feeling nothing but joy, because he knew he was home: the colour, the light and the shimmering beauty of Parallon reached out and welcomed him.

He jumped out of the water and without bothering to dry himself ran straight towards the place where in 2013 he had watched the biker die. The exact replica road shimmered into existence, along with the strange transparent buildings he had noticed on either side of the tarmac. But the patch of road where the biker had been lying was now empty. Matthias stared stupidly at the grey tarmac. He must have got it wrong. He had been so sure the biker would materialize here.

Then he heard a sound that he had heard only once before, earlier today: the sound of a roaring motorbike. He squinted into the sunshine as the biker drove straight towards him. He was about to jump clear when the bike screeched to an abrupt halt. The rider sat for a moment and contemplated Matthias. Then he took off his helmet and dismounted.

'OK, man. I guess you'd better tell me where the hell I am.'

Matthias just grinned, put an arm round him and said, 'Welcome to Parallon, my friend.'

59

Plan

St Magdalene's

AD 2013

Seth was standing in the dining hall with his breakfast tray, scanning the tables for her face. She wasn't here. Had he missed her?

'Seth! Over here, man!' called Harry, who was waving from a half-filled table by the window. Seth absently headed in his direction, glancing across towards the door to check for any new arrivals. As his eyes swept the room, they inadvertently caught those of the tall blonde girl. Ruby. She was sitting with a group of girls at a table near the counter. His eyes flicked quickly away.

But moments after he'd sat down between Harry and Will, he realized with a sinking heart that Ruby had picked up her mug and plate and was coming over.

She plonked herself directly opposite him. 'Morning, Seth,' she sang.

He nodded tightly and his eyes flicked once more to the door. He didn't see the twitch of irritation his indifference provoked.

Seth chewed disconsolately. Was Liv– Eva actively avoiding him? He couldn't reconcile the overpowering emotion he felt when she was near, with the growing certainty that she wanted nothing to do with him.

He looked down at his tray. He didn't have the stomach for breakfast and was about to stand and clear away his plate when his brain suddenly tuned into the conversation. There was a reason, of course. He'd just heard someone mention her name.

'No, that's when I nearly dropped Eva! Oh God, it was a disaster . . .'

'How are we ever going to put on a decent show?'

'Did you manage to learn your lines, Harry?'

'I was up till 2 a.m., trying . . .'

'When's the first night?' asked Ruby.

'Tonight. But *please* don't come. It'll be dire. Wait till the end of the week.'

Ruby laughed and her eyes glinted. 'Don't be silly, Harry. I'm sure it'll be great. Actually, I'd like to come tonight . . . and I'm sure *you* wouldn't want to miss seeing Harry in a show, would you, Seth?'

'Aw, Seth won't want to see me on stage,' said Harry quickly.

'Of course he would, wouldn't you, Seth?' Ruby insisted.

Seth shrugged. 'Yeah, sure.'

'Good!' grinned Ruby. 'I'll pick up the tickets. Starts at 7.30, Harry?'

Harry nodded miserably.

'Meet you at the doors at 7.15 then, Seth.'

Ruby picked up her breakfast things and slipped quickly out before Seth had a chance to change his mind. She walked back to her room, triumphant. She had just manipulated a whole evening with Seth Leontis. A whole evening of terrible theatre, featuring Eva Koretsky. By the end of the show, Seth would definitely be hers.

60

Drama

St Magdalene's

AD 2013

I was standing in the wings of the theatre, furiously wiping my eyes. I had just finished my madness scene, and for some reason it had really got to me. For the first time ever, I totally empathized with Ophelia's sense of loss: her father had been killed, and now Hamlet, the boy she loved but had been forbidden to see (I wonder why that felt so familiar), had turned against her. All through the scene, I kept seeing Seth's face, and suddenly the idea of him turning against me genuinely made me want to scream. I think it was at that point it suddenly dawned on me that my feelings for him had gone dangerously beyond infatuation. And the hopelessness of it all meant that when I ended up breaking down on stage, it wasn't acting any more. Which was why I couldn't stop crying now. And the moment Will came off stage I was going to have to lie as still as a corpse on my tomb, for my funeral scene. Very realistic to have a corpse with tears rolling down her face.

I sniffed and suddenly felt Astrid breathing next to me. She gave me a sharp elbow in the ribs and a wad of tissues. I smiled pathetically, dabbed at my face, and started trying to get myself under control. I had a minute or two: Will was still doing his big Hamlet rant on stage – and remembering all his lines this time, thank God.

I breathed deeply. I could do this.

Then I heard my cue. I brushed my hand across my eyes, collected a couple of stray tears, and took a deep breath.

The blue light came up, and Louis and Harry carried me pretty competently towards the table (tomb), where I'd been directed to lie for the rest of the scene.

Staying totally still at that point was probably the hardest bit of the whole play for me. Because apart from doing my best to suppress the need to twitch, or take a deep breath, or scratch one of a million itches that sprouted everywhere, I had the additional job of shoving down the feeling of total despair.

But I was more or less under control by the time the funeral march began. Harry (playing Laertes, my brother) had just started his grief speech when I heard a groan and a scuffle at the front of the stage. Had someone fallen over? It took every bit of self-restraint I had to keep still. Obviously, I couldn't open my eyes – so I had no idea what was going on. I could just hear a general murmuring from the audience, a door slam and then a sort of silence. A few moments later Harry was stumbling his way through the rest of his lines without a hint of emotion, which I have to admit made my death slightly lacking in tragic weight. Ah, well – I guess I had to be grateful he'd pulled himself together and remembered his lines at all – he'd been pretty shaky yesterday.

When I finally got carried off stage, Astrid cornered me.

'What was that about, Eva?' she hissed.

'Oh, I think he got distracted. He's bound to be better tomorrow,' I whispered back.

'I doubt he'll be coming tomorrow!'

'Oh, come on! He wasn't that bad – just missed a couple of cues and stumbled around the speech a bit –'

'Eva! I'm not talking about Harry! I'm talking about Seth Leontis! It was really weird and a bit scary, the way he ran out just then –'

'Seth?' I went cold.

'Duh!'

'What happened, Astrid?'

'You mean to tell me you *genuinely* had your eyes shut through the whole of that scene?'

'Er – *yes*! I am supposed to be dead!'

'True . . . Well, OK then . . . As soon as the lights went up and we started singing the dirge, Seth – like – stood up – and then he moved towards the stage – like he was going to jump up and grab you! Ruby tried to make him sit down again, but he shook her off – and then a couple of other dudes kind of dragged him out.'

'Oh my God,' I gasped.

'Ruby went chasing after him – and neither of them has come back yet – so I'm guessing they've left. What the hell d'ya think's going on?'

I had no idea what was going on. I was totally confused. And strangely fearful. I had about half an hour backstage before the curtain call and by the end of that half-hour, instead of feeling calmer, I was thoroughly on edge. It didn't help that everyone who came off stage looked at me and said something like,

'What's with you and Seth?' I could only shake my head and shrug.

Then when we were just filing backstage after taking our final curtain, Will (Hamlet) started on me.

'So – is there something going on with you guys then?'

'What are you on about, Will?'

'You and Seth – what's going on?'

'Oh, just drop it, Will!' I hissed, heading for the girls' dressing room.

As soon as I'd changed out of my costume and make-up, I made for the door, but Dr Kidd had other ideas.

'Everyone in the auditorium . . . chop chop.'

Damn.

I shuffled over and sat down.

'Great first night, guys! The audience were loving it – well, most of them,' smirked Dr Kidd, glancing in my direction. I gritted my teeth.

'And great recovery, Harry – I'm sure tomorrow night it will only be Hamlet you're fighting off in the tomb scene' (smirk number two).

'OK, seriously – You all need to go and get a good night's sleep. I'll do notes tomorrow – the call is 4.30. I want to run a couple of the scenes before the show.'

I stood up to make a quick getaway.

'Eva – could you hang on for a sec?'

My heart sank.

The others all filed out, Will more slowly than the rest – he was clearly either hoping to listen in or lie in wait to hassle me some more.

'See you tomorrow, Will,' said Dr Kidd pointedly.

Will skulked out.

'OK, Eva, I just wanted to say well done. Great performance tonight – you were scarily convincing in the mad scene!'

'Thanks,' I mumbled, turning to go. But he was poised to say more. I bit my lip.

'So . . . er – is there anything you want to talk about? Anything you're not quite handling?'

Huh? What was he implying? I felt my jaw twitch with irritation. 'Of course there isn't!' I said fiercely. 'Everything is totally cool. I don't know what happened out there, but it had nothing to do with me. So – if it's OK with you . . . I'm really tired.'

He took the hint and moved aside to let me pass.

'Four thirty tomorrow!' he called after me, scratching his head.

'I'll be there!' I yelled back, breaking into a sprint. I didn't plan to talk to anyone else tonight.

Yeah – like I had any control over my destiny. Guess who was waiting for me outside my room, arms folded across her chest, like a demon from hell.

'Ruby.'

'What have you done to him?' she spat menacingly.

'Who?'

'I'm sorry – didn't I make myself clear?' she hissed.

'About what?' As if I couldn't guess.

'Seth Leontis.'

'Ruby – what did I do? I haven't so much as looked at him since our last little chat.'

'I know what you're capable of, Eva . . . You – you *witch*! Keep away from him. I don't want him looking at you, bumping into you . . . coming anywhere near you. Got it? *Seth Leontis is mine*.'

'What if Seth doesn't happen to fall in with your plans for him?'

What made me say that?

'If you don't stay away from him,' she bellowed, 'I'll make sure your life won't be worth living.'

Hmmm. I had been told.

I slumped down on my bed, trying not to think the inevitable: it was time to move on. I still had no idea what happened tonight, but whatever it was, it was pretty clear to me that my life had got derailed again. Only this time I had everything at stake. I loved St Mag's. The place. The work. My small handful of allies. All the stuff I was interested in, opportunities I couldn't get anywhere else.

And now there was Seth. And that small voice in my head, telling me that I needed him as much as I wanted all the rest.

If I walked out now, I would end up losing the whole lot – St Mag's and Seth.

And if I stayed? One thing was sure. Either way I couldn't have Seth. I could have nothing whatsoever to do with him. I took a deep breath, and bit down hard on my trembling lip. I washed my face, brushed my teeth, and tried to push away the crushing sense of loss.

61

Aftermath

St Magdalene's

AD 2013

'Hey – I thought you were great last night!'

I looked up from my yoghurt, and did my best to twitch a smile back at Rob.

He put his bowl of cereal down and sank into the chair beside me.

'Have you done much acting before?'

'No. I guess madness just comes naturally.' I attempted a hollow laugh.

As he carried on talking about *Hamlet*, my eyes darted nervously around the dining room. No sign of Ruby – or Seth.

We cleared away our trays. Biology was first period. My stomach lurched. I would have to face them both then.

I arrived at the lab early and sat in the front row, so that I wouldn't have to make eye contact with anyone. Rob followed me in and sat down next to me, which, to be honest, was a relief.

I kept my eyes facing forward for the entire lesson, though

annoyingly my concentration was seriously challenged. I lingered at the end until most people had filed out, but I did catch a glimpse of Ruby heading for the door – alone.

At lunchtime I queued at the counter for some vegetable curry, and it didn't take any particular detective skills to spot people nudging each other and pointing at me. I kept my head down. I found an empty corner table, curtained my hair in front of my face and didn't look up. Until the chair next to me scraped out, and Will's tray crashed down in the place next to mine. Then suddenly the whole table was filling up. I stole a quick peek and faced the entire *Hamlet* cast ranged round me.

'Well?' hissed Astrid. She was staring at me expectantly.

I looked back at her blankly. 'What?'

'Where is he?'

'Where is who?' I asked, swallowing hard.

'Seth Leontis, of course!'

'Seth?' I whispered.

'Keep up, Eva,' she groaned. 'He's disappeared! I thought – well, we thought – you'd know what happened.'

I felt the blood drain from my cheeks as I digested this news. 'Do you think he's gone home?' I suggested.

'Nobody seems to know where he is . . . His housemaster's doing his nut, isn't he, Harry?'

'Yeah – he went totally ballistic last night when Seth didn't come back. Called the police and everything. They've been trying to contact his family – in Greece, I think.'

I suddenly tasted blood in my mouth, and realized I had been biting my lip.

I stared frantically towards the door, willing him to walk through it. He didn't.

'Maybe Ruby knows something – she was with him, wasn't she?'

'Ruby's in a total state. She said she never managed to catch up with him – she keeps saying . . . er . . . nah – nothing.'

'Keeps saying what?' I asked sharply. I had a pretty good idea where this was going.

'Well – she just said – "Ask Eva. It's . . . all her fault."'

All my worry and fear suddenly turned to fury. 'She said WHAT?'

Harry wouldn't catch my eye. I stood up, slammed my plate on to the tray and marched it to the service hatch. Then I strode out of the canteen.

Once in the quad, it was my turn to start running. It was either that or smash something. And getting away seemed to be the better option. I could have just run out through the main school gates, sixth-formers were free to come and go at lunchtime, but I didn't trust myself to come back, and I wasn't sure if I was ready yet to make that choice.

Instead I ran blindly through the quad, and then on, past the biology lab. I needed a place to hide out. A place I wasn't likely to bump into Ruby. I glanced wildly around. Students everywhere. Where could I go?

Suddenly I glimpsed Dr Drury leaving the music block. I stepped into the shadows until he'd gone and then darted in. I hadn't booked a room, so strictly speaking I was out of school bounds. Detention if I got caught. Big deal. Someone was practising the clarinet upstairs. I tiptoed to the band room, holding my breath. Sounded quiet. I turned the handle. Relief flooded through me. It was empty.

I moved towards the guitar as though it was a lifeline. I found a stool, nestled into a corner and started to strum. My head was a mess; I needed to log out of my brain. The strumming helped to soothe the cacophony of thoughts, all fighting for supremacy. And the rhythm I strummed did finally begin to impact on the swirling chaos, but not very comfortingly. The strings seemed to be hammering a familiar taunt, 'Useless, Useless, Useless, Useless . . .'

Once I let that word claw through, another stream of annihilating words followed, many supplied helpfully by Ruby. The final sentence that kept repeating itself over and over was *Seth Leontis is mine*. When Ruby had said it, it had felt so wrong. Why?

I knew why. Deep down I had always known. Of course Seth didn't belong to Ruby. Why had I let my fears about stupid school protocol and worry about reputation get in the way of something so obvious? If Seth and Ruby were destined to be together, he would be with her right now. Was that what Seth had been trying to tell me? And now he'd given up.

Which meant he wasn't mine either. He was gone . . .

Where?

Was he OK?

I tried telling myself he'd be back. Nobody walked out of school, never to return.

But I had done exactly that. Twice.

Fear knotted in my stomach and I couldn't swallow the rising panic as I contemplated a future without him.

62

Abyss

Seth jumped into the water before he was really conscious of his actions. It was such a relief to feel the pounding force of the vortex pulling him, pulling him away.

What had he done to deserve such torment? Why was it his fate to watch Livia die over again? As his body submitted to the enormous power that surrounded him, he wished only for oblivion. He had worked so long and so hard for a kind of empty peace, and now his spirit had been torn apart again.

The water spewed him to the surface before he was ready. He didn't want to have to take responsibility for his physical self again. He floated on the water, willing it to enclose him, lose him, wash him clean.

But his arms and legs acted without his consent, and he now found himself on the cool bank of the Parallon Thames. He sat by the water, staring vacantly ahead, scenes he wanted to obliterate playing out in his mind. He no longer cared about Zackary's scorn at his premature return. He no longer cared about the research he had been so obsessed with. He no longer cared about anything. He just blinked into his endless immortality and knew there was nothing he wanted more than for it to end.

He didn't notice the cold. He didn't notice the dark. He didn't notice Matthias emerge from the water nearby, or see the shocked expression on his face. And he hardly felt Matt's arm as it forced him upright, and pulled him away from the river towards home.

Matthias watched over his friend with a growing yet familiar sense of fear. It seemed that Seth had slipped back into that dead pool of misery that he had worked so long to annihilate.

What had happened to stir it up again?

All he'd done was a bit of travelling – nowhere familiar; no possibility of old ghosts triggering buried memories, surely?

Sethos didn't speak to Matthias. He didn't speak to anyone. He slept for two days, and then he ate some olives and started to run. On and on. He ran day after day until the sky changed, blue to pink to velvet-black. By the time his legs found their way home, the stars would be scattering their patterns in the sky.

But he could not run off his pain. He felt slashed and bowed down by it. Suffocated. His breath choked in his throat each night as he returned to his pillared door, wondering vaguely how he had found his way here again.

How had he managed to let the old wound open up? He had worked so hard to cauterize it. And he'd thought he was pretty well healed.

But maybe that was how this second life worked. An inexorable cycle of despair, then numbness, then more despair. He would never be free of it.

Of her.

The name he had avoided confronting for so long now filled his head. Taunting him. Burning him.

Livia.

'Seth, brother?'

Matt touched his shoulder hesitantly. 'Talk to me. What happened?'

Seth just gazed through him, his mind still filled with the images that had precipitated his flight.

'Er – did you find your quantum microscope?' Matt persisted.

Seth turned round slowly. Quantum microscope. One of his original reasons for visiting London. It seemed so long ago . . . But how did Matthias know about it? It had been a secret, between him and Zackary. Curiosity broke through the heavy blanket of his misery. He turned to Matt and stared at him, wondering how much he knew.

'Quantum microscope?' he repeated.

Matt stared back. And then began to speak. 'Your room – it was littered with notes and charts and questions. I – read them.'

Seth nodded.

Encouraged, Matt jumped back in. 'So did you find it? Was the school a good choice for the research? I'd be really keen to hear – because I have begun some interesting research of my own.'

Seth raised his eyebrows. 'What kind of research?'

'Well, when I followed you –'

'Followed me?' whispered Seth.

'To the river. Into the river. To London . . .'

Seth shook his head and managed a half-smile, 'You followed me to London?'

'You and the tall guy. But then I lost you, and I nearly got hit by a massive motorbike, and –'

'I should have known you'd find out. But, Matt, you could

have been killed. We lose our immortality when we go back. And the world you followed me into is so different – I'd had a lot of induction before I made a visit alone. Weren't you terrified?'

'You have no idea,' smiled Matthias. 'But – did you find it – the microscope? I have so many questions.'

'Yes, I did find it.'

'And?'

'And what?'

'Have you found any of the answers?'

Seth shook his head. The last thing on his mind was the microscope. 'No, I have no answers. Only more questions.'

'Questions?'

'There are . . . other questions now.'

'Seth, what questions?'

Seth looked at his friend. Matt had been there for him since the beginning, but could he share this with him? After all, they had made a deal. If Seth spoke of her now, the deal was broken. And it had cost them both so much.

'I – I – can't go back there,' he whispered finally.

'What happened, my friend?' said Matthias

Seth had to risk the truce and speak. 'I saw her,' he breathed at last. 'She was there.'

'Who?' asked Matthias with a sinking heart.

'Who else? L-Livia.'

'But – Seth – that cannot be . . .'

'It cannot be and yet it is.'

Seth shook his head, trying to find coherence. 'I don't understand it, but she was there. Different name, different clothes, different time, but it was Livia . . .'

'Did she know you?'

Seth looked down at his hands. 'Well – no . . .'

Matthias whistled through his teeth. 'Seth – this is all in your head. Livia lives only in your head. And you have to get her out of there. This girl, whoever she was . . .'

'Eva –'

'Oh, Seth, what were you thinking?' Matthias shook his head in disbelief. 'She has a different name. She is a different person. A stranger. A stranger who looks like Livia. Lucky for her, unlucky for you.'

'That isn't all . . .'

'There's more?' sighed Matt.

Seth nodded sadly. 'I was on the point of . . . I don't know . . . trying to find a way to tell her, and then – s-she was – lying d-dead . . . again . . .'

'Seth – you – you – killed her?'

Seth's eyes widened in horror. 'Matthias, what do you believe me capable of? I didn't touch her . . .'

'So what did kill her?'

'No, Matt – it wasn't death, not like – Londinium. It was artifice. A play . . . But when I saw her lying there, so still, I . . .' Seth couldn't find the words to describe his anguish.

Matthias stared at him. Nothing he was saying made any sense. Livia had been dead a long time now. If she had survived, she would be here in Parallon. He, of all people, knew that. And Livia was not here. They had searched and searched, location by location, time and again.

'Seth, man, come inside. Drink some wine. Eat some food. Tomorrow we'll talk again.'

Seth ate some food, and drank some wine. After a dark and

tormented sleep he got up early, dressed and set off for another punishing run. He needed the numbing treadmill of activity. When he finally returned to the villa, he bathed and continued his day in the practice arena, where he fought his invisible foes with the same ferocity that had won him his wreaths.

Matthias didn't dare interrupt.

After seven further days of his solitary savage routine, Seth strode into the kitchen and started cooking. Perhaps cooking would help him to find peace. He didn't much care who would be around to eat his food. The eating wasn't really the point. It was the therapy of blending and stirring that soothed him.

Matthias sauntered over and handed him a glass of wine. Seth smiled, thanked his friend and took a sip. Matthias cleared his throat.

'Seth, is this a good time, or are you going to have to suddenly whisk a turnip?'

Seth shook his head and laughed. 'Matthias, you will never appreciate this art. So, tell me what ails you?'

'Absolutely nothing ails *me*! Huh! But there are some things I need to talk to you about . . . There have been some exciting developments since you left.'

'How long have I been gone?'

'Er – well, long enough . . .'

'Long enough for what?'

'Can you leave that sauce to fend for itself?'

Seth's eyes narrowed as he turned out the flame under the pan, and followed Matthias out of the kitchen.

Matt led him into the living room. It was filled with people. Seth looked around, surprised. He hadn't heard them arrive. They were lolling on sofas, some reading, a few playing board games, some sprawled on the floor watching TV, others crowded round a laptop: a very twenty-first-century scene, a world away from the room it had been when Matthias first brought Seth here. There was no longer any remnant of the cool, quiet and empty Roman room, with its marble floor and pale plastered walls.

The scene he contemplated vaguely reminded Seth of a common room evening at St Magdalene's. He instantly tried to drive the recollection away as it made his gut twist, but the connection had been made, and he couldn't let it go. What was it about the picture in front of him that didn't quite make sense? Why did it remind him of St Mag's?

'Strange-looking party,' he murmured, squinting in confusion.

Matthias cleared his throat. 'Seth, it isn't exactly a party. All these people – er – sort of live here.'

That was it. That was why they looked so comfortable. So *at home*. They *were* at home. Seth frowned at Matthias. They had categorically agreed that their household was already big enough.

Matthias was looking uncomfortable, and Seth started to feel uneasy.

'Matt, what's going on?'

'Well, the thing is, Seth – I had to bring them back here with me . . . because I – er – led them here.'

Seth shook his head, not getting it.

'I brought them to Parallon.'

Seth felt suddenly cold. 'What are you telling me?'

'I've given them immortality!'

'How did you do that, Matt?' asked Seth very quietly.

'Well – you worked it out. I read it in your notes. The fever was the key. The blood . . .'

'What exactly did you do, Matthias?'

'Well, the first one was an accident – I was trying to help him, but I must have bled into his wounds and given him the fever that way.'

Matthias paused and licked his dry lips. This explanation wasn't going quite as well as he had rehearsed. He'd had a suspicion Seth wouldn't feel quite the same way as he did about the 'gift'.

'Go on,' said Seth, his voice icy.

'Well, when Winston arrived here – the guy on the motorbike – I suddenly stopped feeling guilty about killing him – because, after all, he wasn't dead!

'And then – when I'd read through everything you'd written, I decided it didn't matter what the damn thing was called or how it worked, I just wanted to test it out. So I went back and . . . tested it.'

'Tested it?'

'Well, I discovered that the quickest way to bring someone here is with blood. The weaker the person is, the quicker our blood works – it can take anything from twenty minutes to six hours.'

'What do you mean – weak?'

'Well – I guess injured . . .'

'Let me get this straight, Matthias. You went to London in order to injure people, and then – kill them?'

'Seth! You are not listening. They *don't die*! They come here. We are not dead. We are immortal. How many times do I have to tell you?'

'We are worse than dead, Matt.' Seth was staring at his friend as though he were a stranger. '*What have you done?*'

338

He'd thought he knew Matt, but he realized they were worlds apart. He shook his head and started moving out of the room. He felt sick. Sickened.

'Seth – it isn't just blood.'

Seth's head shot round. 'What?'

Now Matthias had stalled him, he wasn't quite sure how to tell Seth what else he had discovered. He had thought Seth would find this piece of information less ugly, but now he wasn't so sure . . .

Matthias stared down at his feet, and took a deep breath. 'On my sixth journey, I arrived freezing, and there was a little café really close to the river . . .'

Seth nodded. He had been there.

'Well – I went in, and there was this girl . . .'

'Elena?' guessed Seth.

'YES! How did you know?' breathed Matthias, looking around anxiously. Seth frowned uneasily.

'Anyway – she was so pretty and so nice . . .'

'Go on.'

'So we kind of ended up in her room . . .'

Seth sighed.

'Well, we'd had some wine. She seemed to like me . . . and we just started kissing – you know how it is. Anyway, I ended up staying . . . we both fell asleep . . . It was nice, cosy, until suddenly, I don't know – four or five hours later, I was woken up by her shivering and convulsing . . .'

Matthias stared ahead, reliving the moment. 'I recognized it at once, of course. She had the fever. Within two hours she was gone . . .'

'Don't you mean *dead*, Matthias?' spat Seth.

'No, Seth, I don't. *She wasn't dead!* She had just changed, disappeared, moved on . . . arrived here . . . found immortality. I had given her the . . . gift – without any injury . . .'

Seth had heard enough. Bile rose in his throat as the full impact of Matthias's revelation hit home. Matt had taken this terrible, contagious disease, and was spreading it, knowingly, intentionally and chaotically. He felt utterly sick and completely betrayed. Zackary had been right. Matthias should never have been allowed to find out about the vortex. His stupid philosophy had blinded him, and the vortex had given him the opportunity to wield a terrible, monstrous power.

Seth ran out of the villa and vomited. Then he leaned against the cool stone wall, weeping . . . wracking tears of grief: grief for that room full of dead people – Matthias's dead people . . . and tears of grief for a lost friendship. He had loved Matthias like a brother. But now he couldn't bear to look at him, so disgusted was he by what Matt had done.

Seth sat leaning against the wall, gazing up at the stars, until dawn began to bleed a soft pink wash through the darkness. He stood up and stretched. Time to go. He walked slowly away from the villa, away from his dearest friend, away from his home.

He wandered around Parallon for the rest of the day, oblivious to the balmy summer breeze, the laughing happy people he brushed past, the women who smiled at him, who turned and gazed after him when he passed. He had lost himself again, and he didn't see any way back.

63

Dreams

St Magdalene's

AD 2013

It was now three weeks since Seth had disappeared, and every single morning I woke up with a dead ache of emptiness. It wasn't like anything I'd ever felt before – and given that I'd done my best to sample the full range of negative teenage emotion, this came as a shock.

I tried to reason with myself. I hardly knew him, he definitely wasn't for me, and it was probably better for the whole school karma that he was no longer around. He had stirred things up way too much.

But I couldn't help it. I missed him. So much. Like the centre had dropped out of my world. It was weird and humiliating. How could I have turned into one of those sappy girls who defined themselves by the boy they have fallen for?

To make matters worse I was sleeping really badly. Terrifying nightmares filled with blood and death were making me scared to go to bed. I tried reading till 3 a.m. – anything to avoid facing the dreams – but eventually I wouldn't be able to keep my eyes open, and the nightmares would begin.

One morning I was sitting on the side of my bed, feeling sick and dizzy with tiredness, when the insistent knocking on my door finally seeped through to my fuzzy brain. I staggered over to open it. Rose Marley stood in the corridor.

'Eva, what's wrong?' she said, pushing herself into my room.

'Nothing,' I mumbled.

She just stood there, waiting.

'I'm fine – just not sleeping very well . . .'

She frowned. 'Eva, you're not relapsing, are you?'

I stared at her. Now that she mentioned it, the dizzying fatigue felt quite a lot like a relapse. I'd been having difficulty making it through the school day, and I was literally dragging myself to band practices.

'No. Of course not.'

No way. Anyone would feel like this if they weren't getting more than three hours' horrific sleep every night.

'I'm just not getting much sleep.'

Rose sat down on the bed next to me. 'What's going on, Eva? Is there something troubling you?'

'*Yes!*' I wanted to scream. 'I fell in love with a boy I hardly knew, and he's disappeared off the face of the earth, and every night I swirl around in a horrible dark cloud of terror, filled with menacing shapes and the taste of death. I run, but I can't work out where I am, or who I'm running from . . . It is like I've got a low-res YouTube video endlessly looping through my brain. Does that count as something troubling?'

But of course I didn't say that. I wasn't planning to spend the rest of my life in a straitjacket.

'Everything's fine – just getting nightmares. Probably should give up cheese . . .'

'Would you like something to help you sleep? I've got some nice herbal remedies.'

I thought about that. Was Rose offering me oblivion? 'Thank you,' I whispered. 'That would be great.'

That night I swallowed two of Rose's tablets, and snuggled down under the duvet. An hour later I woke up screaming. The only thing the drugs had succeeded in doing was adding a further dimension to the horror of my nightmares – I was now paralysed and couldn't run. I got up and gulped down a glass of water, then stood leaning against the sink. This wasn't good.

Wearily, I picked up a book, and set out to spend another night trying not to sleep.

64

Ghost

Parallon

Seth didn't know how to find solace, but then he wasn't looking for it. What he wanted most was numbness. His mind screamed for oblivion. It had worked for him before, sustained him for an eternity. But it had taken him a long time to find it. And he'd had Matthias around to help.

He refused to allow his mind to return to Matt. The betrayal he felt was so profound it was as though a great dark chasm had gashed the world between them. There was no way across it. So he tried to distract himself by walking endlessly around the ever-changing streets of Parallon. His legs took him first towards Zackary's house, but when he stood at the doorway he knew he couldn't face Zackary. Reluctantly, he turned away. When he next stopped, he found himself outside the Natalis villa. And again – he couldn't bring himself to go in. It felt more like a mirage than ever: a pitiful manifestation of his inability to let go. So he turned and wandered on.

He was shocked by the extent Parallon now resembled the London he had just left. A part of him longed for the serene empty streets he had encountered when he first arrived, when there were so few others.

He walked on and on without purpose until finally at dusk he found himself on a familiar street, gazing up at a familiar arch. Only the arch he gazed at this time was shimmering – throwing sparkling spectral colours into the sky.

He walked through it and found himself in the glimmering quad of St Magdalene's. It felt uncharacteristically empty. Silently, he moved across to the biology lab. He flicked on the light. Everything was as it should be. There was even the quantum microscope. But the benches were empty; the desks clear. He turned off the light and gently shut the door. He wandered over to the dining hall: food on the counter – nobody to eat it. Then he made his way to his boarding house, Charles Darwin. It looked exactly as it was meant to. When he pushed open the deep-blue painted front door, he listened out for the usual creak, and laughed mirthlessly when he heard it. Shutting the door quietly behind him, he padded along the corridor to his room. Naturally, it was an exact replica of the room he'd left behind in London. It was, after all, his own creation. He sat on his bed and put his head in his hands.

What was he doing here? Why was he torturing himself? He couldn't be in this room and not think of her. As soon as he sat down, his mind was flooded with images of Eva. Exactly as it would have been had he been sitting on the original bed in the original room in the original St Magdalene's in London. He imagined her in her room, reading, sleeping, showering. He saw her in the biology lab, curious, engaged. He smiled when he saw her on stage with her guitar, singing. And then his treacherous brain recalled the image of her lying on a tomb, perfectly still. As still as she, his Livia, had been on that dark night in Londinium . . .

He shuddered as the pain of the memory blasted through his body.

But then as he sat sobbing his grief into the empty space, another image of her flickered across his brain: Eva sitting beside him on the floor of the common room, looking at him with her beautiful almond eyes . . . not just looking at him . . . searching his face. He replayed the memory over and over, not trusting it, not daring to believe in it. She clearly didn't know him, and yet . . . he had seen something there that he had not dared interpret. Was it recognition?

He stood up. Walked to the door; walked back to the bed. Paced. Indecision was not something he was familiar with . . . but now he felt paralysed by it.

He had run from London – why? Because he had seen the ghost of Livia lying dead again. But she wasn't dead. Not any more. Not yet. His mind spun in confusion. He didn't understand time. He didn't understand death. He didn't understand why Livia was called Eva or who Livia was. All he knew was that he had loved Livia, would always love her, and he had just . . . run away from her. Sethos Leontis, the fearless gladiator, had run away from a phantom.

He cursed himself, and started running . . . out into the courtyard, into the night, towards the river.

65

Decline

St Magdalene's

AD 2013

I trudged through the quad to the biology lab. I felt so weary, so bleak, so alone. Then I sensed Rob's hand on my shoulder. Sweet Rob, always trying to make things better.

'Hey.' I forced my lips to smile.

'Eva – you look terrible. What's wrong?'

How could I tell him?

'Dunno. Just tired,' I sighed, as he opened the lab door and pushed me through. The warm rush of air was comforting, and I slid gratefully on to a bench at the back. I didn't dare sit at the front any more because I wasn't sure how reliably I could stay awake.

Dr Franklin arrived a couple of minutes after us, and strode to the front of the room. When she announced our new area of study, I felt suddenly elated: DNA methylation. We had been looking at DNA epigenetics, so this sounded like a cool tangent to be following. If only I could stop myself falling asleep. But within seconds I was drifting in and out of the lesson, cursing

347

my stupid dreams, and vaguely wondering whether I needed some sort of psychiatric help. Surely all these weeks of nightmares weren't normal?

Dr Franklin's voice had just started drifting away again when I felt myself being gently shaken.

'Wake up, Eva,' Rob was hissing.

I jolted awake, just in time to see Dr Franklin looming in our direction.

Oh God, what did I miss?

But a moment later I was breathing a sigh of relief. She was just heading for the door. I had clearly been too soundly asleep to hear the bell, or her lesson conclusion.

I staggered slowly out, trying to remember blearily where I was supposed to be next.

'You coming, Eva?' Astrid crossed the quad and started hauling me towards the music block.

'God – look at the state of you!' she sighed. 'We'd better keep band practice short tonight.'

I nodded gratefully. I would have pulled out of this rehearsal if I hadn't bailed on the last three. I'd turned into a totally unreliable member. And I didn't even have the energy to feel bad.

When we reached the band room, Sadie was leaning against the kit, looking distinctly uneasy. I sank down on a stool and tried to catch my breath. I was pathetic.

Astrid stood with her arms folded, looking at me through narrowed eyes.

'Eva, Sadie and I have been talking about the band.'

I glanced up at her, guessing what was coming. I was about to be dumped. I couldn't blame them. I had been useless . . .

totally holding them back. I swallowed down the lump in my throat, and managed a twisted pitiful smile.

'Hey, Astrid – I u-understand. It's cool.'

Wearily, I got to my feet and moved over to the door. I longed for my quiet room and soft bed.

'Eva – where are you going?' she asked.

I turned, leaning on to the door frame for support.

'Aw, Eva,' she cackled, 'you didn't think . . .? Ha ha, you did!' She leaped towards me, dragged me back into the room and pushed me back on to the stool.

'Silly girl!' she muttered. 'OK, you idiot, what Sadie and I have actually been talking about – is introducing some keys into the mix . . .'

'A new band member?'

She nodded.

I shrugged. 'Who've you got in mind?'

'Rob Wilmer.'

I bit my lip. Damn. Why did it have to be Rob? Well – obviously because Rob was a great keyboard player. A good choice. Except . . . except I was already seeing way too much of him – and I knew how he felt about me. This was a bad idea.

But then – I wasn't in a great position to have a view.

'Is he interested?' I asked. As if I couldn't guess.

'Totally . . . We – er – tried him out last week . . .'

I shook my head – I was so out of the loop. I suddenly knew why they both looked so uncomfortable.

'He's coming tonight?'

'He'll – er – be here in a couple of minutes.'

I nodded.

'Are you OK with this, Eva?'

'Sure, Astrid,' I said flatly. 'It's your band.'

A tap on the door indicated that Rob had arrived. Astrid swung the door open, and high-fived him. I smiled as he looked tentatively in my direction. Then we ran through the set. About an hour later, Astrid glanced at me and unplugged her bass.

'OK – I think that's a wrap, guys. You OK, Eva?'

I leaned against the wall, and nodded.

But I wasn't OK. I felt awful. My head was spinning and I was having difficulty seeing straight.

'Just need an early night.'

I stood up, replaced the guitar on its stand and walked out of the door, down the corridor, and through the lobby.

Straight into the arms of Seth Leontis.

66

Reunion

St Magdalene's

AD 2013

Seth had no idea how much time had passed since he'd last been in London. He'd been in such a hurry to return that his vortex intentions weren't coherent. And precision was imperative in the vortex. Date and time needed to be the whole mind's focus for accuracy to be possible. Zackary had taught him that. And it had always worked. That was how he had managed to return to Parallon after weeks away with only minutes missing from his life there. But this time his only thoughts were of her. And she continued to be his only thought as he heaved himself out of the river, and ran dripping through the arched entrance.

It was dark when he arrived in the quad, so he slipped into his boarding house and made straight for his room. His stuff was just as he'd left it. He changed quickly out of his wet clothes and headed back into the quad. There were plenty of people about. He stood for a moment, wondering where to look first.

'Seth! You're back – Ruby'll be so relieved!' gasped Mia, who was on her way to supper. 'Come on! Let's go and tell her!' she grinned, pulling him towards the dining room.

Seth glanced around the quad. It was heaving with students now.

'Hey,' he said, trying to remember her name, 'do you know where I'd find Eva?'

Seth didn't like to unleash the full force of his capabilities unless it was absolutely necessary, but he decided that at this point it was. He stared down at Mia. She couldn't look away. Her eyes widened and her lips parted as she tried to summon the answer he was looking for. She was desperate to help him find what he needed, but she had no idea where Eva was. Ruby would have killed her if she took any interest whatsoever in her. But Harry was a couple of metres away.

'Harry,' she called.

Harry swerved towards them, and his mouth fell open when he realized who Mia was standing next to.

'Seth, man! Where have you *been*? We thought you'd disappeared off the face of the earth!'

Seth smiled wryly. *Good guess, Harry*, he thought.

'Seth's looking for Eva. Any idea where she might be?'

'Music block,' said Harry immediately. 'I saw them go off for a band practice after school. Hey, Seth, come and eat. We have some serious catching up to do!'

'Later, Harry,' smiled Seth, heading away.

He didn't have to go into the music block to hear her. Her lovely voice floated softly towards him. He stood leaning against the wall of the building, listening, lost in the sweetness of the sound.

When the singing stopped, he tensed. He was so longing to

see her that his heart began to pound. He didn't know how long he could wait, but seconds later he heard slow footsteps along the corridor and the lobby door opening.

He turned. He was standing face to face with the girl he loved.

'Seth?' she whispered. 'You've come back!'

She was looking at him with Livia's eyes, Livia's warmth . . . Livia's love. Without a moment's thought he gathered her up in his arms.

For one glorious instant her arms were round his neck, her lips brushed against his, and the passion that he had contained for so long burned between them. And then he felt her arms slacken.

'Livia?' he whispered desperately. He stared wildly down at her pale, limp body and knew then for certain that he shouldn't have come back. The Ophelia scene was simply a premonition, his warning. He was doomed to watch her die again . . .

'Please, Livia,' he groaned. But she was absolutely still.

He heard voices behind him.

'Oh my God, *Eva*!' Rob came dashing through the glass doors of the lobby, followed by Astrid and Sadie.

'What have you done to her?' growled Rob, staring ferociously at Seth.

Seth was just shaking his head, lost in misery.

Astrid took control. 'Guys! Guys! Get a grip! Eva's sick. Rob – please don't tell me you hadn't noticed?'

Rob bit his lip. Of course he'd noticed.

'Now, Seth,' Astrid went on, 'do you think you can carry her to the medical block? And, Rob – would you run ahead and warn Matron?'

Rob took off, but Seth stood lost in indecision. He was still holding Eva, but he was convinced that it was his fault that she was lying here, barely breathing.

'I think I did this,' he whispered hoarsely. 'I shouldn't be anywhere near her.'

'Rubbish,' answered Astrid. 'Eva's been sick for weeks – a couple of months ago, before you even came to the school, she nearly died in hospital. This has absolutely nothing to do with you. Now come on!'

Seth shook his head, unconvinced, but he did as she asked. When they arrived, Rose Marley took one look at Eva and rang for an ambulance. She checked her pulse, which was erratic and weak, and her blood pressure, which was extremely low, and noted how clammy and cold Eva's skin felt. She covered her with fleecy blankets and leaned over her.

'Eva?' she said firmly. 'Eva, can you hear me?' But Eva didn't stir.

When the ambulance arrived, and Eva had been fixed up with an oxygen mask, and stretchered in, Rose climbed in beside the stretcher and shooed the gathering crowd away. Word had travelled fast. Between thirty or forty kids reluctantly began to disperse.

But Seth refused to be dismissed. He stood his ground, stared Rose Marley down and within moments had joined her in the ambulance. Rose had no idea why she had allowed this extraordinary boy into the vehicle. It was totally against protocol, but she found his presence strangely comforting. Over the past weeks, she had grown very fond of Eva, and she recognized immediately that she was in the presence of someone with an equivalent affection. She could not guess at the depth of emotion he was trying to control.

354

While the paramedics took a history and Rose gave them all the details of Eva's last illness, Seth gazed at Eva, trying to understand what was happening. He was still convinced that her collapse was his fault. Whatever Rose Marley said about a relapse, he would have to be an idiot if he didn't connect her condition with his proximity – after all, hadn't she nearly collapsed when he had touched her in the common room? Now she was fighting for her life.

Rose watched the boy as he gazed at Eva. He was staring at her with such intensity that it looked as though he believed his will was keeping her alive. She pressed her lips together, fighting a deep sense of foreboding.

67

Déjà vu

London

AD 2013

One moment I was trudging out of the music block; the next I was gazing into those eyes. My heart started to pound wildly. Relief, happiness, I don't know – the feelings overwhelmed me, and it seemed so natural, so right to lean my face up to his.

And then I was falling . . . falling so far through space that I could feel no ending. And finally . . . landing . . . softly, gentle as a feather. Lying on my back . . . eyes closed. Comfortable. Stretching out my arms, my fingers brushing against . . . cool blades of grass. I knew this place . . . the humming of summer insects . . . the scent of wild lavender . . . birds singing in the trees, their song just a pale reflection of the song in my heart . . . breathing deeply, savouring the loveliness . . . a swell of happiness rising inside me, knowing that when I turned my head and opened my eyes . . .

'Eva? Eva? Can you hear me? Eva?'

The scent of grass and summer melted away, my head felt

suddenly heavy, my breathing hurt, and my stomach churned. I stared blankly.

Into the wrong eyes.

Where was I?

Oh God, no. Not back here. Dr Falana was looming over me. I closed my eyes again, willing myself back to the sunshine . . .

No – it had gone.

'Eva? Are you with us?'

My head was pounding. I moaned, and realized at that moment my mouth was covered in a mask. I tried snatching it off, but he held it firmly in place.

'Eva, your breathing has been a little – half-hearted – so I'd like you to wear the mask a bit longer, if that's OK?'

I stopped struggling, and frowned. I could hear an erratic beeping, and turned my heavy, pounding head to see that I was back in the room with a load of monitors.

'What's going on?' I croaked. I wasn't enjoying talking much.

'Not entirely sure, Eva. Some sort of relapse – your case is so . . .'

I shut my eyes again, too tired to listen.

And then I was floating – along strange streets, through a curtained door into a darkened room . . . A man sleeping. Strange scents – vinegar, jasmine, honey . . . Leaning over him, lightly touching his forehead. Burning heat. Sickening fear for him, mingling with the thrill of his closeness . . . Dipping a soft cloth into a bowl, squeezing out excess water, dripping the rest on to his face . . . The liquid running into his hair, across his cheeks, over his lips. Wanting to be that water touching him, tracing the contours of his features. A warm hand enclosing mine. A sense of joy, recognition . . . heat pulsing through me

357

. . . Now more hands . . . pulling me, dragging me from his side
. . . No! Too powerful to resist . . . fighting . . . gasping . . .

'Livia – please . . . come back.'

My heart was thudding . . . the room spiralling away from
me . . . darkness all around . . . and so cold . . . where was he?
Where was I? Spinning in every direction . . . I would never find
my way back to him . . . losing myself . . . dissolving . . .

And then . . . anchored . . . warmth pulsing through my
fingers, through my arm, into my whole body – leading me . . .
back to the light.

I opened my eyes. He was there. Silhouetted against a bright
white glare.

I blinked . . . The wrong room . . . A different room. The
hospital. Monitors beeping. But . . . it was him. Seth. Smiling.
He had my hand in both of his . . .

'You're here,' I whispered.

He looked like he'd been on an even more harrowing journey
than mine. Exhausted. Pale . . . Had he been with me? I shook
my head. It ached. But I needed to try and clear it. I was getting
so mixed up. I couldn't tell what was real any more. I tried to
sit up, but dizziness forced me back.

'Hey,' he whispered, stroking the hair off my face, 'you're
supposed to be resting . . .'

'Seth –'

'Shhh,' he breathed, as the door opened and Dr Falana strode
in, followed by an entire roomful of people. I narrowed my eyes
in confusion. Who were they? And what were they doing here?
Dr Falana was grinning.

'Eva, I hope you don't mind – I have brought some students
to see you.'

Actually, I did mind. A lot. I wasn't feeling quite up to playing interesting specimen to a class full of curious medics. But then I felt Seth's hand squeezing mine, and the overpowering warmth coursing through me filled me with such a comforting glow that I even managed a half-smile.

They all gathered round my bed. I watched them warily.

Dr Falana picked up the chart clipped to the bed frame and cleared his throat.

'This is Eva Koretsky. Nine weeks ago she presented suddenly with pyrexia and collapse, but then on admittance, degenerated almost immediately into ventricular fibrillation and multi-organ failure . . .

'Ms Groves – if you had been the admitting registrar, how would you have proceeded?'

'Er . . . I would – er – begin defibrillating to try and stabilize the heart, intubate, put up a saline drip and – er – obviously do all the bloods – try and find out what was the cause . . .'

'Good. Bear in mind we had no time to analyse the lab results, so was there anything else we could have tried to alleviate symptoms in the first instance?'

The students were silent.

'All right . . . I'll tell you what we did next. We started her on an IV broad-spectrum antibiotic. Now why would we have done that?'

'I guess – hoping for a treatable bacterial infection?'

'Precisely. We assumed some kind of acute sepsis, but obviously we wouldn't be able to identify the bacteria until we had grown cultures – and unfortunately, as I keep reiterating, we had no time. The deterioration was incredibly rapid.'

'So did the antibiotic work?'

'Er – no,' he murmured. 'Nothing we threw at her had any impact on her decline.'

I bit my lip. I could have done without the details. I felt Seth's eyes on me, his hand tightening.

'Unsurprisingly, within hours she had become asystolic, and despite all attempt at resuscitation, including injections of epinephrine and atropine and chest compressions, she remained unresponsive – *yet* at the point of pronouncing, her heart suddenly spontaneously started up with a strong normal beat, no sign of arrhythmia at all. This was followed by complete recovery of all organ function . . .'

He raised his eyebrows, spread his arms and winked at Eva. 'Our own little Lazarus!'

One of the students cleared her throat. 'So what's your theory, Dr Falana?'

He shrugged. 'I have no theory at all. My gut instinct – some kind of virulent infection – was negated by the post-trauma haematology. There was no raised lymphocyte count at all. And whatever other diagnosis we considered (and remember we were working against the clock), the acute period lab results were so anomalous they had to be discounted.'

The students all looked bemused.

I cleared my throat. 'Er, Dr Falana . . . Would you mind letting me look at the – er – anomalous blood results?'

He stared at me blankly for a moment – his face a picture of disbelief. I couldn't tell whether he was just surprised that the patient actually talked, or whether he simply didn't believe that an ignorant schoolkid could possibly be interested in looking at an undecipherable table of numbers. But then he just frowned. 'Sorry, Eva, nothing to show – we had to bin them.'

'You *threw away* the test results? Why?'

'Corrupted somehow. A complete mess.'

'But –'

'I assure you we have done a thorough lab investigation – overhauled the system . . . nothing like that will happen again.' He turned to his students. 'Anyway – two days ago Eva was back in A & E . . .'

Two days ago? I had been in here that long?

'This time no fever, but arrhythmic and hypotensive. Fortunately, on this occasion the arrhythmia has responded to treatment.' He pointed to the steadily beeping monitor that I was annoyingly hooked up to. 'And the blood pressure has improved. We are still waiting on blood cultures, but the absence of pyrexia doesn't suggest infection as a cause. Any ideas, anyone?'

A couple of students shuffled uncomfortably. Then a tall girl with big teeth and a halo of red hair coughed nervously. 'Er – organ function? Was that – um – normal?'

'Yes – apart from respiration, but that's under control now. ECGs have revealed no underlying heart condition or defect.'

The group stood there silently.

Dr Falana turned to me. 'So, Eva, how are you feeling today?'

'Fine,' I said, willing them to go.

He raised his eyebrows at me.

'Fine?' he laughed, 'I think "fine" might be pushing it, but I'm prepared to accept "much better". I'll stop by later. In the meantime . . . *rest*!' He looked pointedly at Seth.

68

Questions

London

AD 2013

When they'd all trooped out, I turned to Seth. 'Could you shut the door please?'

He shot me a quizzical look, stood up, shut the door softly and came and sat by me again. His hand lay on the cover next to mine. I picked it up and felt a little shock of heat, but nothing I couldn't handle.

'Seth, we need to talk,' I whispered. He nodded noncommittally.

'OK . . .' I bit my lip. 'Could you please tell me who you are?'

'You know who I am: Seth. Sethos Leontis.'

'All right then . . . How do I know you?'

He sat mutely, looking at our entwined hands. Then he shrugged and shook his head. 'I'm not quite sure.'

He looked so uncomfortable, I almost let it go. But I couldn't.

'What does that mean?' I asked.

He just shook his head again. I breathed hard, trying to stay calm.

'OK, if that one's too difficult . . . tell me who Livia is.' I had heard him use the name so often it felt almost too familiar.

He spread his hands, and looked at me as though I wasn't getting something totally obvious.

'What?' I asked, exasperated.

'Well – Livia is you, of course,' he smiled.

'No,' I said (in what I considered a very patient voice), 'I am Eva. Eva Koretsky. Livia is someone else.'

He was shaking his head. 'Eva, I know what your name is. But I also know that you are her.' He sighed. 'I don't understand it either, but then – there is so much I don't understand.'

'Like what?'

'Well – the fever –'

'What about the fever?' I asked sharply.

But he was gazing out of the window, frowning, muttering. 'There has to be a connection, but I just don't understand how . . .'

'Do you know something about my sickness?' I asked, my heart thudding.

'I don't know. I only know about mine.'

'You've had a fever?'

He nodded.

'Like mine?'

'I don't know – I don't think so . . .'

'For God's sake, Seth, tell me what you know – *please*! And I'll tell you what I know. Then maybe we can work this thing out. And I can get well like you.'

He looked at me then with such an expression of grief, that I felt a hard lump in my throat. I swallowed hard. 'What? What's wrong?'

'Eva . . . I –'

The door was suddenly flung open, and a nurse with a trolley full of instruments bustled in.

'Please don't shut this door,' she said crossly to Seth. 'We need it left open. Now if you don't mind,' she tilted her head towards the door, 'I need to check over the patient.'

Seth let go of my hand and stood. I panicked.

'I need him to stay,' I said urgently.

The nurse shook her head and tutted. 'He can wait outside until we've finished.'

Seth rewarded her with a fabulous smile, and headed for the door. The immediate chill of his absence shocked me.

'Seth?' I called hoarsely.

He put his head round the door. 'I'll be right here.'

The nurse took ages, and by the time she finally trundled her trolley out, and Seth slipped in, I was feeling too tired to continue quizzing him. I just about managed a wobbly smile. When he smiled back, his beauty made me forget myself and I found my hand reaching out to touch his face. As my fingers lightly brushed his skin, I gasped, as a sudden image of him flashed into my head . . . another Seth – lying on a couch, water glistening across his closed eyes . . .

I tried to blink the image away, but it was becoming more solid, filling my vision, blotting out the hospital room, blotting out Seth's anxious expression, blotting out the light.

No . . . I couldn't let this happen . . . I wanted to stay here. I needed this boy sitting on the chair next to me. I had so many questions. But I didn't have the energy to fight it. Panic started to rise inside me; I could hear my breath coming in sharp pants.

I was finding it hard to fill my lungs . . . 'Help me!' I choked. But I couldn't hear my voice. I could hear nothing . . . see nothing . . .

69

Blame

London

AD 2013

Seth pressed the emergency button and ran from the room, calling wildly for a doctor. Within seconds a team had arrived with electric paddles, which they slammed against Eva's chest. Seth stood helplessly in the doorway watching them save her life, certain that once more her collapse had been his fault.

As soon as he was convinced she was stable and asleep, he walked out of the hospital. He needed to think. He knew that he found it hard to keep focus when he was near her, and he was having difficulty separating what he knew he wanted from what he knew was right.

As he walked, he thought. He wanted to be with her. More than anything. But he was pretty sure that he wasn't any good for her health. He didn't understand the power of the current they shared. He too could feel the charge of energy that flowed between them when they touched, but for him it was simply a delicious glow of warmth. As it had been in Londinium . . . nothing like the staggering shock it clearly was for her. And only her. Ruby didn't collapse when she touched him. Neither did Astrid. Or Sadie or Harry.

So maybe Astrid was right. It was the illness that had left Eva so vulnerable, and when she recovered perhaps he would be able to touch her as he wanted to. Because now at last he sensed their connection returning – he could see it in her eyes. She was remembering.

But would the cost be too great?

And if she had made some sort of journey across time, which seemed the only possible explanation, it had clearly been a difficult one. So while her presence in this 2013 London was still inexplicable, it had to be more than random coincidence. Why would they both have turned up at the same time in the same place otherwise?

He had to go back and talk to her.

He turned round and started to run. But he was so preoccupied that he stumbled across the arterial road straight into the path of a postal delivery van. The loud horn and screaming brakes dragged him back into the present. He leaped in one direction and fortunately the driver swerved in the other, missing him by a hair's breadth. The driver screamed furious abuse out of the window, and drove on. Seth stood at the side of the road, dazed. He wondered what it would feel like to die twice. Would he end forever or return to Parallon?

And at that moment he knew that he didn't want to die. Nor did he want to return to Parallon. He wanted to stay here with Eva, in this cold, noisy, harsh, uncompromising world he now found himself in.

His thoughts turned to Matthias and his growing kingdom of dead. He thought about the motorcyclist – Matt's first, accidental, victim. And then about the girl from the café, Elena. Taken to Parallon by a different route – killed without blood: killed with love.

Seth's mouth went dry as he suddenly absorbed the shocking, irrefutable implication: he could have no possible future with Eva. Even if she did recover from the illness she now fought, how could he stay with her? Matthias's message had been clear. Their love was doomed. If he were to even kiss her, to love her as he longed to, he would kill her. As Matthias had killed Elena.

70

Darkness

I am hurrying . . . hurrying through dusky unfamiliar streets.
I can see a . . . temple gleaming ahead. I feel the gentle touch
of a friend by my side, a heavy dangerous footfall behind me.
I need to stay calm, but my heart beats out a heavy rhythm . . .
I shouldn't be doing this. I shouldn't be here. There are a thousand safer options. Why am I risking both of us like this? And
yet – I know why. He is my reason. And he is waiting for me.
He will be there, under our oak . . . I am moving through the
cool shadows of the temple . . . quickly towards a small side
entrance into a dark narrow antechamber. But ahead, through
the narrow opening, I can see the green dappled light of the
meadow . . . and I am running . . . running. I can see him . . .
leaning against the tree, a cloak pulled round him. He has
sensed me . . . he is lifting his eyes . . . his beautiful eyes. I try
to call his name, but someone is covering my mouth . . . I can't
move . . . I can't scream . . .

I opened my eyes . . . white light chasing the shadows.
  'Eva?'
  I reached a shaking hand up to my face and pushed away
. . . an oxygen mask. Only an oxygen mask. I was back in the

hospital, a nurse standing over me, gently replacing the mask.

'You're all right now, sweetheart,' she said soothingly. 'Everything is fine.'

I pulled the mask away from my mouth to speak, but the only word I trusted myself to say was 'Seth'.

The nurse smiled at me. 'Your handsome boyfriend is just outside. If you promise to stay absolutely calm, he can come in for a moment or two.'

I shut my eyes, relieved. Seconds later I gasped as a warm current charged through my hand. I smiled and opened my eyes, knowing that the face I was longing to see would be there.

He looked awful. Completely ragged.

'Seth?' My voice sounded weird. Damn. I'd forgotten about the mask. I ripped it off. 'Seth, what's wrong?'

His appearance brought back the fear of my dream. Had he been there in the meadow waiting for me? What drugs were they giving me?

Seth leaned across me and replaced the mask. 'You need to keep this on just a bit longer. And – er – Eva, your mother's arrived. She's getting a cup of tea at the moment, but she'll be back in a minute. Are you up to a visit?'

I closed my eyes. No, I wasn't. But I knew she would be worried. So I nodded. Seth touched his finger to my cheek, leaving me with a warm glow. And then he was gone.

I did such a good job of convincing my mother that all was well that she gratefully agreed to get on a train back to York that evening. I was so tired by the time she left that I must have fallen asleep, because when I next opened my eyes daylight was flooding into the room, and someone was clanking dishes down on to a tray.

'Good morning, my love,' a smiley round-faced nurse sang as she wheeled the bed tray towards me. 'Breakfast time!'

I blinked, trying to clear my head. The nurse was pressing a button and I felt my pillows suddenly rising beneath me. Pretty soon I was sitting up. Quite cool! Cautiously, I put my hands to my mouth. Yay! No oxygen mask. I smiled. I felt quite a lot better. Hungry even. The nurse lifted a lid and revealed something just about recognizable as an omelette, accompanied by a wilted lettuce leaf and a soggy slice of tomato.

More tempting was the cup of coffee steaming next to it. I reached over for it, and realized I still had a tube attached to my hand. The nurse kindly pushed the coffee towards my other, unencumbered, hand.

'Do you think you can manage the egg?' she asked, looking at it dubiously.

I nodded half-heartedly, and just before she bustled out I said, 'Does this mean I'm well enough to leave?'

She stood by the door and chuckled. 'Dr Falana will be along later. I think you may find it's his decision – not mine!'

I was getting a strong feeling of déjà vu. And I wasn't enjoying the experience much. I was desperate to get out, and just wondering how easy it would be to pull a cannula out of your hand, when the door swung open.

'Seth!' I grinned delightedly. 'Aren't you meant to be at school?'

'I won't be missed,' he assured me.

'Have you come to spring me?' I asked hopefully.

'Spring you?'

'Get me out of here!'

'Of course not! I've come bearing gifts . . .'

He opened a bag he'd been concealing and handed me a warm almond croissant, and a shiny red apple.

'Seth! How did you guess? I love almonds.' I laughed, sniffing the delicious scent wafting from the bag.

And then I caught his expression.

'You didn't guess, did you? You already knew . . .'

He nodded, his eyes on the bag.

'Tell me what else you know.'

He sighed, slumped down in a chair, and looked at me.

'I know . . . that you love the sound of rain at night. And that when you sing you can restore a man . . . I know that you have five small freckles on your shoulder, and you bite your lip when you're thinking. I know that you are as courageous as a warrior, yet fear to ask a favour . . . I know that you have a tiny scar on the back of your knee and extremely dangerous eyes . . .'

'Dangerous eyes?'

'They nearly killed me once . . .'

'Yeah, right!' I laughed.

But Seth wasn't laughing. 'I know that you speak Latin almost as well as a Roman, and certainly better than a Greek . . . and that you have no idea how beautiful you are. Now . . . eat your croissant before it gets cold.'

I sat for a second, trying to absorb this declaration. When I realized I was unconsciously biting my lip, I rolled my eyes at him and smiled. Then I split the croissant in two and handed him half. As we ate, I watched him. He refused to catch my eye, keeping his gaze firmly focused on the window.

When I had flicked the stray crumbs back into the paper bag, I crumpled it up, aimed the screwed-up ball at the bin and . . . missed. He smiled, reached out and threw a perfect shot.

'Seth,' I said quietly, 'where did we meet?'

He cocked his head on one side, looked me straight in the eye and said, 'Londinium. AD 152. The arena.'

I laughed, but something about his expression stopped the sound in my throat.

I stared at him. Why was he doing this? It wasn't funny any more. Tears of anger began to prick my eyelids, and I chewed my lip furiously, to try and stop them spilling over. I had really begun to think that he might care for me a bit. But here he was playing with me, treating my confusion as a game. Some stupid boy joke. Why had I let down my guard? How had I let him get to me? Unconsciously, I had balled my hands into fists. Dumb thing to do when you have a cannula and drip shoved in one of them. 'Agh,' I gasped as blood seeped out from under the plaster.

Seth sighed deeply, covering my injured hand with his. As he did so, the strangest image flashed through my head . . . Seth – half-naked, bleeding, crouched on the sand; a giant of a man standing over him . . .

'Protix,' I gasped. The name came into my head from nowhere.

Then the vision faded and I was back in the hospital room, only now Seth was staring at me, his eyes wide.

'You remember!' he breathed.

I lay back against my pillows and shut my eyes. What was going on? Seth touched my face and started to whisper.

'You came to watch me fight . . .'

*

And I am there, sitting on a purple silk cushion, perched on stone steps facing a huge circle of sand. Surrounded by a noisy massive crowd of people.

'A date, Livia?' The woman next to me is offering me a basket filled with fruit.

'Thank you, Tavinia,' I hear myself say.

I pick out a date. The golden bangle on my wrist flashes in the sunlight. It's lovely. I lift up my eyes and gaze out at the sandy arena in front of us. I am feeling sick. I do not want to watch this fight, and yet I need to be here.

I look down at my lap, wondering if I have made a terrible mistake. My hands lie helplessly against a long white dress. I run my fingers along the fabric. It is soft, beautiful, edged with gold thread.

Music starts and the crowd begins to cheer. My stomach clenches. Then the wooden gates are thrown open and they all burst through . . . the gladiators. And the fifth gladiator through the gate is Seth. God, he is so beautiful. I hear Tavinia inhale sharply next to me, and I glance across at her. Yes, it is Seth she is watching too. I hear the women around me whisper his name excitedly. I feel lost, insignificant in this sea of women, all longing for the same man.

He is gloriously oblivious. He is almost naked, wearing no more than a leather half-tunic and shoulder strap, yet he walks round the arena like a prince, muscles taut, head high, chest broad. And I can't take my eyes off him. The gladiators all stop to salute governor Cnaeus Papirius Aelianus and then one by one they greet the crowd. Some wave; others roar. Seth simply touches his hand to his forehead, barely looking at us. The women around me scream with excitement. He is the one they have all come to see. I bite my lip nervously. Then the music stops; there is a loud crash and the fighting begins. They split into four pairs, and I am horrified to see Seth now facing a huge armoured monster of a man. I can hardly bear to watch.

'Protix is a devil,' I hear Tavinia hiss. 'He has never lost a fight. But then he has never faced Leontis – another date, dear?'

How can she eat? I bite my lip so hard I can taste blood. It is my first time at the arena, and I am sickened by the pleasure everyone around me seems to be taking in this horrible, horrible entertainment. As Seth dances round Protix, I glance across at the other fights – they seem more evenly matched . . . equivalent-sized gladiators fighting with equivalent armour and weapons . . . which makes Seth look all the more vulnerable when my eyes travel back to him. But he seems tireless. He ducks and jumps without any sign of effort, though the sweat that glistens across his shoulders and chest belies the show. Protix is getting wild, flailing indiscriminately. Seth continues as before, watching. He seems to have an uncanny ability to predict each move the giant makes – ducking a second before the sword is thrust, diving moments before Protix lunges, and then Seth has thrown his net and the giant is caught. I am so relieved and put my hands up to my mouth, and at that moment Seth suddenly shifts his focus and moves his eyes from the struggling gladiator in front of him to me. For a split second it is just him and me, and then I see Protix has grabbed his moment – he has disengaged his sword arm, raised his sword, and is thrusting it into Seth's shoulder. I scream . . .

The scream pulled me back. I was wrapped in Seth's arms, shaking.

'What did you see?' he asked, stroking my cheek. 'It's OK. You're safe now.'

Seth's words soothed me, and the warmth from his arms helped to ease my fear. But I needed to understand what I had seen. I ran my fingers along the fabric of his white T-shirt, across his chest to his shoulder. I could feel the unmistakable raised line of a scar.

'You see? All healed,' he smiled, and the happiness I felt was so overwhelming it left me with only one impulse. I leaned my head up to kiss him. But instead of feeling his lips against mine, I felt him stiffen and turn his face away.

'Seth?'

He unwrapped his arms from around me and moved across to the door.

'Eva – I can't . . . we can't . . .' he groaned, and was gone.

What had I done? And how could he leave me now – in some crazy halfway place between two lives? A crazy place that he had brought me to.

'Seth?' I called, hoping he was still outside the room.

Nobody answered.

I felt totally abandoned. And – rejected. And yeah, yeah, it wasn't like I was a stranger to rejection, but – but . . . the way I had started to feel about Seth . . .

Stupid! Stupid! Stupid! Why could I never learn? Why had I let him in? And how could I have allowed him to take me by the hand, lead me into all this weirdness and then walk out on me? I felt my lip trembling, and big fat tears plopping down my cheeks.

I wiped them away angrily with my good hand, and stared at the mess of dried blood on the other.

I had to get out of here. I was like a chained prisoner, strapped to tubes and unable to move. I looked around the room, wondering where my clothes were. I couldn't make a break for it in a stupid hospital gown. The tears began to fall hard again. I was starting to feel overwhelmed by the enormity of what Seth had opened up in me . . . and by my feelings of inadequacy in confronting it alone.

Who was I? And how had I lived that other life, as Livia?

I totally didn't believe in reincarnation. Past-life rubbish was the stuff of idiot charlatans conning the gullible masses, just a stupid deception to convince people that they need not face their worst fear: death.

Did I fear death?

I knew I did. Death was haunting me. Since my near-death experience I had been dreaming of little else.

I reached across to the table next to my bed and grabbed a tissue. As I dabbed at my eyes, I took a deep breath and decided this had to stop – this pathetic self-pity. I was not going to be a victim here. I was tough. I had dealt with enough bad stuff in my life to get through this. And I was determined to find out what was going on.

The first thing I had to do was get hold of a computer.

I looked down at the cannula in my hand. It hurt. It was seeping blood. Would it be a big deal to pull it out? It was the only thing I was still attached to. The heart monitors had been unplugged, which meant once I was free of the cannula, I could get up and . . . leave.

I was just peeling off the soggy plaster when – typical – Dr Falana strode in.

'Eva? What are you doing?'

'Er – I think – this has come loose. It feels kind of bad,' I said lamely.

He narrowed his eyes at me, and came to take a look.

'Yep. It needs to be changed,' he said, ripping off the plaster. 'Good Lord, Eva, what have you been up to?'

I looked down. The skin was all swollen and bruised. Not a pretty sight.

'Hmm – we can't go back in there,' he said decisively, as he carefully removed the cannula, cleaned up my hand and covered the messed-up skin with a big white plaster.

'Er – Dr Falana . . . I don't think it needs to go back at all . . . I – er – I think I'm better. I'm ready to leave.'

He sat on the side of my bed and stared at me. I realized I might look a bit of a mess. I wiped my face quickly, checking for stray tears. Then I gazed up at him with the perkiest, healthiest expression I could produce.

'Well . . .' he said slowly, reaching over for my chart, 'your blood pressure is good, and your heart rhythm has stabilized, but . . .'

'Please!' I begged. 'I'll go crazy if I have to spend another day in here.' I couldn't disguise the pathetic hiccup in my voice. He shot me a reflective look.

'A-and I've got loads of stuff I need to do . . .' I said, trying to sound a bit more powerful.

'That's exactly what worries me, Eva. If I let you go, you have to promise to take care of yourself. You only have one body. You only have one life. Don't mess with it.'

Way too late for that, Dr Falana.

'So – am I free?' I gulped, grinning.

He sighed, stood up, and said, 'I'll give Rose Marley a call.

But I will only discharge you if I can have an assurance from her that she will be looking after you.'

'I'm not a child, you know,' I said, sounding alarmingly like one.

He laughed and left the room.

71

Rift

London

AD 2013

As soon as Dr Falana had gone, I hauled myself out of bed. Whoa. Head rush. I'd forgotten this bit. I sat back down, cursing my useless body. When the dizziness seemed to be under control, I tried again. I made it over to the cupboard in the corner of the room, and opened the door.

My clothes. Thank you, God. I grabbed them and brought them back to the bed. But before I could get myself dressed I just needed a little rest. So I laid my head down, and shut my eyes for a moment.

When I opened them again, Seth was perched next to me.

'Hey,' he said.

I didn't trust myself to answer.

'Eva,' he whispered, and then looked at his hands. 'I'm – sorry. I didn't mean to . . . it's just that I can't – we can't . . . I'm no good for you . . .'

I stared at him and swallowed.

I had never been on the receiving end of the brush-off speech, but I had given a few. So I recognized the vocabulary. And I guess I wasn't surprised . . . Numb . . . Annihilated . . . Sick . . . But not surprised. After all, everyone had a greater claim to him than me. And if my most recent little vision was telling me anything it was that they all wanted a piece of Seth. He wasn't mine . . .

'I know,' I said.

He reached his hand over to touch mine, but I moved away.

'Eva –' he groaned, but I pressed my lips together and turned my head. I wasn't going to let him in again.

'Seth, I need to get dressed. Would you mind –'

He sat there, staring at me.

'I need you to leave,' I said, not daring to make eye contact.

'Eva –'

'Now.'

I heard him scrape back his chair and slowly walk out of the room. When I was sure he'd gone, I staggered over to the door and shut it.

It took me a ridiculously long time to put my clothes on because my eyes kept blurring, but I'd just about tied my trainers when the door swung open and Rose Marley appeared.

'Happy Groundhog Day,' I smiled weakly.

72

On the Trail

St Magdalene's

AD 2013

Although it was good to be out of the hospital, and Rose's calm and efficient presence was soothing, I found it hard to settle. I was twitchy and on edge. I had told Rose that I didn't want to see Seth, and though she frowned at me and behaved like she thought I was making a big mistake, she didn't argue. I nearly caved once, when I heard him in the corridor, but I knew I couldn't afford to let him in again.

After a couple of weeks, I was back on the morning school timetable. Ruby couldn't believe her luck when she clocked how far away I was keeping from Seth. I couldn't bear to be anywhere near him. I didn't look at him or for him. I refused to let anyone mention his name in my presence, which meant conversations could get quite awkward, as everyone was so damned interested in him. I refused to give Astrid, Sadie or Rose Marley any explanation whatsoever.

Each lunchtime I came back to the medical block to eat with Rose – who kept a beady eye on everything I put in my mouth.

After lunch I was supposed to rest in my room. Which I did (a bit) along with my research.

Being sick had made me feel kind of desperate about time. To be honest, I didn't know how much I had left. So I couldn't afford to sleep it away. Although I was low on energy, sitting for two hours at a laptop didn't exhaust me nearly as much as – say – taking a shower. So research was actually the perfect occupation.

I needed some clarity on the 'anomalous' blood results: the ones that Dr Falana had binned. I'd noted he didn't say *deleted*. Which gave me a little thread of hope. Surely everything had an e-trail? I was banking on it.

The first thing I had to do was hack into the hospital intranet. I'd made up my mind during the student ward-round that I would have to get in, so from then on I memorized name badges: doctors, medical students, nurses, anyone who I thought would have access to the site. In the end I decided Dr Falana himself was probably the best cipher, as he would have been accessing all the data I needed. So I had to first research him a bit, which was easy – he did a spot of Twittering and had a Facebook page. I soon knew his full name (Danso Jojo Falana); where and when he was born (Accra: 12 November 1968); his favourite band (Nirvana); and his wife's name (Melanie). He had two children, Sisi (born 2 March 1999) and Kurt (born 17 May 2003).

People were lazy with PINs and passwords. They usually went for something easy – a middle name; a birth date. In fact Dr Falana was marginally more imaginative. His password was *Aneurysm*, which I guess was kind of witty – being a Nirvana song title and a medical condition. As soon as I got his password, his PIN was easy: 5494 (the date of Kurt Cobain's death).

Once I was in, I could start accessing patient files – well, mine . . .

It basically reiterated stuff I already knew . . . I was admitted with the fever, my condition deteriorated rapidly for four hours, I flatlined and then recovered.

But I couldn't find any record whatsoever of any blood-test data during that crucial four hours – just the twelve tests taken subsequently, which were deeply uninteresting, as all levels analysed fell within normal ranges.

So I needed to contact the haematology unit direct and find the technician who had done the lab work. It took me a couple more days to get into the unit as Rose Marley would randomly visit my room on some pretext or another, so I had to keep logging out.

Then one evening she was called out to one of the boarding houses for a suspected appendicitis, and I got a bit of time.

When I found my way into the hospital haematology database, I realized that all test results were referenced with a pair of initials, followed by the patient name and hospital number, then the consultant name. I couldn't be sure, but I began to hope that the initials were those of the lab technician responsible for the data. To test this theory I cross-referenced the initials against the human resources databank of hospital personnel. They had thoughtfully listed all hospital employees by department in alphabetical order.

My theory held. The haematology lab technicians' names matched all the initials I found. Except one set.

Around the time I was admitted the first time, there were thousands of results recorded by A.N. And the initials dated back twelve years.

But two days after my admittance A.N. had disappeared.

Hmmm. Coincidence? Sabbatical? Or was A.N. the technician responsible for my anomalous blood results? Was A.N.'s disappearance the result of the lab investigation overhaul?

I was staring at the screen, trying to prioritize my questions, when I suddenly heard a sound behind me.

'Eva? What are you up to?'

I jumped, and simultaneously cleared my screen. Rose Marley had crept in as silent as a cat.

'You are supposed to be *resting*, Eva, not working.'

'But –'

'No buts now. I promised Dr Falana. So please don't give me a hard time, or I'll have to take your laptop away.'

I gritted my teeth, torn between deep frustration and total panic. I couldn't live without my laptop. So I shut down, and reluctantly submitted as she hauled me across to the bed, drew the curtains and closed the door.

As I lay on my bed brooding, I decided that I had no choice. I would have to set my alarm and do the research during the night. Much safer . . . Rose would be asleep, and unlikely to prowl. And although a hospital was open 24/7, I hoped that not too many legitimate users would be accessing the databanks at that time. It was always a bit of a risk to be hacking when the system was busy: observant users could occasionally spot unauthorized use.

So at three the next morning I was blinking blearily at my laptop as I skipped my way through the spyware back into the hospital database.

I was trawling through human resources – looking for anyone with the initials A.N. I found four: Anushka Nepali, nurse on the paediatric ward; Ashanti Nokombu, a consultant neurologist; Arleen Nateman, pharmacy dispenser; and Arthur Newland, dermatology lab technician.

Naturally, I honed straight in on Arthur Newland. He was doing the right kind of job, in the wrong place. I needed to know how long he'd been working in dermatology.

Different damned database. Different passwords; different entry codes. But by 5 a.m. I was in. And by 5.30 I had everything I needed. Arthur Newland had stopped working in haematology two days after I was admitted. He took up employment in the dermatology labs the day after that.

Got him.

I thought about emailing him, but I couldn't afford to leave any sort of trail: secure sites like those in a hospital would have too many backup systems. So I decided I had to phone him.

I looked at my watch. 5.35 a.m. . . . . Unlikely to catch a dermatology lab technician working at night. I yawned, wishing I could say the same about myself. But I had just about done all I could right now, so I shut down my PC, turned out my light and gratefully closed my eyes.

73

Blood

The next day I was too tired to think. I sleepwalked my way through morning classes and staggered back to the medical block for lunch. Rose didn't need to tell me to go to bed that afternoon; I took myself off without any prompting.

I woke up several hours later, screaming.

Breathless and disorientated, I opened my eyes to find Rose Marley standing next to me in her dressing gown.

I tried to get my breathing under control while she sat on the edge of my bed, and offered me a glass of water.

I sipped it gratefully.

'Eva,' she whispered. 'What happened between you and Seth?'

I blinked back at her, suddenly realizing why she was asking. I had been shouting his name. I tried to remember my dream. It had been so dark. So frightening. And Seth had been there.

I shrugged. What could I tell her? I didn't even know myself.

I felt pathetic tears squeeze through my lashes and down my cheeks. I wiped them away angrily.

I thought I'd been doing a pretty good job keeping the Seth door shut, and now here it was wide open and he was blasting through again.

Rose put her arm round me, and said, 'For what it's worth, Eva, I think he really cares about you.'

I shook my head furiously. 'You couldn't be more wrong, Rose,' I croaked.

I didn't trust my voice to say any more, but I felt again the sharp pain of rejection in my chest, as I relived the moment when he'd walked away as I had started to kiss him.

Rose sighed deeply and stood up.

'Eva, I brought you some supper earlier, but you were fast asleep. You must be starving.'

I wasn't.

But she brought the tray over and perched it on my lap. 'Would you like some hot chocolate?'

I shook my head and hazarded a smile. 'I'm fine, Rose, thank you. Now please go back to bed. I'm really sorry I woke you up.'

She shook her head, patted me on the shoulder and headed back to her room.

I picked at a vegetable samosa, finished my glass of water, and put the tray on the floor. I wasn't sleepy any more, so I went and got my laptop.

I didn't have the energy or focus to do any of my schoolwork, and I had hit a wall with the blood-test research until I was able to make my phone call, so before I knew what I was doing I found myself accidentally typing *Seth Leontis* into the search window.

No direct hits.

I typed in *Sethos Leontis gladiator.*

Oh – my – God . . . A hit . . . The British Library site: a small photograph of a Roman carving, with a short entry:

This is a relief carving (AD 152) on a slate found in Newgate Street. It depicts the fêted gladiator Sethos Leontis, one of the most admired Retiarii of the period. He is said to have won nine wreaths by the age of eighteen – an unrivalled achievement. The Retiarius was a gladiator who would have fought with only a trident and net, which made the achievement surprising, as these gladiators wore no armour.

I stared at the words for ages, reliving the fight I had witnessed. It had been so brutal, yet so . . . compelling. I had promised myself to cut him out of my life, and now here I was aching for him. I was such an idiot.

I cleared the screen, shut down and switched out the light.

Bad idea.

As soon as I closed my eyes, his face found its way under my eyelids. Not in the scary, visionary I-was-there way, but in the girl-with-a-stupid-obsessive-infatuation way. Why did it have to be my fate to find myself linked with the only boy I knew who wasn't interested in me in the way I wanted him to be?

I pulled the covers over me, and forced myself to push him away. I started thinking about Arthur Newland instead. Was he really the guy responsible for the blood results that night? What would he be like? I was desperate to talk to him and I had intended to try this afternoon, but had slept the chance away. Then I realized that if I didn't get some more sleep I would be doing the same thing tomorrow. Eventually, I found peace by reciting the periodic table, and I must have finally dropped off, because when I next opened my eyes my alarm was ringing and it was 7.30 a.m.

I sat up tentatively. Not bad. I felt pretty good, actually. I jumped out of bed, took a quick shower, ate some breakfast and headed across to my first lesson. Art history.

Rob came running up behind me, and linked my arm.

'Hey, Eva, how are you doing?' he asked, giving me a little squeeze.

'I'm good, Rob,' I smiled.

'That's such a relief – you have no idea how worried I've been.' He was standing in front of me now, staring into my eyes, and brushing a stray strand of my hair behind my ear.

Whoa. He was way too close.

I stepped back quickly and glanced uncomfortably across to the art history room. And suddenly I was staring into the eyes of Seth Leontis. I glanced quickly away, but I had registered the look of pain I saw there.

I breathed in hard. Anyone would think I was the one who had walked out on him! Anger knotted in my chest, making it hard to breathe. Literally. I suddenly couldn't catch my breath. I was gasping.

'Eva? What's wrong?' Rob was holding my shoulders, and looking wildly around for someone to help. I slid down to the floor and put my head between my knees, until I began to get control of my lungs again.

Damn, I thought. *And this morning started so well.*

As I crouched there, working on my equilibrium, Rob's agitation began to get faintly oppressive, so, pressing my knuckles down hard on the ground, I hauled myself back into an upright position. Well – pretty upright, I thought. Rob was less convinced.

'Eva, I'm taking you back to the medical block,' he announced, propelling me firmly back across the quad. I started to argue, but frankly I'd used up most of my energy reserves on the last manoeuvre, and I didn't have the stamina to face Seth again any time soon, so within a few minutes I found myself back in the calm peace of my blue room.

'Sorry, Rose,' I sighed, as she took my blood pressure.

'Nothing too serious,' she smiled. 'I'd like you to just stay put for the rest of the morning, and if you're feeling up to it after lunch, you can do the afternoon timetable. OK?'

I nodded.

'Now I need to run out and pick up a couple of prescriptions. Can I trust you to rest until I get back?'

I nodded again.

'The doctor is in the surgery this morning, so if you need anything just press your buzzer.'

'Sure,' I said, suddenly recognizing that I had just acquired the perfect little window of opportunity I'd been looking for.

As soon as Rose had left the building, I pulled out my mobile and dialled the hospital number.

The receptionist asked me what department I required. When I said 'dermatology', she put me through to appointments. It took me ages to get round the system, and in the end I had to pretend to be Arthur's sister with an urgent family message.

Finally he came to the phone. Very suspicious.

'Who is this?' he hissed.

'Arthur?'

I could hear him moving away from a room full of chatter.

'Ye-e-s,' he said slowly.

'Arthur Newland?'

'Yes, I am Arthur Newland. Who are you? And I am guessing *not* my sister, as I didn't appear to have one when I left home this morning.'

'Er, no . . . I'm actually someone you don't – er – know at all. My name is Eva Koretsky . . .'

I heard a sharp intake of breath. 'Geez – are you . . . OK?'

I bit my lip. He knew who I was.

'Er – sort of. Look . . . you handled some blood results . . .'

At first he was really cagey, but when I told him that I'd seen some weird T-cell microbiology the day I got sick, he got really excited. I liked this guy. We talked the same language. And – yes – he had copied the data on to his own external hard drive. And he was prepared to email it to me.

'So tell me what you saw?' I asked.

'Well, we did the routine automated lab tests, but when your results came through they were so perplexing that I checked the bloods again under a microscope.' I heard him swallow. He then described a microbiological event uncannily similar to the one I had witnessed with Professor Ambrose. And, it turned out, he had managed to explore further than I had.

'I tried to freeze a T-cell – to identify the invading pathogen. But although the freezing process is pretty instant, it proved too slow to catch it. A pathogen multiplying at that speed should have been absolutely lethal. So, I – er – assumed the host – er, sorry, I mean *you* – had to be dead.

'I was completely gobsmacked when a few hours later I was

presented with sample after sample of healthy T-cells. I began to assume everyone was right . . . some chemical agent must have compromised the slides.'

I sat with the phone to my ear, my heart pounding. This was exactly what I was expecting to hear, but it was still a shock.

'Hey, Eva – I've gotta go. I'll send you those files,' Arthur said suddenly and hung up.

I was so lost in the implications of the call that I didn't hear the door open, or the feet pad quietly towards me. It wasn't until I was blasted with the heat of his touch on my shoulders that I realized what was happening.

I turned to face him, my resolve evaporating at the sight of his face. He looked so unhappy.

'Eva,' he choked.

He pulled me into his arms and we both wept. Then he began to speak. In Latin.

'Do you remember how after the fight with Protix, I was taken to your villa, to be tended by the physician Tychon?'

I shook my head slowly. But as he talked a picture of an elderly man came into my head . . .

'The Greek?' I whispered.

He nodded.

'While I was sick you sat with me, and your songs echoed around my dreams . . . reminding me that there was somewhere to go, someone to return to. That was when I fell in love with you.'

I could see him lying on the couch, water trickling across his skin.

I did remember.

'And I fell in love with you,' I breathed.

He squeezed my hands. 'But I was just a slave and you were a noble woman and – betrothed . . .'

'What?' I spluttered

'To Cassius Malchus. The procurator.'

And as he said those words I felt my heart start to hammer. A cold chill went through me, and suddenly I couldn't catch my breath . . .

'Breathe, Livia,' he urged. 'Please . . .'

'Seth,' I gasped. 'He found out!'

I lost my hold of Seth, and I was falling through darkness . . . alone again.

Standing waiting. Waiting for him. My love. Sethos. The river sparkling in the moonlight. Beckoning. Vibia has got us passage with a merchant ship, and soon we will be on a boat, swishing through the water, heading far, far away. I'm nervously tapping out little tunes with my feet to distract myself. I run over the plan in my head, praying nothing has gone wrong.

Tonight's our one and only chance of escape. Tomorrow Seth is to leave Flavia and Domitus, to return in chains to the gladiatorial barracks. And Cassius is away – travelling to Camulodunum on business, taking most of his garrison with him. Sabina, my handmaid, has helped me drug the two remaining guards.

But Seth's not here. What's happened to him? I shiver, though it isn't cold – I am just so full of fear. For him. For me. Has he been caught? Has Flavia found out? If Cassius were to hear about our escape, he would have Seth killed. And me?

I stare out into the darkness. Then I hear him. My darling boy.

'Livia –'

He is running through the shadows, his cloak billowing behind him. Reaching out to me.

I run towards him, but before I can touch him he is gasping, 'We have to get out of here – I think they –'

He never gets to finish his sentence, because they are here. They've been waiting. Waiting in the darkness. Watching me. Waiting for him. Ready to ambush. I know this as soon as I feel the iron grip around me. There were no footsteps, no chase. I gaze towards Seth, and see that he too is now held by guards. He gasps in pain as they ram his injured shoulder against a wall. And while we struggle to get free, Cassius Malchus walks slowly towards me, his mouth twisted into a menacing smile.

'You honestly didn't think you could get away, did you, my love?' he hisses, placing his disgusting hand under my chin and lifting it so that I have to look at him.

'Your naivety astonishes me. Did you not know I *own* Londinium? Nobody defies me. I have bought everyone. No friends, no allies would stand by you and defy me. Foolish girl. Even your father –'

'He is not my father.'

Cassius's eyes narrow dangerously. He does not like interruption.

'Even your father,' he continues smoothly, 'has been bought.'

He is stroking my cheek, almost wistfully. 'Such a waste. You are so – lovely . . .'

I shudder and turn my head away, my eyes catching Seth's look of furious hatred.

'And to throw in your lot with – *him*! That slave *scum*! A mangled gladiator! What reckless idiocy. I had believed you cleverer than that.'

His fingers come together, spitefully pinching my skin, as he turns to Seth.

'You have won your last fight, gladiator,' he spits. 'This time you have overreached yourself. Nobody takes on Cassius Malchus and lives . . . especially vermin intent on getting their polluted hands on my goods.'

I watch in horror as Cassius moves slowly over to Seth and kicks him savagely in the stomach. Seth doubles over, groaning. Then Cassius unsheathes a long curved knife, and uses it to rip off Seth's cloak, and tear away his tunic. He laughs when he sees the bandaged shoulder.

'Was this apology for a man worth it, my darling,' he snarls, slashing his knife across Seth's chest again and again. As the blows strike, Seth moans, and falls forward.

'Call yourself a gladiator,' he jeers as he ruthlessly kicks and kicks the curled-up bleeding man at his feet.

'*Stop!*' I scream, knowing now that Cassius is not planning a quick ending for us.

Cassius turns. 'Ah, thank you, my sweet Livia, for reminding me not to get carried away. I wouldn't want the slave to miss the next part.'

He leans down, pulls Seth up off the ground and throws him against the wall. I hear the crack of Seth's skull slamming against the bricks. His head lolls as he tries to stay conscious. Cassius grabs his hair and pulls his head up. Then he slaps him viciously across the face.

'Pay attention, gladiator. This is the part where I cut your sweetheart's pretty throat . . .'

I see the knife flash as he walks slowly towards me. I struggle against the men who have me clamped fast. Cassius is leaning over me, his features distorted by the ruthless purpose in his eyes. His hard mouth is suddenly against mine, in a mocking parody of a kiss.

I hear Seth's snarl of rage, and then as Cassius draws away I feel the sharp heat of the blade as it runs across my throat.

I shut my eyes. I can hear my breath bubbling, my blood splashing as I drift down.

'NOOOO!'

From far away I can hear Seth screaming . . . fighting, men grunting . . . And then shouting . . . feet running . . . and just as I float away, Seth's voice . . .

'Livia . . . please . . . breathe . . . Livia . . .'

74

Together

London

AD 2013

I gasped, trying to find air . . . My lungs burning.

I opened my eyes and I was staring wildly into Seth's eyes. He was holding an oxygen mask over my face, and I could feel my heart thudding, and my lungs begin to fill.

'We got away?' I gasped.

'No, my love.' He shook his head sadly. 'We didn't.'

He held me tight in his arms, until I stopped shuddering. Then he carried me over to my bed, and laid me down. He sat down beside me.

'Cassius got away. Almost clean away . . .'

'Almost?'

'I managed to get just one slice at him . . .'

'How? There were so many of them.'

'When I saw the knife at your throat, I flung off the two holding me, and hurled myself at Cassius – but I was too late to save you. I got hold of his knife and went straight for his heart, but he twisted and got away with a slash across the arm

– just a scratch. Then the whole pack was on top of me. I didn't have the strength or the will left. You were dying . . .

'I could hear the shouts of some Roman soldiers who'd just shipped into the harbour, presumably soldiers that Cassius hadn't yet managed to corrupt. So he called his guards away. They gave me one last kick, assumed I was dead, and ran off. But Cassius suddenly turned, drew the knife and hurled it into my leg, laughing mockingly, "Just in case you ever think of running . . . Scum . . ."

'I was more dead than alive . . . I could barely keep my eyes open, but I wanted to die next to you – so I began crawling towards you. And then I realized you were gone . . . they'd taken you . . . I was alone. And suddenly Cassius's words seared like fire in my head . . . I couldn't let him win . . . so I hauled myself on to my knees and dragged myself back towards the barracks. I didn't make it all the way – Matthias found me – but by then the fever had got me anyway . . .'

'What fever?'

'The fever that killed me . . . The fever that brought me here . . . The fever I will *not* infect you with. Eva, I am not like you . . . I am – dead.'

'I died too.'

'No – you got here another way. You were born here. I wasn't. This isn't where I belong. I travelled here to find out how the fever works, but . . . then I found you. And – I can't bear to lose you. Not again.'

'You won't lose me. I am yours,' I said, leaning up to kiss him.

He turned his head away. 'I love you, Eva, but I am lethal . . .'

'I don't believe you,' I said, running my hands over his perfect face. I couldn't get rid of the image of it bleeding and bruised. I kissed his eyes, his cheeks, his neck, his jaw . . . and moved towards his mouth.

'Eva, stop,' he moaned. 'A kiss from me could kill you . . .'

'Then it would be a good death,' I breathed, taking his face in my hands. And when our lips met, I knew that wherever this love took me, it was a place I wanted to go.

Acknowledgements

When I was a little girl, writing stories and drawing pictures on the living-room floor, my parents kept me supplied with a stream of encouragement and notebooks even when times were hard. They have continued to offer unconditional support for all my endeavours ever since, and I can't thank them enough.

Thank you to my kids, Axie and Max, for talking endlessly with me about Eva, Seth, Parallon and String Theory (and for maybe inspiring one or two of the characters!).

Boundless thanks to the talented Shannon Park, my lovely editor, who has nurtured this book with such immense care and skill. Thanks also to the amazing people I've met at Penguin: Francesca, Zosia, Jen, Jess, Camilla, Jo, Susanne, Katy, Helen, Samantha – and to all the ones I haven't met yet, working so hard to help make *Fever* happen.

Living in London is like a daily adventure in time travel – modern buildings growing right next to ancient ones. I've always walked down these streets picturing ghosts from previous lives, so time travel wasn't such a big conceptual leap for me. But *viral* time travel was, as well as inventing the science to support it. I am indebted to my sister Caroline for reading the manuscript and correcting my more glaring medical blunders – how could I have confused hypertension with hypotension? I am also grateful to Dr Mark Zuckerman of King's College Hospital for checking the passages concerning virology without flinching.

Many thanks to the real Dr Mylne (no relation to the one at St Mag's) for conscientiously reading *Fever* all the way through – even the romantic bits – in pursuit of classical historical accuracy.

Thanks also to the host of scientists and historians who generously post up their research on the Internet, and to those who have published their research in books. Particularly helpful to me were: *Roman London* by Jennie Hall and Ralph Merrifield, and *The World of the Gladiator* by Susanna Shadrake.

Every effort was made to contact Michio Kaku for permission to use his quotation at the beginning of Part II. I do hope he will appreciate the tribute.

Writing is an immensely selfish and solitary occupation, so if writers have partners they are usually generous, forgiving people. Nobody could be more so than my husband, Chris. I thank him for patiently listening and incisively commenting on my numerous plotting quandaries, and for wholeheartedly giving me the licence and strength to shut my door and disappear. I couldn't have done it without him.

GET YOUR
NEXT DOSE OF
THRILLING ROMANCE
AND
ADVENTURE
IN:

DELIRIUM

THE
**HEART-STOPPING,
PULSE-RACING**
SEQUEL
TO

FEVER

CAN SETH AND EVA'S LOVE SURVIVE AS OLD
ENEMIES THREATEN TO DESTROY THEM?

COMING APRIL 2013

WWW.FEVERBOOK.CO.UK

Prologue

Londinium

AD 152

There was a loud hammering on the front door. Ochira, one of the Natalis family house slaves, paused in her vegetable chopping. Both porter slaves were currently in the cellar, mopping up water from a leaking drainage pipe, and all the other house slaves were out on errands. Ochira had no choice.

She walked quickly across the atrium to the door. A tall, angular man wearing a richly woven toga stood leaning against one of the marble pillars.

'Greetings,' he began.

Ochira bowed low.

'I have come to visit the lady Livia. Is she at home?'

Ochira's face paled, and her hands began to tremble. 'The . . . the l-lady Livia is n-not here.'

'Then I'll wait,' he said, pushing past her towards the atrium.

Ochira stumbled backwards, overpowered by his unexpected entry. She darted quickly after him, wringing her hands. 'The lady Livia was married three months ago –'

The stranger instantly froze, then slowly turned back to face her, his dark eyes narrowing dangerously. 'Impossible!' he hissed, taking hold of Ochira by the shoulders and shaking her. Ochira gasped in pain.

'Forgive me,' he said quickly, dropping his hands. Then he massaged his temples wearily. 'Was she willing?' he asked evenly.

Ochira bit the inside of her cheek and stared at the ground.

'Who is he?' the stranger spat.

'C-C-Cassius Malchus . . . the procurator himself.'

'And Livia is at his house now?' he asked, striding back towards the door.

Ochira was too afraid to answer.

The stranger suddenly swung round and fixed her with his black eyes. 'Is – the – lady – Livia – at – Cassius's – house – now?' The chilling restraint of his voice served only to amplify the slave girl's fear.

She trembled and shook her head. 'No, sir! Th-the l-lady Livia has disappeared.'

'Gone?' he choked.

Ochira bit her thumbnail nervously. She had been absolutely forbidden to talk on the subject, but there was something so powerful about the stranger that she was unable to resist the overwhelming compulsion to confide.

'Some say she r-ran away . . . but –'

'But?' he hissed impatiently.

'Others think . . . she was . . . m-murdered . . .'

The stranger's sudden stillness was terrifying. Ochira didn't dare meet his eyes. She stood staring at her shoes until he turned and strode from the house.

With a shaking hand she shut the heavy wooden door and slumped against it, a deep sense of foreboding tightening in her chest.

FOR FICTION TO MAKE YOU

GASP out loud
STAY up late *and*
MISS your stop

Get into **Razorbill**